Victory Ruins

Victory Ruins

Troop Brenegar

To all generations of the faithful heart.

But in this case, as always in life, alongside a man's open course there moves a mystery, to him dark and shining at once. The mystery here is change, whose god is Mutability. In the shifting relation between ourselves and the new order lies the profoundest source for our living, I mean change in that almost mystical sense by which, so long as we are alive, we are not the same and yet remain ourselves.

- Stark Young,
"Not In Memoriam, But In Defense,"
I'll Take My Stand

PEACE

I

The two men were standing right where they should, the same as where they wanted to stand, and the same as where they had intended to. Right out there in the field, surrounded by the ripe winter wheat that was ready to harvest under these hot early June skies. They liked being here, the two of them side by side, one barrel-chested and one long-limbed and wiry, and not half the pleasure came from what they knew was about to happen. Yet still they waited with patience, looking at their wheat, grown from their own seed for generations, talking of the yield. The older, barrel-chested one nodded toward the corn which sat in the bottom section of the farm. The stalks were still hardly out of the soil, but it was a good start and if they had the usual amount of rain, the corn would be knee-high in a month. The younger, wiry one nodded knowingly. He had seen a fair number of crops come in, but he knew of the harvests of decades past more, for he listened to what the older man said.

The older man's head turned, and his eyebrows lifted slightly with his head. He had caught wind of something. Then there was a squeal of brakes from behind and the younger man turned around. There was a thin cloud of dust drifting through the branches of the oak beside the house. A black Ford was now parked beneath the oak.

"That'll be Earl, Pa," said the young man.

"Reckon so," said the older one. He dropped his eyes from the distance to his son there beside him. "All right now, just like we planned."

And they set off walking away from the house and the barn, walking as they had stood, side by side, into the field. The young man could not help but look back as they walked. A thin woman, his mother, came out of the front door and looked down from the porch onto a man in a hat. He could imagine what his mother was saying: "They'll be in directly."

But they were not. They walked out through the wheat, pausing here and there to talk, but only for effect. They reached the far end of the field, swung across its far limit, arcing back along the edge of the wheat where it petered out in a tangle of brush until the treeline began. As they slowly walked through

3

the wheat, the full ears bounced against their thighs. Looking across the acres of field, they could see the man in the hat standing, just to the side of the barn.

"Earl's lookin' at us, Pa."

"Reckon so. Let him look."

They drew closer, although the field of wheat still separated them from the house and the waiting man. The young man could see the visitor was down to his shirtsleeves on this hot day. He was looking at them, eyes following them as they walked. Earl must have wanted the two of them to see him. After all, when they did, they should come in and greet him. It was the polite thing to do, for he was a visitor. And as much as he might expect them to, so too did Earl need them to come in. He had business with them. The two men kept walking, taking their time, although not as they pleased, for they were biding their time very carefully, very consciously. They were just about abreast of the house, on the far side of the field, when their visitor raised his hat in his hand and shouted, "Wade!"

The young man looked to his father. The older man just gazed straight ahead as he walked. "Let him holler one more time."

Earl shouted again, flapping his hat around, and at last, with a slow and surprised air that came from careful thought and planning, Wade looked across the field, paused for a moment as if not perfectly comprehending, and then waved back. His son made a start as if to cross the field, but Wade held him back. "No, no, not yet. Give him some time."

And they walked on, down along that far edge of the wheat, until they reached the end of the field down next to the road. Then they walked along the edge in the direction of the house. Surely Earl thought they must be coming in. But then Wade turned and his son did, too, and they wandered back out into the middle of the field and then all the way down to the end of the field farthest from the house. Earl came out into the field, shouting after them, waving his hat, but they paid him no heed. When they turned around at the far end, the visitor had retreated to his spot next to his car, against which he leaned with folded arms. They meandered their way back along the edge of the wheat, just above where the higher land began to gently run down to the lower sections with the corn. Slowly they approached the house and the barn and all the outbuildings clustered around a handful of old oaks. There was a small ditch bordering the field — Wade crossed it slowly and stiffly and with half-whispered obscenities, while his son nimbly hopped across. And then they were there, right in front of their visitor who had stepped away from his Ford and approached them. The older, barrel-chested man smiled and offered an open paw. "Well, stranger, been a while since we've seen you," he said.

Earl took Wade's hand. "A little over a year, Wade. Good to see you again."

Wade Breckenridge nodded slowly. "Been that long? Well, don't time fly.

Earl, you remember my son, Arlen. Arlen, Earl's the ag extension agent, if you don't recall."

"Arlen, good to see you again." Earl reached out and shook the hand of the lean young man, who nodded his greeting without expression.

They walked into the shade of the barn and Wade, mopping his brow, leaned his shoulder against the open barn door. "Hotter'n Billy-be-damned already. Earl, you'd better loosen up that tie. Don't do farmers no good if you drop dead from the heat."

Wade and Arlen Breckenridge chuckled. The extension agent ignored the jibe. "What were y'all doing out there, Wade?"

"Out there?" Wade reached into the front pocket of his overalls and pulled out a pouch of tobacco and a rolling paper. "Just enjoyin' ourselves."

"Enjoying yourselves?" said Earl.

Wade did not lift his eyes from his rolling paper. "Reckon a man's got to appreciate what he has, what he's done with his hands. Whether he eats it or sells it or both, reckon a man's got to look at his handiwork before it's gone for another year."

"The wheat, you mean."

"That's right."

"I see." said Earl. "Do you have an idea of what your yield will be?"

A cigarette appeared from between Wade's thick, rough fingers. Arlen reached into his pocket and produced a match. He struck it on the head of a nail that protruded from the barn door and offered it to his father. Wade drew on the cigarette until it began to burn. Satisfied with how the cigarette drew, Wade let it hang between his lips and said with a faint curl of smoke from his lips, "No. Ain't got no idea. And you know, Earl, that don't bother me much."

That last comment was provocation. Arlen knew it. Perhaps Earl knew it, too. If he did, the ag extension agent would not rise to it. He stood there, looking at Wade expectantly. But Arlen's father did not elaborate. Wade just puffed contentedly on the cigarette. Arlen stood beside him, thumbs through his belt loops, examining Earl silently. He tried to put on his best sullen, defiant face. Earl's eyes flicked over for a second, not once, but twice, and each time returned to stare at Wade, as if feeling the hostility from Arlen's gaze.

At last, one of them could not stand the silence any longer. "Wade, are you ready to talk about the farm? And I mean really talk."

Wade did not say anything to Earl. The cigarette drooped in an arc of ash from his lips and he just stared back. It was common attitude for Wade, and for Earl. Farmers have their own particular stubbornness. Around here, the Breckenridges had a reputation for it above others. This section was the oldest part of Catawba County, and even in this Year of Our Lord 1940, it had the most entrenched ways. The Breckenridges did more than their fair share to keep it that way. But that had never dismayed the extension agent. Delayed in his desires to improve this farm, yes, Earl had been, and Arlen was proud that he and his father had put him off. But Earl was never completely put off, not by the mules unmoved by cars spraying clouds of dust across their pasture, nor by the crooked, nearly toppling corn crib and unchinked log barn of yesteryear. No, Earl was far too certain to be dismayed to the point of giving up. For he brought with him the solution to all the woes of the farmer: the success and security of a good crop, scientifically grown and shrewdly sold.

"Come on, Wade, it's been a year, you've had time to think, like you insisted on last time. I want a commitment from you," said Earl.

The barrel-chested farmer carefully plucked the cigarette from his lips with his thick, calloused fingers and tapped off the ash. "Commitment to what?"

"A new plan for bringing this farm up to the times. Growing better crops, diversifying, making some investments in the land."

Arlen watched Wade's face brighten, and he saw the surprise in Earl's face. "That's right. I remember. What's the plan?" said Wade.

"That's what we've got to discuss. Maybe we should go inside, have a seat at the table?"

"No," said Wade. "No, reckon that won't do. Can't smoke inside. Legenia won't allow it." Plucking more tobacco from the pouch, Wade began rolling yet another cigarette.

The extension agent wet his lips. "If it's all right, then, I'll go ahead and tell you my thoughts for improvements," he said.

Wade looked over at Arlen. Beneath that calmly uncaring visage was a look of mischief. Arlen tried hard to keep from smiling. "Go on," said Wade, licking the rolling paper and deftly turning it.

And then Earl set into it. With the most even tone and clear words he could muster, building and building his case so that there was no escaping its logic, the extension agent explained what he thought the farm needed. No more of this growing wheat, corn, and oats, only to just eat most of it themselves. Such was nonsense when a fair price could be had. No more scraping out an acre of cotton every now and then for a little cash. No more truck patch of vegetables and beans to haul into town a few times a year. And they had to put an end to their mule breeding; there was no point anymore, tractors would replace them all. Quite simply, the family could not persist as they had and hope to survive. They needed to come up to speed, get modern, join ranks. They needed to start growing raspberries, said Earl — a profitable new opportunity. Or sweet potatoes, those had years of proven success here in Catawba County, perhaps more so than any other county in North Carolina. Extra acreage in lesbedeza and alfalfa would round out the crop. And above all

6

else: get a tractor and stop relying solely on three mules for all their horsepower.

Wade nodded slowly at all of this, though he hardly looked up at Earl. He finished rolling that second cigarette and handed it to his son, saying, "Arlen, what do you think?"

Arlen took the cigarette, but did not light it. He waited until Earl was looking at him and then and answered quickly. "'Bout these sweet potatoes — how much of a yield are we talkin'?"

"That depends," said the agent. "You can probably raise it up to thirty percent above average if you treat it right."

Arlen laughed. "Treat it right? You mean talk real sweet in its ear?" Wade smiled a bit.

The extension agent bit his tongue for a moment. "Treat it with fertilizer, I meant. Nitrate, acid, potash — that'll bring up the yields."

The humor in Arlen's face disappeared as if by command, replaced quickly by a suspicious, almost defiant mask. Oh, yes, he could act this way, he was his father's son. "Fertilizer — you're talkin' money, ain't you? We ain't got money," said Arlen.

"It'll be more expensive if you don't apply the fertilizer — that extra yield will pay off the investment and then some."

"No, I mean, we ain't got enough money to buy it all in the first place."

"We can fix that," said Earl. "I'll look into arranging a mortgage."

Arlen stopped there, his eyes narrowing. That was one thing he did not know how to respond to.

"It's the best thing for the farm." said the extension agent. "No one wants to go back to the old days, now, do they? Where everyone made less and less on one crop each year?" That was not how the Breckenridges had lived, Arlen wanted to say, for he knew his heritage. Nor was it the truth in general, but before Arlen could say anything, Earl continued. "You can't keep saying no or doing nothing. That's a recipe for disaster. Only growing the right crops will turn this place around. Y'all can be something to talk about in this corner of the county. But it takes commitment, it takes money. You'll see in the end — the black ink in your books at the end of each year will prove it, Wade." Earl finished and was silent.

Wade's eyes rose from the dirt to meet the agent's, his eyebrows crinkling almost completely together like a pair of woolly worms moving toward each other. "Well, now, I ain't sure what you mean by black ink. I mean, ain't never kept books."

"Never?" said Earl. The shock in his voice was palpable. To some men, that seemed impossible in this day and age. But, then again, so did the survival of this old farm.

"To tell the truth, I just let Arlen remember what we need," said Wade. "Hell, he finished the eighth grade, that's one more than me, so I figure he's got a better head for sums. But now, don't go askin' him 'bout last year's crop or nothin'. A hundred bushels or three hundred, it don't ever figure into this year." Earl seemed about to interject, but Wade just kept on. "Ain't no reason to, as far as I see. 'Cause some years are wet and some are dry. Sometimes winter stays long and comes early, or the other way 'round. Now, my father used to believe a little bit in the signs of nature — he knew a bunch of 'em, though I reckon everyone did back then — and he taught me a few and I don't think that highly of some of 'em. But I reckon he had a point. You got to look at what's around you. So that's what I done. Taught Arlen here the same. So really, I reckon it's just going by a feeling. I might think to myself, 'Well, now, I put in fifteen acres of wheat last year and I got 'bout a hundred and fifty, hundred and sixty bushels out of it, which weren't quite enough for us, but last year was dry and this year proved to be pretty steady in heat and rain so far, so maybe I'll plant the same number of acres.' See, like that. But sometimes I ain't even got to think about it. I just know."

Hardly had Wade paused than Earl butted in. "Wade, that's not what I've been saying. You've got to put in the right crop, not just one that has always seemed to work. And you've got to fertilize it right, harvest it right, store it right. You don't need a little surplus here and there, but a whole crop to sell for a good price."

Wade's strong face, stained from the sun, remained calm, almost understanding. With great, almost bovine slowness, Wade moved his mouth once as if he were ruminating. And when he finally spoke, his voice was not defensive, but almost contemplative. "Earl, 'least in my experience, ain't no call for that. If I get exactly what I need, I ain't got to put in more work than I have to. Hell, more I plant, then the more days puttin' it in, bringin' it in, more worry 'bout the weather and what not. Rather just not work and do without if it really comes down to it."

"You'll starve, then," said Earl. "That's always the fate of those who won't change."

He was pressing his attack. Earl had always intended to see how far he could get, and from the look on his face, he knew was almost inside their defenses now, close to making these two farmers see the truth.

Wade shook his head slowly in response. "Now I ain't said we starved, neither. But I still ain't seen no good reason yet to work more than I care to. 'Cause that much work gives us what we need. Now, this land's seen better days. A little worn out in spots. Ain't gettin' nowheres close to the yields I used to. Y'all got me rotatin' crops, that's fine, that's free to me. Of course, that ain't everything. Maybe the soil does need treatment, like you said. Reckon you can see that, Earl. But that don't mean this place is finished. She's got life in her yet. We're keepin' on keepin' on, and I ain't got no reason to expect that it ain't goin' to be the same for Arlen here. That's really what matters, whatever we do." Wade clapped his hand proudly on Arlen's shoulder.

Earl wasn't listening, not by this point. Arlen could see it and he knew his father could see it, too. Earl had a reputation among farmers for convincing, but surely he was weighing whether there was any convincing to do here. The perpetual neglect, slipshod accounting, and complete indifference in progressive agricultural ways was obvious in Wade's tale, brief as it was. Perhaps Earl was wondering, could it all be true? Earl was no fool, he surely did not believe all of it. But then again, how could he corroborate the falseness of the story? He had nothing by which to measure this farm by: no numbers, no dollars, nothing. All Earl had was the long, rambling word of a barrel-chested farmer, who knew not the report, only the anecdote, and the silent hostility of the only son.

Or maybe Earl was wondering how had they survived this long. It was no wonder to Arlen, for he knew it from having lived it and having heard it from the lips of his father. It could only be mysterious to those who looked upon change as a blessing in and of itself. Many talked about the miracles had been worked in this county, indeed, in the whole state and across the South. Many in Catawba County had given up their old dependence on cotton and tobacco, the twin millstones around the neck of the farmer, and put behind them the poverty of the past seventy-odd years. Farm after farm had gone over to new and diverse cash crops, to intense and scientific farming, and still they who converted, for all their progress, had struggled to live through the decade-long depression. But the Breckenridges had survived without doing so at all. Corn, wheat, truck patch and oats, milk cows and mules, they adhered to the old balance and ate all the same. They were behind the times, true, but, at the same time, they had escaped the ravages of the age. Maybe that was the thought crossing Earl's mind and tuning out his ears, the brief thought that it was as if all the change of the last forty years, and the forty before that, had hardly happened. As if the Breckenridges, taking God's word that a man's bread was made by his own sweat, had simply watched all the turmoil pass with temporary interest, a reproachful remark, and not a lick of fear.

But perhaps that wasn't what Earl was wondering. His eyes sharpened and he shifted his weight, squaring up his stance to the two farmers. Then Earl said evenly, "I know how you feel about this, Wade."

"Ain't 'bout how I feel, it's just how it is," said Wade.

"That's fine, and I'm sure you and I could go back and forth to no end over what's right for this farm. I'm willing to leave it at that. But I'll ask this one last thing: what does Arlen think?"

9

Arlen jumped a little in his skin. The skin on the back of his neck prickled and he felt his cheeks flush a little.

"It'll be his farm one day, won't it?" said Earl. "Well, Arlen?"

Arlen didn't speak. Instead, he began to gnaw nervously on his lower lip.

"Earl, leave the boy alone."

"Do you think you can keep on like this forever?" said Earl. Was he speaking to Arlen or to Wade?

"'Til kingdom come, but I ain't gonna live that long," said Wade, insistently.

"That's right. This farm works, for now, but that will change. You'll have to change. Especially if Arlen were to ever go away."

The hairs up Arlen's neck prickled coldly. "Go away? Like hell I will," he barked, like a scared dog at an intruder.

Earl just looked at him skeptically, as if at a small child who simply does not know.

"I'm stayin' right here, Earl. I'm farming with Pa and I'll take over the farm when he can't no more. That's the way it is and that's the way it'll be."

"I've heard boys say the same thing and they all leave," said Earl.

Arlen was inclined to retort, but he knew what Wade would say: he did not need one.

That Earl is wrong, so wrong. This land's in my blood. I'm meant to live here and work it.

"Don't think too long on what I've said, Wade" said Earl. "You wouldn't want to lose the farm because you wouldn't get with the times." And with that, Earl dropped his hat onto his head and tipped the brim down, as if the flourish would distract from his defeat.

Wade spat contemptuously. The gob welled up on the hard-packed earth at his feet. "That's about how much good you've done me and my family, Earl."

"Well, then, y'all think it over for a while. I'll swing back around eventually, to see if y'all changed your minds."

"You take your time, Earl," said Arlen, his face defiant. "We ain't going nowhere."

The extension agent backed the black Ford backed carefully down the drive. Neither of the Breckenridges waved farewell. Arlen watched the car roar away down the county road in a cloud of dust that gathered slowly upward and, caught by a breeze from over the tree tops, rolled up the slight hill toward the house shaded by the old oaks. He felt relief.

We showed him. I ain't leavin'. I'll never give up on this farm.

No matter what. They would live on, like they always had.

Legenia Breckenridge came out of the narrow front door and waited on her husband and son. Wade looked to his son and Arlen looked back. His father cracked a smile. Arlen did too. They had won, for today. They walked slowly toward the house and the smiles became devilish grins that turned, with each step, into hooting and cackling from the depths of their empty stomachs.

Their boots clomped up the bare front steps to the front porch and at the top, Arlen gasped painfully for air. The gut-shaking laughter had given him a stitch in his side. His mother swung open the screen door and from eyes between a set of deep crow's feet watched them come up onto the porch. Wade pecked her on the cheek, which softened her face very slightly. Arlen leaned in and did the same. Before entering the house, he remembered to tap his toes firmly before the threshold to shake the dirt from his feet. He must at least pay lip service to one of Legenia's commandments. Wade was whistling — just fragments of a song, a half-stanza here and there, broken by residual chuckles that still shook his barrel chest.

"What did y'all do to him this time?" said Legenia, slipping by Arlen as he hung his hat by the door on a peg.

"You make it sound like we bushwhacked him," said Wade. He had already taken his spot in his chair, which creaked as he settled into it.

"Well, did you?" said Legenia from her spot at the Big Boy stove, which sat in the middle of things like a bloated tick.

"Bushwhack him? No, ma'am. Maybe I just pinned him down while Arlen tanned his hide with a switch."

"Y'all ain't laughin' 'cause he got the better of you, I know that," said Legenia, moving the warm food from the iron stove to the table.

"Seems like you'd be happy that he didn't," said Wade.

Arlen's mother did not respond. She continued moving dishes to the table. Arlen's hands bounced apprehensively on his knees. He felt he would starve if he waited much longer.

"Wade, would you bless it?" said Legenia, taking her own seat.

Wade scooted his chair forward with a squeak. Bowing his head slightly, he closed his eyes and delivered a rapid-fire prayer: "Thank-you-Lord-bless-this-food-to-our-bodies-and-our-bodies-to-your-service-in-Christ-Jesus-name-we-pray-Amen."

Arlen's hand shot out to the cornbread, grabbed a slice and passed the rest, just faster than Wade could. His father, though, was not perturbed; his mind was still on the nascent argument with his wife: "Well, if you're curious, Earl didn't get us to commit to nothin'. We'll keep on as we have."

"At least for another year," said Legenia.

"Another year? I'd wager more than that. I knew what Earl was going to try to get from us, from the moment he first approached me in town. So Arlen and I needed a plan. We had to play Earl the best we could. And it turned out all right, 'cause we planned it together." Wade looked at his son knowingly.

Arlen grinned back and watched his father's gaze swing back across the table.

Wade's coloring of the story got Legenia's response: "Then what did you plan?"

"Well, let me tell you." The farmer shifted forward to the edge of his chair, leaning on the table with his forearm. Legenia hated that, but it was as a part of him telling a favorite story as was moving his tongue. But Wade stopped, cocked his big head, and looked over at Arlen. "No, I'm gonna let Arlen tell you."

Arlen wasted no time. "It was a good plan. We knew what Earl was gonna say: we've got to modernize, got to change everything. And I said, let's draw the line in the sand, a firm 'no,' make it real clear that ain't nobody going to push us around. But Pa said that ain't going to keep Earl away. He ain't one to take 'no' for an answer. We had to made it look like even if we said 'yes,' it wouldn't change nothin'."

Legenia arched an eyebrow. "How's that?"

"Like even if we did everything Earl wanted, things wouldn't be any different." Arlen could see she still did not understand. "Ma, Earl wants us to change the farm because he thinks it's broke-down. Used-up. Nothin' but trash." Arlen glanced over at his father and got an almost imperceptible nod of approval. "Earl wants us to be new, growin' all kinds of crops we ain't got the money for. He thinks it's the better way, but it ain't."

Legenia had stopped eating and was just listening to her son's story now. Her face was as set as it ever was; it betrayed no sympathy for Arlen's words, which were Wade's in genesis. Arlen knew she had heard all this again and again, so perhaps she was merely unmoved by its repetition across the years of marriage to a Breckenridge and the incessant assertion of how things were supposed to be. *Wish she'd at least be a little happy for us standin' up for the family. Standin' up for her as well as us.* But maybe she didn't see it that way.

Still, Arlen continued. "Pa said, we can't act like we're willin', but we can't be stubborn neither. We had to show Earl what he thought we were, only without any hope of changin' it at all."

"We had to get Earl to give us both barrels," said Wade. He never could resist chiming in. "The whole hog. That way when we gave him a story 'bout us barely scrapin' by and not caring a whit, he'd realize that even his fancy pitch wouldn't do a damn thing for us. I figured, then he'd have to think, well, then we're just a lost cause. So I told him a story, the one I wanted him to hear. Now, I acted amenable and Arlen acted a little suspicious and I reckon that helped us get him where we wanted him." Wade grinned, as much to himself as anyone.

Arlen mopped the plate with a last piece of cornbread and Wade leaned back in the chair. Legenia nodded slowly. At last she spoke in that even but hard tone of hers that had become harder since Arlen's sisters had moved away. "Don't see why you had to do that." And that was all she said.

"Legenia, you don't understand," said Wade. "You just can't tell these folks like Earl 'no' anymore. None of 'em. Don't matter whether the Federal government or the state or the county sends 'em. It's my land, it's my crop, it's my livelihood, but they think it ought to be theirs. Right now it's all mine and it's serving us just fine. My belly's full, thank the Lord, and I'm gettin' and giving a fair price to any man who wants what I sell. Ain't easy to do and it certainly ain't got any easier, not since my pappy's time. But to Earl, us livin' the way we do, he thinks we're singlehandedly holding back the whole goddamned United States."

"Don't take the Lord's name in vain like that," said Legenia, staring hard at her husband with her dark eyes.

Wade would repent later; he had to finish his point. "Earl and the rest of them will tell any farmer to change their ways, to go to a money crop. What matters to them is the numbers, the numbers and the money. Everyone's scrambling, just flat out trippin' over themselves to get money, get secure, and get stable, all at the same time, but I tell you, there just ain't no doing it. 'Cause what damn good is it if I got to scramble to get more? Every time I've talked to Earl, he's had a different crop for me to try, a magic crop that'll get me the cash I need. Do I have change everything about this farm every three, four years just to get by, just to make sure the money's coming in? Pay off one mortgage and take out another just to put in whatever new crop they say I need, just to pay taxes, hell, just to eat? I'll wear myself out, and this farm out, for that matter, before I ever find any peace in that."

Wade finished and was silent. He could be silent because the rest needed no argument. His wife, his son, and his daughters, who lived elsewhere now, knew the other half of the story. He could resist, he could survive, he could use appearances against the extension agent because he knew what mattered and what didn't. A rickety barn, a bunch of stubborn mules, a house still without a single electric bulb: if all these things looked used-up or broken-down, it was because they had a different usefulness, one beyond Earl's comprehension. They meant the independence of the farm, tenuous as it might be, and, in turn, the independence of the family. The three of them would eat from the land's gifts no matter what. And so too, as long as Breckenridges could live without selling themselves to others for their daily bread, they would pay back the farm for what it had given them. Just as they had today.

Legenia was looking past Arlen, over his shoulder, her eyes far off. Arlen searched for any trace that his mother was considering what her husband had said. In the back of those hard dark eyes of hers, hidden between delicate folds of eyelid, there was something stirring, something she was ready to say, but would not. It was almost like she was fed-up with something. Legenia had heard all Wade's reasons before, yes, time and time again, but she had never failed to give her assent to Wade's wisdom and direction. But now, after all these years, had she something to say against it? That wasn't right. How could she? She knew how they lived and worked, the order of things; she had taken part, with joy and skill, for near on three decades.

But she never growed up in it. She married in.

That was true, wasn't it? Legenia wasn't privy in the way that blood and raising makes people. She thought differently about the farm. Arlen wanted to know and opened his mouth to speak.

The contented quiet that hung over the table was broken by a prolonged roar, hissing and tumbling all together. Rubber on rocks and dirt. Brakes squealed and from beyond the open front door, a terrible rending crash, bending and rupturing metal and shattering glass. Then quiet.

Arlen wiped his mouth with the back of his hand and was out of his chair and through the front screen door in one motion. He paused on the edge of the porch. There was a brown Studebaker on its side in the ditch on the far side of the road. "Pa! Come see!" he shouted and leapt from the porch. He ran down the drive, squinting through the thinning cloud of dust, his hands ready to help. When he got to the road, Arlen could not tell if there was anyone in the car. He approached the car, but the pinch of gasoline in his nostrils stopped him. The tank must have ruptured.

"Arlen! The mules!"

Arlen turned around. The mules had spooked, whinnying and stomping around the front pasture.

"Get in there and get hold of 'Thu!" shouted Wade.

The oldest mule, Methuselah, was thrashing about harder than the rest. If he tripped and broke his leg, they would have to put him down for sure.

Arlen stepped back from the car and moved to the fence. With one leg already over the top rail, an instinct to look back held him. Turning his head, he saw a hand grasping through the passenger window. The fingers and wrist stretched tautly like they were reaching for an apple on a high branch. The skin was very white and young. Arlen froze, teetering atop the rail. The thin white hand grasped around, padding down the outside of the door until it found the handle. It wrenched at the handle, trying to open it, but the angle was too great.

One of the other mules whinnied and jumped out of the way as Methuselah rampaged across the pasture.

"Arlen!"

"Pa! Look!" Couldn't Wade see? The woman's hand, which Arlen was sure

14

it was, yanked at the door handle. The smell of gas was getting stronger, even over here on this side of the road.

"Get 'Thu!"

The mule was stomping something terrible. He was into one of his fits.

That hand grasped at the door one last time, then let go.

Arlen smelled the fire before he saw anything. He swung down off the fence and dashed across the road. He could see the gasoline turning the dirt into an inky delta. Holding his breath, Arlen grabbed a hold of the door and wrenched on it. The metal strained and popped. He braced his boot against the body and heaved again. With a *whunk*, the door burst open and he fell back, flat on his rear. Standing, he quickly stuck his head into the vehicle. There was a young woman in there, in a white blouse and print dress. "Ma'am, you all right?"

She didn't respond. Arlen grabbed both her arms and, as gingerly as he could, lifted her limp body up through the door. She had passed out from the fumes. He hefted her up onto his shoulder and pulled her completely clear, carrying her quickly across the road. Her breasts pressed gently against his shoulder. He had not felt a woman that way before.

"Arlen, you smell that?" said Wade.

"Lot of gas."

"I think I'm on fire," she said.

Arlen almost dropped her in surprise. She hadn't passed out after all. "Oh, Good Lord, yes, ma'am, you are." Her dress was burning.

"Oh, put it out!"

Arlen set her down in the grass near the fence. There was smoke now, a lot of it.

"Oh, please!"

"Lie down!" said Arlen, forcing her down into the grass. The flames wooshed suddenly as they caught gasoline on her clothes. Arlen reached through the flames and with firm hands rolled her over and over through the long blades of glass. She must have rolled twenty feet until the flames died and there was only the smell of burnt cotton and singed hair.

"Pa, help me lift her up!"

The two Breckenridges pulled her away, carrying her up the hill to the house. As they reached the porch, the gasoline caught and the Studebaker sent black flames into the air.

"Thank the Lord, but that was close," said Wade.

Arlen knelt next to the young woman. "Ma'am, you all right?"

"It hurts." She looked up. "My legs."

At last Arlen got a good look. Her face was small, with a delicate chin but high, full cheeks that gave her a girlish look; her nose was in proportion, too, save for the end of it, which grew round, just enough to be endearing. Her eyes, though pained, were not fearful and were hardly upset. Behind everything, they were calm and gentle.

Arlen looked at the bottom of her legs as much as he felt propriety would allow. The skin was red and blistered. "They look a little burned," he almost said, but held his tongue. "Do you feel anything broken?"

She wiggled her feet and winced, but shook her head. "No."

Arlen looked up to Wade. "Pa, she needs a doctor."

"I'll go fetch one," said his father. "You're a lucky woman, ma'am."

She looked up, not understanding.

"You crash out in front of any other house, you won't have Arlen to run in there and pull you out so quick." Wade took his hat from inside and went without another word to the truck.

"Ma'am, can I get you anything? Some water?"

"Can I just rest my head on you?" she said.

Arlen swallowed against a dry throat. "Ma'am, what's your name?"

"Caty, Caty Cline."

"Miss Cline, you can rest your head on me."

He sat down next to her, her feet on the steps, his long legs dangling off the porch so far his toes almost touched the ground. Caty Cline turned to him, reaching across his chest with her arm and grabbing his shoulder. She pulled him closer and buried her face in his chest. Arlen did not object. He did not even realize when his mother came out onto the porch; seeing there was nothing she could do, Legenia left them be. Caty kept her face buried in his chest and he held her rigidly, not knowing how else to care for a woman like this. Perfectly still though he may have felt to her, Arlen trembled until it was long since dark and Pa arrived with the doctor, his heart even then pounding deep and steady, as if he'd just run a mile.

II

It was the next Sunday in the afternoon. That meant it was after church, when folks had to have something do. When it was this hot, most folks would sit at home and talk or the young folks would go for a swim somewhere. But if you had a Ford or a Chevy, you could get a pretty good breeze coming through the open windows at about twenty or thirty miles an hour and that would cool you right off. That was better than just sitting for the rest of the day, especially sitting at the camp meeting. Some folks didn't have quite as much tolerance for that today. Better to get out and see things, wasn't it?

But although there were a fair number of folks driving up and down the length of Startown Road, no one much noticed the modest house off to the right. A freshly painted white fence separated the house from the road and the motorists that trundled by every minute or two. If you looked closely, it was obvious that the paint had been slapped on without scraping off the old, chipped coat beneath. There was a nail on the gate hinge that needed hammering in and the flat flagstone of the front walk had popped above the level of the grass around it. Other than that, it was a decently-kept little house. Nothing to remark about, but nothing to be ashamed of either. The mailbox said "Cline."

"Son, you gettin' out?"

Arlen was in the passenger's seat of the black Chevy ½ ton. He ignored his father and kept his eyes set on the house.

"She don't bite, you know."

Arlen shook his head. "Pa, quit it."

Wade paused dramatically for a second. "Sorry. Didn't mean the dog. I meant the girl."

"I'll tell you if she leaves a mark."

Wade chuckled, mostly to himself. Cocking his hat back on his head, he rested his hand on the shifter, jiggling it about slightly. "You want me to pick you up on the way back from town?"

"Don't worry, I'll hitch a ride." Arlen's hand grabbed the door handle and yanked it. As soon as his feet were out and planted on the verge of the uncut grass beside the road, his father was off, bathing Arlen with warm exhaust from the tailpipe. Arlen looked past the white fence to the house, also painted white. There was no going back. Even if he turned right now and walked away, Caty might happen to come onto the porch and see him and he would have to explain why he was there. He didn't want to have to explain anything. He just wanted her to see that he had come. That was enough.

Arlen swung open the gate and walked up the flagstones. He winced at the clomp of his boots on the steps. The front door was open and the screen door closed in its place. Arlen rapped on the frame as loudly as he dared and stepped back, so that a little sunlight would illuminate his face and they might see who he was. Unsure of what to do with his arms, Arlen let them hang akimbo but that felt awkward. Hands in pockets, too casual. He hooked his thumbs over the top of his belt: that felt more like him.

A silhouette moved in the house. It was not Caty, he knew from the shape. Heavy footfalls approached the front door. A short, stocky man with a big balding patch and thick forearms came into the light. He squinted through the screen. "Can I help you, son?"

"Mr. Cline, sir, I'm Arlen Breckenridge."

Mr. Cline's eyes looked hard at Arlen and his mouth fell open as if to say something. Then it hit him: "Breckenridge, Arlen Breckenridge, that's right." Mr. Cline swung the front door open. "What brings you here?"

Arlen's face flushed hot. "I came to call on Miss Caty, sir."

Mr. Cline's face was a tad surprised, as if wondering what really happened the day of the crash.

Arlen shuffled his weight from one foot to the other. "What I really meant was to check on her, Mr. Cline. Just make sure she's doing all right."

Mr. Cline's face brightened a bit. "That's mighty fine of you, Arlen. Caty's just cleanin' up dinner. Why don't you have a seat on the porch and I'll send her out when she's finished." He disappeared back into the dark of the house.

The blue checked shirt was already plastered to Arlen's back and neck by the sweat that poured out in torrents. He already felt greater exertion than plowing a hundred acres of stone-ridden earth. Casting about the porch and seeing the motionless swing, Arlen moved to sit down. But he stopped just before he did. It would not be right for him to sit with Caty on the swing. That was presumptuous; it would make a bad impression on her as well as her parents. But there was nowhere else and it would be too awkward for him to remain standing. He sat down half-heartedly. His weight barely rested on the swing. It didn't feel right. As he convinced his legs to stand up, the screen door swung open. Arlen jumped to his feet and his thighs kicked back against the swing. It went jangling on its chains, twisting about like Arlen's stomach.

Caty Cline was smiling, though, when she came out of the door. Her smile was not broad, but one that rested naturally, as if she had carried it comfortably for the whole time she finished the dishes. "Hello, Arlen. I wasn't expecting you."

"Ain't got a phone," he said apologetically.

"Why, we've got a phone, Arlen."

"No, I mean, I ain't got one to call with."

"Oh." Now she seemed to understand.

They stood awkwardly for a moment, unsure of what to say. Mr. Cline came out, carrying two chairs with him. "Arlen, would you like the paper after I'm done?" said Mr. Cline, waving the *Catawba News-Enterprise* at Arlen. The headline stood out in thick type:

NAZI DIVISIONS ARE HELD BACK BY THE ALLIES. GERMAN INFANTRYMEN WALLOWING WAIST-DEEP IN FLOODWATERS AT DUNKERQUE. HEROISM CITED.

"No, thank you, sir. Don't care much for newspapers myself."

"You sure? Lots of good readin' in here, 'specially about the war."

"No, I appreciate it, Mr. Cline."

"All right. You'll wish you'd kept up with it all when it all comes here. It will, you know. Always does, always does." Mr. Cline looked at his daughter, then back to Arlen. "Well, I'll leave y'all to the talkin'." He sat, unfolded the paper, and starting from the back worked his way slowly to the front page.

Caty sat down on the swing and her weight stilled its eccentric dance. Arlen pulled the second chair over, though not too close as to be presumptuous. He looked at her and her eyes caught his. He quickly looked away and pretended to look at the flower bed along the length of fence. He couldn't bring himself to say the first word.

"How have you been?" she said eventually.

His mind raced, wondering what to say. "Well, Pa and I've been real busy. Been gettin' ready to harvest the wheat in a few weeks. And we've got a mule that's givin' us trouble — he'll be a good mule if we can just get him broke, but he's ornery. And between that, I've been cultivatin' and workin' the truck patch."

"Oh, I see. Is that all?"

"Yes, ma'am."

"Do you hang around the filling station and talk about cars? Or go to the theater? I thought that's what most young fellers did."

"No, ma'am."

She didn't reply. Arlen looked at her, then away. What to ask her? He didn't know how to talk to woman much at all. Arlen looked to Mr. Cline at the other end of the porch, as if the older man might introduce a convenient topic of conversation. But her father paid them no heed.

"It's mighty hot weather."

"Yes, ma'am." This was painful. He wished he'd never asked his father to bring him here.

Caty crossed her leg. Arlen by instinct looked down as a bit of skin showed. Only it was a lot of skin, nearly half of her calf. The big patch of red, blistered skin was still there. It looked worse than it had in the moment of the fire. How awful that it should happen to such a pretty girl. Caty noticed him staring at her burn and quickly pulled down the hem of her skirt. Embarrassed, Arlen looked away.

I should have gone to her faster. Shouldn't have bothered with those mules. Awful for a pretty girl like that to get burnt. I should've known better.

Arlen clammed up even tighter than before.

"Arlen?"

He was so thankful. The silence was unbearable. But would she ask him about the burn? "Ma'am?"

"It's not comfortable here. Come with me," said Caty, rising from the swing with greater grace than Arlen had. He followed her down the steps.

Mr. Cline looked over at them. "Where're y'all headed?"

"Out back, Pa, to the garden."

"All right, y'all be good, now," said Mr. Cline absently, his eyes still glued to the *News-Enterprise*.

They walked around the side of the small white-painted house, Arlen following Caty at a few paces' distance. The uncut grass tugged at his boots as he walked. She stopped next to a bare patch of earth, brown tinged with red. Stakes were stuck into the ground at intervals. The earth was dry and crumbly on the surface, but when Arlen stepped forward and nudged it with the toe of his boot, it seemed more moist beneath. The sun was baking it for no good reason.

"Y'all puttin' in tomatoes?" he said. He felt the confidence to speak, now that there was actually something to speak about.

"Pa's got to string the wire." said Caty. "If he'll ever get around to it."

Arlen almost asked why her father had not gotten around to it, but in truth it didn't matter. Because he would do it for her, regardless. Arlen had seen Caty Cline only twice, but he wanted to do a thousand things for her. Not talk, not get to know her, but help her endlessly. He did not know why.

"Where is it?" he said. "The wire."

She pointed to the small shed near the edge of the property, the door askew.

He went there and took the bale and, without gloves, proceeded to string

20

all the wire between the stakes that she would need. Caty returned from the house with a pair of nippers for him. "Oh, you're bleeding," she said, reaching for his hand. "Oh, I wish I had gloves for you."

"Don't worry. Just a scratch." The blood from his calloused palms stopped after a minute, well before he was finished with the wire. Finally, he stood up, looking at his creation.

"Thank you, Arlen," said Caty. She touched his elbow lightly. The hair on the back of his neck stood up.

"You put in the seed yet?"

"No, I haven't."

"It's almost too late. Better do it now." Arlen paused and gnawed on his lip. "Better turn over that soil, too. Ain't real rich, from the looks of it. Got to plant those seeds deep."

She brought him the seeds but she had no trowel. He didn't care; he rammed his fingers into the already-broken soil and dug deeper. He set the seeds where they should be, ready to grow into fine plants for her family. The Clines would eat from it, Arlen was confident. He brushed the dry, cakey soil off of his hands.

"Thank you, Arlen." Caty's voice was very soft. There was no forced enthusiasm, done for the sake of politeness. "I appreciate it." She meant it.

They stood there for a bit, not really looking at each other, but just around. Caty looked down at the fresh earth and poked it with her toe. Arlen looked around for other things to do. He didn't see any, at least that wouldn't be too presumptuous to take on himself. He didn't want to undermine Mr. Cline and put him off of Arlen so quickly, just when—

Just when what?

He was scared all of a sudden. Like a little boy, he knew he had to run away. It was all too embarassing and what he was secretly hoping for was even more embarassing to think, let alone admit to anyone.

"Well, I reckon I better be going."

Before he could take a step, Caty grabbed his arm. Lightly, with a feminine touch, though. "Arlen, thank you."

"You already said thank you, ma'am."

"I meant thank you for pulling me out of that car."

"Oh." Now he was the one looking down.

"It was very brave of you."

"Ma'am, I didn't think I'd say this, but I feel bad I didn't come to you sooner." He swallowed against his dry throat. "Pa was yellin' to me and I thought—"

Caty shook her head, her lovely face brushing aside any guilt he might have felt. "I'm alive, Arlen."

21

"But you got burnt. I just feel bad 'bout that."

"That will heal. I'm alive and your father was right, Arlen. That's what you need to know."

"Right about what?"

"Don't you remember?" Caty said. She had a knowing, almost mischievous look in her eye. But her words were proper, conveying sentiment with a homely decorum. "I feel like your father is always right. Make sure you listen to him."

He smiled. It was the first time he had ever smiled for her. He still felt he should go, but he felt better about doing it. The way was open for him. He was free to go right toward the thing which he wanted ever since she buried her face in his shoulder on the porch.

"Ma'am, may I call on you next Sunday?" he said.

"I'll be waiting," said Caty.

III

The sun was sinking low against the trees, but the late August heat still had many hours before it dissipated. That heat held the smell of threshed wheat over the farm. Arlen could smell it everywhere. Or maybe it was just his shirt. He gave his sleeve a sniff. It certainly was there, along with a plethora of other unsociable odors. He should get washed up quickly.

Arlen had just started brushing himself off on the porch when he heard the car horn raucously screeching behind him. He turned around and recognized the car. The Cass boys were here.

Was it this week that he had told them to come by? Yes, it must have been. He should have specified a night. Really, any night but tonight. But when he had set the date, he hadn't been thinking about anything or anyone except Caty.

Arlen poked his head into the front room where his father sat. Wade didn't look up from his magazine. Arlen was willing to bet it was *The Progressive Farmer*. Though he surely knew more by intuition than he gained from the magazine, Wade still perused it once every few months, as much to learn something new as to make a fair judgment about how much the American agricultural mind had slipped. Wade was always sure it was slipping, but he was also curious to see for himself to what extent. His memory of its annals was nearly encyclopedic; he could turn its contents for or against whatever it claimed was right and true, and Wade did not ingratiate himself with his peers for it. But when Arlen looked more closely, he saw that it was *Time* magazine. A strange choice, Wade never read that sort of thing. There were two helmeted generals on the cover — probably European, fighting in that war over there.

"Pa, the Casses are here."

Wade crinkled his eyebrows and muttered to himself.

"Sir?"

His father looked up finally. "Did you finish gettin' everything ready for tomorrow?"

"Yessir. Pa, the Casses are here."

Wade nodded and went back to the magazine.

"What do you want me to do?"

"What else? Sell 'em the mule."

"What price are we askin'?"

"Use your judgment, son." Wade went back to reading, his eyebrows crinkling even closer together, and muttering again. He was in a mood, Arlen could see, one that came periodically between long months of steady determination and thoughtful joviality. *Ain't 'cause of me that he's bein' curt. Something else, I reckon.*

At the top of the drive, two young men stood beside a Chevy truck. One was lean like Arlen, the other was a tall, broad-shouldered, and barrel-chested. The lean one nodded to Arlen. "Hello, stranger."

"Calvin, how you been?"

"Been a while since we've seen you."

Arlen smiled to the other one. "Roy, we've missed a whole summer of fishin'."

Roy nodded regrettably. "We ain't kids no more. Too much else to do."

"We'll make up for it come the fall."

"Hope so."

"Arlen, what's this I hear about you seeing a young lady?" said Calvin.

Arlen's lips sealed up tight.

"Heard you two were courtin' in your daddy's truck here." Calvin pushed on the fender and the truck bounced up and down on its springs. "He let you use his gas or you gotta haul some hay for him to pay for your courtin'?"

Arlen's face burned a little, but he held back. Calvin was like this to everyone. He didn't deserve a thrashing for it. Not yet, at least.

"Cal, shut up and leave him alone," said Roy. "Arlen, don't pay him no mind. He's just full of himself. He thinks he's a war hero in the makin'. Don't you, Cal?"

Calvin gave a sour half-sneer. "Little brother here is a little slow to do what he knows he should."

"What is it they say? 'Discretion is the better part of valor?'" said Roy.

Arlen was confused. "What exactly are y'all talkin' about?"

Calvin put his hands on his hips resolutely. "I'm thinkin' about joinin' the Navy."

Arlen was not particularly impressed. Calvin thought about doing a lot of things. "And why's that?"

"Ain't you seen a newspaper recently, Arlen?"

"How long's recently?"

"Look at this one." Calvin pulled the *News-Enterprise* from his back pocket; it was but a day old. "You can see right there in black and white." The

24

words were no less bold than the last time Arlen had seen the front page of the newspaper:

NAZIS TAKE CHARGE AS TRUCE ENSLAVES FRANCE.

"And next Hitler'll invade England," continued Calvin. "Ain't stopped for nothin' yet. England and then we're next."

Arlen snorted in derision.

"What's that for?" said Roy.

"Ain't no Nazis gonna make it here."

"Not if the Navy gets 'em first," said Calvin.

"Can't wait to see, Arlen," said Roy. "Can't wait until it's too late."

Arlen said nothing.

"He's about convinced the rest of us," said Roy. "Me and Paul, I mean. We've been talkin' 'bout it. Danny, though, he ain't got no mind for it, he's a married man."

"It ain't Calvin here whose got your mind made up," said Arlen to Roy. "He's tellin' you what the newspaper thinks you should do."

"You're damn right," interjected Calvin. "Got to read the news, stay abreast of things. And why not? How else we gonna know when it's time to do our duty? I'll be the first to step forward. And the Navy will be fightin' first. I read that they're lookin' to enlist twenty five thousand."

"So when're you enlisting?" said Arlen.

Calvin looked annoyed. "Soon, Arlen. It depends what all those politicians up in Washington decide on. You have to stay abreast of it, you know, pay attention to it all."

Arlen could not understand that kind of language. Nothing had happened to him. Nothing had changed in his life, nothing except the pretty girl that was now in it. She would be here soon. "I ain't got all day," said Arlen. "You want to see this mule or not?"

Calvin sighed. "Fine, fine, Arlen. Show us the mule."

They walked to the pen, which occupied a small space to the rear of the barn. In the center was the mule. At the sight of the newcomers, the mule turned its head away and laid back its ears. The animal seemed to lean forward a bit, as if wishing to move away. Then whatever invisible harness was restraining the mule gave way and the animal walked steadily away from them to the far side of the pen, and, upon reaching the farthest spot, slowly turned back to face them.

"This one from the same mare and jack you've had for the past few years?" said Roy.

Arlen nodded. "Same pair."

"Did the other mules turn out well?"

"Just like you want 'em. A little high-spirited at first, but smart as a whip. Like to be worked. Only problem is, some of the folks we've sold 'em to ain't got enough work for 'em."

Calvin scratched his head. "I wonder if we will."

"Why wouldn't y'all?" said Arlen.

Calvin shrugged. "Pa's got his team already, and if there ain't gonna be any of us to work the others we already got, don't see the point in addin' another."

"Pa might hire on some hands," said Roy.

"And let them take on a wild, half-broke mule?" Calvin shook his head. "I don't see why Pa don't just replace the whole lot with a tractor."

The mule snorted once.

Arlen was not one to talk a man into what he did not need. But selling this mule was what the Breckenridges needed. Could he try telling the Casses that a mule didn't need oil and spare parts? No, that wouldn't work. Arlen had tried to explain his view before, that this poor animal, as sullenly stubborn as he might appear, was how folks like the Breckenridges made their way in this world. But their ways were not the same, not anymore. The Casses had been, as long as Arlen had been aware of adult matters, squarely into money crops. And they were good at it. That was one reason why Arlen did not see them, especially his old school friend Roy, much anymore. They were always working on that farm, changing crops, putting up new buildings, improving everything endlessly, streamlining and modernizing it all, furrowing their brows as much as the land: Arlen could see the lines in Calvin's forehead already.

From the corner of his eye, Arlen saw the mule lower his head. Arlen was for but a second reminded of a man digging in his heels before he took off running. Out of instinct, Arlen's head swung around toward the mule, which was now halfway across the pen in a lope. Arlen took a step back in anticipation, but neither of the Cass boys, conversing with each other, noticed. The mule hit the side of the pen square on with his head. For all his bulk, Roy jumped back a few feet in surprise, almost tripping over and toppling Calvin. The whole pen shook, and the top rail came loose and fell to the ground right where Roy had stood before. The mule backed away from the side of the pen and stared at them resentfully.

"Good Lord, Arlen," said Calvin. "I reckon he wants to get out."

Arlen grinned. "He might be a gelding, Calvin, but one good look at your pretty face and he's liable to overcome the limitations of nature."

"Shut up, Arlen."

"That mule ain't broke," said Roy.

"Never said he was."

Calvin glared at Arlen. "We ain't payin' for a mule that can't be broke."

"Ain't broke, not can't be broke," said Arlen. "Some are ornery like this, but they'll come around." The mule rammed the side of the pen again; the rails rattled and creaked, but no more fell off. The Cass boys stepped aside again and talked with each other intently and quietly. Leaving them to their private discussion, Arlen stepped up to the edge of the pen. The mule stared back at him with an equine fierceness. Arlen almost regretted selling this one, he wanted to see how it turned out.

"What's the mule's name?" said Roy.

Arlen had not bothered with a name until now. But one came quickly from his lips: "Jeremiah."

"Like the prophet?" said Calvin. "That's fittin'. Bangin' his head away against what he can't change." He looked down at his wristwatch, a dainty looking affair even on Calvin's thin wrist. A strange affectation, Arlen thought: too easy to smash to pieces on a fence post or with an ax handle. "We've got to be going," said Calvin.

Without much further talk, they all walked back. As they drew closer and closer to the house, Arlen kept looking and hoping his father would pull himself away from his magazine and come out to talk the Cass boys into buying the mule. Wade could rope folks into stories that always illuminated the immense worth of anything he chose. No one could resist the tales, not at least in the moment, for he made them see themselves as a part of it. Later, perhaps those folks felt disappointment, for they had not the mettle of Wade nor the order natural to the Breckenridges and that same story could not live for them in the same way. But, had they asked, though they never did, Wade would have told them that for his story to be theirs was not the point.

But Wade never came out of the house. The three young men stopped at the Cass' truck. It was time to put this down to a word and a handshake. "What do y'all think?" said Arlen.

Roy folded his arms. "Well, only so much we can tell lookin' at him. Don't really know 'til he's broke."

"You've got my word he'll be as good as the others."

"Ain't doubtin' your word." Roy paused. "What are you askin' for him?"

"One hundred fifty."

"Too much. If he was broke, that's another matter."

"I can get him broke, but that's a matter of time. Can y'all wait?" No answer from the Casses. "Fine, how about one hundred thirty?"

"One hundred ten," said Calvin.

"You're robbin' the family blind," said Arlen.

"You ain't got to take it," said Calvin.

Roy spoke with a serious finality from the depths of his big chest. "One hundred fifteen, Arlen. Best we can do."

Arlen shook his head and kicked a stone at his feet. "I reckon I can talk Pa into it," he said eventually. "But at that price, I'd appreciate Roy's help breakin' him," said Arlen.

Roy laughed. "I might stand a better chance in the Navy than in the ring with that animal."

"I'm countin' on you for it," said Arlen.

"And I'm countin' on you to do the right thing," said Roy.

"What do you mean?" And then he understood. "You want me to enlist?"

"We've all got to eventually."

"I ain't got to do a damn thing if it ain't time."

"How are you going to know it's time? Don't seem to me like you care to know."

Leave me alone. My family's always done the right thing. But we ain't done it 'cause anyone made us.

Arlen almost told them this. But he held the words back, where they stayed. He had to hold them back, for he saw a car turning up the drive: it was Caty.

The two Cass boys saw her, too. They grinned knowingly. "Well ain't this been a day," said Calvin. "We get to see if not one but two of Arlen's pets have all their teeth."

"Y'all get out of here." They didn't move, so Arlen pushed them into their truck. "Go on, now. Get out of here."

"All right. We'll let you know what we decide," said Calvin.

"Don't keep me waitin' too long," said Arlen. "I want an answer."

Roy reached out of the truck window and plopped the copy of the *News-Enterprise*, headline facing up, right in Arlen's hand. "Uncle Sam is, too. Don't keep him, either."

Arlen didn't look at the paper and he didn't care to watch them go. He felt distance between Roy and himself. They had been in school together and their families had swapped work before, back when it was still a custom, one dying out but useful all the same. He had thought they would carry on the relationship of their fathers, and perhaps even make it stronger, work giving new meaning to the play of their youth. But that seemed almost impossible now. They had come from the same place, grown up in much the same way. But where had the path split? They each took their own now, but Arlen's did not feel wrong or lonely. He felt he was entering another season, the same but with its minor changes, in the kind of life he had seen lived out and heard passed down in a thousand family memories. The accumulated weight of lives long since passed but still here were with him all the time — everything he did was in their light, and that did not bother him, for he was little different.

But this newspaper: this would not do. It wouldn't do anyone any good,

Caty least of all. He took the newspaper and, averting his eyes from any more of it, ran to the outhouse and tossed it inside on the gap-toothed floorboards.

The table had been at first well laid, but perhaps laid to waste was a better term now. The remains of supper were growing colder and colder, but nobody noticed, for they were caught up in conversation. Or at least Wade was. He was holding court from his chair at the head of the table, delving into stories about the family. Tonight, Wade told many about the three girls who had once expanded the table. He thought anyone would be glad to know what a handful they had proven to be. Having finished one more story, Wade inclined his body toward Caty, causing his chair to creak badly. "But Miss Cline, I hope you know that ain't no reflection on Arlen here. He's been easy in comparison."

"I thought the baby of the family was the wild one," said Caty. "Wild and a big talker."

Arlen flushed in his face. Was that him? He didn't think so, but perhaps Caty saw him that way. He looked over at Caty and with his keen eye, saw her suck in her lower lip a bit, as if holding back a smile. She was simply teasing. She knew he was anything but.

A grin crept up Wade's face. He saw through Caty's deadpan expression and he liked her, Arlen could tell. Arlen knew that after supper, his father would tell him not to let her slip through his fingers.

Legenia, though, was not as perceptive as the other two. Or perhaps she was but felt the need to set opinions, and especially Wade's, a little straighter. "It weren't Arlen. Elizabeth was always the troublemaker," said Legenia of their second child. "It's because she was so tall."

Wade had not intended to conversation to turn away from the subject of his son with all these stories. Better that they all pointed back to the subject of the boy. He had told many a story of Arlen to his daughter's suitors in order to make them appear more angelic than perhaps they deserved. But the conversation had gotten a bit away from him and so he had to continue down the path he had started. "Yes, Elizabeth was taller than Rebecca by the time they were nine and ten," said Wade.

"And Rebecca's the oldest?" said Caty.

"Yes'm. And couple years later, Elizabeth was almost as tall as Legenia. Everyone she met thought she was older and treated her like it, so she got a big head. Sweet girl now, but she tormented Rebecca and Ruth something terrible. Arlen got the worst of it, though."

Legenia rocked her head side to side as if considering the veracity of those words. "I remember when Arlen was real little, Elizabeth would pick him up and threaten to drop him if he didn't stick his arms up high. Then she'd walk to a tree, make him grab onto the branch, and walk off. She'd tell him that she'd only take him down if he promised to do her chores every morning for a week."

Caty looked at Arlen. "Did you?"

The young man shook his head slightly. "Not the first time. It was high, but I figured I could drop down without hurtin' myself. Except I about broke my ankle and couldn't walk for a week. Ma and Pa didn't believe me, though, when I told 'em who did it."

"Took us a while to figure out that Arlen was tellin' the truth," said Legenia. "Those girls were good at hidin' what they did."

"And I couldn't hit them back," said Arlen.

"Now, Arlen, we let you hit back once we found out how bad they were to you," said Wade.

Arlen nodded. "I suppose I got a few good licks in on Elizabeth and Rebecca, at least before they left home."

"Where are they all now?" said Caty.

Wade stretched his arms. "Rebecca lives in Hickory with her husband. Had her first child a year ago. Elizabeth got married last year and lives down in Charlotte. No children yet."

"And Ruth?"

"Ruth's in Winston-Salem. She's a typist at R.J. Reynolds." Wade nodded to himself. "Yes, they're all gone now. Just Arlen here."

"It must be hard running this farm with just the three of you, Mr. Breckenridge," said Caty.

"Most of the time ain't all that bad. Harvest is the hardest time. Seems like we have to hire help more and more. Folks don't swap work as much as they used to. Of course that's the problem with everything these days, the money." Wade sighed at length and his chest seemed to settle down further onto his big frame. "Been a problem for us, I'll say it. Wheat prices ain't all that good, I'm findin' out, and the feds holdin' them up ain't solved it neither. I ain't ever tried to make all my money off one crop; that's a fool's errand and we've always known that. But there's got to be a margin somewhere, enough to break even at the end of the year. It's one thing to have bad prices for a year or two or even a few more. We can weather it. But I'm concerned ain't no one buyin' our mules, cotton ain't high enough, and ain't enough profit on truckin' the garden patch to town. I ain't worried 'bout it for me, I'm worried 'bout it for Arlen here. This place is as good as his now, but I still can't help feelin' that I've got to keep us from the worst of it."

He did not mention what the worst of it was, although perhaps Caty should have known: going into debt, losing money every year, and watching the farm slip away, little by little, then all at once. It was their realest fear, for it had been happening all around them for the past couple of generations. Only tenacity — or pig-headed stubbornness, as some neighbors saw it — in their ways, ameliorated by a natural simplicity, kept them from darting here or there, trying to get ahead or get away; they stayed put and persisted. They grew, but they did not measurably change. They were no different than corn.

The farmer raised his gaze, buried deep into the table, up to the level of Caty's eyes and forced a smile. "But with the Good Lord's help we'll weather it somehow. Always have before. Few needs, few troubles, that's what I've always said."

"A thousand times," confirmed Legenia.

Caty cocked her head thoughtfully. "If you don't mind me asking, Mr. Breckenridge, why are you still worried?"

"Ma'am?"

"You survived having money and survived not having it. You survived other folks having it and also not having it. Y'all survived this long. What else could there possibly be to worry about?"

Wade was speechless for once. He thought to speak, but his lips just sat pursed. After a moment, he sat back in his chair and nodded with a smile. "Yes, ma'am, I reckon you're right."

Caty looked to Arlen. Her look wondered if she had done right.

What could he say? It was always better to say nothing. After all, there was no reason to contradict her. She had spoken plainly and fairly. Arlen could tell Wade was put off by it. But perhaps Wade was wrong. After all, Caty was right: what else was there to worry about? What could possibly threaten the family and the farm if they kept fighting off every danger through their own cunning, their careful choices, and their natural discipline?

Maybe Pa just ain't as certain as he used to be. Maybe all this struggle has got to him. Things'll be better when I take over. Ain't like I'll forget the lessons, I know 'em all. I just ain't been battered down by learnin' 'em.

Arlen drifted away for a moment. He thought about his father and how perhaps the old man wasn't as sharp or as endlessly right as Arlen once believed. Wade had his flaws that marked his manly limitations as surely as any other. He was a father, a patriarch, a titan of the community, but he was a man, too. He was not greater than the son, in the final reckoning of it all.

A rousing chorus of laughter and Caty's hand on his arm brought Arlen back. It must have been quite a joke that Wade had told. Even Legenia laughed as she cleared the plates from the table. Then the laughing tapered into a sated quiet. Eventually, Legenia finished clanking dishes in the kitchen and came back out. Caty did not wait for Legenia to sit back down but stood up. "Thank you for a wonderful evening. I really, really do appreciate your welcoming me here."

"Our pleasure," said Wade, standing slowly. He smiled. "Any time, ma'am."

"Yes, any time," said Legenia. "As I'm the cook, that's my offer to make too. Any time, Caty."

"Well, thank you again," said Caty.

"Are you really going to drive all the way home alone?" said Legenia. "After the last time?"

"I've just got to get right back on that horse," said Caty. "I won't let myself be afraid. I just won't."

"Arlen, you want to follow her home, make sure she gets back all right?" said Wade.

"No, no, I'll be just fine," insisted Caty.

They all headed toward the front door. "We'll have to have you over again, when Arlen's sisters are back home. They'll love to meet you too," said Legenia.

"I look forward to it," said Caty. "Good night!"

Arlen and Caty walking down to her car. It was used but new to her. He felt conscious that Wade and Legenia were looking at them. He turned around and gave them a stare until they went back inside. Once they were alone, Caty laid her hand on his arm. It seemed to be her mark of affection. "I wasn't just saying that. I really did enjoy them."

"I know they did too."

"How do you know?"

"'Cause my mother talked to you."

"Oh!" Caty laughed. But her laughter did not last long. "Arlen, what's on your mind?"

He gnawed his lip for just a moment. "Caty, why are you so interested in us? I mean, in how we survive?"

She looked down at her feet. "I grew up on my uncle's farm. He looked after my father. We moved to Hickory when I was seven, right before the crash. My father worked in Highland, at the mill. He survived the furloughs and everything else, but he couldn't survive his drinking." Caty shook her head and her hair bounced tautly. "They finally fired him last year and my uncle, once again, was the only one to give my father work. And me, too. I do the books for him." Caty looked up. "Whether the mills stops or a man drinks himself out of a job," she said, "I know a farm will always have work for as many folks as want it."

Arlen nodded, understanding suddenly his great unacknowledged blessing.

"Don't ever say a bad word about your family, Arlen, because there ain't nothing about them to be ashamed of." Caty sounded defensive, as if Arlen himself had spoken ill of them. Caty's eyes did not move to meet his; she looked off across the fields, which were hazy in the quickly failing light.

"There's no reason to be ashamed of yourself either. Don't ever be that way. I know it ain't an easy life. Although maybe you don't have to get up every day and look it in the face and say that you're going to stick with it. Maybe it's easier for you, even though it's a hard thing for most folks today. I can tell you got that from your father and your mother."

She kept on. "Arlen, I saw it in you first, and now I see it in them. Your family works hard, but work isn't everything to them. They love simple things and don't need a lot. And, Arlen, they didn't stand on airs. Not that I expected them to, but they took me right in tonight, from the moment we got to the porch and your father held the door for me and commented on you bringing home light to the darkness, in that funny little way of his, and your mother hugging me when I came in and telling me all the good things you'd said about me. They didn't drown me in affection, and they weren't cold. As if they'd known me for years! That's why you came down to the road that day we met. I know it. I know it's why everything else has happened the way it has."

Caty was looking at him now, eyes full, brimming not with tears but with feeling. He leaned closer to her and, to his surprise, she leaned toward him. Their lips met softly, had one kiss, and then pulled back. Arlen saw her eyes were closed. He leaned in farther, with greater strength, and set his lips on hers again, this time firmly. Caty reached up and pushed him away after a second, her fingertips pressing firmly on his chest, pressing him away from her. Arlen could not resist. He felt his will, though not his desire, drain away from him through her fingertips, as if they were greedy roots drawing every bit of water from the soil. Arlen stepped back, almost empty, wanting to gasp for a breath, but not daring, only looking at her.

Caty wiped her eyes, but she was smiling as she did. "Good night, Arlen. Thank you."

"See you soon?" he said. He wished he hadn't. He sounded like a little boy.

But she did not look at him like one. She looked at him like a man. "Very soon." And with that, she started the car and was gone for the night.

IV

"Y'all call a doctor!"

But how? There was no telephone. If someone could have hollered for the doctor, they would have. But even if one of them had the lungs for it, who around would have known what the holler meant? Things weren't quite that way anymore.

Still, there was plenty of shouting from Arlen as he came toward the house. "A doctor!"

From the barn, Wade came running. Legenia and Arlen's sister Elizabeth emerged from the back door of the house. They shielded their eyes against the August sun. They didn't seem terribly worried.

"One of y'all want to help?" shouted Arlen. The weight was about to break him. Only then did Wade begin to scoot over to them.

"Come on Roy, just keep breathin'. Keep it coming." Arlen pulled Roy's arm further over his shoulder and hefted his huge friend as much as he could bear.

"Ain't like I can — aw, shit — ain't — ain't like I can stop Arlen. Just — shit — just hurts like hell when I do."

"Reckon you broke a rib."

It had been a long hobble from the mule pen and Arlen could not bear the weight anymore. Just as his strength was about to give out, Wade caught Roy's other arm and hefted the big young man. "Y'all make way!" said Wade as they came up to the back door. Legenia and Elizabeth both got out of the way as they threaded sideways through the door with their gasping neighbor.

"Put him in Arlen's room," said Legenia.

"Ain't no way we'll get him upstairs," said Wade, clearly feeling the strain himself.

"Just lay me down on the porch," wheezed Roy.

"The porch? That's no place for the boy," said Legenia.

"Aw, hell, just put him out there!" said Arlen. They dragged him through the house, out the front door, and laid him down.

"No, prop him up, Arlen. He'll suffocate himself like that!" said Elizabeth.

"Don't tell me what to do," said Arlen.

"Pick him up."

Roy batted away their arms. "Leave me here," he gasped.

"What happened to him?" said Wade.

"Mule kicked him square in the chest," said Arlen.

The women gasped. Wade's eyes went wide. "How come you ain't dead, Roy?"

"Pa, ain't like he ain't wondered it himself," said Arlen.

"He should be thankin' the Lord Almighty. A kick square to the chest should have burst his heart. Did you see it coming, son?" said Wade, putting his hand on Roy's shoulder.

"Pa, leave him be, he can't talk."

"That might've saved him." Wade cocked his head back. "Or maybe it's just 'cause you're a hoss, Roy."

Roy nodded through a grimace of pain. "I'm a big ol' boy," he choked out.

"You think he needs a doctor?" said Arlen.

"You run out in the truck to fetch the doctor, by the time you come back, Roy'll be fine or dead."

"If I'm gonna die," said Roy, "I need one thing."

"Oh, Arlen, do it for him," said Legenia.

Roy waggled his head. "Don't want it from Arlen." He raised his eyes. "I need just a peck from sweet Elizabeth here."

Legenia gasped. Elizabeth snorted, less offended than her mother was. Arlen stood up. "You sonuvabitch, she's a married woman." He gave Roy a sharp kick to the side with the toe of his boot. That set off a spasm of racking coughs. "Hope that mule did bust something up in you."

Elizabeth shook her head. "Arlen, don't be too upset. Just the courage of a dyin' man. Brave enough to ask for now what he had years to try and steal but never did." She leaned over Roy. "Ain't that right?"

Roy grimaced and it was hard to tell the real pain from the fake.

"Mama, we got to go," said Elizabeth. "That train ain't going to wait."

Wade sighed. "Reckon I got to drive y'all to the station now, don't I? My work's got to wait on the world, world can't wait on me, can it?"

Nobody said anything. Wade was not mad at the world. He was upset that his children wanted their parents to come visit them at their homes, when Wade thought they should come to visit him at his. Elizabeth had tried to split the difference and came for a couple of days before taking Legenia back to Charlotte to help decorate her new house, but it was not enough for Wade. His mind was set: this was the family seat and life did not take place out there.

The woman gathered their bags and took them to the car. Elizabeth bid a farewell to her brother. "You stay safe. Don't let yourself get kicked. You ain't got the sense to stay down like Roy here."

Arlen nodded. "I'll be seein' you." Roy moaned a farewell.

The mule would not be broken today. But Arlen would not give up on it. He went back out to the pen and kept at it until the mule was worn out. Not broke, but worn out. Neither of them had prevailed for the day, but there was always tomorrow. Roy would spend the night and maybe would be feeling better in the morning.

Arlen ate cold biscuits, buttermilk, and ham for supper. The inside of the house was orangish-yellow from the oil lamps on the table. Finishing his meal, Arlen opened the kitchen window. The night air, slightly damp on the skin, came wafting through the house from the open front window. Outside on the porch there was the sound of Wade tuning the fiddle. Short little squawks of the bow on the strings, rough like bristly hairs or pea gravel. Longer strokes — A-A-A-D——A-A-D-A went the notes — were smoother, but not by much. Wade had the bow too tight. Arlen heard him work his way through the beginning notes of several songs, skipping from one to another. Filling a cup with water, he went out on the porch.

Roy was now propped up against one of the porch columns. Arlen handed him the water. He sucked down about half of it before he began to choke.

"Easy now," said Arlen.

"That mule busted you up pretty well, Roy. You feel any better?"

"Don't feel better, but I'm feelin', that's for sure."

"Well, that's something," said Wade. "What do you say we celebrate feelin' something. That and the womenfolk not being around." Wade looked up at his son. "Arlen, you pick a little and I'll fiddle."

Arlen knew that picking and fiddling meant more than just that. He was excited. When he came back out on the porch with his guitar, twilight had almost passed, but it was still light enough to see the glint of the bottle Wade held in his hand. Wade was running his finger over his chin. "One of y'all tell me: what did you do to that mule to make him kick?"

"Nothin'," said Arlen. "That mule's just a loose cannon. All over the damn place. Couldn't get the halter anywhere near his face."

Wade rested the fiddle on his knee. "What changed?"

"That mule's the same as the day Calvin and I came over to take a look at him," said Roy. "Ornery, that's all. Angry, even." Roy shifted his weight and winced in pain. A racking cough shook his body. He recovered his breath and his face seemed to ease. "I wasn't sure if we should buy that mule in the first place, but, I'll tell you, I got even more reservations about it now."

"Well, we'll figure out something." Wade handed the bottle, the cork gone, out to Roy. "Take a few sips of that, son. It'll help that cough."

"That what it smells like, Mr. Breckenridge?"

"Drink up."

They sat in the dark, the lamp light from inside nearly imperceptible to them. They played music and drank one by one from the bottle. Roy said nothing the whole time, for pain and whiskey silenced him, and hardly a dozen sentences passed between Arlen and his father. They only spoke about the songs they played. And play they did, each in his own way. Wade did not fiddle with speed or passion. He certainly could if he wanted to, dropping the fiddle down off his shoulder almost into the crook of his arm and bowing with a sharp, snapping motion of the wrist, hand gripping the bow quite high. At gatherings with neighbors — which came fewer and fewer than in days before — he played like that and some folks found his rhythm so infectious they couldn't help but make an impromptu dance. But that was Wade in the light, amongst people. He was not a man to wear a mask, but he knew what people thought of him. If he showed them a good time, they would question their own judgments upon him. But any time he gave them mystery and complexity, they found him a baffling character, an eccentric whose set ways seemed to provoke more and more confusion and revulsion as the years went on. He was a living reminder of an uncomfortable fact and both he and they knew it.

Wade knew, too, that manners meant knowing what to show and what to hide and when to do each. So it was here, in the dark, that Wade played, not with speed but with feeling. He had loosened up the bow and Arlen could tell from the sound that it had a better touch on the strings. The tempo seemed to slow and slow some more. Arlen picked the harmony on his cheap guitar, just simple notes backing his father Wade would hit one note softly and the next one with a quick but deep burst of effort, letting the note blossom from the full weight of his hand on the bow. Then the note would die off in a lonesome taper and there was a nearly soundless pause between it and the next note, which Roy and Arlen hung onto, waiting for the next one, like waiting for another breath that might not come. Each song ended and with only a few words, the next one began in the same pattern. Eventually, Wade stopped and set the fiddle on the porch and folded his hands across his stomach. "You play one, Arlen."

"I ain't good leading. You know that."

"I ain't tellin' you to lead. I want to hear just the guitar."

Arlen fingered the stubble under his chin. "Which one?"

Wade leaned back in his chair. Its joints creaked. "Long way back, I taught you a couple of tunes. You were too little for that guitar, but you got the fingering just fine." Wade stretched out his hand toward Arlen. "Let me see that." Arlen handed over the guitar. Wade tucked the guitar in close and hunched himself over it, face intent. He was silent. The crickets chirped and droned out in the thick, warm darkness. Then Wade's fingers set to the strings and began to play for a minute. He stopped and handed the guitar back to Arlen. "Wasn't the first one I taught you, but it was the one you played the best."

Roy finally broke his silence. "What's the name?"

"*Old Stepstone*," said Arlen. "Now that you played it, the tune's back in my fingers, but the words ain't in my head."

"Then I'll sing it." Wade licked his lips, leaned forward with elbows on knees, and waited for his cue from his son. Arlen played the tune through one time, then nodded to his father.

"*I stand on the doorstep at evening time now, the wind whispers by with a moan.*" Wade's voice was clear but he had added an edge of ache to it. "*The fields will be white and I will be gone, to roam o'er this wide world alone.*"

Arlen kept playing, head down, listening to the words.

"*Goodbye dear ol' stepstone, goodbye to my home, God bless those I leave with a sigh. I'll cherish fond memories when I'm far away, to roam o'er this wide world alone.*"

Wade abruptly stopped and leaned back in his chair. Arlen quickly finished off the tune, but let the last notes ring in the guitar, fading and giving way to the sound of the crickets again.

"Where did you learn that one, Mr. Breckenridge?" Roy said. His words flowed whiskey-smooth over the cracked rib.

Wade was absolutely stock still and perfectly silent. After a moment, Arlen started to wonder if he had fallen asleep. Then his father's voice rolled out into the night air. "A feller in the Army with me taught me that song. He was a mountain boy. Can't quite remember where he was from, maybe up Madison County way. He came down to Hickory, worked in the Piedmont Wagon factory there, and joined up with the rest of us when the war started. We were all nervous, 'cause we didn't know where we were going. And this feller, his name was Buckner, and he said he already knew what that was like, leavin' home. Said he'd learned that song when he was young, but he didn't know how right it was until he moved down to Hickory. I don't think he ever liked working in that factory. The Army didn't suit him neither." Wade took a sip from the bottle and let it wash around in his mouth. "Some of the other fellers didn't care for him, and I don't know how much he cared for us 'flat-landers,' but I liked Buckner. He taught me that song."

There was a length of peacefulness after Wade finished speaking. He cradled the bottle in his lap for a while, then set it down on the porch, within reach of them all.

"Was it bad, Mr. Breckenridge?" said Roy loudly, shattering the quiet. He was quite drunk.

"Was what bad?"

"Going off to fight. In the war."

"Which part? Leavin' home?"

"All of it."

"Leavin' home was hard. I hadn't ever been farther than Statesville before that." Wade stopped.

Roy persisted in his questioning. "Well, how was it hard?"

Arlen felt a little sour. He and not Roy should be asking Wade these questions. *But I ain't ever had no mind to ask. Pa never talked about it.*

Wade drank from the bottle again before he replied to Roy. "I never had been away from this place and I didn't know what was out there in the wide world. I was excited, of course I was, but it got to my nerves at times." Wade stopped. Arlen could not see if he was pondering a point or just had nothing more to say. But eventually his voice cut again through the dark. "Reckon that was because everything was always changing. We were always going someplace, packin' up, unpackin'. They'd give us an officer, then switch him out after a week 'cause he was a fool, or sometimes promote him because he was too good, and then they'd assign us a fool. There was a lot to learn – marchin', salutin', all the little bits of drill. And then we had to just about forget all that when we were put on the line and we had to learn how to fight all over again."

"What do you mean? They didn't train you the way to fight?"

"No."

Arlen had never ever heard Wade's voice that terse. He felt the need to put himself between his friend and his father, just in case Roy went a little too far. "Pa, I reckon Roy was just curious. Just tryin' to get an idea of what it was like."

"I reckon there ain't much to tell. I didn't do nothin' too important. Hell, I didn't even see a German worth shootin' at. Only ones I ever came across were already dead or prisoners."

"So you ain't ever shot a man?" Roy said.

"I was in charge of laying the wire for the field telephones. I spent all my time hoofin' back and forth between the major and the telephone exchange in the rear."

"That's all you did? Lay wire?"

Wade's disembodied voice rumbled sternly through the humid purple-black air. "It was an important job. All the shellin' kept you busy, 'cause the shells would cut the line and you'd have to run out and replace it. There were other fellers who rotated in and out, but not many of 'em liked it. Weren't much good at it, either."

"How's that?"

"If the wire's cut, most of the time you got to get out of the trench and run out in the open to fix it. If the Germans had a crack shot or a machine gun sighted in, they'd put bullets around you. They'd snap around your ears. Most fellers didn't like that. 'Course, I didn't either, but I was good at the job. You boys should have seen me back in my day. I could carry a hog on each shoulder and go anywhere with 'em, even up a ladder. Runnin' with wire, that was nothin'. There was only one other feller who could do it. He was farm boy like me, from Minnesota. He'd been doing it longer than me, showed me a few tricks. We got on real well, we'd lay wire together. Thing was, he was a mite tall. One day, we ran out of wire and needed more. He told me he'd go back and get more. He scooted down into a shell hole and I reckon he stood up a little bit too much as he went across the bottom. German shot him through his helmet." Wade cleared his throat. "His name was Arlen. He didn't have no family of his own, so I named my son after him."

Arlen's face flushed. Roy looked over at him, as if he could feel the heat from Arlen's cheeks. "How about that?" he said. Arlen said nothing. He knew he had been named for his father's friend. But he had never heard the truth until now. It was a strange time to mention it, strange for Wade to talk about the war so freely. The whiskey was not lubricating the way, there was something else pressing it out of Wade, some other need that did not come from within, but from out there.

Why now?

Before Arlen could speak, though, Roy was at it again. "It was a rough time, then?" Roy asked Wade. "Did you have some close calls?"

Wade's voice was very low. "Yes."

Roy forged ahead with his questioning. "Mr. Breckenridge, I just want to know what it was like," he said, his words slurring from the drink. "And I reckon I wanted to know what we have to do if there's a war. I mean, what do you think we should do, Mr. Breckenridge, when we get into a war?"

Wade took his time and his voice was very low when he did speak, but reply he did: "Do what's right. Do your duty."

"I'm gonna do my duty, Mr. Breckenridge, I guarantee you that. You mean my duty to my country, don't you?"

"If that's what your duty is."

"Well, ain't that duty, Mr. Breckenridge? Weren't that your duty? Why'd you go to fight?"

Wade's voice was no louder than before when he eventually spoke. "I won't go into why we went, what we thought we were fightin' for. Doesn't matter now, because none of it came to pass, not like folks said it would. But going was the right thing. Not going would've been worse. And a man's duty ain't a terrible thing."

The hairs on Arlen's neck prickled in a wave to the top of his scalp.

If it ain't terrible, then why does he sound like it is? And how can stayin' here be worse?

Wade hefted his bulk out of the chair and slowly bent over to pick up the fiddle and bow. "All right, boys, now that's enough. I'm going to bed. Roy, you going to be all right?"

"If I'm still warm to the touch in the mornin', you can count on me for breakfast."

"Arlen'll fix up a place for you to sleep. See y'all in the mornin'."

"'Night, Pa."

"'Night, Mr. Breckenridge."

They didn't say anymore. Arlen just took the bottle from Roy and had another long pull, then set to barely picking the guitar, no louder than the crickets.

Morning came all too soon. Arlen had tried liquor a few times, but never quite that much, and he knew from the moment he awoke it would be a long, hard day. With a pinch in his temples and a dry mouth, he stumbled through the morning chores. The cow milked, Arlen headed straight for the kitchen, his hand already out for the coffee pot on the back of the Big Boy iron stove.

"Just what do you think you're doing?" said Wade, sweating before the stove.

"Pourin' coffee."

Wade lifted a piece of hog jowl out of the skillet and dropped in a fresh slice. Grease popped like foam under a mill wheel. "The chickens."

Arlen rubbed his eyes, nodded, and went back outside to let the chickens loose.

When at last he had coffee in hand, Arlen went to check on Roy. His friend was not where Arlen had left him, in the girls' old bedroom, feet sticking over the end of the bed and arms sprawled across the whole breadth of the coverlet. He found Roy resting in a chair on the porch, rocking slowly back and forth. He had his shirt off. In the center of his chest was a large purple bruise stippled with black spots, the shape of a gibbous moon. "Goodness, Roy, look at that thing."

"Almost the size of a dinner plate, ain't it?""

"You want coffee?"

"Oh Lord, I think I need a whole pot."

"Come on in, we'll eat."

The pork was passable, as was the cornbread if you washed it down with coffee, for it was a little dry. Wade was not much of a cook. Nor was he much of a conversationalist this morning. He sat there staring past the boys, who just ate silently, wholly in the grip of their aching heads. No acknowledgment was made of the night before. It was as if it was already a secret past not to be dredged up for light and transient reasons.

Pushing back his chair, Wade left his dishes on the table and walked to the front door. He donned his hat, a two-toned fedora, faded from the sun and stained from sweat. "Roy?" called Wade through the house.

"Yessir?"

Wade stepped back to the table. Even now there was no acknowledgment that the deep conversation of the night before, nor evidence of even the slightest offense at Roy's drunken probing. "Hope you heal up quick."

"Thank you, sir."

"And if your father changes his mind on that mule, I'll understand. Wouldn't blame you."

"Yessir, thank you."

And Wade was out the door, saying nothing to Arlen. He did not even glance at his son. His eyes were set confidently in the shade of the hat brim: so guarded, they were ready for work and nothing else. They wanted above all else the consoling solitude of long, hard labor.

"Well? You want to stay on and break that mule?" said Arlen to Roy, his voice hopeful.

"Arlen, I ain't in any shape to break anything or anyone today."

Arlen concealed his disappointment behind a long slug from his cup of coffee. "Reckon I'll drive you home."

"Reckon you'll have to."

They were well down the road in the truck before either one of them spoke again. "Did you hear about Luther?" said Roy.

"Heard how liquored up he got just to have the courage to stand at the altar." said Arlen. "Can you blame him? Reckon that was the only way he could go through with marryin' that Harriet girl."

"That ain't the half of it. Harriet's gonna have a baby."

Arlen guffawed. "Already? Luther's a real Davy Crockett."

Roy paused and then laughed. "Oh, he don't miss on the first try, that's for sure." They both chuckled. "I thought you meant it's 'cause he wrestled down a bear," added Roy.

"That's Daniel Boone, Roy."

"Oh."

They were nearly to the Cass place when Roy tapped on the glass and nodded to a dirt lane that led off into the woods. "Would you pull off here?"

Arlen was surprised. "What's down there?"

"Just drive, would you?"

The long, thin drive snaked through hickory and poplar and arrived at a tiny white house. The paint was chipped and cobwebs and mud dauber nests accumulated under the eaves. There was no grass around the house and a broad carpet of leaves, twigs, and hickory nuts wholly undisturbed by feet or wheels. As soon as the truck stopped, Roy lumbered out.

"Where are you going?" said Arlen.

"Inside. Come or stay, whatever you like."

Roy went right up the brick front stoop and pushed in the front door, which was cracked halfway open. As Arlen followed, he saw the windows were wide open. As soon as he stepped into the house, he heard chirping and fluttering. He peeked into each of the rooms. They were damp and dank. Cautiously, Arlen stepped into the small parlor to see where Roy had gone. A pair of birds went chirping and twittering past his head. He ducked instinctively. The two chickadees alighted on separate perches, one on the window sill, the other on an upright of a chair back, holding itself sideways and twisting its head about for a better view. The chair was marked with tiny scratches, so fine they could only have come from birds' feet. There were crusty white-black splotches of bird feces scattered across the floorboards, dripping down the front of the dresser, and carpeting the windowsills. There was nothing painted or colorful or lacy in the house. Arlen heard the sound of rummaging and he followed it into the lone bedroom. Roy was poking around in the bottom of the wardrobe. "Good Lord, Roy, what is this place?"

"This is my Uncle David's house."

Arlen remembered Roy's uncle now. He was a strange fellow who sold seed and farm implements from time to time, but most of the time never worked. He never married, and while he was friendly toward children, most found him an awkward man. Arlen looked around the bedroom. The posts on the cannonball bed were scratched up and shat upon. "The house is ruined. Why has he let it go to pot like this?"

Roy shook his head. "He always liked birds, so he'd open up the house most days and let the birds fly in. I'd bet that bowl on the kitchen table was full of seed at one point."

"Ain't he gonna be mad that you're going through his stuff?" Arlen saw over Roy's shoulder into the box in his friend's hand. There were a couple of medals, darkened and discolored, and a stack of letters written in thin, slanting script. Roy closed it and set it back in the corner of the closet.

"Roy, ain't he gonna be mad?"

"He passed away, Arlen."

"Roy, I'm sorry. I didn't know. When?"

"Back in the spring. You were busy with the planting, I never told you."

"I would've come to the funeral anyway."

Roy waved a dismissive hand. "He was peculiar, didn't want no funeral. Just to be buried in his uniform."

"Uniform?"

"He fought in the war," said Roy.

"He was mighty talkative around us, but I don't remember him ever sayin' that he was in the army."

"Your pa didn't say much to you about it neither," said Roy.

A damp and moldy silence hung between them as Roy dug through the mess in the bottom of the wardrobe. "There something in there you're lookin' for?"

"Hopin' to find his diary. I know he kept one. Might tell his thoughts about the war. I've got to—" Roy shook his head and sighed. "Never mind. Ain't gonna get the full truth from anyone anyhow. Certainly didn't get it from your pa."

Arlen jerked bolt upright. "What's my pa to do with it?"

"I asked him what we should do if there's a war, and what did he tell us? You tell me, 'cause I sure couldn't figure it out." When Arlen did not respond, Roy continued. "I wanted to know what was good and what was bad, the right way and the right side. I want to do the best for my country, be the best soldier, be one of the ones who wins the war if we have one, and what did he tell us? Do your duty, that's all. And not even what that is. I'll tell you now, Arlen, when your pa said that, I about made up my mind to enlist. Not 'cause I took his words to heart, but 'cause they don't even know why they fought. Well, I know. I made up my mind for myself and if I stick with that, ain't ever gonna be in doubt."

And Roy could have just left it at that and Arlen would have silently wavered between the vague insult and the sharp fact that were in fact one and the same. But Roy just couldn't do that.

"You ought to join up, too, Arlen. Don't you wait around for your pa to tell you the right thing to do. I ain't waitin' for Cal to quit runnin' his mouth about joinin' the Navy. I ain't waitin' for the war to get here or the politicians to make up their damn minds, neither. You ought to be more serious 'bout this."

"Don't you tell me what to do," said Arlen.

"Then who will?" said Roy, raising an eyebrow. "You gonna wait for your pa to tell you?"

Arlen was silent.

Roy muttered under his breath.

"What was that? You call me a coward, Roy?"

Roy glared back at his friend. "I did not."

But look at those eyes of his. Those are the eyes of contempt, the kind of contempt that only a friend can have for a friend.

"You sonuvabitch, you take it back."

Arlen shifted his weight in preparation for the moment he thought was coming and Roy was quick to read the motion. The bigger man's arm cocked back as if to throw a punch, a big, barrelling roundhouse. But Arlen saw the motion and stepped in with a short, quick strike. He wasn't as strong as Roy, but he knew where to place the punch. He drove his fist right into the tender bruise on Roy's chest. His friend bellowed like a bull and then squeaked like a mousey, frightened woman and collapsed down on the floor. Arlen stepped back, fists clenched, ready in case Roy rose up and came at him. But the jab had taken all the fight out of the bigger man. After a few minutes, Roy was able to rise to his knees. He tenderly probed his ribs. "All right, Arlen, I take it back."

Arlen reached out and helped his friend up.

Roy looked around the house once again and then at his friend. "You want to take me home?"

The Cass farm was just around the bend in the road. It was vibrant and busy: Mr. Cass and Cal were spreading fertilizer while the hands were chopping weeds in the sweet potato field. Arlen stopped the truck in front of the house, which was surrounded on three sides by all kinds of machinery, some new, much of it old and rusty.

"Roy, tell me, why did your uncle David not work? Your family gave him food and firewood and always looked after him; why'd they support a man who wouldn't work?"

"He couldn't work, Arlen. Couldn't do much of anything. Uncle David was gassed."

"Gassed?"

"Mustard gas. From a German shell. Burnt his lungs all up. He didn't take much interest in anything after that."

Arlen drove straight home. For once he did not take even a passing interest in the land around him. He did not stop, as he once might have, to watch a field of corn stretching upward in the full-on heat with an audible creak here and there, nor a herd of languid Jerseys, the grass between their teeth tautly ripping from the ground. He felt so unsettled. He felt acutely that there was much building outside all of this, this land of small places where food and raiment grew called Catawba County, North Carolina. Yet all was fine here, for all that had changed: this place continued on and on and on, the forms persisting, and strongly with some, with the few like the Breckenridges. Theirs was to continue on doing right, and doing it well, though not in any hope of a great arrival at somewhere wonderful, where the harvest was full every year and the rain and sun just right and never a lame mule nor sick wife. No, theirs was simply to persist until what was building out there came here and did its

45

ambiguous work and then left, and then they would persist some more.

And maybe that moment would come just like this gray, heavy storm that had drawn larger and larger as Arlen had headed west across the county toward home: surprising him from over the horizon, dark clouds rolling in, full of intent, but not releasing their purpose yet. The clouds covered the light of the green and golden upland tracts and the river bottom pieces and the small farms with their darkness, but did nothing yet. They had their own way of waiting, of a strange providence, letting Arlen reach the house, park the truck, and make his way to the barn where Wade was putting away the cultivator, before opening up and letting the rain fall, steady, heavy drops that did not cease for days.

V

Slowly, with crusted eyelids, Arlen awoke for good. The rain was on the roof, an embracing low roar. Staring at the ceiling as he blinked the sleep away, Arlen found the sound the only thing he could focus on. Not a single individual drop could he make out, not even water dripping from the eaves on the roof. Something about the rain sounded different. After a period of lying beneath the thin sheet, listening with an empty mind, in that blissfully unhurried, unworried time of the day when there is no momentum placing demands on thought, Arlen was struck by the strength of the rain. The falling water was not simply in the background, but rolled with seamless resonance to the fore. And Arlen could not help but listen, for he was already building his own store of knowledge of the seasons and their patterns; so he noted it in his mind as the hardest rain he had ever heard. The farmer in him felt anxious.

Anxious expectation, directed at nothing. Arlen could not know the object of his trepidation, but he felt it all the same. With a start, a jump of the mind that marked the beginning of his working day full of conscious thought, he realized it was later than he thought. The clouds were heavy enough to keep the light out and perhaps the rooster could not be heard through the rain.

Why didn't Pa wake me up? Arlen rolled out from under the sheet and right into the legs of his overalls where he'd let them drop the night before. Buttoning his shirt, he went down the narrow stairs and put on his boots at the front door, followed by the rain slicker. Covering his head with his hat, Arlen went out the door and, as he stepped from under the porch roof, felt the rain drop on him like a loose bale of hay. The rain pressed against his shoulders and back and vibrated through the brim of the hat as he walked to the barn. The animals were all in their stalls, nervous and shifty from roar of the rain and the spray that wafted in through the unchinked gaps between the logs of the ancient barn. Arlen had to put his shoulder into the two cows and pin each up against the side of the stall just to milk her. There wasn't much milk to be had today, it seemed; or perhaps he wasn't as careful as he was to get it all out. Milking done, he fetched oat straw from up above and fed the cows and the mules, and the ass and the mare as well. The livestock seemed less nervous now that they could eat and he hoped they would remain so long as the storm continued. Ducking through the narrow doorway cut from the logs to the henhouse added onto the side of the barn, he found the hens unusually still and quiet. He had to shoo them away to take the eggs they had laid. Having forgotten the basket in the house, he set the eggs gingerly in the pockets of the slicker and, judging his chores done for now, made his way carefully across the softening earth to the house.

Arlen had to wait at the breakfast table not for the food, but for his father. He drank a cup of coffee. Miracle of miracles, Wade had cooked biscuits, and there was country ham, too. At last Wade came through the front door, shedding water like a duck all over the floor. His slicker and hat hung, he dropped himself into his chair. "Lord-make-us-worthy-of-these-gifts-we're-about-to-receive-in-Christ-Jesus-name-Amen," he said quickly and took the biscuits.

"A mess out there," said Arlen.

"Yes, it is." Wade spent time carefully fixing his plate with victuals before continuing. "Was steady last night, but it got even stronger right before dawn."

"Where did you go?"

"To check on the oats. The shocks should be fine, so long as this rain lets up soon."

Arlen poured more coffee for Wade, then himself. "Can't be good for the corn, neither."

Wade just stared down the length of the table, never looking to either side. "It'll be fine. So long as this rains lets up soon."

From the kitchen window came a flat slapping sound as the rain dashed the glass like a fat wet palm. Arlen finished his breakfast and rose and went to the front door, reaching for the slicker again. But he stopped; would it even do any good? The roar of rain on the porch roof seemed deafening even through the door. Curious, Arlen opened the door and stepped out. The rain rolled like waves toward the front of the house and the heavy, wet air rippled against his skin. Rivulets ran from the roof and gathered in puddles below the porch. He could hardly see the road at the end of the drive and could make out nothing of the trees on the other side. The sky was not there: it had disappeared under the falling rain which pulled one's attention downward toward the ground blasted with drops. *Now ain't this something?*

Arlen was grinning when Wade came out onto the porch with him, feeling child-like wonder. He could not remember rain like this. But he saw the serious look on his father's face. Best to get his slicker. When he came back out onto the porch with it, Wade still stood staring out into the deluge, the toes of his boots overhanging the porch and just inches from the driving drops.

"We going out?" said Arlen.

Wade was thinking. He crossed his arms and did not look back. Arlen stood there with the door half open, waiting. "You got something in mind for us, Pa?"

Still Wade did not move. At last, Arlen closed the front door and stood there, waiting patiently.

Wade turned around, his face glistening with the spray from the rain. "You say something?"

"Just wonderin' if we're going out in this."

"The day's about shot," said his father. "Might as well enjoy the storm."

Wade settled into a rocking chair. Arlen fetched his guitar and tried to pick a little, but the roar of the storm was too much; he could not make out out the notes. Finally he gave up and put the guitar inside the front door, next to the .32-20 Winchester that leaned in the same corner, and returned to the porch to sit and watch.

The storm occupied them for a long while. The fall of rain would lighten slightly and give the illusion that it was about to break. But then that lightened fall would remain steady, for perhaps an hour. Then the intensity would increase rapidly and drive on harder than before, each time the size of the drops and their fall greater. A channel of water cut down the length of the drive, taking red clay and twigs with it. The water spurted up over an exposed rock, then tumbled over itself and streamed on down toward the road. Rain gathered on the flat patch of dirt in front of the house where they often parked the truck. A patch of grass beside the porch, already flooded, rippled with falling rain like waves on a pond.

"Ain't never seen anything like this," said Arlen.

"This ain't anything like the big flood," said Wade. "You should have seen it. There were two storms that came in together, one from the west and one from the south, and they poured rain like you wouldn't believe. It brought down all the telephone and telegraph lines and we didn't hear a thing for weeks. 'Course we never heard much anyway out here in those days, but there wasn't a breath from the outside world. Couldn't even tell you what was happening in Newton. Couldn't take the wagon on the roads, and everyone was too busy fixin' their roofs and findin' their livestock that got washed away to do much visitin'. The corn crop was ruined, too."

"Would you say the rain was about as bad as this time?"

Wade only nodded.

"What year was that, Pa?" said Arlen.

"1916. Year before I went off to war."

"Pa, can I ask you something?"

Wade slowly said, "Go ahead." His mind was elsewhere.

"Would you tell me about the war? Your war, I mean."

His father chewed on his lip, the same habit as Arlen's, though Wade tended to gnaw on the inside. "Reckon I've said about all I want to say about the war, Arlen."

"I don't want to hear about battles or how many men you killed or anything like that. I just want to know why you went off to fight."

Wade sat with his arms folded, his eyes cast away from Arlen.

"Was it because of the draft? You had to join up or get drafted?"

There was still silence. Arlen had asked too much, he was sure of it. He sat back in his chair, feeling guilty, not aware that his father's forgiveness, albeit slow, was coming, in terse but hard truths. When Arlen had almost put his hope for an explanation aside, a story finally came from Wade's lips:

"It was a strange time, Arlen. Still seems strange to me today. When they declared war, the whole country about had a fit. It was like a fever, seemed like anyone could catch it. Reckon we'd heard stories about all the folks the Germans had killed and the poison gas and what they did to those nuns over there, and everyone knew how bad the war had gotten in Europe and I think that set a lot of folks against the Germans and everything they stood for. Those kind of folks went sniffin' out the Dutchies around here, pickin' on some folks for their last name. Ain't no difference, of course; they settled here, married everyone else, and they raised good crops and families; they were good folks, ain't a lick of difference 'cept the name. But they had to prove they weren't loyal to Kaiser Bill. Made me sick, like every time anyone stepped up to put on uniform with U.S. buttons, he got a big pat on the back and they told him what a good boy he was. And then there were the folks on the other side, callin' it a rich man's war, but a poor man's fight, sayin' we had to stay out. Said it weren't no different from the war with the North. And I asked Grandfather Alexander if that was so and he said it was true but weren't the whole truth. You see, he was alive then and still had his mind with him. And I asked him how it was, what he remembered, and he told me that all the war talk was for folks full of envy. Full of love for things that ain't theirs and hatin' other folks because they ain't givin' what they expect from them. We never had nothin' except this land, he said, and it never made us rich, but we fought for it and there ain't no one who made us go do it. He went to go fight on his own, and his brothers and his father too, and it ain't for envy that he would've gone or stayed. I reckon I didn't understand everything he was sayin' at the time, but I understood enough to keep my head on straight. I was blessed to have Grandfather around."

Arlen caught his father's eye. "But Pa, why did you go?"

Wade looked down at his feet. He seemed to sag a little bit, the recollections weighing so heavily upon him. "'Cause it's my country. I had it in my head that it was and that meant something to me. But it wasn't an easy thing. I knew all the things that Grandfather Alexander had said, how much he had bled and how much this family had given up to have our freedom, and how we still had some, but not the best of it — the best part was taken away, and not just in his war but in all the decades after that. And he didn't have to say who took it but I knew who he meant all the same: it was that Uncle Sam I was going to fight for. Maybe he would rather me not have gone, because of all he knew. But I reckon I thought he was still fightin' his old man's battles, and that mine were different. We were one country, not divided like in his day, and it had been that way for a good long while. I knew what had happened to our family and the place where we live and how it ain't been pretty; but I knew too our family had always gone off to fight, no matter what. It's my country and this, Arlen, this land — it ain't going nowhere, it's stayin' right here. And, well, I reckon I believed what the newspapers and the politicians fed us, sayin' we'd end all the wars and make the world safe for democracies like ours. But it didn't turn out like they said." Wade blinked several times, drawing deep breaths. He cleared his throat and rested his forearms on his knees, eyes closed. "It don't weigh on me, though. Weren't up to me after all."

"Duty ain't a terrible thing," said Arlen.

Wade looked up, eyes blurry. "It ain't at all."

They each sat back in their chairs, saying nothing further. Eventually the rain began to roar on the roof again.

But the rain of that morning was nothing compared to the afternoon that followed. Water cascaded in sheets off of the roof and filled the new pond in front of the house where grass and bare earth had once been. The drive disappeared underneath a long set of whitish riffles that carried an unbroken line of brown water all the way from the house to the flooded road. Tree limbs sagged lower and lower and some weaker branches of the old oaks dropped with a damp snap to the ground. Arlen moved from room to room in the upstairs of the house, emptying the pots that caught drips of water in the bedrooms. Coming down the stairs with a pot brimming with water, Arlen found Wade donning his slicker. "You going out in this mess?"

"Pour that out and come with me," said Wade.

Sealed up as best they could be, they went out into the downpour. The ground was saturated. The leather of their boots soaked quickly and soon they were squishing cold water and grit between their toes. Wade led, walking as best he could across the unstable ground, or rather through the ground at points, as both of them sank up past their ankles. He did not stop to look at the the oats. Though cut and shocked, they looked to be mostly ruined; but the oats were for the animals and feed could be bought in a pinch. The corn was the real concern. It was the warm-weather backbone of the farm, just as the

51

wheat was during the cold months. Without it, there was trouble. It was planted down along the branch, which was spilling over its briar-shrouded banks and running more and more of its watery course through the corn. Wade and Arlen slipped and stumbled down the slope to get down to the crop. The ground was even softer down here and big Wade sank to his knee at one point. Struggling and grunting, Arlen helped tug his father free of the deepening morass. Wade's foot popped out of the hole without the boot. Arlen reached in and gave several hard tugs before it came loose. Gasping for breath, Wade shook the mud and water out of the boot as best he could, stuffed the dirty sock into the slicker pocket, and slipped the grimy boot back on. At last upright on more solid ground, he set to walking up and down the rows of corn. On the farthest outside rows, water lapped at his ankles. The corn sagged and a few stalks had broken under the weight of rain and the ever more saturated ears. Wade wiped rain from his eyes. "Bad, Arlen, just bad as it could be. All this water'll sour the corn if it don't let up soon. Soon, Lord, soon."

"What'll we do?"

Wade wiped his eyes again. "Get to prayin', Arlen."

And maybe that was what Wade was doing when they got back to the house and dried off and cleaned off what mud they could. He sat in that rocking chair again without a word, without his magazine, just staring out at nothing, for he couldn't see anything through the storm. Arlen had said his little prayer, saying it silently and then done with it, like a young man always did, his trust in Providence quick and easy because he had seen little of life yet. His mind moved on while Wade dwelt on the storm, turning to the not-terrible thing: *duty*. It was here suddenly and for good now, unshakable, hewn from stone, set in the corner of the farmyard for him to see every day. It was a part of this place, this piece of land and its handful of people, as much as the house, the barn, the crops in the seasons, the old mule who would not die. It was the final piece of his upbringing, the hardest part saved for last.

War was not good, but dishonor to this place was worse. There was no draft yet, though it might be coming. Whether it arrived as law or not, Arlen could not wait for it. He had to go fight.

Arlen's face flushed hot, followed by a prickly sensation that ran from his cheeks to his ears. Suddenly everything from this long, good summer had faded in its vibrancy; all the richness of any given moment, where the promise of life seemed assured, where he could toil and exhaust himself and know it was for something worthwhile — something of his own making and not just keeping whole the heritage others had passed down — had receded to the background. The farm and the way it ran, his mother and father and even his distant sisters, and Caty Cline most of all, were not as bright as they had been now that there was this other great thing he had to do.

I can't go. Can't leave it all, not like this. Good Lord, there'll be a hole in me without it all.

But it ain't just me. They all need me, too.

His thoughts turned past his fears for his girl and what she might say and do, past the separation from his aging mother and father, and settled on the land, which each minute was ever more submerged under the falling storm.

What if the crop is ruined? Corn soured, nothin' to eat and nothin' to sell. Oats might be 'bout ruined too; we'll have to buy feed for the livestock.

No, Pa will have to buy it. If I'm not here. If I join up.

And perhaps Wade would have to even if Arlen stayed. There was no way of knowing. But Arlen's absence would certainly make the trials of the farm all the harder. At planting and harvest, even in simple chores like chopping weeds, Wade would have to hire on hands to help him: spending money they didn't have.

If I join up, I could send home my pay. That would help.

It might not be enough, though.

An emptiness opened up in the pit of Arlen's stomach.

I can't go. Can't let this farm fall apart. Everything else depends on it.

His family certainly did, but so too did Caty. She was not just a woman to him, with a life as malleable as his own. She would live with him right here on this piece of land one day. Practically one of them already, she needed this land as much as they did. And as much as they needed him, he needed all them. It was all knotted up together, the farm and the folk and the way each lived because of the other. Arlen knew no other way to live than to be all knotted up with the others like that, and he did not need to, for what could be better, as hard as this life was? There were no greener pastures, none that were not already his, merely needing to lay fallow, carefully spread with clover and potash.

The wind drove the rain up onto the porch and into the faces of the two Breckenridge men, who scooted their chairs as far back against the house as they could. Perhaps it would not matter if Arlen stayed or not; perhaps the cataclysms of nature, the will of Creation meeting man's precarious toehold on the surface of the earth, would make his choice to stay irrelevant.

But I can fight it, can't I? Ain't it better to fight my own fight here than someone else's fight over there?

Would he say that when German tanks landed at Wilmington and drove up the rivers through the endless pine stands and dive bombers brought down the rail bridge over the Catawba River?

Those're Roy's kind of words, fearin' what ain't even likely.

But Wade's words came back to him: nothing of his war had panned out like his generation had thought it would. They had fought Germany and expected peace, and yet here was Hitler, conquering more lands than his nation ever had before. Disappointed Wade had put his own war behind him, but what if he had never gone? What burden would he have felt? Wade had done what he could and could feel no shame no matter what had come out of it all.

I got to do the same. Ain't nothin' else to do.

So it would be. He said as much to himself. But his guts were still churning. His mind followed his viscera and circled around again, right back to the farm and what it would be without him there. There was no one else to carry it on after his parents, and without Caty, he could not carry it on, and even the two of them could not keep on together, not as themselves, not as the thing they had started together, without the farm. Could he accept that?

Lord, I can't. I can't do that to them.

But I still got to go.

Good Lord, what am I supposed to do?

He waited there on the porch until dark for the answer. And he waited some more. Life remained silent and as night fell, the rain was louder still.

The rain stopped about noon on the second day. The clouds lingered, but the chill from the storm quickly abated and one could feel warmth squirming its way through the gray curtain above. The sun came out and its glint off of standing water caught one's eye sharply. Wade did not disturb Arlen, did not even go to check on him once. Perhaps he knew he should leave his son be. After all, a Breckenridge knows another as himself.

Arlen had laid awake in bed nearly all night. It was not the rain that kept him up, but the pain in his belly. An uncomfortable, gnawing feeling had started the afternoon before and by night it had turned into a fretful stabbing. Arlen had tossed and turned from side to side in the hope that the pain would subside. By some miracle, exhaustion had overtaken him and he fell asleep. But he awoke eventually, hardly rested, and as the rain continued to drum the roof, he felt he had not left the day before. He lay there under the quilt, waiting for something, anything at all, to change how he felt. But nothing did and only the *thwack* of the front door and Wade's heavy steps descending the porch at last pulled Arlen from bed.

He went down to the porch. Wade was nowhere to be seen. Arlen leaned against the door frame and winced. The burning and periodic jabs had returned. Oh, they hurt. He straightened up and a sharp jab got him right under the ribs, quicker than any knife. Arlen gasped, his mouth drawn wide quickly but the sound stilled in the back of his throat before it could get out. He doubled over, clutching at his stomach with both hands, trying to pull at the invisible blade. He sat down in his chair. Head hanging, arms folded, body laying forward against his thighs, Arlen waited for a while, eyes scrunched shut. His boot heel tapped over and over on the boards of the porch, toes tensed to the point of cramping as they drove his foot up and down.

The anxious knife stabbed at him again and again and Arlen was helpless against the alien pain. He had no defense, having never once experienced this before. The bile built and built and he could feel awful, corrosive fire sending burning tendrils up and up, reaching out to ensnare his heart. In pure instinct he sat bolt upright and gave a shout as the bilious fire washed around inside him, and yet relief came too as he abandoned quick and shallow breaths for deep, purging ones. He gasped and gasped and the pain seemed to hold and then fade gradually like the passing storm. His right leg bounced gently now, his heel barely tapping the porch.

Where is Pa? I need to talk to him.

But what else could Wade to tell him? He had been silent about his war for a long time and Arlen had never known otherwise. Then, when it came time to know what war was, Wade had spoken only with reluctance. Arlen still sensed that his father, even at his most candid, had not shared everything. Silence had returned.

But Arlen had heard all he needed. It was not example he lacked. It was the vision to see what example would render in the great unwritten future, vision which no man had.

Arlen rose from the chair and stepped off the porch. He walked away from the house, hat-less, stepping carefully between puddles of water, squinting against the sun. Beyond the shadow of the house, he stopped and closed his eyes in relief. The warmth of the reflected sun felt good. If only he could just stand here like this forever.

Ain't got forever.

He opened his eyes. No, he didn't. Sooner or later, he would have to choose and that was what his whole body was fighting.

His stomach began to gurgle and Arlen decided it was time to begin walking again.

His steps were not leisurely, though. Despite the sodden earth that sucked at them, his feet moved faster and faster. But where were they getting to? Arlen knew the bounds of this place; what good was it to move over this fold of ground and down past that tree so fast? He would reach the limits eventually and have to turn around back to what he knew and then cross it again. There was no purpose to speed when you had what was and would be yours.

But will it be mine? If I lose this farm — if we lose it — ain't no one's fault but mine.

He raised his head up from the ground before him, looking out across the field in which he stood. He saw the green of the corn and the gold of their tassels and a blue sky that seemed to be preparing a farewell to the hardness of prolonged summer heat and readying itself for the hardness of short days that were coming. It would be good to stay for such days. And Arlen thought he might just wait and see if the war really would come. There was still time. He could harbor his secret inclinations to duty inside and follow his work through the seasons. He could work harder than ever for the farm and then if war did come, drop it all to go fight just as hard.

But what if the war came too fast? His thoughts returned to German tanks slashing across the state until they were at the Catawba's banks. Look at how quickly France had fallen and how Britain was the next apple to fall from the tree. Perhaps it would be too late to join the fight when the Germans did strike. And then their farm might be put to the torch, all while he had waited to see what would pan out.

But if I go enlist and there ain't no war, without me to help, we could lose the farm. What good is my duty then?

He was right back to where he had been.

The shallow breathing was back, too. This time it was almost panicked in its ferocity. His eyes were wide open and dry as a bone, but he felt like he wanted to cry, just to sob a couple of times.

Oh Lord, how is this so hard? How?

Ain't never had to make a decision like this. Always been one way, our way. Always took that and gone with it. But I can't now. Got to work it out on my own. And I can't be sure.

Can't be sure. No matter what I do, can't be sure.

He saw movement in the corn. A head bobbed along in between the stalks and then disappeared. Arlen walked along the outside of the corn until he saw his father squatting amongst corn rows. The big man looked as if he was hiding behind the shoulder-high stalks. Of course Wade would never hide; he had nothing to be ashamed of. No failing of his own had fated the green ears to the souring that was not yet upon them. There was no possible preparation for a storm like this one. No one deserved shame for what nature did to a man's work, so long as the work was not done in hubris. And Wade had never asked so much from the land for it to be that. Wade neither moved nor spoke as Arlen came squishing through the soil behind him. The broad back of his white shirt was the face presented to Arlen. "It's a downright shame," said his father. His words were slow and carefully spoken. "Ain't never lost a crop like this."

"All lost, Pa?"

"As good as lost, if it ain't completely. I'll bet we got ten, twelve inches of rain all at once. Don't matter how good this field drains, ain't seen a crop yet that can come back from that." Wade's head dipped forward, his face even more invisible to Arlen now. "We need lots of sun, plenty of dry weather. That's my prayer, Almighty Lord. Dry all this out."

Arlen did not say anything.

It was as if Wade could read his son's mind. "You set your mind on it?"

"Sir?"

"I know what you've been thinking about. You gonna enlist?"

Surprising himself, Arlen said, "Yessir."

Wade made no comment after he rose up to his full height. His narrowed eyes did not seem enthusiastic nor disappointed by Arlen's response. They were captured by the sight of that drowned green and gold crop. All else paled in comparison to that. How could they do anything else first, or even do it well, if they did not care for the crop? But the two Breckenridge men could not: their attention would not save this year's corn, and there was another matter that demanded their time and energy. So Wade followed his son, his feet plopping and sucking until they had climbed the slight incline to drier ground. Wade turned and looked at the crop again. "Well, it's settled, then."

Arlen almost fell to his knees, head hung in sickness. But he would not cry, would not let his anguish over what might come to pass because of him show before his father. His father, for as strong as he was, must not be hurt by Arlen's own troubles. The son was beginning to be the one who cared for and looked after the father in his considerations, as it was always meant to be in the end.

"Son, you all right?"

"Yessir." Arlen's voice was strained to the point of cracking.

"You keep stewin' like you are and you're liable to bust."

"Sir?"

"Come on, now, tell me. What is it?"

"It's nothin'."

"It ain't nothin'. Go on and tell me. Ain't nothin' I ain't ever heard before, I'm sure."

"It's like I know it's the right thing, but I can't bring myself to want it. Not now, at least. But I got to."

Wade nodded slowly. "You doing it to run away? To get away from Caty? From your mother and me?"

"No. You know I ain't like that."

"I know. I know you're doing it for the right reasons."

"Don't want to leave y'all, don't want to leave the farm." He gnawed his lip once. "I'm just worried that you ain't gonna be able to run the farm without me. I don't want that to be your burden."

"Always has been," said Wade.

"But I don't want my decision to make us lose the farm." Arlen looked away from his father: this was all too hard to say to his face. He shook his head to himself and let it hang down in near despair. "But I know I got to live with it either way."

"What about if you can do both?" said Wade.

"Do both?"

"There's a National Guard company down in Shelby. Join the Guard. You serve on the weekends, maybe a month in the summer. You stay on and farm the rest of the time. Then you ain't leaving me and your mother on our own, if that's what you're worried about."

"And if I get called up?"

"Then fine, you'll go fight. Ain't no shame in it, either way."

Arlen's still head hung down, unable to look at his father. "Can't do no better than that, I reckon." He choked. "Tell me if there's another way, Pa, 'cause I can't see it."

Wade heard the desperate edge in his son's voice, and comforted him, not with a manly clap on the shoulder, but with provoking words. "Then go on. Go join up. You got to, you know. And it ain't me tellin' you. Who's tellin' you?"

Ain't my choice, I know. But he's leaving it up to me. Arlen didn't understand the conundrum, but, for once in his life, he realized he could not wait until he did.

"Who's tellin' you, Arlen?"

VI

One, two, three good whacks, and the stalk was free, coming loose into the crook of Arlen's arm. One, two, three whacks and another stalk fell and he caught it with his chest, letting it topple over against the others in his arm. He let them all drop in a pile and paused a moment, letting his strained left arm get some feeling back into it before he stepped forward again to the next stalk. He swung the long-bladed knife again, caught the stalk, and moved to the next one. His mind was clear, his attention on the corn. He made sure each bit of work was his best, that he carried the most stalks he could before dropping them, and that he cut with fast and clean strokes. That was what Arlen could do with this moment and he found pleasure in that.

Arlen reached the end of the row and looked back down the distance he had cut. Wade was a few dozen yards behind, cutting stalks just the same. He would bundle fewer in his arms than Arlen before dropping them into a pile, so he moved slower, but his cutting stroke was stronger than Arlen's: one long, slow swing and the stalk came free. Arlen mopped his forehead with his rolled-up shirt sleeve. Wade hacked his way up to Arlen and dropped his bundle. They both stood breathing hard, the rhythm of the air in and out of their nostrils slowing little by little as they rested. This was the third day they had been cutting the corn and they had many more to go. There was nothing to make it come any quicker or any easier and they accepted that. It was frustrating that they would not get a crop from this. They could get silage from the stalks and leaves, and the ears themselves could be fed to the hogs — Wade was even arranging to buy more swine to fatten up, both to slaughter and to sell; his resourcefulness could only be delayed, never entirely stopped. But keeping much of the crop to grind for their own meal, as they had always done, and selling the rest: that was impossible this year.

Hell, we've seen it before. One season ain't made the farm and ain't gonna end it neither.

Wade looked up at the sky. "What time is she gettin' here?"

"Who?"

"Caty. She should be here soon."

59

Arlen stopped. Was it today that Caty was coming for supper? He had almost forgotten. He had been so wrapped up in his work. "I reckon so."

"She'll be here soon, then," said Wade. "Or ain't you pickin' her up?"

The corn knife dangled pendulously by the leather strap from Arlen's wrist. "Shit."

Wade laughed as Arlen began running to the house. "If you'd just marry the girl, you wouldn't have this problem!"

Arlen cleaned up as quickly as he could, combing his unruly mess of hair and putting on a fresh shirt. Wade's words dogged him as he ran to the truck and bounced down the drive, potholed from the storm of the previous month. He had other matters to handle with Caty, news to break that deserved the presence of the family.

When he arrived at the Cline home, Caty was waiting on the porch for him. She did not get up, but waited for him to get out of the truck and come up the front path to her. "I'm sorry I'm late," said Arlen.

"Is that the most important thing?" she said, raising an eyebrow.

He paused, mind racing to figure out what she meant. She stood facing him, looking down from the porch. She looked good tonight. What was it? Hair was the same, dress was the same. "You got new shoes."

She brightened. "I saved for two years for them."

"They look mighty fine."

Now she came down to meet him. "Let's go."

"Don't I need to tell your pa?"

"He's sleeping."

Arlen did not ask why, but he could guess it had to do with a bottle of something strong.

The roads were just as rutted as the front drive and it was slow going back to the farm. Caty was very talkative today and Arlen just nodded and murmured his assent as he wheeled the truck around dips and holes in the road.

"And Pa said that storm was just as bad as 1916, but the government's built all the bridges and dams better so that's why they didn't all get swept away," said Caty.

"Mmm-hmmm," said Arlen.

"Don't you think that's a good thing? What the government's done for us? I think it's just fine."

"Don't factor into my thinkin' much."

"Now that sounds like a Breckenridge thing to say," said Caty. "Y'all don't hold no truck with the government at all. And after all they've done for us."

"That ain't true," said Arlen. He mashed the clutch and the brake just in time to avoid a deep pothole.

"Oh, you know it is," said Caty.

Why was she so ornery today? Was it that time of the month? Arlen grew up with sisters, he knew there was that one week out of four when they took everything out on him. "Stop it, Caty."

"Arlen, it's just you. I'll bet you wouldn't even enlist unless we were really in a war. You don't hold no truck at all with Uncle Sam's plans."

He did not reply. This road was tricky, especially now that the light was falling and the shadows were muddling the outlines of the potholes. He nearly missed a gear as he shifted.

She nudged him playfully. "What, cat got your tongue?"

"I ain't no coward, Caty."

"Oh, Arlen, I didn't say you were. I just meant you don't give anyone their due until you really have to."

"Then why do you think I signed up last week?" snapped Arlen.

The whole inside of the truck went cold as Caty clammed up. Her eyes were hard and wide like marbles.

Sonuvabitch.

He said nothing.

"When were you going to tell me?" Her voice was quivering.

"Tonight, Caty. Tonight. That's why I wanted you to come to supper."

"You enlisted? In what, the Army? The Navy?" Before he could answer, her voice broke and she began to cry.

"No, the National Guard." Arlen pressed on with the driving. He had to get her to the house.

"The National Guard."

"Yes. It ain't the Army. I just serve on some weekends and some training a few times a year."

The crying subsided and only sniffles remained. "I just can't bear the thought of you going far away."

"It's just down in Shelby. Ain't far."

"I can't bear to be apart from you for even a few days," said Caty. "Don't you know it's hard for me just to be at home, waiting on the next time I'm going to see you? I love you, Arlen. I love you."

She really did. Those eyes could not lie.

"If you're gonna go—"

"Caty, I ain't going nowhere."

"Then can we—" She stopped.

"Can we what?"

Caty's head turned in surprise. Why, there was Legenia, standing down at the fence next to the road. Her arms were folded, hands tucked up under her armpits. They were already at the house — Arlen almost missed the turn up

61

the drive and had to turn the wheel hand over hand in order to squeeze through the open gate. Legenia came toward them and Wade came down off the porch as well. Strange: they should both be inside, Legenia cooking and Wade changing from his work clothes into something more presentable. Caty wiped her red face and looked at Arlen for his answer. Wade and Legenia were now close to the truck, looking at him, not at her. Arlen opened the door and got out. "We ready to eat?" he said.

"This came for you," said Legenia. She held a piece of yellow-white paper in her outstretched hand: a telegram.

Arlen took it. "Who's it from?" Neither his parents answered. Arlen unfolded it. The words typed out in blurry ink were not many, but it took Arlen a second time, and a third, and a fourth to comprehend.

"What does it say?" said Caty, who stood beside his parents.

The words on the page were so simple, so direct, that they seemed impossible.

Can't treat a man like that. Can't make me go like that.

But who could he argue with? This telegram had been composed by a man in a far-off office, with the law and the swelling sentiment of a massive nation behind every stroke of his typewriter, and it demanded of Arlen what the young man had already promised. He had promised it not even two weeks before, when the roads had dried out and Wade had driven him down to Shelby to sign the papers and take the oath to join up and serve his country.

"Arlen, please tell us," said Caty.

Arlen folded the telegram shut. "The National Guard's been mobilized. I have to report immediately."

The crickets covered their stunned silence.

"One year's federal service."

Wade said nothing. Legenia took her hand away from her mouth and said, "But you haven't even reported for training yet."

"Don't matter. I'm being called up."

His mother clapped her hand back over her mouth. Wade cleared his throat. "All right, then, what do you need to do?"

Arlen opened his mouth, but no words came out. He had known this moment was possible, but how could he have ever anticipated it? No one had ever compelled him in his whole life, not like this, compelled him to do what he had pledged but was not prepared for.

Wade took his son by the arm. "Come with me."

Arlen stumbled along, unsure of what was happening or what he was moving toward. The two women fell in behind the men and their steps were out of time as they all moved faster and faster. Wade spoke what felt like right in Arlen's ear. "Legenia, I will get him packed. You take Caty to the kitchen and look after her."

"Oh, let me do it, Wade."

"No, I know what he needs. You'll send him with too much." Wade marched his son upstairs and fetched a bag for him. "You need just enough to see you through until they issue you a uniform."

Arlen sat on his bed, silent, thinking of his orders. The plainly printed words were folded up and tucked away in his pocket, always there for him if he forgot or if he simply did not believe that he really was being pulled away. He could not argue with them, for he had committed himself to their expectation.

Good Lord, what have I done?

There wasn't time for that. He was far beyond the decision that had landed him here. He had to get packed. Arlen set into frantic movement, reaching for things of meaning and usefulness almost at random. He grabbed undergarments and a spare set of trousers and crammed them hastily into the bag. He wasted time considering whether to take his hat; which shoes to take, his nicer church shoes or his work boots? He reached to his dresser and grabbed the pocket New Testament and the photograph of him with Caty on the street in Newton during the Old Soldier's Reunion. She was smiling in the photo, broadly and spontaneously, and he had a satisfied but firm look, mouth set, eyes slightly narrowed, appraising the camera's intent. He set that in the bag and then with it the small photograph of Caty alone that she had given him. Wade brought him a spare shirt and several pairs of socks Legenia had finished darning. "Not like that, it'll all wrinkle," Wade said. He proceeded to remove everything and repack them for Arlen.

Arlen descended the stairs and Caty grabbed him in a desperate embrace, her hands gripping onto his rolled up sleeves as she buried her face in his chest.

"Do you have to go tonight?"

"Orders said immediately."

"But don't you think that could mean tomorrow? Or maybe in a few days? Surely they can give you that much time." She put her head back on his chest.

Maybe they did mean that. Perhaps he could bend the rules and maybe get away with it. But the words on the telegram: who could argue with them? Not even Arlen, here on his farm, with his family and his friend and his girl, his life free and no different than it ever had been if the telegram had just disappeared. Not even him, of all men.

"No. I got to go tonight. Ain't no way around it."

"But what about us? Arlen? What about us?"

Arlen took Caty by the hand and led her out of the house, out into the fading light. He dropped her hand and she stopped in her tracks. But he kept on ahead, stomping along, breathing hard. Acidic trepidation was boiling up inside him, that now-familiar feeling. He stopped many yards away from Caty and stood akimbo, head hung down, eyes screwed shut, the moment eating through the bottom of his stomach.

Good Lord, why does it have to be like this?

I ain't ever wanted much. Just what my family expected of me. Just to work on my own, for myself and my family. To be left alone enough so I could do it all right. Live right, live with a good woman and raise up my children in that way, free as I ever was.

Just that, Lord, nothin' else. Nothin' more than what you wanted. And nothin' more than what my grandparents and their grandparents wanted. And nothin' more than what they got — they got that, Lord. You gave it to them and they did their best with it. And you ain't givin' it to me.

Arlen almost swore at God in the words he formulated in his mind, but he dug his teeth into his bottom lip to stop himself. But he had made the words in his heart and he knew he meant them.

Lord, I just did what I was taught to do and it's always been enough and it was supposed to keep this farm and this family livin'. But now it ain't. It almost ain't even enough with me here, and here I am leavin', 'cause I have to. 'Cause it's the right thing. But I don't want to do it.

His jaw and cheeks were slack and almost numb, listless in the absence of hope. The inside of his head was curtained from the rest of the world and he could not see the trees and fallow fields and clear early autumn skies, so heavy was this care, dizzying him with its sudden weight. Running over his grievances like a tongue over cracked teeth, he could find no solution. There was no hoping for that now. But perhaps he could at least know now that he was the one who suffered.

What guilt Arlen felt. He should have known that his clever avoidance would come to no good. Farm and duty could not be drummed into formation and made to serve together.

Maybe it ain't my fault. Maybe it's just the time I live in.

He then thought of all those who came before him and had it so much better, but their successes were small consolation. They were dead and he lived. But they had had their own struggles to keep those good things. Wade had his war and Great-Grandfather Alexander had his, and Alexander had stood with the Farmers' Alliance, too, at risk to life and livelihood and reputation. They had done what they had to do to keep the world at bay, well away from the farm gate. Perhaps they had not wanted their fights any more than he did — after all, Arlen was no different from them. What else could he expect, and what else could he do?

He was going, tonight. He wouldn't see morning on the farm again for a year. A whole year. He would spend every day thinking of that day when he would come back, his duty done, the whole matter settled.

Or perhaps it would not be so easy. The war might come.

Don't think it couldn't. Don't make that same mistake like you did when you signed up. Should have picked one or the other. Not what Pa said.

For the first time he realized Wade wasn't always right and that he had a better instinct for what to do, a clean and clear choice. Maybe that was a Breckenridge virtue that skipped a generation or two. It felt good to think so.

All right, then. Go and serve. Fight when the time comes. With honor and to protect this place. When it's done, come back to it.

There were footfalls behind him. A slender hand laid on his back and another on his chest, and then a familiar head rested on his shoulder. Arlen tried to gather himself, knowing he needed to speak. He felt a warm dampness bleeding through his shirt sleeve. Caty pulled away, sniffling, as he turned around. Her eyes brimmed but did not run now, though her cheeks were red and puffy.

Speak, Arlen, speak. A man must say what was on his mind. But only with men. He could not spill his guts to her, even though she believed she would accept and understand everything about him because she loved him. She was anticipating — no, she was already carrying — the burden of having to love him when he could not be there with her, day by day, whenever she missed him or needed him. She kept looking at him. "Don't you have anything to say?"

"You want me to tell you again?"

She sniffled again

"Caty, ain't a thing to do. I'll go and I'll come back."

The sniffles grew bigger and Arlen reached out and smothered them in a embrace that nearly crushed the breath out of her. "You stop that now, all right? Ain't nothin' to be sad about. No, ma'am, not at all. Because you know we will."

"Know we will what?" said Caty.

"Get married."

"We will?"

He smiled as she looked at him. "Now don't you look so surprised. Just as soon as this National Guard service is up, we will. I promise you."

"Oh, Arlen, what about now?"

"Naw, ain't no time now. Wish there was, but there'll be plenty of time later."

"How long, Arlen?"

"One year. That's all. Then I'll be back here on the farm, with you."

"You promise?"

65

"That's what they tell me."

She didn't want to hear that. "You promise?"

Fine, then. "I promise."

WAR

VII

The din of the rain on his steel helmet sounded like a tin roof under a hurricane.

"Why couldn't he have picked a place under some goddamned trees?"

No one should be talking now, not with the enemy close by. He turned his head to see who. A rivulet of water that had gathered on a fold of his poncho hood poured down his back. Cold Tennessee rain. Indian summer had gone. He pulled his M1 rifle in closer and kept his hand over the action to keep it dry. The platoon was exposed, silhouetted at the crest of a hill. The road was a morass of red clay.

"All right, up and at 'em. We're moving out."

The whole squad rose to its feet quietly. Sling rifles, heft gear, look ahead, and wait: one, two, three, four, five paces — now step off. Long strides covered distance quickly. The rain began falling harder. It was really hard this time. Hitch up your poncho, lower your head, press ahead through the muck. Legs spattered with mud, red clay dripping down calves. The heavens opened like a spigot. The deluge shook tree branches and drummed through the poncho like fingers on a piano.

"Halt!"

They stopped in the open. He felt warm vapor rising from his collar and caught the rancid smell of his wet, dirty self. The squad stood perfectly still, taking the brunt of the downpour, the din against their helmets a choir of misfit bells.

Time rolled back: it rained like this once. But when? The past year's rains at Camp Blanding were brief, soaking showers of a warm Florida afternoon. Before that, the rain at Fort Jackson was a steamy patter. This rain was hard and steady, unrelenting, nourishing or destructive, the difference between its gift and its wrath all in the duration of its uncontrollable volume.

Rain like this sours corn and leaves it fit only for the hogs.

Why did that cross his mind? It was familiar for some reason. Familiar, but not immediate.

"Move out!"

69

They stumbled along again, a few who still did not know left foot from right. What good had all that drill done? All the back and forth, stirring up dust that coated their eyes and choked them. Certainly it gave them endurance. Or perhaps they had the officers to thank for that: endlessly obsessing over the tiniest hanging thread or unkempt necktie, they taught you to bear with anything, for there was no dignity for you, not even for the volunteer. And a volunteer he was and deserved respect for it. He fought them back, overtly and covertly, and his time was filled with KP and sentry duty, and the squad suffered for his sins just as he suffered for those of others. The only thing he understood was the march and the rifle, the two things he had thought of when he thought of war before he thought of going to war. He had tough feet and shot expert, so in the end, the Army forgave all. He did not.

Be magnanimous. Look at what Uncle Sam made you. Stronger, quicker, a razor edge put on his woodsman's senses: he was more than he ever had been. And in secret he could admit that he loved his new strength and that while he regretted the way it had come to him, he gladly accepted that it had and thought of no other way it could be. They beat him down and they built him up and he had vowed that though it was worth it, his Army days would be over.

Yes, he had, hadn't he? So certain at the end of year one. Then the politicians made noises about keeping the troops, enlisted and conscripted, in the service longer. All in the name of national defense. Along with the other soldiers, Arlen had scrawled on the barracks wall *O.H.I.O: Over the Hill In October*. Word came filtering down from on high: Old Hickory, the 30th Infantry Division, his outfit, would be demobilized in December. Worry not, they would have Christmas at home.

Pearl Harbor came first. In truth, he could hardly remember before that. Much of what he knew of the Army came after, even if it felt like before. Yes, it all blurred together as it grew faster and more complex. The division was like a deck of cards flying through the air. One regiment was split off for another division. Soldiers were transferred to other divisions or branches. New volunteers and draftees poured into their places. The regiments and companies had been filled with North and South Carolinians and Tennesseans and Georgians, each one drawn from a small town or modest city. Overnight, those transplanted communities vanished and an olive drab wind blew in, new draftees and volunteers from the North and the Midwest. They all had two left feet and odd accents and outlooks, and there was no trust to be had. The division began again from scratch. A year lost.

Yes, that was how it was. But why think of it now? For all that had changed, it was all still the same.

Indeed, he had remained. Men came and went, the propaganda slogans changed, and the officers were replaced. Nothing stayed the same, but he stayed right where he was. Almost another year at Fort Jackson, almost two total, close enough to home that maybe he could have gone, if there were not a war on. No liberty for him. Not even for home.

Home: where Wade had to hire men for planting and harvesting, shiftless men who wanted more money than they deserved for their work. His father had fired them and hired a few Negroes. They worked better than the white men, except for the one who said he was glad to do be working for Wade because he didn't have to go fight this white man's war. And Wade had kicked the man off the farm for that and cussed his name up and down for weeks. So Legenia said in a letter.

There was more than that, but what?

And then Florida. Forced marches and calisthenics under rays of sun so harsh they could make a man sick. Drill, shoot, march, and repeat. That was where he qualified as expert and his already calloused feet became impervious to any road. And the division having been gutted, filled up again, and hammered back into shape, the big brass ordered Old Hickory to Tennessee, to these mock battles in the hills against the Second Army.

And only now were they finding out if they had the skills to fight.

How long had that taken? He counted: *Camp Forrest this year, Camp Blanding last year; Fort Jackson for most of '42; Jackson for all of '41. And I got there the September before that.*

That made it three years. Almost to the day.

For all he knew now, it could have been the only three years in his life that mattered. He was a soldier now. What else did he know? Oh, yes, home, that's right. There was a home for him. Wade and Legenia and all that, that something else.

Three years, a long time for a young man. It could have been thirty times longer in reality. What did he know? How could he measure? Only the growth of his calluses seemed to mark the passage of time, like rings on a tree.

"Halt!"

The sergeant appeared through the grey rain. "Corporal, you've done your orienteering work, come with me."

At the front of the long column, the lieutenant huddled under the platoon guide's poncho, scowling, contorting his peach-fuzz cheeks into all manner of wrinkled shapes. "Ah, Corporal, there you are. The sergeant here says you know your way around a map and compass. Maybe you can settle this for us." He pointed to a mess of contour lines. "I think we're here, but the sergeant disagrees. I know for a fact I've maintained a north-by-northwesterly course and haven't deviated one bit. It's the damn map that's wrong."

"Lieutenant, I don't think the map is wrong," said the sergeant. "Arlen, tell him what you see."

71

His eyes told him the truth before the sergeant even spoke. They were not lost. The lieutenant was simply shooting azimuths down the road every time they halted and matching it to a miniscule section of road on the map. A fool's way to navigate.

"Well, Corporal? Who's right?"

He snatched the map and compass from the lieutenant and hopped out up onto the overgrown grassy bank and vaulted a barbed wire fence beside the road. The lieutenant and sergeant both shouted hoarsely at him, but not too loudly, for fear of alerting the opposing side. Crossing a small field at the double, he began climbing the small hill on the far side. Bent nearly in half, he slipped again and again on the long, wet grass. The rubber tread of his boots went *wee-ick, wee-ick*. Near the treeline, he stopped for a second, leaning forward and resting slightly on his fingertips. He crept around the curve of the hill until the treeline moved up higher and the view of the land opened. Crouching behind a knobby piece of ground, he flattened down a patch of grass and rested the map there, with the compass atop. Find magnetic north, adjust the compass, shoot a bearing on that hill off on the left — from that peak crease the map with his thumbnail along the azimuth. That hill over there: do it again. The spot where the two lines was where he stood. It was actually far to the front of where the lieutenant thought they were. Check again: yes, it was right.

He didn't walk down the hill, but just tried to control his slide on the wet grass with an outstretched hand, the other clutching his rifle sling. He was moving too fast to stop and the momentum carried him across the small field right to the fence. Climbing over, he sank almost immediately up to his ankles in the red mud. He put the map in front of the platoon commander.

"Marvelous, Corporal. How did you know how to do that?"

The sergeant's face said, Don't say anything.

"But, Corporal, don't you ever go off alone like that. Never again. You need to wait for orders, and take a buddy with you when you do."

Dutifully, he just stood there and let the lieutenant lay into him for another minute or two. He didn't even nod in acknowledgment. He just stood there and resisted the temptation to gnaw on his lip. "All right, let's move out," the lieutenant said with absolute confidence in himself, as if everything was moving according to plan. And look here, it's the company commander, marching up the road with his entourage, surely upset about the hold-up. The lieutenant puffed himself up like a peacock, drenched though he was, and strutted toward his commander. With his skinny shoulders thrown back and fists confidently on his hips, there was no doubt in the looie's mind who made the map solution.

That sonuvabitch, I made that solution. You bastard, you officers are all the same, I ain't no draftee, ain't no greenhorn, I volunteered, I'm a Guardsman, I've been in three years and you can't treat me like that, not no more, no sir, you bastard, you come here—

"Hey," said the sergeant, grabbing his sleeve before he could charge at the lieutenant.

Fuckin' greenhorn looies, bastards gonna get us all killed, ain't gonna get me killed, you come here—

"Arlen!"

The jerking on his sleeve was fierce now.

I ain't going to war with the likes of you, you sonuvabitch, this ain't what I signed up—

"Arlen!"

His eyelids burst open to bright light. He blinked painfully until he could see again. The skies were a dull silver, sun shining from somewhere behind a thin, even ceiling of clouds. The air was damp, but no smell of rain.

"Arlen, wake up."

Arlen smacked away the hand that grabbed his shoulder. "Don't touch me."

"Oooh, testy, aren't we?" The short man next to him took a last drag on his cigarette and flicked the butt away.

Arlen sat up. His head was pounding as if he had a hangover, but he hadn't touched alcohol, not since they were moved down to the staging area.

"You were grinding your teeth. What were you dreaming?"

"We were back in Tennessee, on maneuvers."

"Oh, God, that's a nightmare. Was I there?"

"We got any coffee?"

"It's one o'clock in the afternoon, no, I don't have any coffee. You were asleep for a couple hours. Was I there?"

"Where, Paine?"

"In your dream," said Paine.

"No."

"Why not? I was on maneuvers with you. That was the first time we shared a foxhole."

"Paine, I don't know. I don't remember. I don't remember a lot of things."

His fellow soldier snorted. "Then what do you remember?"

The dream had slipped past him, like a skinny woman in a crowded corridor who turned your head but was gone. You looked back, trying to catch a glimpse of her as she was farther and farther away, but there was so much that was closer. Like General Hobbs telling them a week before that it — the big it, the invasion — was coming soon, and the very next day they awoke to thousands of planes in the air, headed south. And then the division was turned

73

out of its billets in a frenzy and loaded into trucks and driven here to the big tent city, where they had waited and filled out wills and written letters — oh, how the officers insisted they should — and waited some more. Waiting to board the boats that the big brass said were here. Waiting to get across the Channel and through the narrow door into Fortress Europe that the Allies had knocked in. Waiting for the fighting.

None of that was in his dream. He knew that there was something missing from it and it wasn't Paine. He rolled back and back in his mind, wondering where it was. He remembered rain in the dream and tried to recall what kind of rain, but the only rain he could picture at the moment was the perpetual English drizzle. Good Lord, had this place become all he knew? Back and back, grabbing for that sensation that had left him wondering what he was missing, but all he got was the frigid walk up the gangplank onto the troopship in Boston harbor. The winter seas had scared them all to death. The ship would crest a wave and then pitch forward steeply down the other side; the screws burst from the frigid water into the air and the ship's engines screamed through the hull as the propellers turned without resistance; and then as every G.I. stomach heaved, they plunged back in and a muffled hum fell over the ship as the screws churned along through the water as they began to ride up the next wave. Eighteen days of constant sickness and anxiety. Every ship had to take its turn as the last one in the convoy, the "graveyard position." Colonel Ward ordered life jacket drills, and the men practiced putting them on and scrambling topside from the lower decks. Arlen had questioned aloud what good a life jacket would do in icy black water that would freeze you as surely as suck you down. The division had landed in Glasgow and there was the solace of rich green hills and solid ground under their feet. They entrained and moved south under bombing raids. Soldiers and equipment packed the island so tightly it seemed the whole of the country would sink under the weight. Everywhere you went, there was war and preparations for more of it. The big it was coming, although nobody knew where or when. A few times a week, they escaped their drafty quarters to a pub and drank watery war-time beer and swapped rumors, always betting on their next destination. Half said France, half said Norway; the next day some switched from one to the other, and on rare occasions, threw a curveball: Denmark, or Holland. Or no invasion at all: they would be transferred to the Italian front. Or the Rooskies would cut a deal with Hitler and no more second front. Paine would often tell a newcomer to their table that Field Marshal Montgomery was taking command of the division. Nobody wanted that cocky Limey s.o.b leading them into battle and the G.I. would swear endlessly until the others assured him it was all a prank.

That was all there was. He had not left anything out.

"Arlen, wake up."

"I just closed my eyes for a minute."

"You want me to go find you some coffee?"

Arlen shook his head.

"Look alive, Sarge is coming."

Arlen sat up. Sergeant Gunderson was nearly on them. "Private, Corporal, do you have any final letters? Last chance before we get on the boat."

"When are we going?" asked Paine.

"Soon," said the sergeant. It was the perpetual answer. "Letters?"

"Not me, Sarge," said Paine.

Arlen hopped to his feet. "Sarge, you got any mail for me?"

"It's not mail call. I'm asking you for letters."

"I was just hopin' something came through."

Sergeant Gunderson laughed. "What, are you afraid your gal forgot you?"

Arlen felt a chill up his spine.

Oh Lord, that's what it was. I forgot her.

He plopped down on the ground.

Paine's mouth moved, but the sound of passing trucks drowned him out. He looked in annoyance at the convoy, then turned back to Arlen. "What is it?"

It would do no good to admit anything to Paine. He still hardly knew the boy. Arlen thought of him as a boy, for although he was only a few years younger, he had been with the division only a year. He was a randy, foul-mouthed, energetic boy who lusted after — and bedded with shocking regularity — every red- and tow-headed nurse and lonely girlfriend he could. Paine had no self-control, what could he possibly understand about holding onto the hope of the same girl for so many years? How could he understand? They were not the same men.

How could I forget you, Caty? How could I let you go? Why did I let myself?

But he did not. It was not his doing. It was the dream. He had no control over the dream, indeed, no control in it. He did what he did, remembered what he remembered, suffered what he must, and that was that. There was no guarding himself against his baser impulses, no yearning for his Caty that sustained and tormented him. When he had no control, she did not exist to him.

Oh, Caty, I'm so sorry.

But she did not know and never would. What did it matter?

"Arlen, what is it?"

Too embarrassed, Arlen blurted out, "Caty forgot to write me."

"Oh, hell, you can't be worrying about her."

75

"Dammit, Paine, I do."

When his comrade spoke again, it was with a more comforting tone. "She didn't forget you, there's no way she could."

"I don't want her to forget me." Arlen looked at Paine. "How do you forget all those girls?"

"Is that what you want to do?"

"No, I don't."

"I'll just say this: I don't spend my time writing them letters and looking at their pictures every fucking day."

Arlen looked down dejectedly. "I just want to put everything right. I had so much time . . . I wish I had put things right. Reckon I didn't. Got to carry that with me."

Paine snorted. "No way, Arlen. Don't do that. That's an extra piece of gear. One piece too many. You carry a woman like that, checking on her all the time, wondering if she's still there, one day she might not be and then what were you so worried about? And think about what you'd miss in the meanwhile."

He was not a complete fool, that Paine. Arlen could miss a lot of things: a sniper in the trees, a machine gun nest, an ambush.

"You can do that," said Paine, "or you can take her, your little piece of kit, and just put her in your foot locker. Lock her up tight and send her on ahead. She'll be waiting there for us in Berlin. But you gotta forget about her until then."

Another convoy rumbled up. The G.I.s shouted and made rude gestures to Paine, who hopped up and gave it right back to them. "Those Company L bastards! Look at them, they get to ride in the deuce-and-a-halfs! Those sonsabitches. We get all the hard breaks."

Paine's gleefully griping grin was wiped away as he turned back up the road. He grew serious and reached for his helmet. "Grab your pot, Arlen. We're going."

And down the road came the company commander, Captain Smith, carbine in hand. It was indeed time. They were going to the boat.

So the final movement was here at last, the time they had prepared for all those years. They were so prepared, it seemed routine. And so perhaps that was why Arlen did not hesitate too long before putting on his helmet. He reached into his chest pocket and pulled out the photo of Caty that he carried there. She had sent him a new one last fall — she looked better than ever. He gave her one last look, like a long drink of cool water from the bucket before walking to the plow and taking up the reins. Then he put her picture inside the front of his helmet, nestled in the liner. He set his helmet on his head, but took it right off again. Too easy to see her there. He moved the photo to the back. There, now she could see where he was going, and he could just look ahead. It was only war that he needed to see now.

"Arlen, let's go."

"All right, all right, hold your horses."

"I'm pissed about having to march. Wish we had those deuce-and-a-halves."

"You quit your bellyachin'," said Arlen, smiling suddenly. "You're gettin' an all-expenses paid tour of Europe courtesy of your Uncle Sam. You never had it so good."

"Jeez, aren't you sore," said Paine.

"I ain't. I'm just tired of hearin' you run your mouth all damn day."

"Well, you're stuck with me now," said Paine.

"And don't I know it."

The platoon formed up and fell in with the rest of the company. The long, olive drab column tramped its way down and down, the smell of salt air growing stronger. The smell of the English Channel. Yes, the war really was coming.

Lord, it's just you and me now. I might forget you at times, Lord, but don't you forget me.

VIII

"Corporal, get up."

Arlen awoke into a clear twilight. He blinked twice, then sat up on one elbow. "Sarge?"

"Get up. Get your section up, too," said Sergeant Gunderson. "We've got hot chow. Get some in your men's bellies and then get them ready to move out."

Arlen nodded, rubbing his face. The sergeant disappeared into the dark. Arlen sat up and put his helmet on. "You sleep all right?" whispered Arlen to Paine, who was assembling his gear.

Paine's voice was taut: "How could I?"

None could have slept soundly after their orders the night before: attack in the morning. The officers had given them no grand destination, nor described a fine battlefield: they would just attack.

As the company roused itself, the remaining darkness quelled the instinct toward noise. The smell of this field was powerful in that inky dark: dewy grass and days-old manure. And with the smell of the sea, and of dry, dusty days, and of wet, muddy nights, it was the smell of France, the land they were liberating, the place to meet the Germans.

It was not what they had imagined. All the way across the English Channel, the troopship had tossed the G.I.s so badly, they had needed no encouragement to climb down the nets into the landing craft. But no sooner than they had set off for the beach, the men began to puke, vomiting their tension and nerves over the side and onto the deck. Arlen was no exception. Weak down into his guts, he had stepped off into the surf where rocks clattered in the waves and raised his eyes to the shore: he instantly saw corpses. They wore olive drab like him; they were Americans — *Americans* — unburied, more than a week after the invasion landings. Paine had refused to believe it. "Those are wax dummies; the Krauts left them there," he said. What comfort to believe that; but Arlen would not lie to himself like that. It was all but for the luck of the patch on their shoulders, the luck of being the 30th Infantry Division and not the 29th. The shock had struck most of them, leaving the men of the 3rd Battalion, 120th Infantry Regiment quiet in the dizzyingly frenzied push up to the front line. March, halt; march, halt; they did it in silence. Standing during a halt, Arlen would wonder whether to drop his pack in the hope of a long pause or just bear the shoulder-cutting weight of the straps in the belief that the column would start moving soon. They all had to decide such things themselves and many times they were wrong and they simply had to bear it. And fighter-bombers loitered overhead and artillery echoed from far ahead, reminding them of what they were moving toward and that soon they would have to bear that, too.

Here came the hot chow at last. Buckling up his gear, Arlen slung his M1 rifle and fell in. The cook slopped franks and beans in their mess kits — army chicken, once again. But he ate up. It would be only C and K rations for a while. He sat the lip of the foxhole, eating with Paine. With each passing minute, they could see each other more clearly and they began to shovel the army chicken down faster. Finishing, they checked their gear, strapping down everything tight, hanging hand grenades in the right place, checking their rifles once, twice, three times.

At last, they were done. To check again would do no good and they might make a mistake. Now to wait for the order.

Paine's hoarse whisper broke the still air. "Arlen, I'm ready to get at those Krauts." said Paine.

"You're higher than a Georgia pine," said Arlen.

"I feel a little jumpy."

"Cool your heels. We'll be in it soon enough."

Arlen could not stay still. He rose and checked the rest of the men in the section, correcting their mistakes, giving a word of advice here and there, for what it was worth. He had barely finished before the call to form up came, just like that, as easy as any maneuver or training march. Platoons came together and once Company K had formed, its elements fell in on the dirt road and begin their march forward from the assembly area. Boots beat irrythmically on the road and harnesses and rifles slings clicked and clacked. The company halted alongside the road for a while, the reason unknown. It then formed again and moved ahead.

The sun was up when the artillery started, the 105mm shells ripping the air overhead. Arlen looked at his watch: *0631 hours*. They were still not to the line of departure. The battalion marched on and the regimental guns continued throwing shells to the unseen front. Arlen touched his cartridge belt, his bayonet, the trigger and operating rod of his rifle over and over, just feeling that they were there. He looked up and down the column, checking on his section again. Sergeant Gunderson did the same. The sergeant's face was frozen, mask-like.

At last they were close to the line of departure and each company split off from the others. Carefully each platoon formed into columns of twos and moved down narrow lanes between the hedgerows. The signal came for Company K, known as King, to halt. They were the battalion reserve. Company I, called Item, and L, called Love, deployed ahead, melting into the hedgerows and the trees. They would lead the battalion across the plain toward their objective, the Vire et Taute Canal. The abstract descriptions of the night before ran again and again through Arlen's head, the form but not the shape, nor the color, of the attack. He looked at his watch: *0712 hours.*

"Get over to the side," hissed Lieutenant Iannucci, their platoon commander. First Platoon shuffled into the roadside ditch and hunkered down next to the hedgerow, a long earth and rock berm festooned with bushes and trees. One felt safe, well-protected just being next to it. The lieutenant walked up and down, checking on everything, consulting with his sergeants, quiet but conscientious. The men liked Iannucci; he was better than that last whistledick lieutenant.

Slap, slap, slap, slap-slap-slap, slap. The unseen artillery bursts pushed on their eardrums and chests. Then the tearing crackle of 105s was overpowered by a dull, freight car-like roar. Arlen looked up and thought he saw the shell. He blinked and it was gone. "Good Lord."

"Did you see that too?" said Budowicki, a private.

"Where'd that come from?" said Arlen.

"Battleships out in the Channel," said Paine. He was grinning ear to ear. "Won't be a Kraut left after they're done."

Yes, it seemed so. The G.I.s waited for the artillery's work to be done, smoking one cigarette after another.

The shells stopped falling little by little, then all at once. Now came the double bass signature of air support. Silvery P-47s lumbered overhead, carrying bombs to targets far ahead. They circled back around. Black streaking clouds appeared from the fronts of their wings as the planes swooped down, pumping out machine gun fire. The first flight was replaced by a second and then a third. Finally the last few bombs burst and the planes disappeared, and there was a whispering void that seemed to be beckoning them.

Then the order came, the one of many in a long chain, leading up to the very moment of trial. The shouts rippled across the Norman fields, although not for King Company. The other companies rose and with steady steps moved across the open fields towards the dissipating clouds of smoke and debris to their front. King Company, officers and men, peered over the top of the hedgerow, trying to get a good view, of Item on the left and Love on the right.

Peering through the foliage, Arlen felt his jugular throbbing against his collar. The moment was very ordinary, for it was as his eyes saw it and not his imagination. Beyond the still-unfamiliar terrain and the surprising might of the artillery, Arlen could not distinguish this attack from any exercise they had ever been through back at home. The steady advance, all the platoons spread apart, went quietly, the fear of land mines or enemy fire seeming to disappear with each step.

Of the same mind, Paine shouted: "Hey, Sarge, did we ever leave Tennessee? It's maneuvers all over again."

The advancing companies passed from view, disappearing into a long fold in the ground. The soldiers watched patiently, trying to pick out any movement, but catching only glimpses of G.I.s as they crossed hedgerows. At last, the advancing soldiers appeared as the land began to rise again on the far side.

Machine guns broke the silence. Arlen's heart jumped a foot high, then sank like a rock into his stomach. More automatic weapon fire and then individual rifle shots lashed the advancing Americans. There were no flashes from the Germans, only a din of rifle fire and the black puffs of mortars shells that began to drop. The men of the lead companies fell like sacks of meal. Indistinct shouts rolled up the slopes toward Company K. Arlen stood up to get a better view, but jerked ducked back down as an ear-splitting crack tore the field of battle. An explosion amongst the Company I boys followed. Then another, and another, each feeling as if it could rend granite.

"A goddamn 88," said Sergeant Gunderson.

Oh, Good Lord, is our goose cooked?

More unseen fire poured from the German positions. Item and Love returned the fire and the heavy thirty caliber machine guns fired long, searching bursts toward the German positions, yet none could seem to match. Time stretched on, the fire did not slacken. No one could see what was happening.

Captain Smith's voice caught every ear: "King Company! Let's go!"

The soldiers rose out of the ditch, hefting rifles, mortar tubes and bases, light machine guns, spare ammunition, in column, each platoon to its assigned starting place: First Platoon on the left, Second Platoon on the right, Third Platoon waiting in reserve. Captain Smith, seeing all was right, passed the word, which filtered along through platoon commanders and squad sergeants, to advance. "All right, let's go," said Lieutenant Iannucci in his subdued manner.

Arlen climbed over the hedgerow. The dirt and roots gave way under his weight and he half-sank into it. Pulling himself out with difficulty, he moved ahead with his squad. The din of small arms fire and the crump of mortars continued far off to the left. Arlen could see nothing from that direction. He suddenly took a deep breath, as if he had been holding it back this whole time.

81

Here he was, and he almost did not know how he got here. He looked back and they had already come so far. And yet, look ahead: it was still so far to go, to get up there to the ridgeline which seemed to withdraw behind long and wide fields broken only by hedgerows and their intertwined trees. A bead of perspiration ran down his side under his shirt. His mouth was dry.

The men moved as swiftly as they could in the high grass, stretched out in columns of twos. They crossed hedgerow after hedgerow, and the scouts pushed ahead, probing for the enemy, but there was nothing. Perhaps the Germans had retreated and were already on the run. *Good Lord, are we ever gonna get to fight them?*

First Squad, leading the platoon, came to the next hedgerow. In twos, just as in the column, they climbed over it.

A shot rolled over the land.

The sound of the bullet hitting home was clear to them all. Private Budowicki, straddling the top of the hedgerow, fell forward, over the other side and out of sight.

"Goddammit," said Sergeant Gunderson. "Medic!"

Arlen threw himself against the hedgerow, trying to make himself flat against its earthen sides. He looked back at the rest of the platoon. Almost every man had frozen where he was, dropping to the ground. "Get up here!" yelled Gunderson. But not one of them moved. "Come on, get out of sight!" Not one of them moved, they only seemed to burrow deeper into the shin-high grass, trying to hide.

"Where did that shot come from?" said the sergeant.

Arlen shook his head. "I don't know."

"The left, up ahead somewhere," said Paine. He crouched down right next to Arlen, almost leaning against Arlen's leg like a dog.

"I know I'm not supposed to do this, but—" Gunderson raised his eyes just above the lowest part of the top of the hedgerow. Arlen felt the sweat course coldly down the small of his back. *Don't get it, Gunderson, don't get it in your damn head.* The sergeant slid back down, shaking his head. "I can't see shit."

The medic arrived and Lieutenant Iannucci was with him. "Where is he?" said the medic.

"On the other side."

The aid man did not hesitate, but grabbed hold of a few broken roots and scrambled over the top. A belated shot snapped overhead just after he dropped to the other side.

"Sniper," said the lieutenant.

"I'm not losing a man sending him over the top."

"We have to get into that next field, sergeant. Get your squad through any way you can. Provide cover for the rest of the platoon once you do." He turned to leave. "Now, sergeant."

No man could be convinced to go over the top; they could hardly be dragged from their spots hiding in the grass. So they had to go through. With rifles butts and entrenching tools, First Squad beat away at the weakest part of the hedgerow until it had crumbled enough and the men could step through crouched over.

When Arlen climbed through, he looked to the right and saw Budowicki. The young man's face was covered with his poncho. The body was still but seemingly undisturbed, except for a small pool of blood that soaked the grass and his jacket. Each man in the squad paused as he passed through. Each wanted to say something, to look and wonder, just as Arlen did. "Let's go, let's go, no time to gawk, let's go," said Gunderson, nudging the men along with his rifle butt. "Corporal, get your section moving, now. Let's go."

Arlen nodded and turned away from Budowicki. He pushed himself, putting one foot in front of the other, resisting the urge to look back. He got his section together and waited for further orders, head locked straight ahead.

The platoon moved onward, drawn ahead by skinny Lieutenant Iannucci, right out in front. Nothing more happened. It was quiet to their immediate front again, though to the east there was plenty of artillery and machine gun fire to be heard. Once again, on the far side of this field the platoon reached a hedgerow. Arlen crouched down at its base, almost out of instinct. He pulled out his canteen, fumbling with the top. Finally, he got it open and drank the whole thing. It was not enough.

Sergeant Gunderson hunkered down with the squad. "The Krauts are holding up Love Company out there on our left," he said. "We will provide covering fire along with the mortars, while Second Platoon takes the far side and defilades the German position. Understood?"

They had trained enough. In that sense, and only in that sense, was this like maneuvers: there was a problem and they would have to fix it in the only way they knew how. The squad was deployed, the objectives of each section were clear. There could be no questions. Satisfied, Gunderson said, "Now, do me one favor, boys. For Pete's sake, spread out."

The machine gun fire ahead and to their left grew thicker. Arlen pulled back the bolt on his M1 enough to see if there was a round in the chamber. The dull brass cartridge sat patiently. Arlen closed his eyes for a moment. *Good Lord, here we go. Let's do it right.* He heard the men breathing raspily.

Sergeant Gunderson gave the order and Arlen opened his eyes as the platoon found places along the hedgerow, each man drawing his weapon to his shoulder. The hedgerow was high here, and Arlen kicked a step into it. Feet slightly off the ground, he poked the rifle over the top of the hedgerow.

Arlen saw nothing, so he drew a bead on nothing in particular and settled into his pattern of breathing: in, hold, out, hold, repeat.

Lord, let me shoot straight.

He jumped when the light thirty opened up. The machine gun fired several bursts, searching the corner of the hedgerow ahead with fire. Second Platoon poured over the hedgerow on the right.

"Keep your eyes open!" said Sergeant Gunderson.

Look to the front, Arlen.

Second Platoon reached the middle of the field and then it came down on them: machine gun fire and the black puffs of mortar rounds. G.I.s fell irregularly, their cries audible.

Oh, Lord, there they go. Our boys. The Krauts are gettin' our boys.

"Goddammit, give them some covering fire!" shouted Lieutenant Iannucci, his voice shrill.

Arlen held his weapon in his hands. He had felt no impulse to fire at all. He was frozen up.

The lieutenant came down the line slapping the back of their helmets. "For Christ's sake, fire! Fire, dammit!"

With the lieutenant there, they all began to open up. Arlen wasn't even sure exactly what he was shooting at. He fired and fired until the clip pinged away and the bolt locked back. He reloaded in a frenzy, and settled back down behind the sights. *Come on, now, get it together, Arlen, get it together.* He breathed in and out, in and out, and a forced calm followed. He found some capacity to speak: "Where the fuck are they?"

"Tall tree, you see it?" shouted Paine.

"No!"

"That one! Missing the branches low on the right side, see it?"

"No!"

"Fuck, Arlen, they're there, just to the right of there. Machine gun!"

"I can't see it."

Gunderson came up behind Arlen. He pointed. "There, see it?"

"I see, I see it now."

When Arlen settled back down with the rifle, he took aim at a slight gap in the bushes on the opposing hedgerow. The light thirty seemed to be firing there, so he did too, squeezing off shots. Theirs was not to kill, but to suppress.

The situation dragged on. Second Platoon could not move and the German fire continued to hail down on them, as much as they tried to work their way forward. The machine gun and rifle fire of the rest of the company did little good if Second Platoon could not advance.

"Keep up the fire," said Arlen to his section. Dropping the M1 down onto his knee, he pulled a fresh clip of eight rounds from his cartridge belt. He set it atop the follower as he held back the locked operating rod with the blade of his hand. He pushed down the clip into the receiver with his thumb and when the clip was all the way in, the operating rod unlocked and he whisked his hand away as the bolt slammed home, with eight rounds ready again.

At last, the 60mm mortars began to plaster points along the far hedgerow and the German fire slackened. The sound of American weapons now echoed ahead and from the left, a surprise to both sides.

"Cease fire, cease fire," said Lieutenant Iannucci. "Let Third Platoon do their worst."

Gradually the firing died away and the men reloaded. They had just broken out their canteens when the order came to move ahead. Many of Second Platoon lay in the field, tended to by aid men, their white circles with red crosses bright against their drab uniforms. Their platoon pushed up to the broken hedgerow on the far side. As Arlen stepped through a hole in the hedgerow, his foot nearly landed on a body. He stumbled and caught himself. Turning, he saw a German lying on his back. The man's helmet was missing and his hair was tousled with blood. His eyes were closed, but his mouth was frozen open, teeth slightly bared, as if he were about to bite an apple. Arlen could not see a single mark on the body. He felt the dead man's pulse. The body was still warm. Arlen's hand jerked back. He gnawed on his lip as he took a few steps back, then forced his eyes away and tried to catch up with the platoon.

"Let's go, keep up!" shouted the lieutenant to the stragglers. Arlen picked up the pace, his toes snagging on the thick grass. A huge field curved ahead and to his right, the land disappearing before it began to rise gently again to the distant ridge. Eventually he slowed, though he had not caught up with the rest. There was no hurry, despite the lieutenant's insistent commands. Every soldier moved with the same deliberate pace, upright, alert, but confident in his stride. Arlen felt the same. There was shooting and the crump of artillery far to the east, but here there was nothing. This was his war right here, not way over there. How could he be anything but thankful for the respite?

Lord, if only the whole war was like this right now, I'd be mighty thankful.

And already he felt shame at all the boasts they had made, and he remembered their professed and secret eagerness to get into combat. It was gone in an instant and now he would beg for a reprieve if it was not so dishonorable. Older he was, by years within mere hours, mere minutes, old enough to know what he should have all along.

But still they advanced across this green, open field. He saw Paine looking back, to his left, then to his right. Arlen whistled to him. His buddy turned around. As Arlen came close, Paine lit two cigarettes and handed one to Arlen. "Have a Lucky." Arlen took it gratefully. "Hey, Arlen, look at this: I pissed myself." Indeed, Paine's crotch was wet.

Arlen didn't know what to say. He puffed on his Lucky. The lieutenant's urgent hand signal put him into motion. "Best keep movin'."

"Did you piss yourself, Arlen?" Paine took a last drag on his cigarette. "I don't want to be the only one."

A sound like an enormous sheet ripping broke over them. Words from another life in another place came to mind: *And the sun was darkened, and the veil of the temple was rent in the midst.* The sheet ripped again and bullets snapped in between the men of the platoon, arcing over the land from just out of sight.

Arlen's chest hit the ground and his helmet bounced on his head. He couldn't see anything to the front. The lieutenant was screaming orders, but Arlen could not make them out. More rounds snapped around them, the ripping sound of the MG 42 machine gun very distinct across the wide open space.

Sticking up like a statue in the vast field, Gunderson swept his arm and the squad began to move forward at the signal, creeping through the grass. From the right, Second Squad cracked off rounds in reply: their BAR chattered, but the light thirty was distinctly absent.

Endless grass and piles of cow dung passed under Arlen's chin and his elbows crushed wilted wildflowers. He poured sweat and felt the salt building on his temples. At last the sweat stopped and his tongue began to swell, but there was still far to go, for there was Sergeant Gunderson, urging them forward at every chance.

The light thirty started in on the Germans and the bullets overhead slackened a bit. Arlen dared to lift his head. There it was, the inevitable hedgerow, where the German surely were. His stomach sank. It was in sight, but still so far.

Again the temple veil was rent and the rounds snapped all around the squad and Arlen threw himself face-first into the grass.

Good Lord, don't let us have to attack that hedgerow. Lord, please no.

The sergeant was not privy to his prayer, nor the lieutenant. Again the sweep of the hand pushed them ahead, all their trust in God and the suppressing fire of the rest of the platoon. Closer and closer they inched, until the yards were cut to less than a hundred. And now it was really too hot. The German fire was no longer merely snapping overhead, but tore up the grass around them. Where were the friendly mortars? Where was the heavy thirty to lay down those long, driving bursts of fire that would keep the Germans behind their stone and tree wall?

"Covering fire!" called Sergeant Gunderson to Arlen. The sergeant's section was getting ready to rush and Arlen's was to support.

Sarge, no, that's too damn far, don't do it.

Arlen's thoughts were one thing, but his actions were wholly another. Automatically, he hunched himself up on his elbows and began firing at the hedgerow. "Fire, dammit!" he shouted to the men in his section. They joined in one by one, the BAR in the hands of Private Hardin the last to join in. The sergeant went with his section up the left, where another hedgerow marked the far side of the field. The Germans did not see them. The tight bursts of the MG 42 reached for Arlen's section and he lay back down again. The incoming rounds snapped all about and Arlen dared not raise his head to fire back. The pumping, ripping sound of the MG 42 echoed again and again. There were cries from the left. Arlen strained his ear. Again the German machine gun fired. Cries again.

"Medic!"

Oh, Good Lord, no, no.

"Medic!"

He raised himself up again and began firing back at the hedgerow, trying desperately to pick out any semblance of a German uniform or a gun barrel. Rifle rounds reached toward Arlen one by one, but he stayed up and eventually his section was up and firing back, too. He squeezed off round after round, reloading and firing through another clip and then another and another. The front sight began to waver in the heat rising from the barrel.

A dull thud from the hedgerow in front of them. Shouts, sporadic shots, then another thud. And Arlen saw a big-framed figure in olive drab hunkered down in front of the hedgerow, reloading. The German fire slackened and then stopped suddenly.

Arlen motioned his men forward at the double, running half-hunched to the hedgerow. Far off to the right there was still shooting and a few rounds snapped around them, but Second Squad held the Germans' attention. When Arlen reached the hedgerow, he practically collapsed against it. Sergeant Gunderson, that big, olive drab figure, was there, peering through a gap in the roots and earth. "Fuckin' Kraut, there he is."

"Good Lord, Sarge, Krauts are on the other side?"

"Yeah, that one got what he fuckin' deserved." The sergeant mopped his brow with his sleeve. "We took two casualties. Martin and Donovan."

Arlen's stomach sank. "How are they?"

"Martin got hit, he's all right. Donovan — he's gonna bleed out if the aid man doesn't get here quick."

That was three from the squad in one day. Three of twelve.

"Sarge, you got any water?"

Gunderson handed Arlen his canteen. Arlen drained it, desperate for anything to restore a sense of life.

The lieutenant was shouting and signaling again.

"He wants us to move forward, Sarge," said Arlen.

"Like hell we will."

Arlen licked his lips, which were dry again already. "We gotta clear out those Krauts in front of Second Squad."

"Don't you move a muscle. I'm not losing any more men, not today. Hell, the medics aren't even up." Gunderson looked right back at the lieutenant and shouted across the distance, "Where are the goddamned medics?"

Arlen's section was looking at him and at the sergeant, and Arlen to Gunderson and the lieutenant, and the lieutenant's anger was pulsating like incoming rounds across the hundred yards. Arlen reloaded his rifle and peered over the hedgerow. Who knew how many more Krauts there were out there? And how many more Americans would it cost to kill even just one? Arlen looked at his men: Paine and Hardin and Kelly and the rest. He could not imagine ordering them to go die. But if it was not them to risk their lives, it was the others of the platoon, pinned down under the German fire off on the right, growing stronger all the time. The lieutenant was screaming and his sergeant was hounding him and his men were looking at him.

"Gimme a boost," said Arlen to Paine. The smaller man locked his fingers together and Arlen stepped on his hand and then swung himself over the top of the hedgerow.

He sank down into a leafy darkness on the far side. It was an orchard of apple trees, their branches heavily laden. The air was sickly sweet with the smell of fruit rotting in the grass. A pair of dim bodies lay in the mottled shade of the branches, both contorted in death. There were no other Krauts to be seen. Paine slid down the wall behind Arlen. "Which way?" he whispered.

Arlen motioned into the orchard. He wanted to stay off the hedgerow. It was too easy to just shoot along it. They would sweep around and get the Krauts from behind. Their faces were tight, their jaws were shut even tighter.

And then there was sunlight beyond the orchard and he stopped under the boughs of the last apple tree. Arlen heard nothing, but his senses swung his head to the right and his rifle with it, the hunter's instinct returning after many years away. And there went a German machine gun crew through the sunlight, scurrying along. One of them turned a surprised head. Arlen's front sight grabbed the lead one and held, and the aperture set around the post, and in one smooth stroke he took up the two-stage trigger and — *boom, boom, boom-boom-boom-boom*, the whole squad opened up, and the Kraut brought the machine gun off his shoulder, but the hail of thirty caliber hammered him down onto his back, and his comrade went down too, falling into a lump on his face, still clutching the ammo cans in both hands.

The breathing of the G.I.s caught up with them at last, rustling through dry throats like bullets in the leaves.

"Jesus, Arlen, that was quick," said Paine. "Who got him? The one with the MG."

"I don't know," Arlen said, not loud enough for anyone to hear.

We got them. But they could have gotten us.

He was quick enough this time. But he did not know why he was. He did not feel like it was enough.

"Corporal!"

Arlen nearly jumped all the way to Berlin.

"Get a move on!" said Gunderson, now behind him with the rest of the squad.

And they pushed on, to do it again.

With hands bereft of dexterity, Arlen chucked the empty C ration can out of his foxhole into the last gloom. He had eaten the meal cold. It sat heavy and greasy in the pit of his stomach. He needed water, but there was none in his canteen. Perhaps he could get some more in the morning.

Night was closing in at last, though it was almost ten o'clock. Sentry duty was his later on; he should sleep now. But he was almost too tired to sleep. Even the worst training, those long thirty-hour marches and flanking maneuvers, could not compare. His muscles felt used up beyond any renewal.

Paine, across the foxhole, eyed Arlen but said nothing. He must have been upset at having to stand sentry first. Well, they drew straws, it was only fair, nothing to be bitter about. Or perhaps he was just tired like Arlen, tired from the rise and fall of fear, of the imperative of pressing ahead, of realizing for the first time that one could never know where the enemy lay. Tired from taking field after field, pushing to the crest of the ridge, only to see a slightly higher crest a few hundred yards ahead. Tired from digging a foxhole in the wet, sucking earth and settling down in sweat-sodden clothes that trapped grime against one's skin.

They had done well, that was the word, passed down from the brass hats. After all, the attack had gone forward, as intended. It took all day, into the evening, but the regiment had done it.

The lieutenant came by, kneeling at each foxhole, saying a few words. Conscientious, he was, if nothing else. Squatting next to Arlen, their commander shifted back his helmet from his eyes. "Well done out there."

"Thank you, sir," said Arlen.

"You doing okay?"

"I reckon I'll be all right, sir."

Arlen couldn't read the lieutenant's face perfectly in the darkness, but it looked surprisingly calm and understanding. No sympathy, nor empathy, just simple knowing, the equality of having suffered just as another had. Yet the lieutenant did not seem withdrawn, concerned with his own little world of equipment and entrenchment, sentry and spade, rifle and rest. *Afraid as me, ain't he? But he's got a lot more to do, and he's doin' it.* Who could not regard such a man?

"Keep your chin up, Corporal," said the lieutenant. "Today was everyone's first day."

"I'll remember that, sir."

The platoon leader nodded and stepped off a few yards to the next foxhole, already disappearing into the falling night. Arlen checked his M1, the safety snicked into place, and made sure his bayonet was in easy reach, in case a Kraut snuck over a hedge that night. Then he settled down into the hole as best he could. "'Night, Paine."

"Two hours."

"Yep."

His sore and weary muscles settled down to sleep. But not an ounce of tension faded. Arlen's mind still raced ahead. It darted and dodged, from thought to fear to another fear and back again. He kept his eyes closed, knowing he should sleep, hoping the thoughts would disappear and he would nod off. But they remained, repeating themselves in endless, inescapable loops.

Arlen dozed in that half-aware world between life and sleep. Crimson waves and lines like tides of blood filled his unconscious sight. His body jumped involuntarily. He opened his eyes and sat up. It was pitch dark. Paine turned his head toward him, but said nothing.

Arlen pulled his helmet back down, but left his eyes open, staring at the darkness of the inside of his helmet.

Ain't nothin' prepared me for today. Ain't no substitute for the real thing.

I ain't as good as I thought I was.

We ain't as good as they say we are.

He fidgeted.

Only one thing keeps me from going there, with the rest of 'em. Dead in those fields, bleedin' in the aid station. That can be me.

He shivered unexpectedly.

Ain't up to me.

All that remained was a sense that it was all was in his Creator's hands. He was not comforted. If God had the whimsy to take some men and not others, would He be so whimsical with him?

Death ain't to be feared. I know that. But most folks ain't seen death like this.

Arlen tried to pray away the sovereignty of the God who watched him, telling God that He could not do certain things, let certain things happen, He just couldn't — even though He could and did, just not to Arlen, not yet, at least — for wasn't he more deserving, more honest, more faithful, more — well, anything — than others?

Lord, ain't I done right? Ain't I done what you asked? Ain't that enough to get me through?

There was only silence in response.

He turned the thought over and over in his head, rolling it about, trying to make it disappear, but it was like a candy that would not melt under his tongue.

IX

The Pall Mall burned almost to Arlen's finger before the ash broke. Flecks fluttered down onto his knees. Gripping the butt farther back, he drew one last time, stubbed it out, and field stripped it. He reached into his pocket and felt the last cigarette left from his C ration. No, not yet. He blew the last bit of smoke out of his nose like a silent steam whistle and waited.

He shifted the heavy M1 rifle from the crook of one arm to another. Paine was peering silently down the dirt lane, Private Xavier watching the other direction. The rest of the squad said nothing, just waiting and smoking in the ditch. No one talked much anymore, at least, no more than was necessary. Small talk filling empty space served no purpose; it could not even distract them from the matter at hand. Indeed, it should not. They should be watching, waiting, listening, prepared. Only replacements talked a lot.

Paine raised his rifle slightly and Arlen laid hold of his, too, and the others began to bring their weapons about. But then Paine stopped and at last broke his gaze. "It's the looie."

Down the shady lane came the lieutenant. He squatted down with the squad. He refused a cigarette from one of the soldiers. "Where is Sergeant Gunderson?"

Paine grinned. "He's seeing a man about a horse."

"Oh." The lieutenant said nothing else. He looked around at the road, the trees, the hedgerows, and the G.I.s. There was no friendly recognition, nor awkward shyness, nor stern acknowledgment. The lieutenant was simply seeing the ground and the men. It all meant something in that strange head of his, the source of his intense, penetrating way of leading men. Arlen liked him for it. He could follow a man like that.

Gunderson came through the bushes, buttoning his fly. "Lieutenant, are we on the move?"

"I want you to come recon with me."

The sergeant looked surprised. "The two of us?"

"Yes, I need your sharp eyes."

Without question, Gunderson picked up his rifle and followed the lieutenant back down the road. Arlen looked away for just a moment and when his eyes flitted back, the two superiors had disappeared. Arlen let out a sharp breath. He would have gone rather than just sit here, waiting. Anything to get this damn war over with. It was time for that last cigarette.

The squad smoked all they had. Overhead, a P-47 wheeled about and strafed a distant target. The spent brass came tinkling through the tree branches. They all asked each other for more cigarettes, but they were all out.

"Coffee, anyone?" said Xavier.

"Ain't no time," said Arlen.

"Says who? When are we moving out?"

"When they come back."

"And when's that?"

Arlen didn't know. He shifted his rifle again from one side to the other.

"I'll take some," said Paine.

The smell of the burning chemical tablet got right up in Arlen's nostrils. He rose and walked down the dirt lane. Second Squad was down there somewhere. And Third beyond that. He had half a mind to walk down there and ask them for cigarettes.

That P-47 was back and it had a partner. They were strafing the hell out of something on the other side of those woods. Arlen watched with interest. They circled around and around and around until he started to wonder how they could still have any ammunition left. Must be a hard target to hit. Or a lot of them.

He walked back and settled down in his old spot. He didn't feel any better than before. No, he was more restless.

"Coffee?" said Paine, offering his cup.

Arlen shook his head.

The fighters came back. This time it was a racing throb that cut the air: P-51s, zipping past so fast there was no seeing them through the trees.

"What do you think that's all about?"

Arlen looked at his watch. How long had the lieutenant been gone?

He started to stand up again, but why? Where was he going? He plopped back down. "Gimme some of that coffee."

"Not much left," said Xavier.

"Whatever you've got."

The coffee only made him want a cigarette more. Should never have smoked his last one.

A thump pushed through the woods and rolled over the hedgerow on the other side of the lane.

The soldiers all looked at each other. "That wasn't artillery, was it?"

"Sounded like a tank."

"Not one of ours."

Their eyes flitted between the direction of the woods and Arlen.

Another thump, that sharp wave of air pushing out in all directions. Yes, a tank firing. High-velocity gun, 75mm, maybe 88.

"Arlen, that's a Kraut tank," said Paine. "Are they coming our way?"

Arlen stood up and looked down the road. The rest of the squad was hidden away in the leafy ditches. He could not see any concern among them.

Maybe it ain't nothin'. If it's a Kraut counterattack, they'd be gettin' ready.

He gnawed on his lip. Squatting down, he cocked his ear. Were those rifles shots? Maybe, or maybe not. He returned to the ditch and settled down. He felt the eyes of the squad on him.

What're they starin' at? I ain't in command.

Again — a thump. It had to be a counterattack.

Sergeant Fuller or Sergeant Gillis was surely getting the platoon ready to meet the Germans. The order would come any minute.

Thump.

The stares on him were so intense that Arlen dared only look straight ahead in desperate desire of clairvoyance, as if the branches and earth and distant woods would send up an image like a truthful mirage which would tell him for sure, for sure, for sure what was on the far side.

Thump.

Ain't my place.

Thump. Thump.

I ain't in charge of the platoon.

Thump.

One of the sergeants should get the platoon ready. They know they have to if the looie's gone.

Thump. Thump.

If they did know, they would.

"Hey, Arlen," said Paine.

But he was already up. There was a machine gun burst in the distant woods and the matter was settled.

"We got to get the lieutenant and Sarge," said Arlen, rolling his sleeves down. The others didn't know to whom he was speaking. "I mean, I've got to go get 'em. Y'all hold this hedgerow until I get back. Get word down to Second and Third Squad. See if they've got a bazooka lyin' around somewheres."

"I'm coming with you," said Paine.

"All right, but you give Mathis the rifle grenades. Drop your musette bag."

Paine stripped down until, like Arlen, he only had his cartridge belt, two hand grenades, a canteen, his bayonet, and a K ration jammed into his jacket pocket, plus his M1.

"Don't be gone too long," said Private Mathis, fitting the launcher for the rifle grenades.

"I just got to find 'em before the Krauts do."

"Don't let them find you two first."

Arlen did not answer, but set out down the road at a brisk pace, headed in the direction that Gunderson and Iannucci had gone. Paine, though small, was nimble enough to keep up with Arlen's long-legged double-time. There was artillery fire now, the low, flat rumble of American guns to the rear, and then the whistling crackle of incoming mail from beyond those forbidding woods.

Arlen raised his hand and they stopped, crouching in the roadside ditch. The hedgerow sprouted like unkempt hair, but Arlen could see a little break in the green growth: a thin branch pushed unnaturally behind another, a dozen leaves crushed into a darker green under a boot, a scuff in the dirt. He took a swig from his canteen, the water stinking of chlorine from the halazone tablets. "Reckon they went through here."

"You sure?"

"No."

He stepped through into the next field all the same.

Come on, Sarge, where are you, where are you, Lieutenant, which way did you go

Thump.

The tank fire was a real slap on the eardrums now. Arlen stopped at the far side of the field, hunkering down behind a tree. Now he could hear the wheeze and whine of an engine and the occasional squeak of a metallic track. It was very close. It would be shaking the earth soon.

Lord, I should have brought those rifle grenades.

What to do, what to do.

He looked to Paine. His buddy's sharp face, which could mug for a camera or be serious like a general or even approach some semblance of debonaire charm before a woman if his loins required it, was scrunched up, as if he was just waiting for the shot. But then it released and his eyes brightened. He signaled to the north. "Moving that way."

"What?"

"The tank, moving that way."

A relief. Perhaps the woods were too thick. The hedgerows turned from boon to curse and back with ease.

"Hey, let me have some of that water."

A lone rifle shot.

From the left.

Another rifle shot, followed by a second.

95

Ain't an M1. The report didn't have that booming thump. This was a sharper crack.

Crack. Crack, crack. Crack.

Now the M1's thump resounded.

The ripping of an MG 42 and a hail of rifle cracks replied, and the M1 sounded lonely as it tried to reply.

"Fuck's sake, Arlen, is that the platoon?"

"You know it ain't."

And he got out and began worming his way along the hedgerow, moving toward the sound of the gunfire. He winced with every step and every echoing shot.

What am I doing out here, should have stayed back, gotten the squad ready and the rest of the platoon, ain't gonna do no good gettin' my ass shot out here, Good Lord, no I ain't, Good Lord, what am I doing out here

Fire, fire, fire, the fire in the woods would not stop.

Arlen knelt at the corner of the field, tucking himself under a drooping branch. The hedgerow was very low here. Paine crept up behind him, watching the rear. "Arlen, what are we doing? Where is the lieutenant and Sarge?"

"Don't you reckon that's them?" said Arlen, jerking his head toward the gunfire. He slipped his rifle between the branches of the hedgerow and carefully peered over the top. He ducked back down as German fire crisscrossed the field on the other side. But none of the rounds came close. He peered over again. In desperation, an olive drab figure was running across the field, rounds tearing the ground around him.

"Paine! It's the looie! Get down there and get his attention. Get him over on this side."

"What about you?"

"When you can, cover me and I'll scoot down to you."

Gingerly, Arlen threaded himself between branches, resting himself against the hedgerow. He undid the lockbar on the rifle's sights and twisted the dial until it said 2, then twisted the lockbar back into place. It wasn't quite two hundred, so he might have to hold a little low. Arlen hunched down, set his cheek against the stock, and got a sight picture. The front post wobbled, slowly steadying itself in the rear aperture.

Breathe, Arlen.

Come on, you Kraut bastards, show yourselves.

Their rifles gave no telltale smoke, but at last he saw grey-green uniforms moving on the far side of the field. There were plenty. No reason to pick one over the other. The front post settled on a German. He was out in front, standing boldly upright, firing across the field at the fleeing lieutenant. The front sight wobbled a bit. Pushing his left arm through the sling, Arlen wrapped his arm back around again, holding on tight to the rifle. The taut sling pressed tightly against his chest. The sight picture steadied.

Finger against the trigger, Arlen took up the slack of the first stage. He took a breath, let it half out.

The front sight was clear, sitting almost motionless on the faintly-seen German soldier. The rear aperture had disappeared almost altogether.

Arlen squeezed the trigger the last little bit.

The rifle thumped and spit a brass case into the brush. Coming down out of recoil, the sight picture was still good. Arlen took a couple more breaths, a hot knot rising above his stomach. He held again, let half a breath out. The front post settled on another German, the only one who was still upright. Slack out of the trigger. No wobble in the front sight. Arlen squeezed it the rest of the way.

Another thump from the M1. A burst of burp gun fire ripped through the trees overhead. Arlen slipped back down behind the hedgerow. His heart was racing like a V8 Ford.

Steady shots from down the way: Paine was covering him.

Arlen popped up and went running. Bullets snapped around him. He slipped and fell onto his rear. A bullet hit a rock and he felt little fragment peppering his face. He tried to swing his rifle around to fire a few blind shots in retaliation, but his arm was still wrapped up in the sling and the shots went wildly into the air. Now the German fire descended on him. The earth and stone portion of the hedgerow was still very low here and the incoming rounds cracked and split the brush that festooned the top. Rolling onto his belly, Arlen began to crawl. He squinted and pressed his face down into the dirt. The air was alive with German fire. He heard a lone M1 rifle again. *Lord, let that be Paine, let that be Paine.* He wormed his way along, trying to press himself flat, sucking in his buttocks as if it would help make him smaller.

The fire about him shifted elsewhere, but did not slacken. Screams mixed with orders. He heard a BAR somewhere. Who had come to help? He raised his head up. The MG 42 and the BAR dueled a bit. More shouts. The American fire intensified. An M1 fired nearby. It was very close. It had to be Paine. Looking up, Arlen saw that he had a little bit better cover. Springing to his feet, he ran forward, head and shoulders hunched forward. The hedgerow grew bigger and he was safer. And up there, that must be Paine.

He had a second or two to see the German before the German saw him. The soldier appeared suddenly through the brush. He saw Arlen and swung his burp gun around. Arlen had his rifle up. There was no time for the sling. The gray of the front post disappeared into the gray-green of the German's uniform. The distance was not far; Arlen squeezed—

A thump — sights back down, they barely settled.

Thump.

The German pitched forward, oddly, almost straight onto his face, as if someone had nailed his boots to the ground. The burp gun fired a harmless blast into the soil as he fell.

Arlen lowered his rifle. He began breathing again and felt his neck and face prickly hot. Expecting the Kraut to move, he approached slowly. He almost willed the man to move, to be wounded, to be a prisoner like the others they would round up and hand over to battalion for questioning. *Come on, you Kraut bastard, just twitch, just make a move.*

But the man was still. Two neat holes came from his back. Not with his toe but with his hand, Arlen reached out and rolled the German over. Two holes were there in the front, still languidly pumping black blood. But Arlen saw the man's face. The man's helmet had slipped down and broken his nose, which lay flattened to the side. His front teeth were broken, too, and the chipped pieces lay squarely on his tongue, white against the red all around.

The hot bile rose quickly and Arlen staggered away a few steps and heaved up one long warm stream. Another small vomit followed, and then there were only dry heaves.

Lord, I'm sorry. I'm so sorry.

Jesus, forgive me.

He had shot at men before and shot shapes of men before. He knew in his head he had killed. But this was the first one he knew for sure he killed, the first one that his body told him so.

Who ever said it would be so close like this? Who ever said war was this close?

"Jesus, Arlen, you all right?"

Arlen jumped.

When Arlen didn't see him at first, Paine waved from down the way, his hand poking out from the brush. Collecting himself, Arlen made his way to his buddy. What solace there was in a close buddy.

"That was some fast shooting," said Paine.

Arlen dropped down next to Paine. "He could have been faster."

"No way, not faster than you."

"Who's that out there?"

"Second Squad. Third on the right. First bringing up the rear." Paine motioned with his head. "Look who I found."

Arlen smiled in relief. "Sarge, it's you."

Gunderson was squatting, helmetless, weapon-less, his face a mask drawn as tight as drum.

"Glad you made it, too. I thought it was just the looie we rescued."

Paine touched Arlen's arm. He shook his head slightly.

He understood soon enough. Second Squad came back, four of them hauling a body on a poncho. They set it down and Sergeant Fuller lit a cigarette. He motioned to Arlen.

No, Lord, I can't.

"Corporal, come here."

Don't rub my face in it, I know he's dead 'cause of me.

But he went anyway. He took the Lucky Strike offered by Sergeant Fuller and drew on it and at last had the strength to look down at the body on the poncho. Lieutenant Iannucci was peaceful, if pale. His thin, feminine wrist had spilled from the poncho and lay bare on the dirt, its fingers curled like a hand Michaelangelo might draw. The other G.I.s standing around sniffed and coughed, holding back what they felt. Arlen could not cry; he had nothing left in him. He drew on the cigarette one more time. *Lord, why'd he have to get it? Why?*

Cry, he could not, but the sickness in his gut was still there, worse than ever.

If only he had not waited so long, maybe the lieutenant would be alive. Maybe that fucking Kraut, too. Maybe they all could have skipped killing for a day. Maybe they could have put it off for another day, when they could get the upper hand and kill easily and at a distance and with the knowledge that it might help in ending this damn war. Not just killing like this, swapping one for another.

The lieutenant got it, and Arlen didn't. And the Kraut did, too, but Arlen didn't. The looie had looked out for Arlen and the rest of them, and he had sent them out again and again to kill Krauts and take ground, which cost lives, American and German. Who was going to make it? Who was going to get through? Iannucci didn't; the Kraut didn't; and Arlen did, because he got the Kraut.

That was it. All there was. Didn't matter why or how, right or wrong — you got them before they got you or any of your men. And if they got some of your men, you still get those Krauts so they don't get anymore. So someone can make it. So someone can say, *It was me or him,* or its corollary, *It was us or them.*

Even so, it didn't change a thing. More men were going to die. The lieutenant was a good looie, he was smart and didn't sacrifice men unless he had to, which was all anyone could ask. Who knew who would replace Iannucci. Few could be better. Many could be worse. Someone would come along who would send them all — even Paine, even Arlen — to their deaths.

Death grew more death, it was its own manure. It would come, it would come. Until then, it was to be given and not received.

99

Goodbye, lieutenant. Rest in peace.

Arlen stepped away, sucking his cigarette down to a nub. It was his fault. He should have said something, done something, anything at all. It was no good to say he didn't know what would happen. He would not accept that for his own death — should Wade and Legenia lose their son because someone just shrugged and said, "I didn't know?"

Arlen looked up at the sky. He added one more to the deaths God must forgive him for. He offered the prayer up simply, though the weight did not go with it.

The P-47s and the Mustangs were gone. The artillery was rumbling again.

We ain't even out of France yet.

X

Arlen awoke for no reason. His hand reached out for his rifle all the same. Sliding his helmet back from over his eyes, he squinted in the July sun. Paine dozed in the corner of the foxhole, arms wrapped tightly around his M1. No one was on sentry. Arlen sat up and winced as a cramp shot up his side where his canteen had jammed against him.

But Sergeant Gunderson was guarding them all. He sat wordlessly on top of his helmet, watching over the sleeping squad. Deep dark circles lined his eyes and his cheeks sagged. He stared straight ahead, right into the hedgerow to their front, but his eyes did not move.

When Arlen rose from the foxhole, at last Gunderson blinked. He looked at Arlen wearily. "Sleep tight?"

"Didn't mean to. Paine didn't wake me up. You want me to take over, Sarge?"

Gunderson shook his head. "They're pulling us off the line."

Arlen's heart skipped a beat.

The sergeant squinted in the sunlight, taking in Arlen's surprise. "Just for the day. One platoon at a time, sending us back to get showers and a hot meal."

Arlen's stomach gurgled and popped and he squatted down next to Gunderson. "Showers."

"Finally."

They woke the squad an hour later. The G.I.s gathered their equipment and walked with the rest of the dirty, weary platoon a few hundred yards to the rear. There a small convoy of four two-and-half ton trucks sat with engines idling. Their new commander, Lieutenant Colby, talked with the lead driver and the platoon sergeant checked the roll as each man climbed aboard the deuce-and-a-halfs. Arlen dropped his gear at his feet and took a cigarette offered by Paine. They lit up and leaned over the side as the small convoy began to roll.

The road was hardly wide enough for one truck, let alone two passing, and the G.I.s marching alongside the road had to jump out of the way to avoid being crushed. Dust boiled up and covered the poor dogfaces laden with weapons and gear. Arlen tapped Paine on the shoulder. "Replacements."

"How do you know?" Paine shouted back over the growl of the engine.

"Still got creases in their pants."

Mischief seized Paine in a fit and he leaned over the side so far Arlen thought he would fall out. He kept tipping the brim of each marching soldier's helmet with his finger as they passed. At last, he found a loose one and snatched it from the dogface's head. He hooted. "Hot potato! Hot potato!" he cackled, tossing it. The squad passed it around laughing until grim Gunderson grabbed it and threw back to the dogface.

Arlen laughed at the mischief until he saw the marching soldiers staring up at them — at him — in bewilderment and trepidation.

Quit your lookin' at me. What'd I ever do?

He scratched his jaw and his fingernails bristled. There must have been almost two week's growth. He looked around the truck. All their faces were filthy, smudged with Norman earth and fine black grime from firing and cleaning rifles and machine guns day in, day out.

We look like real haints, don't we?

And maybe we should. We came out of the place where the dead lay.

He thought of the body on the poncho and the curled up fingers. A shiver ran up his spine and he wanted to run off. Standing, he reached out of the truck and tried to grab leaves from the trees alongside the road.

This road was the same one they had fought the length of this past month. How strange to be going back instead of forward along it. The sky was big and a warm blue, puffed with clouds. Through breaks in the trees, the rest of the Norman plain appeared briefly, stretching to a far horizon, spotted and lined green on green. Arlen imagined those distant fields with a yellow-gold tint, and he could see home. Dark plumes of smoke rose here and there across the scene, though, but that was like home, too. That was like Hickory and all the factories there, pumping out smoke and goods for the people in the cities; it was like that part of Catawba. *But it ain't like my part. My part's safe from all that.* His head swiveled around, following a burnt-out German tank as they passed it and it faded down the road behind him. *Safe from all this.*

Safe indeed. The inexorable flood went away from Catawba County and not toward it. It brought Arlen here, it brought all of them here, and even as they stepped away for one brief day, it kept marching on: bowl-like helmets and olive drab stretching in both directions, marching to the front, always moving onward, always replacing what broke and fell, pushing the shattered, the burnt-out, the destroyed out of the way, into the ditches, left there until someone came to clear it away, not because they cared but because they were ordered to, picking up shards and moving on to once again find behind the vanguard the inevitable waste in the wake.

Paine leaned up next to Arlen as they passed a jeep, seemingly unscathed, sitting silently on the side of the road. Around it lay a couple of Germans, their weapons long since taken, the bodies unmoved, unburied. Paine snorted a stream of cigarette smoke, which whipped around his head and dissipated behind him. "That's the difference for you."

Arlen couldn't hear from the road of the truck engine. He leaned closer to Paine. "What's that?"

"That's the difference between how America fights and how the Krauts fight. We burn dollars, gasoline, and machines. The Krauts? They burn courage."

Arlen furrowed his brow. He loved the kid, but he said foolish and offensive things at times. "That ain't right."

"What?" shouted Paine.

"That ain't right. Ain't the America I know."

"What America is that, then? There's only one."

Arlen did not know what to say to that. He shut his mouth and looked back out over the land.

Every worry dissipated when they turned the corner and saw steam rising from behind a long line of hanging tarpaulins. The trucks had not even stopped before the whole platoon jumped from the tailgates and sprinted toward the showers. The G.I.s disrobed with lightning speed. Arlen was so fast that he forgot to unbuckle and unlace his boots before he stripped off his pants. He shoved Paine out of the way with a playful push and his buddy fell on his back, also caught by his pants over his boots. The shower attendant slapped a bar of soap into each man's hand and said, "Don't leave the water running. Wet yourself down, lather up, then rinse off, and you're done. Get out so the others can have their turn." But no one listened. It would have taken a company of MPs with fixed bayonets to drive the G.I.s out.

Arlen stood motionless under the hot water. It beat against his neck and back and unspeakable relief soaked through his muscles and trickled its way slowly to his fingers and toes. He lathered and rinsed twice. He dug incredible filth from inside his ears. Scrubbing under his fingernails did no good — they were too long and the thin line of black stayed under them.

Finally, the clamor of the men outside the shower tent and the harsh words of the attendants forced Arlen's squad out. Each man jogged naked and laughing back over to the pile of equipment. Arlen stood dripping dry for a minute, then reached for his pack. "Aw, shit." He picked up his fatigues. They were stiff with sweat and dirt. He did not have any other pants nor a jacket. None of the G.I.s did. Their spares were sitting in their footlockers, stashed safely somewhere in the division's baggage train, far to the rear, or perhaps even still in England. Reluctantly, Arlen slipped the fatigues back on. The old feelings returned. His mind was clear and alert now, but the rough olive drab cloth still rubbed against his skin and the weight of his equipment still hugged his waist.

The hot chow made them feel a little better. The men sprawled in the grass or propped up against packs or leaned back on a hedgerow or tree, food in hand. Arlen and Paine sat together. Gunderson sat with the three new replacements who had come to them a few days before. One of them was in Arlen's section.

"I don't trust him," said Paine through a mouthful of food, nodding in that direction.

"Who?" said Arlen.

"That kid, the greenhorn who talks all the time, even at night, the one that's gonna get us all killed. What's his name?"

"I can't remember."

"He probably won't be with us long anyway."

"Ain't no way to talk, Paine."

Paine snorted and then began to splutter. He coughed up a piece of chipped beef back onto his toast. He wiped his watery eyes. "Why? You think it's bad luck?"

"That ain't the point."

Paine shrugged. "Fine. Don't see why you have to get all bent out of shape about it."

"How'd you like it if you were one of 'em? They need someone to show 'em the ropes."

"Oh, and is that going to be you?" said Paine sarcastically. "I'm not sticking my neck out for them and I know you won't, either." Paine lit up a cigarette, reclined on an elbow, and sighed. "Arlen, it's hard being an old timer."

Arlen laughed loudly. "William Buford Paine, what do you know about being an old timer?"

"I've been in since late '42, I think that qualifies," Paine said. "How long have you been in?"

"I joined the National Guard right before the draft bill was passed."

Paine's eyes ticked upward for a second as he thought back. "Jeez, Arlen, what was that, 1940? You've been in for four years?" Paine shook his head. "All these things I don't know about you because you're so damned tight-lipped about everything."

"No, I ain't."

"Yes, you are. You never tell me anything about yourself. I know your girlfriend's name, I know you're from South Carolina or some hick place like that, and I know you grew up on a farm. That's it. You never tell me anything else. I've told you everything about myself," said Paine, "and you never share it back."

"You ain't sharin' nothin', you just talk regardless." Arlen reached out toward his buddy. "Give me a cigarette."

Paine shook one out of the pack. It was a Raleigh, the worst of the worst cigarettes in Arlen's eyes. But Arlen held it up in front of Paine. "In case you forget, it's North Carolina, not South Carolina. And Raleigh is the capital."

"Hope it doesn't stink as much as those coffin nails do."

Arlen slapped Paine upside the head. "I am sick and tired of you mouthin' off to me."

"What did I do? What did I say?"

"All of it. You just say too damn much, all the time."

"All right, all right." Paine lit another cigarette. But he really could not stay quiet for long. "Is there really a lot of difference? Between North Carolina and South Carolina."

"We are a vale of humility in between two mountains of conceit."

"What's that mean?"

"Oh, it's just a little sayin' we have."

"You've lived there your whole life, haven't you?"

Arlen nodded.

Paine snorted. "I can't imagine that. Being in one place forever — that would drive me crazy." He flicked ash off of the cigarette. "My old man was like me. A rolling stone gathers no moss and, boy, did he roll. We lived in Lowell in my early years, and then the old man dragged us to Scranton and then Pittsburgh and then Chicago and Milwaukee after that. Then I think we spent six months again in Chicago before we ended up in Gary. And that was all, oh, I don't know, maybe from when I was six to about fourteen. Lived in Gary until I graduated from high school. Then I went out to Seattle for a little while but came back, I didn't like it out there."

Arlen sighed. Here Paine was, talking about himself again. But what could he do except humor the boy? "I know. You told me."

"Screw you, Arlen." Paine shrugged. "You know, the Army gives you a lot of time to think. And I think my old man never was happy with what he had. He was always scheming about something. Always had a plan to make it big, here or there. He did all kinds of work to make a buck, but he never stuck with anything too long. Started out just doing assembly line work, then got into machining, but it was too boring for him. He always wanted something new, something fast-paced, click, click, click. He tried running a bar, but he always argued with the owner and the customers, and he left for something else. Traveling salesman for a while, but got bored of that." Paine scratched his chin. "I couldn't really say what he did. But I know he was happiest when he had a new plan and a new city in sight. He always told us kids he was close to making it big and that one day we'd see and be proud of him."

"Were you?" said Arlen.

Paine fingered the corner of his mouth. "We already were, he didn't have to do anything. But he kept at it all the same." He drew on the cigarette. "Is your old man a farmer too?"

"We've always farmed."

"On the same land?"

"Same land."

"Never moved? Never wanted to?"

Arlen reached over and took another cigarette from Paine. "Never thought about it. Strange now, thinkin' 'bout it. Never'd been out of the state 'til I volunteered."

Paine shook his head over and over. "I can't imagine. Weren't you ever tired of it?"

"It?"

"You know, the whole thing: farming, living in the same town, all that."

"Ain't nothin' worn out 'bout it, so there ain't nothin' to be tired of."

"Jeez, Arlen." Paine stubbed out his cigarette butt and lit another. "It's like you live in a different country."

"Well, when this war is all said and done, come on down and you can see yourself it ain't so foreign."

"I will, if we make it," said Paine. That stilled the conversation, leaving them both puffing away, trying to enjoy the cigarettes on full, warm stomachs. Arlen looked at the Raleigh between his fingers. He remembered Iannucci turning the cigarette down that fateful day. The looie never smoked.

Wish the lieutenant could've gotten another hot meal. And a hot shower, too. He deserved it. More than we did.

I should have gone with the looie.

Paine looked with concern at his buddy. "We'll make it, Arlen. Quit worrying about it."

"I ain't worrying 'bout that!" snapped Arlen. "Hell, I hardly even got time to think with your constant jabberin'."

"Well, I wish you'd let it off your damn chest rather than take it out on me," retorted Paine.

"I ain't gonna make it and you ain't either, that's what it is," said Arlen. "'Cause the lieutenant didn't—" Arlen felt a catch in his throat and had to stop until he could swallow past it. "The lieutenant didn't make it and that's on me. And one day I ain't gonna make it because someone else didn't do their job."

"Arlen, you didn't kill the looie. The fucking Krauts killed him."

Arlen hung his head. "But if I—"

"If you what? Told the looie not to go? He was going to anyway. Went with him? Maybe it would be you who got shot and not him. Or maybe you both would have. Or maybe you would have given your position away to the Krauts. Or maybe the looie would have gotten you killed. There's no way to tell." Paine jerked the cigarette pack again and let Arlen take another. "There's no knowing anything except the fact that it was the Krauts that killed the looie. And that's all."

Arlen hung his head, the Raleigh sticking from his lips, unlit.

Should have been there, Lieutenant, but I wasn't. And maybe I wouldn't have been any use anyhow. Maybe I wouldn't have got the Kraut that got you. 'Cause I didn't know what I had to do. Hope you know I'm sorry.

Immediately Arlen felt a twinge of disgust at himself. What good were apologies to the dead? Their race was run, and if it was a short one, it was because he, Arlen, had come up short in his duty. There was no changing that. All that was in his power was to never let it happen again. Never, never, never.

I got to do for the living what I should have done for the dead. For both their sakes.

Arlen sighed and lit the cigarette. "You're right, Paine. Just don't you leave me, 'cause I'm liable to forget."

"I wouldn't do that, Arlen." Paine knocked his knee lightly with his fist. "You're my good luck charm, my rabbit's foot. That's why I keep you around."

"Appreciate it."

"You should, it's an honor."

A clean-clothed G.I. with a large camera wandered around the platoon, stopping at each little cluster of men. He came to Arlen and Paine and said, "You gentlemen interested in having your picture taken?"

"Well, ain't gonna look any better any time soon, I reckon. Is it for *Stars & Stripes*?"

"No, I just do it in my spare time." He jerked his thumb toward the rear. "I'm at regimental HQ, so I can take all my developing equipment with me."

"Well, I'll be," said Arlen. "How much for a copy?"

"How about a Luger?"

"You want a Luger," said Arlen evenly. He thought about it for a moment. "Ain't got one now, but I'll find one if you'll make a copy for each of us."

"Say cheese."

Arms around each others shoulders, Arlen and Paine looked into the camera, eyes easy, mouths shut and relaxed. The shutter went click. The G.I. went off to the next group, but he didn't get another exposure off. The trucks had arrived again, engines rumbling. The next platoon was dropped off, and it was time for First Platoon to go.

107

XI

Click, clack, click, clack.

Arlen checked his rifle, his ammunition in the cartridge belt and the cloth bandolier, his grenades, and his canteen. He took a swig of water and rinsed it around his mouth several times before swallowing. It did nothing to allay the dryness of his cheeks and tongue. He was getting jittery.

Click, clack, click.

Arlen shifted his weight from one leg to another so he could get a better look at his section. At the far end of the line was Sergeant Gunderson. He caught Arlen's eye and motioned with his head toward Private Kelly. The poor kid had toppled forward and was resting against the hedgerow, his head cocked to the side and eyes shut serenely. With a stick, Arlen jabbed him a few times in the leg. Kelly blinked several times. His breathing was hard and his right hand reached down to the trigger of his rifle. But he saw and heard no threat, and Arlen's narrow gaze at him made him wet his lips and nod silently in apology.

Clack, click, clack.

"Buddy, come on, now, what is it?" said Arlen.

Paine stopped flicking the safety of his M1 on and off. He scowled. "They're going to make us take that hill, aren't they?"

Arlen peered over the hedgerow briefly. "Reckon so."

"We couldn't do it yesterday, what makes them think we can do it today?"

Arlen didn't have anything to say to that.

"You think it's those Kraut paratroops again?"

"Maybe," said Arlen quietly.

"Those sonsabitches had brass ones."

"We killed enough of 'em, I reckon they learned their lesson."

"Who screams like that when they charge? They've got to be crazy." Paine shook his head. "We shouldn't go up that hill." He clicked the safety a few more times. "We should plaster that entire hill with arty. You think we'll get a good bombardment before we jump off? Or you think it'll just be mortars? We're screwed if it's just mortars, we need more than that."

"Would you quit fucking talking about it?" said Private Kelly.

Paine shut up. He unwrapped several pieces of gum and jammed them all into his mouth. He chewed them with a ferocious intensity.

The G.I.s kept waiting. A few ate K rations in the meantime. Arlen did not, he took the cigarettes out and threw the rest away. He did not want anything sloshing around inside his stomach if he got hit.

They were still sitting quietly when Lieutenant Colby came down the line. "Artillery is starting. Keep your heads down, it'll be close."

Heads down, the soldiers waited, their bodies firm and still in expectant tension. The first shell whistled and ripped through the air and each man drew a fortifying breath. The falling rounds plowed into the earth several hundred yards ahead, the bursts slapping the ears and chests of the G.I.s. When the occasional round fell short, shrapnel sent green twigs and leaves fluttering down onto their helmets. The shelling went on and on. The G.I.s began to trade looks: the Krauts were really getting it. No expense in shells was spared. At least they had that going for them.

The artillery stopped. Without hesitation, Lieutenant Colby signaled with a forward-falling arm and Sergeant Gunderson said hoarsely: "Scouts out." Two G.I.s went over the hedgerow and began working their way forward through the narrow field, each clinging close to one of the sides. The way looked clear and Gunderson ordered the squad forward. The G.I.s followed quickly over the hedgerow, their boots scratching for grip on the crumbling berm and their equipment jangling softly. Not an unnecessary word was said.

The squad strung out in column and Arlen brought up the rear, making sure none fell behind and that they kept pace with Gunderson and the scouts. But most lagged badly. Too much had been asked of them these past few weeks.

The inevitable: a German machine gun burst passed down the length of the squad, miraculously missing every single G.I. Another burst, from the same direction, this time finding home, and one of the scouts went down.

"Skirmishers!" shouted the sergeant, sweeping his arms to either side.

The squad broke column and formed a single rank stretching the breadth of the field. The German machine gun reached out again for the G.I.s. Sergeant Gunderson was shouting to Arlen, who raised his hand to his ear symbolically. But Gunderson didn't see the motion and turned toward the front. Arlen picked up his pace, catching up with two of the replacements whose steps slowed as they drew closer and closer to the German lines. Arlen gave them a nudge: "Get along, now, get movin'!" The two replacements began a quick-step, knowing Arlen would nudge them next with the rifle butt. Satisfied, Arlen looked back.

Good Lord, where is Second Squad?

They were not there, not even the scouts preparing to push out and maintain contact with First Squad. Arlen stopped and shielded his eyes, trying to see through the glare if—

As if yanked up by wires, Arlen was lifted from his feet. He landed hard, right between his shoulder blades. Dirt rained down around him. He coughed and gasped several times as he rolled onto his side. He burrowed into the grass and stayed down, barely daring to look up. He felt himself all over. He didn't feel hit.

Though his ears rang, he made out bellowing and screeches of panic. He raised his head up. First Squad, here and there in the grass, was worming its way forward. In his peripheral vision, from up the slope, dust rose in a thin cloud. Then the earth rose up and dropped down and clods of dirt rained around him and shrapnel clanged against his helmet. He still was holding on to the earth when it ceased to move.

"Kraut tank!" shouted Paine.

Even if those screaming German paratroopers had taken a shellacking from the bombardment, those tank crews were safe from all but a direct hit.

Two more shells burst in their midst. Arlen looked up to Gunderson, hoping for orders. But his sergeant was bewildered, too, looking hopefully toward the rear for Second Squad or their new lieutenant, Colby.

Bullets snapped overhead. Arlen flattened himself again against the grass. His jaw was clenched so tight he felt like his teeth might crack.

Good Lord, where's our supporting fire? Machine guns, mortars, anything, just give us some cover.

The BAR fired short bursts. Gunderson shouted orders, but Arlen could only catch a word here or there. The shells burst closer and closer. If only he could make himself into a piece of paper, to get that flat against the ground. He pulled his helmet down and closed his eyes, and just in time. Two rounds burst to his right, so close he felt the air ripple from the shrapnel. Screams followed on the wake. There was a ferrous taste in his mouth. Arlen felt his face and his hand came away from his mouth touched lightly with red. He touched his mouth again — bloody. He had gnawed on his lip too hard.

Another shout — didn't that sound like Paine? Arlen raised his head, looking around for that great reciprocating jaw, chewing on a massive ball of gum. He could not see, so he boosted himself up onto all fours.

There was a thin cloud of dust up the slope.

Pierced to some unknown knot within that held him together, Arlen collapsed. All command of his limbs and faculties was gone. Agony lanced him from his first breath.

Oh, Lord, I got it, I really did, I got it finally finally oh finally Lord

A familiar voice was beside his ear. "Shit, Arlen, shit, you're fucking hit."

Arlen tried to turn his head, but nothing happened. He just lay there frozen.

Oh, Lord, I can't move why can't I move

"Ah, shit, that's a lot of blood," said Paine. "Hey, hold on, all right, just hang there."

The medic appeared over Arlen. What incredible comfort, even greater than that of Caty or mother in a moment like this. "Hey, Doc," Arlen said. He was surprised — he could talk.

"Hey, Arlen. You're gonna be okay." And the medic went to work.

He lost track of time. Lying there in the grass, he was unable to see anything except the sky and Paine's face occasionally popping into view. He heard heavy automatic weapons fire to the front, the burst of mortars, the blast of the tanks.

The medic's face reappeared. "You feeling that morphine yet?"

"You gave me some?" said Arlen. He couldn't remember.

"Hey, grab his feet and let's get him on this poncho. One, two, three."

Arlen felt the world lazily swirl and his shoulder and neck ached dully. They set him down. "Okay, you think you can drag him back like that?" said the medic.

Then he was sliding across the grass, head bobbing around. He felt something in his shoulder, or was it his neck? The hill was out there — big poofy trees. Dust clouds. Snap, snap go the bullets. Where was he?

With a thud his head landed back on the ground. The Norman sky and little speckly stars above him.

"Arlen?"

"Huh?"

"I've got to go." Paine swallowed hard. "You're gonna be okay. You've got good luck, you're my rabbit's foot, you know."

Arlen nodded.

"You gave me a fucking scare, you know?" said Paine. "I swallowed my damn gum."

Arlen wanted to snort in derision, but he just sort of coughed.

"All right, I'm going now. Bye."

Arlen tried to reach out to his buddy, but Paine was already gone.

He was looking at the sky again.

Lieutenant, I'm going out just like you.

Lord, it ain't ever enough, is it? Ain't it ever gonna be enough?

I will see you soon.

He let everything go and just lay there.

Doc appeared and sprinkled sulfa powder in the wound to disinfect it. Setting a bandage on the wound on his left shoulder, the medic wrapped gauze tape over the bandage, then under his arm, back up again, and over and over in the same pattern.

At some point, G.I.s with unknown faces came with a stretcher. "One, two, three," one said and they lifted him up.

"Doc," called out Arlen.

The medic appeared next to him. "They'll take you back now. I've got to go ahead. There are a lot of casualties." The medic grabbed Arlen's hand with both of his own and squeezed it tight. "You'll be fine. You need some surgery, but they'll take care of you, all right?"

"All right, Doc." Arlen laid his head back and closed his eyes.

"Get him out of here."

Up he went into the air and then the jarring steps began. He tried to keep his eyes shut and wait. The steps never seemed to end. He didn't think or feel much. The steps just pounded on and on until he thought in the darkness of his closed eyes that was how it was going to be forever now, just an endless walk to the aid station. Then they set the stretcher down. He opened his eyes and managed to turn his head a bit. He was in another field, surrounded by wounded. Medics hovered about, tending to wounds, holding bottles of plasma high above G.I.s that lay quietly on stretchers. There were so many dying out there, but they were so quiet when they went out, hardly offering a shout or a whimper. The Krauts, on the other hand, went out screaming and howling, Arlen had seen it plenty.

He lay there for a long time.

The pain began to come back. The morphine must have worn off. Arlen screwed his eyes shut, trying to ignore it, but each passing moment became less bearable. He lay there helplessly, squirming occasionally, thinking of nothing but the pain now, all else gone from his mind.

The orderlies came and lifted his stretcher up. Arlen opened his eyes and grabbed a strange arm. "Morphine."

"You've had enough."

"Morphine."

"You've already had one."

But that had to be hours ago. Don't they know that? "Morphine."

"You'll get some when you get to the hospital." The orderlies loaded Arlen onto the rack of the ambulance jeep and the vehicle jolted into gear. The wind whipped over Arlen and chills began to wrack his body. When the jeep stopped, another set of orderlies carried him to an open area near a tent. They set Arlen down roughly, banging his shoulder. He felt the pain from deep within his bones, as if they would split, and then the pain spread its thousand nimble fingers and grabbed for his stomach. He felt sick. He would be sick. Arlen tried to roll to his side so he would not drown in his own vomit. But he

112

had no strength. He tried to call out, but the orderlies had disappeared. Slowly, Arlen tried to move himself, but he found his left arm did not want to move. He tried but he could hardly lift it or make a fist.

Oh, Good Lord, I'm gonna lose my arm, gonna lose my arm, I'll be a cripple, I'll never be able to work again, oh Jesus my arm

Summoning all his strength, Arlen used his right arm to shift himself as best he could, but it was too painful to lay on his side and he rolled back onto his back. Cold sweat poured down his chest — he was exhausted.

An orderly walked past. He wanted to call out for morphine, but it would do no good. He would just have to bear it, silently. For G.I.s kept everything in. They didn't scream to others, they weren't like the Krauts.

Jesus I need some morphine it hurts so bad so bad Good Lord get me some morphine don't let me be a cripple don't let me be a cripple

The turbulent sleep of fear and pain eased away. His head was groggy, but his body perfectly at ease. He felt another's touch. It was not a man's touch. He tried to open his eyes, but they were sticky. He tried to wave his arm up to wipe the sleep from them, but his arm did not want to move. Still, he knew it was there, it was not missing. With effort, he scrunched his eyes shut and they popped open.

He gasped like a man who had been gassed. There she was at the end of the bed, tucking the blanket under his feet. Her fair hair hung uncharacteristically loose and she wore olive drab like the dogfaces, but he knew it was her.

He tried to say her name. But she put her finger to lips and he was instantly silenced.

She had volunteered. He had no idea. She volunteered and they sent her here and to this very field hospital and there she was on duty, just when he came in. The war put the two of them together.

No. No, it wasn't like that. She came to him. It was no coincidence. She knew he would need her and she was there just when he did.

He was so happy he could sing out. But she put her finger to her lips and again he was stilled as if he was a weak, helpless child and she a mother. He hated that feeling. He wanted to speak her name, tell her he loved her, tell her to come over here and kiss him. He lifted his arm and she forced it back down. He tried to speak and again she hushed him. *Dammit, woman, let me speak!* He began to throw his weight back and forth on the cot. *Get this damn blanket off of me! It's too hot and I want to grab you and I want to tell you that I love you! Don't be like one of them! Let me go!*

Her eyes were deep wells and he dove into them, but the fact that they understood didn't stop her from pulling out the hypodermic needle and drawing off several hundred ccs of morphine. *God, no, don't let her do that! Let me tell her! Let me tell her!* And the needle went in without a prick, only a dull thud, and he felt heavy like a tired swimmer and the cot wrapped around him viscously. He opened his throat and tried to call out to her. But she stood over him and did not hear anything. He thrashed and thrashed with the last of his worldly strength, not knowing if he would come back up. Why would she do that? He needed to see her, not to sleep! It was not painful to be awake if she was there — he could bear anything. Then why, oh, why was she doing this?

Had she changed her mind? She took his hands in hers as he thrashed. She folded his hands across his chest. *No! Stop that! Let me hold you! Don't you force me down!* He sank and sank and sank and sank and she was still up there and she lifted his feet again and tipped him head first so he would slide down into—

Arlen gasped again and was awake. He saw the tent roof first. It was dark outside, he sensed, and there were moths fluttering around the hanging lamps. He tried to raise his head, but it was difficult, as he was lying on a cot, swaddled up. Bandages and gauze encased his torso like a cocoon. The pressure felt comforting now. The pillow was soft. The sheets and blankets were perfectly clean. He must have passed out at some point, perhaps for a long time, but now he was in a hospital somewhere — in France? in England? He would be all right. It was against orders to die if you got to a hospital.

"You're a fidgety one."

He realized there was a nurse at the foot of his cot. He craned his neck around and saw her tucking the mussed-up blanket in.

"No, no," she said, "don't strain your neck. You need to lie there and rest."

She came to him and tucked the rest of his blanket in. He got a good look at her. It was not Caty. He was relieved and sad.

But how good this woman looked. If she was a plain jane back home, if no man would ask her to a dance, Arlen did not care. She was an angel right now.

"You're awake now, that's good. Your fever finally broke."

"Where am I?" Arlen croaked through a dry throat.

"You're at the division general hospital."

"In France?"

Her face was tired but she managed a smile. "Yes, in France." She looked at his chart. "I think you will make it. It was touch and go there for a while. You were in and out, in and out for a few days." She fiddled with his bandage. "Now we just have to see what happens with this wound."

"Am I gonna be crippled?" Arlen cried out. His voice shocked him: it was gravelly and weak.

"Crippled? No, I don't think so. Has anyone told you what happened to you? You were wounded at the base of the neck. The surgeon removed a large piece of shrapnel from your trapezius." She raised her eyebrows. "You were very lucky. Another two and half inches to the right and the big piece would have cut your spine clean in two."

"Will I heal up all right?"

"You need rest, but the wound should heal completely. It's too early to say, but you should have full use of your left arm again. At the worst, you'll have a stiff neck."

How thankful he was. He would work again one day. His parents would not have to care for him. He wouldn't be like Roy's Uncle David, a useless old bachelor that everyone had to humor and pity.

But the thought occurred to him: "It's not a million-dollar wound, then?"

She knew what he meant and, as she rolled him over to give him a shot of penicillin in his buttocks, looked at him with sympathy. "Not a million-dollar wound, I'm afraid."

Then the Army would have him back. He was not going home.

"Ma'am?"

"Yes?"

"Would you mind gettin' me something to eat?"

She nodded, patted him on the leg, and disappeared out of the end of the tent into the darkness. Arlen lay there for a while, thinking of nothing, for nothing was all that he had, nothing but his little course through this war. He was buffeted here and there by its winds and waves like a rudderless dinghy, going whichever way the storm wanted, no matter how hard he leaned against the current. There was no magic end to the war. Victory, that word bandied about everywhere, would come in no way other than killing Germans and taking ground. And to take lives and ground, you had to give lives, or pieces of them. He turned his head to the side to get a view of the quiet and the maimed and the crippled. That what this hospital tent was, the gift of flesh and blood that was necessary to accomplish what was sacrosanct: Victory with a capital V, Churchill and Roosevelt flashing two fingers, dot-dot-dot-dash, cellos and violins playing *bum-bum-bum-buuummm.*

He'd been given once; he might be given again. In whole, in part. It was not up to him.

He thought of writing home, but he had no strength. His eyes fell shut and he was sound asleep by the time the nurse returned with the food.

XII

The deep growling started from where he had come from. Closer and closer, louder and louder until he knew it was right behind him and then Arlen carefully stepped off of the road and into the ditch, as he had countless times now. The deuce-and-a-half roared past him and the tail of the heavily-laden truck swung a little bit toward him. Arlen stumbled into the ditch, tripping over cans and torn boxes and bits of wood and wire and other backwash of war. "You sonuvabitch! Watch it!" But his curses were lost in the roar of the convoy. What a way to go: crushed by a half-asleep driver, miles and miles from the front. Although was it any safer to be in the cab with one? If one of them stopped, he would be sorely tempted to hop in. He was tired of walking.

Walk he would have to, for now. The trucks were not the only concern. At the last town, the MPs were out in force and he was without orders. It took nearly all day to sneak through alleys and back streets without being seen and once he had put the outskirts behind him, dark had fallen and he had slept out again. In the morning, he cadged a C ration and a pack of Pall Malls off a sentry and set out again, trying to stay off the Red Ball roads, where the fast gasoline convoys ran. Who knew, maybe he should have sought those out, he could catch a ride and perhaps the sentries were less likely to stop the express trucks. Still, he would march if he must. The soles of his feet were hard as nails: a month in the hospital had not softened them and the old callouses had come right back again within a week.

A couple more miles passed under those iron feet. Arlen heard a growl like a jeep and his head started to swing around, but he stopped when he felt his belly gurgle. Yes, it was well-empty by now. It must be after noon. He did not know for sure; some REMF — a Rear Echelon Mother Fucker — had stolen his wristwatch at the hospital.

When the growl from behind came sneaking up on him, Arlen almost did not turn around. He knew from the sound it was just more trucks. He didn't expect anything from them. Now, tanks, that was a different matter. The tankers would let him ride along in a heartbeat. They were always happy to have dogfaces along for the ride — in never hurt to have some rifles around to clear out an ambush. He could hear it was a big convoy. He pulled his garrison cap down tighter. His helmet was lost when they moved him from one hospital to another, and he felt foolish looking in this cap, like a lost boy soldier and not a veteran. He dared not look back and show his face. The trucks came rumbling up, led by a jeep. This convoy was going slowly, as if it had all the time in the world to get to the front. Dust boiled up under the tires and Arlen squinted and coughed and at last stepped far off to the side to let the convoy pass.

Boy, it was a long one. It stretched as far back as he could see. He looked at the one of the trucks rolling up. It was oddly familiar. The numbers on the bumper read: 30-117-I-C-6.

Hot damn, it's the 117th! It's Old Hickory!

He ran up beside a passing truck. "Hey, y'all are with the 117th, ain't you?" The G.I.s packed inside were surprised. "That's us!" called down one.

"Old Hickory!"

"You too?"

"120th!"

"120th is up the road, in Belgium," another said. "You need a ride?"

"'Long as it ain't to no Repple Depple!"

They stretched out hands and Arlen pushed his tired legs as faster he could get them. The dogfaces leaned out a little farther and Arlen at last got hold of a hand. The big hand yanked him straight up and Arlen thought his arm would pop out of his shoulder. He fell onto a dozen boots. Hands pulled him upright and dusted him off.

"What outfit did you say?"

"120th. 3rd Battalion, Company K," said Arlen.

"What are you doing all the way back here?" said one big man in a Chicago accent.

"Left the field hospital back in Normandy 'bout two weeks ago. Tryin' to get back to my platoon."

That elicited a few cheers from the G.I.s. "You really didn't want to be sent to a Repple Depple!" Many slapped him on the back and he winced and gasped in pain as they hit his tender scars.

"Careful, boys, last thing I want to do is spend another month in that hospital."

A swarthy sergeant laughed. "Aw, bullshit, you know it wasn't that bad."

"At least you got to see some broads," said another soldier. "Come on, tell me there weren't some gorgeous nurses there."

Arlen grinned and tapped his temple. "I memorized 'em all for later."

The afternoon was long and full, for Arlen was back amongst his kind: dogfaces like himself, men who had seen the enemy and lived. They happily shared smokes and talked loudly to make themselves heard over the truck engine. He happily shared stories of the world back there, replete with hot food and clean sheets, thieving orderlies and Red Cross packages. Their faces fell in wry disappointment before they told him what they knew best, about how the division was bombed by their own planes at Saint Lo and then were bombed by the Krauts in return, a first in this campaign.

"Yeah, you got wounded at the right time," said one of the G.I.s. "You missed out on all that, and Mortain, too."

"What happened at Mortain?"

No one spoke first. After a moment, they all cast eyes at each other, raising eyebrows in an attempt to see if someone else wanted to answer. The sergeant snapped a pack of Luckies against his thigh and pulled out a coffin nail. "Krauts hit the division pretty hard. Big counterattack, panzers and all. Lot of the division almost got cut off. It was a pretty hard fight on us all. Lot of us wouldn't be here if it weren't for our air support." And with that the sergeant went into the gory details: the endless artillery, the close-in tank attacks, patrol after patrol to flush out infiltrating Kraut attacks, the incoming fire of all kinds that came from every direction, the scarcity of water and the lack of ammunition.

"Don't ever want to fight like that again," said another G.I.

"Lot of casualties?" asked Arlen, taking a Lucky offered to him.

"A lot. Our 1st Battalion lost probably half its strength." The sergeant could tell Arlen was thinking. "What outfit in the 120th did you say?"

"3rd Battalion."

The sergeant waggled his head back and forth. "Don't know about that outfit. But the 120th got hit pretty hard."

What was done was done. It wouldn't do him any good to think about it.

Arlen lit that Lucky and looked out the back of the truck. Other than the convoy and the occasional burnt-out hulk of a German truck, there was little sign of the war. The sun was getting close to the horizon now, casting long shadows ahead of them as they motored steadily up the road.

The convoy began to slow. Arlen stuck his head out. They were approaching a fork. A roadblock was set up on the branching road and an MP directed the trucks to the left. Other soldiers stood around a pair of jeeps, one with a bazooka set across the hood and rockets laid out, ready to go. He squinted in the dying light, but could not catch the unit markings. As the deuce-and-a-half drew abreast, Arlen shouted out, "Are y'all 3rd Battalion, 120th?"

The MP looked back to the other soldiers, who realized after a moment Arlen was speaking to them. "That's us," said one.

"Company K, where's Company K?"

"Up the road there. Why?"

Arlen grabbed his musette bag. "This is my stop, fellers!"

G.I.s slapped him on the back, shook his hand. "Good luck!"

"See y'all in Berlin!" Arlen leapt from the truck.

The dogfaces waved casually as the convoy pulled away.

"Which Company was it?" said the MP as Arlen turned to him.

"K, King Company."

"Where are you coming from?"

"Hospital."

"Why don't you drive him up to the company?" said the MP to the squad sergeant.

The sergeant climbed behind the wheel of the jeep. "Let's go, I want to be back before dark."

They sped up the road and crossed the river over a bridge, which was entirely intact, left untouched by the Germans. On the north side, near the town of Antoing, or so it said on the sign, the sergeant stopped the jeep and pointed up the road. "That's Company K headquarters, I think."

"Appreciate it." Arlen shook the sergeant's hand and set off. Drawing closer, he saw the sentry standing guard by the road. He wore the fresh young face of a buck private: a replacement. Arlen strode up to the sentry. "Where's company HQ, Private?"

The young G.I., almost certainly no older than eighteen, was shocked. He eyeballed Arlen's dirty, worn uniform and fumbled about for words. "W-what's the password?"

"You ain't even given me the challenge. But don't bother with that, now, I'm here to see Lieutenant Reaser. Or did they make him captain by now?"

"Lieutenant Reaser?"

"He's still commandin', ain't he? Good Lord, don't tell me he got it, too."

"H-he's right over there, Corporal." The gangly kid pointed to a copse of trees. Arlen brushed past the private and walked straight to the headquarters section. And there was First Lieutenant Reaser, the company commander, shaking his head in astonishment. Arlen came to attention and saluted. "Corporal Breckenridge, reporting, sir."

"Is that really you, Corporal?"

"Yessir."

"What are you doing here?"

"Reporting, sir."

"Never thought I'd see you again. Do you have your orders with you?"

"No, sir."

Reaser frowned. "Did you come from the replacement depot?"

Arlen opened his mouth, about to speak, but shut it just as quickly.

"Go ahead, Corporal, tell me."

"Left the field hospital, sir, when they told me they were shipping me back to England to keep recuperatin'. But I weren't about to wait there and then get sent to some Repple Depple and get thrown in with a bunch of replacements."

"You left the field hospital? When?"

"Reckon almost two weeks ago, sir. Came on foot, and by truck, when I could."

"You've got steel ones, Corporal, that's for sure." Reaser's tired face was pleased to see him. "I'm glad to have you back. Things are chaotic. We've advanced pretty quickly. A lot of training to do with all our new replacements, a lot to prepare for. I could use an old hand like you here with the headquarters section."

"Thank you, sir, but I'd like to go back to my old platoon."

"First Platoon, wasn't it? Well, they are short of squad leaders."

"What about Sergeant Gunderson, sir?"

Reaser sighed. "Gunderson lost an eye to shrapnel at Mortain. And his replacement got his leg taken off by a mine a few days ago."

Lord, Sarge finally got that million dollar wound.

"If you're going back to your platoon, I'm promoting you to sergeant."

Arlen nodded sternly. "Yessir, thank you, sir."

"There's no doubt you've earned it. I'll let your lieutenant know." Reaser raised his eyebrows. "New lieutenant, at least to you."

"Yessir."

"Are you sure you don't want to stay here? I need a good supply sergeant."

Arlen bit his tongue.

"All right, then. Go rejoin your platoon, I'll fill in your lieutenant tomorrow."

A soldier from the headquarters section led Arlen to First Platoon, which sat in reserve in a grove of trees behind a farmhouse. It was dark underneath the canopy, but Arlen could see men silhouetted against the faintly lit fields beyond the trees. The soldier from headquarters left him there and Arlen stood in the darkness, feeling some heads and eyes turn toward him. "Who's that?" voice said.

"I'm the new sergeant," said Arlen. He wanted to see the surprise on their faces when they came up to him and saw who it was.

A figure approached out of the dark, striding toward him with a muscular swagger that made it look like his shoulders were doing all the walking. The orange dot of a lit cigarette moved smoothly with it. The figure clicked on a flashlight, its red filter on, right in Arlen's face. He squinted painfully. The face with the flashlight was unfamiliar — surely a replacement. But the G.I.'s face was confident, stoic, and a little worn — like a veteran. He clicked off the light. "Best get you to the looie." His footsteps led away through the darkness and Arlen followed after him, trying not to stumble in the dark.

There was a single light coming from the kitchen of the farmhouse, which they entered through a back door. Sitting a table was a soldier in olive drab, without insignia on his collar, sifting through a stack of papers with a business-like hand. When Arlen came through the door, he looked at Arlen with narrow eyes beneath a tall, cliff-like brow that was topped by a shock of unruly blond hair falling over a receding hairline. The man's high nose seemed strangely thin under the light of the kerosene lamp.

"This is the new sergeant. Just got here," said the other G.I.

"Thank you, Sergeant. Dismissed." The lieutenant set the papers down and tapped a cigarette over a coffee cup. "And you are?"

Arlen saluted. "Corporal Breckenridge, sir."

"Two stripes, not three? I thought he just said you were the new sergeant."

"Indian Joe said he'd put me in for it."

The lieutenant nodded. "I'm Lieutenant Venters. What outfit were you from originally?"

"This one, sir."

"Is that so?" Arlen expected a change in his voice, but there was none. "Where were you?"

"Field hospital, sir."

"And you came back."

"Yessir."

Lieutenant Venters rested the cigarette carefully on the lip of the cup. "I won't ask why, I don't care. Do you really want to fight again?"

"Sir?"

"Or do you just want to be back with your old pals? It's got to be a powerful motivation to get a man off of a comfortable hospital cot."

Who does this sonuvabitch think he is?

"I want to fight with my old squad, sir."

"Which one was that?"

"Sergeant Gunderson's."

Venters drummed his fingertips on his lips and looked off into the aether, somewhere up near the ceiling. "Gunderson. Gunderson. Ah, yes, I recall him. Wasn't around for much of my tenure." He swung those narrow eyes back to Arlen. "I don't know if that's best. I'm inclined to put you with one of the other squads. Your old squad needs someone with experience."

Arlen neck prickled in two parallel lines up to his scalp. "I've been with them from the beginning, sir. I know them well."

It was as if Venters had not even heard him. "Where were you wounded?"

"I took shrapnel in the shoulder."

"Have you healed?"

"I'm ready to fight," said Arlen. He let the last word hang a little on his tongue, just to emphasize.

The lieutenant did not smile. "You'll need a new rifle, I assume. Where's your helmet?"

"They lost it, sir. At the field hospital."

"You lost it, Corporal."

That's Sergeant to you.

"Yessir."

"We'll sort that out tomorrow." Venters folded his hands on his lap. "You think you can lead your old squad?"

"I know I can, sir."

"I will take your confidence in trust. But do not disappoint me. I expect you to be a leader, not the men's older brother."

"You'll see what I can do with any men," said Arlen. "Just show me to them."

Venters nodded to behind Arlen. "Looks like most of them are here already."

Arlen turned around, his heartbeat swelling. Outside the door, cheeks and chins and helmet rims burnt harshly in the farmhouse light. He could not make out any eyes. The olive drab bodies were not of the size and shape he remembered. That one over there could be Xavier, he was tall enough, but the shoulders were too big. Was that Mathis on the left? No, too skinny. He did not see a single familiar shape.

Arlen's throat began to rise. He swallowed hard, bottling up whatever was rising and jamming it down into that big empty spot that had opened up within him. With that, he could look back to these men, his face never betraying a bit of turmoil. A few G.I.s gave half-hearted salutes and he returned them. "We're over on the far side, if you want to come along."

He followed. He remembered a solemn, heavy tread like this once before, at Great-Grandfather Alexander's funeral. The men and women alike had worn black and the September dust puffed from the feet of the pallbearers who were all far too old but still bore the coffin as a horse would a loaded cassion. Tramp, tramp, tramp, tramp, their feet marked time on the march, slower in their old bones than once, but with no loss of the familiar rhythm of younger days, and Arlen swayed on his father's shoulders and wrapped his arms tightly around Wade's forehead. And that was all he remembered from that day, the only mournful part of it, for over the grave the preacher spoke of Alexander's sure heavenly reward. Loss was earthly, it stuck to ground which those who remained must tread in full cognizance of the calculus. All were counted at some point.

Lord, I can't stay here with them. I ain't got not place.

Maybe he should have taken Lieutenant Reaser's offer. Supply sergeant? It could be worse. It would be leading, just in a different way, just not leading men — his men, his buddies — into the fight. The other soldiers peeled off in singles and pairs to drop down into their foxholes. The fighting positions were neatly made, with squared-off sides. Hard to do in soft earth; someone must have showed them how, some soldier from long before, long since passed. Gunderson, Xavier, Kelly, any one of them. These men lived and they lived off those who had come before.

That's all that's left in the end, ain't it?

He could not go back to Reaser. He had to stay. It was his squad still. It would be his even when it was not. And maybe one day he would begin to feel for these men, too, just as he had for all the old timers.

Arlen stood there, looking around. Everyone else had a buddy for their foxhole. It was time to dig his. "Anyone care to let me borrow their entrenching tool?" he said loudly.

A blanket draped over the top of a well-dug, deep foxhole was thrown back, illuminating the ground. Silhouetted by the light of a small fire of cardboard cartons was a familiar shape — that head, the ears, the way his squirrely body hunched forward and sprung upright again. That could only be one person. "Arlen?"

"Buddy!"

He leaped all the way to the foxhole, like a drowning man lunging for a life preserver.

The two soldiers hugged each other tightly, slapping each other on the back. They broke the embrace and look at each other. "Goddamn, it is good to see you, Arlen."

A shout from across the way came: "Hey, put that light out!"

Paine grabbed Arlen by the arm and pulled him into the foxhole. Paine pulled the blanket shut and adjusted the forked branch that held the blanket up in the middle over the foxhole like a tent, making it higher for Arlen's tall frame. "I'm making coffee. You want some?" said Paine.

"You make the best damn coffee in the world, of course I do."

Paine added water to his canteen cup and then held it over the tiny fire and waited. Arlen waited, too. Any moment the flood of stories to begin pouring out of his old buddy. But Paine did not say anything. His eyes were focused somewhere else.

"Buddy."

Paine looked over as if he had not even left. "Hey, Arlen." Paine smiled. It was not the same old smile. "You look good."

123

"I feel good. Feels good to be back."

"You really wanted to come all the way back."

Arlen simply nodded, looking right at Paine, right into his eyes. It is not often that men really look into each other's eyes; when they do, there is no need to explain the look or elaborate on it or ever reference the moment again. That one time of the eyes says it once and for all. Paine smiled and he began to talk. "We missed you — I missed you — at Mortain, Arlen."

"What happened there?"

"You didn't hear?"

"I heard a little bit."

"Well, the whole company got cut off by this huge Kraut attack. We were stuck on top of a hill for five days. The Krauts shelled us and attacked and tried to push us off, but we stayed. They tried to get us to surrender, but we stayed. We lost of men. A lot of 'em." Paine's voice trailed off and stopped. He blinked a few times and swallowed, then looked back at Arlen again. "Wish I'd had my lucky rabbit's foot there with me."

Arlen wanted to reach out and hug his buddy again and cry together with him and tell him that everything would be all right. But his tongue had swollen up and stuck to the roof of his mouth. Paine's pencil-thin gaze moved away and Arlen turned away to clear his throat.

"You owe my brother a Luger."

Arlen looked back to Paine. "Why's that?"

"I had to give up the one I'd saved for him," said Paine, fishing into his musette bag, "to pay for this." He produced a photograph.

Arlen took it. He and Paine were sitting in the Normandy grass, hair clean, clothes filthy, grinning. "Well, I'll be."

"You can have it."

Arlen smiled. "Thanks, buddy. I'll get your brother that Luger."

"With interest."

"Interest? What do you mean 'interest?'"

"Maybe get him an SS dagger to go with it."

Arlen guffawed. "That ain't interest, that's usury."

"At least a Hitler Youth dagger."

"You'll be lucky if I get you Luftwaffe butter knife."

Paine's mask cracked a little as he smiled with a long-lost warmth. He poured instant coffee into Arlen's canteen cup and they clinked them together.

"Christmas in Berlin, buddy."

"Yeah, Berlin."

They drank the coffee in silence, happy.

XIII

The faint rustle of OD cloth, the click of a loose sling swivel, the clank of a piece of tin reached Arlen's ears. He looked off to their left. Thick morning fog obscured his view of the company's position as well as the muddy plain before them. Again came the scratch of uncut fingernails on tin. He craned his neck as far as he dared, but he still couldn't see. He wasn't so interested in the sound that he dared raise his head up over the lip of the foxhole.

Another clank. "Who is that?" he said in a nearly-voiced whisper.

"Sarge?" came back a voice equally hoarse. "It's Mueller."

"What are you doin'?"

"What?"

"What the hell are you doin'?"

"Sarge, do you have any C rations?"

"Why?"

"I gotta piss and I filled all my C rat cans already."

"I got one can left, and I'm savin' it."

There was a pause from the unseen voice. "Can I just put in a little? I've gotta let off some of this pressure. Just a little, Sarge."

"Hell, no. If you start, you ain't gonna stop. You'll fill it on up and then there ain't a mite of space for me." Arlen wormed his way further down into his foxhole and tucked his cold, bare hands further under his armpits, hunching up his shoulders once more as a cold breeze stirred across the plain.

"What about Paine?"

Arlen scowled for no one that could see him. "Ask him yourself."

"Is he there, Sarge?"

Arlen didn't answer. Paine was dozing in the corner of the foxhole, a fleck of drool hanging from his lip, about to drop onto the heavy blanket. The patrol he had come back from had been long and cold.

"Sarge?"

"I ain't stirrin' him." Arlen's annoyed tone belied his sympathy. They all had to deal with the same problem. They sat along a highway running through sugar beet fields, flat as flat could be. The battalion had been in this position

125

for the last two days, digging in after hitting the Germans in a big attack. But this spot along the divided highway, though a stationary position, offered no rest. The Germans, to the south of them in the town of Wurselen, and perhaps farther away, toward the horizon, could see their every move. The Krauts continually plastered the battalion's position with artillery and mortar fire. Arlen had lost two men — one killed, one wounded — the day before. The only respite came with the fog that surrounding them this time every morning, and the G.I.s dreaded it burning off, for that meant a clear view for the German artillery observers. Each man had to piss into their ration cans, for to get out of the foxhole even for a minute was to invite an 88 or a mortar to take a potshot at you.

"You think this fog will hold, Sarge?" said Mueller.

Arlen was already squinting in the rising sun's rays, amplified by the grey mist. "Not much longer."

"Think it's enough cover for me to take a leak?"

"If you make it fast."

"Actually, I've got to do more than that."

Arlen was exasperated. "Just quit talkin' and go, dammit." He heard Mueller crawl out of the foxhole and scramble toward the rear through the mud. The fog was really clearing now, and Arlen rose up a little to look behind him, suddenly concerned for Mueller. He saw the soldier duck around back of the battered brick house to the rear. The Germans had pounded down the top story on the first day and smashed down most of the first story last evening. All that remained was the cellar, with a load of shattered bricks resting on top, but some poor fools still insisted on taking shelter there. Arlen knew they wanted to smoke and cook coffee over cardboard boxes without being seen, but he knew the Germans knew that too. As much as he wanted, no cigarette or lukewarm cup of joe was worth the risk.

He removed his helmet and ran his fingers through his hair. It kept receding all the time — ran in the family he supposed. What was left was stiff and bristly from weeks without a wash. Still, at least he had some, better than going bald. Then the young replacements really would have grounds to call him "the old man."

Old man at twenty-five! Arlen knew he wasn't old. He was faster, stronger, smarter than ever. He had the edge in everything that only comes at the pinnacle of youth. He was all that any young man could hope to be and still be young. But he felt old. He felt that he had forgotten more than most could remember. There were some things a man held onto even when he lost everything else, but what was the cost of holding on? Arlen looked down into his upturned helmet like it was a bottomless pit. There should be a photograph inside, but ever since the field hospital—

He heard the tearing crackle of a shell only a second or two before he felt the burst, but he knew it was incoming and instinctively threw on the helmet and threw himself down into his foxhole. A deafening blast slapped his ears, shoved his chest, and raised hairs on his scalp and neck. Paine threw off the blanket and grabbed about madly for his M1, the other hand patting his own helmet to make sure it was still there. He was as alert as Arlen in mere seconds. "Jesus, Arlen."

"Incoming mail."

Another shell crackled inbound toward them and its blast stilled Paine's words in his mouth. After its reverberations dissipated, Paine gasped, "That's no 88."

Arlen said nothing and did not move a muscle. Another crackle, another explosion. The company was buttoned up tight now; nobody dared raise a head or move. The Germans used artillery like a sniper his rifle, taking shots at men alone or in pairs. In France, the Germans husbanded their shells, but here at home, they had all they wanted and could shoot as much as they wanted at whatever they liked. Another shell burst among the company, farther down to the left.

"I wish we could get some counterbattery," said Arlen.

"Venters never calls it in. Why doesn't he call some in?"

The shelling had stopped, but neither Arlen nor Paine dared lift their heads. Each kept hunkered down, holding his helmet on tight by the rim. Paine's face was pale and drawn, but his eyes were full of energy. Shelling was the worst. Whatever callouses that combat had raised to the killing and destruction around them, bombardment cut right through them. It touched any man in his soul.

The silence began to fill with shouted orders. Equipment jangled as men shuffled about and dodged from here to there along the constricted line.

A shell cut its high arc through the air again and before it exploded, Arlen heard another and a third right behind it. Shells pounded the earth one after another, without rhythm. The sky darkened in the aftermath of each blast, clumps of earth raining down on both Arlen and Paine. The shells kept coming. They lay in their foxhole, silently enervated, hoping and praying for the maddening barrage to end. After a while, the fire slackened to just a few shells every minute, then stopped.

"Don't move! Don't move an inch!" Arlen shouted out, not even daring to raise his eyes above the edge of the foxhole. Somewhere, a familiar voice screamed for a medic. But nobody moved. They would not be fooled. The G.I.s just sat wordlessly in their holes, anticipating the next barrage, almost wishing it to begin just to get the interminable wait done with. But they knew the Germans were biding their time and letting the respite drag out a little longer, and then a little longer still, just to see if someone lost his nerve and moved.

Finally, the shelling began again. This time, it didn't let up. The shells came thicker than ever. Arlen's jaw ached as his clenched his teeth to keep them from chattering. Faster and faster, the tempo increased. He clenched tighter, jaw and eyes. *Lord, let this end, let it end.* The blasts overlapped and he could not tell one from another. *Please end it, Lord.* Dirt rained down on them, pouring in from above and the side, falling in clods and specks and cascades, filling in all around them, getting down in all the little crevices around and behind them, just like it was meant to be one day.

Then there was silence.

Arlen waited and waited for one more barrage, but no, it did not come. He raised his head and peered over the edge of the foxhole. The Germans must be following right on the heels of the bombardment with an attack. But the muddy plain was empty all the way to the horizon. He slunk back down into the hole, shivering even as the sunlight began streaming down on him.

There was the rumble of artillery in the distance again and the sound of shells overhead. This time it was outgoing mail.

Paine peered over the back of the hole. "Mueller got it. They've got him on a stretcher."

After a while, there was stutter and crack of small arms fire off to the south. The rest of the battalion was pushing into Wurselen. A plume of smoke rose from somewhere amongst the neat rows of brick houses and paved streets. The G.I.s waited, smoking, wondering if and when the order would come for them to attack as well.

It was late afternoon and the squad was heating C rations. Lieutenant Venters, clad in muddy olive drab, no different from the rest of the G.I.s, strode up to Arlen's position. "I've got a patrol for you, Sergeant."

"Sir, get down. Come on, get down in the foxhole." Venters slipped down into the wet, sticky hole and Arlen and Paine made space for him. *Bastard ain't as careful as he should be.* Call Venters careless or bold, there was no doubt the man could fight. He pushed the platoon harder than anyone had before, and out-thought and out-fought the Germans at every turn. He knew the best spot and time for an ambush, the best way to take a wooded ridge, and the best men to lead patrols. That was why he was here.

"Lay it out for me, sir."

Venters jammed two cigarettes between his lips, lit them, and passed one over. Arlen noticed it was a Camel. Had to hand it to the man, he got the little things right. "Orders from battalion. We need reconnaissance on the ground ahead of us."

"Are we going on the attack tomorrow, sir?"

"You said it, not me." Venters uncovered a map and produced a pencil. "There is a railroad line running almost parallel to our position out there on the plain, about eight or nine hundred yards out. I want you to take five men and reconnoiter the railroad line and beyond it. I want to start here," said Venters, pointing to the map, "and end down here. We need to know what kind of forces the Krauts have out there, if any." Venters tapped his lip with the pencil. "I think it would be best for you to make a loop. Start from up here on the far left, then straight across to this point on the railroad line. Figure out what sort of connection the Krauts have on that end to their positions up in Euchen, if there's any at all."

"All right."

"Then work your way south-southeast through these fields on the far side. Figure out where the Kraut flank on the north side of Wurselen is. If you don't find it, don't go farther than, say, here." Venters made another mark on the map.

"What am I lookin' for?" said Arlen.

"OPs, assembly areas, obviously any Kraut units dug in over there. I want prisoners, most of all, if you can get any."

Arlen nodded and flicked the ash off of the cigarette. "Yessir. How long do you want me out there?"

"No more than four hours."

Arlen shook his head. "It'll take me at least six hours."

"Impossible."

"Sir, it's flat out there all the way to the railroad line. Reckon we might have to crawl over a good part of it. Might have to hide out if we run into any Kraut patrols. It'll take longer than you think."

Venters glared at Arlen, but he had to concede the point. "Six hours maximum. And I want you to report back to me by 0500 tomorrow."

Arlen looked at his wristwatch. "Yessir. I'll take the patrol up to the left flank about 2100 so we'll be ready to leave at 2200."

"Fine. It'll be dark in about an hour and a half, so draw whatever supplies you need."

"We'll go light. Reckon I can get a tommy gun for us?"

"Yes, if I can find one. Who are you taking?"

Paine sat forward. "He's taking me. I'm not staying behind."

Arlen gnawed his lip, looking at the map. Should he pick the best, those men with the keenest field sense and sharpest shot? That would make sure they all got back. Or should he take the most expendable, the replacements in particular, so that even if the whole patrol was killed or captured, a few veterans would live to teach the next wave of greenhorns? Yet a patrol of nervous, jangling replacements was likely to get Arlen killed as well. There was no criteria. Every patrol was different, and each time he was presented with the choice, Arlen was a different man, a different soldier.

Paine had to go. He was the most experienced one in the squad. Arlen couldn't leave him behind, for he was still just a private first class and Corporal Sedgwick was second-in-command of the squad. *I'll put him at the back, bringin' up the rear.* Arlen took another cigarette from Venters, lit it himself, and then spoke. "It'll be Paine, Goodson, Hirsch, Curtis, Schaeffer, and myself."

Venters mulled over the choice. "Good. Go ahead and tell the men, then come with me down to the OP and we'll take a look at the ground."

By night, the plain was cold and empty. The fighting had long since stopped in town and there was an eerie quiet. The sky was cloudless and there was no moon. Arlen checked the time under the red filter of his flashlight. *2145 hours.* Time for a final weapons check. The all carried rifles, except for Hirsch, who carried the submachine gun. Each man brought his bayonet, its blade blacked out, and a few also had knives they had acquired by hook or crook. Paine carried a blackjack that he kept tucked into his cartridge belt, and Arlen had a .45 automatic that he had bartered off of a wounded tank gunner. Other than weapons, each G.I. carried only ammunition, two grenades, a canteen of water, and a single K ration. Arlen shook their webbing and cartridge belts to make sure nothing clanked or clicked. He smudged burnt cork on their faces until they were as black as miners. Did they remember the challenge and password? Yes, each knew what to say. There was nothing left to chance, then.

What soldiers they had become. New by Arlen's judgment, these dogfaces had quickly turned into crafty veterans. Of course, what choice had the past month had given them? Since Arlen had rejoined them near Tournai, the division had driven across Belgium, taken the fortress at Eben Emael, where the war on the Western Front had started four years prior, and crossed into Germany. With tenacity the division threw itself against the feared Siegfried Line. It had been pure, relentless fighting: creeping up on impregnable pillboxes to take them from the rear, battling through drab hamlets of brick and stone, and suffering punishing counterattacks and artillery bombardments. The mad dash across France was done. Now they were in for a long, grinding slog. It broke a man or he lived through it. These men lived, so far.

Arlen checked his watch again. *2202 hours.* He motioned to the patrol and they went forward, filing past the observation post, whose sentries bid them a whispered "Good luck." In a loosely staggered column of twos, they moved from the morass of the company's position down into the beet fields. The leafy tops swished against the boots the soldiers and flashed faintly silver under the light of the stars. It was a very clear night. Arlen crept down one row for many yards before gingerly stepping over the beets into the next row. The patrol carefully mimicked his movements. It was slow going, though, for many times there was the snap of a fingernail against a matchbox — a prearranged signal for a halt — and the vanguard had to wait for the rest to catch up.

Arlen's eyes had adjusted to the dark and he could see their objective well ahead of them, a faint line where the plain crested ever so slightly and ran perpendicular to them. They pressed on steadily. Finding a dirt path, the patrol walked beside it, not on it, for fear of mines. And, too, there could be German patrols passing in the opposite direction to reconnoiter their own lines, or waiting to ambush them at the opportune moment. The Krauts were careful, they would leave only the faintest hint. But the faintest hint would do. Arlen just had to catch it. He snapped his finger against a matchbox. The squad halted and crouched in place. The path had reached a junction of paths. Arlen watched and listened and smelled with patience that rivaled that of the German gunners. The junction was empty. The calves of the G.I.s went numb. Still, he waited. He would not rush this. The junction, still empty, began to radiate a sense of safety. Arlen felt it and his instincts were assured. At last daring to move, Arlen signaled the patrol and the G.I.s crossed and continued on.

The patrol ended its long, slow creep at the railroad line. They reached it at its highest point above the plain, which was dangerous, but also intentional on Arlen's part. One German could effectively observe the whole length of the rail line as well as all the ground around, but he could also be easily seen. At Arlen's signal, the G.I.s put themselves himself to the ground and crawled to the railroad bed. Private Hirsch, on point, drew a knife and Arlen produced his .45, and on hands and knees they crept to the top of the embankment. Other than the rails running into the dark, there was no sign of any Germans. Cautiously, they waited and watched. Again Arlen felt safety come to him. Sharp-edged stones crunched slightly under his feet; he knelt on the railroad bed, listening again. Nothing. It was far too dark to use Venters' field glasses. They would have to reconnoiter farther on foot.

They followed the plan. Pressing north and then looping back south, their torturous route went deeper and deeper into what should have been the German lines. But there was nothing. No abandoned positions, no tank tracks, not even spent cartridge casings crackling underfoot. The wind kicked up and began to sing in the helmet straps around Arlen's ears. He shivered and looked up. Was a front blowing in? No, the sky was still clear. They should stay out and finish the patrol.

There was a shout and splash from behind. Arlen's heart jumped up into the back of his throat. His breathing quick and shallow, he fumbled for the matchbox in his pocket. He finally got hold of it and the box slipped from his fingers and tumbled to the ground, gone forever in the dark.

Shit. Arlen whispered hoarsely, "Hirsch!" The scout came to Arlen and they retraced their steps until they found the rest of the patrol, all whispering.

"What happened?" asked Arlen.

"Paine fell in a shell hole," said Goodson.

"You all right, buddy?"

"Y-y-yeah, Arlen," Paine said through chattering teeth. "Got w-w-wet, but I'll be fine."

"Shhhhhhhhhh—" hushed one of the others.

"Can you keep going?" asked Arlen.

Then his head whipped around.

What was that?

"I'll be fine," said Paine. "Let's keep g-g-going."

There it was again.

Arlen turned to Private Schaeffer. "You heard that, didn't you?"

The private shook his head.

"It was German."

Schaeffer knew German, but even he was skeptical. "Are you sure, Sarge?"

Arlen knew what he had heard. He grabbed Paine by the sleeve. "You still all right to bring up the rear?"

"I'll be f-f-fine, Arlen."

The patrol spread out in a diamond, ready for contact, and began to circle back toward the rail line. At the embankment, they stopped and Arlen took the lead. The patrol followed him single file, making slow but silent progress down its length. Still, contact eluded them. They should not have been surprised. Sound could travel considerable distances on cold nights.

I ain't crazy. I know I heard it.

It was getting very cold now. Best he call a halt and let the men rest.

Arlen squatted on his haunches and reached into his pocket for a K ration. A cigarette was *verboten*. The chocolate bar would have to do. He wolfed it down in a few bites. Shielding his watch under his jacket, he checked the time under the red flashlight: *0353 hours.* They had little time left. They had struck out badly.

"Johann?"

The voice was faint but clear through the dark and Arlen froze, not even reaching for his rifle. He held his breath and listened again.

"Johann? Wo bist du?"

Arlen signaled to Paine and the blackjack was passed forward, hand to hand. With Schaeffer behind him, Arlen moved slowly below the railroad embankment.

Pfffffffffffttttttt.

Arlen froze.

A muffled clapping sound. Like gloves smacked together, just a few yards away.

Arlen's hair stood up so straight, his helmet nearly fell off his head. He slowly handed his rifle back to Hirsch.

Pffffffffffftttttttt. The muffled clapping followed. Someone keeping his hands warm.

Arlen waited, crouched like a sprinter.

I'll get Venters his damn prisoner.

Arlen possumed forward on all fours, up the little slope to the rails themselves. The sensation of shape, of darkness on darkness, planted itself in his mind. Yes, there was a man there, standing in a hole dug into the edge of the embankment. The dark sensation blew on his cupped hands and clapped them again and then turned around. Arlen froze.

"Johann, kommst du mit ein—"

The blackjack hit him clean across the face. Arlen dove into the hole and hit the German again and again. The soldier cried out like girl and Arlen shoved his hand over the Kraut's mouth as he fumbled for his pistol. "Sarge," hissed Schaeffer, crawling up behind him.

"Gimme some light!"

The red light clicked on. The Kraut's eyes bulged with fear and defiance above Arlen's hand. Black blood was smeared from nose to chin and leaked between Arlen's fingers and oozed from a gash on his eyebrow.

"Ask him if there are any others," said Arlen, his .45 in his other hand.

Schaeffer growled in German at the prisoner. Arlen removed his hand from the prisoner's mouth, but the Kraut only started to shout. Arlen clamped his hand down tight and shoved the pistol right up in the prisoner's face. "What did he say?"

"Said the Fuehrer is going to drive us all back into the sea."

"Sonuvabitch."

"One of those fucking Hitler Youths, I bet."

"We'll see how tough he is when Venters gets to him. Help me get him out of this hole. And you tell him that if he makes a peep, he's a dead man."

Schaeffer took the Kraut. Arlen looked around the position. It was a neat little post, just a man with a field telephone and a trench periscope sticking up just a few inches above the tracks. But it had cost Arlen three men.

Should have given that Nazi sonuvabitch a few more whacks.

Arlen kicked over the periscope and stomped the optic to pieces.

When he stepped from trench, Schaeffer said to Arlen, "Any sign of the other Kraut?"

"Other Kraut?"

"He was calling out for someone."

Shit.

The patrol was over.

Arlen led the squad over the tracks. They crunched across the railroad bed, slid down the other side, and pushed through the beets. Sending Hirsch ahead again, Arlen looked back. Paine was back there on his own. He should never have let Paine come along, let alone bring up the rear. And sopping wet on a cold night, at that. Paine could get separated and lost out there in the beets, and the Krauts might snap him up before he could find his way. And all for what, getting Venters his prisoner? Swapping a Paine for a Kraut: that was no trade in Arlen's book. Maybe he should go replace Paine. But they would come upon the sentries soon — did Hirsch remember the password? In the off-chance that the guard was switched, they wouldn't know a patrol was returning and the nervous sentry might rake them with fire. He should stay up close.

A single shot broke the night. The deep report was followed by another and another. Then an M1 opened up from far behind — and he knew Paine was firing in return.

Like fireflies strapped to an express train, a handful of tracers winked overhead and a loud, ripping report followed. The MG 42 fired another burst and the tracers passed through the patrol and spluttered amongst the beets. Arlen threw himself on the ground and began worming his way forward. "Get moving!" said Arlen as loud as he dared. "Get back to our lines!"

The rifle fired again in the rear. What was Paine doing? Dueling with a machine gun in the dark? The MG 42 stopped for a minute, then fired a quick burst.

There was rustle in the dark ahead. Arlen pushed himself up and peered over the row of beets. A hunched figure leaped the row of beets and began to run. One, two steps, and he ran right into Arlen. They both tumbled to the cold, hard earth, tangled up. Each threw blows at the other. Arlen hit out with the butt of his rifle, but he couldn't get it up for a good swing, his arm was tangled in the sling. A boot caught him in the face and hobnails scratched his jaw. It was the fucking Kraut.

Levering himself up with the rifle, Arlen jumped on top of the German. Pressing his arm against the Kraut's throat, he fumbled for the blackjack, the knife, the .45, anything.

"*Nicht schiessen, nicht schiessen!*"

Arlen set his hand on the blackjack and pulled it out.

But it was the flashlight in his hand. Swearing, Arlen switched it on. The scared prisoner's face was black with blood and dirt.

Arlen growled, "Get up!" He grabbed the Kraut's belt to pull him to his feet. What was this? Arlen felt again and knew. A grenade, stuck in the Kraut's belt and hidden by the overcoat.

Schaeffer, you sonuvabitch. Lost control of the prisoner and forgot to search him, too.

Fumbling, Arlen tried to pull the grenade free of the belt. The Kraut pushed and flailed at him.

"Arlen!" It was the voice he had been waiting for. Paine was nearby. He fired and the clip pinged from the rifle.

The MG 42, seeking out the flash of Paine's rifle, tore the beets with rounds — *plock, plock, plock.* Arlen threw himself to the ground. The Kraut pushed free and scrambled away. The MG 42 fired again. Paine muttered in anger, his teeth clicking and chattering.

Arlen reached for his rifle in the dark, but his hand only grabbed dirt. The Kraut swished away through the beets.

"Arlen, my rifle's jammed!"

"High tail it, buddy, just get out of here!"

Groping blindly again, Arlen set his hand on the cold steel of the rifle barrel.

There was a loud thud and the jangling of gear. "Fuck!" Then nothing.

"Buddy!"

"Arlen! I just ran into a fucking Kraut!"

And there was that damned prisoner again, backing off, hands up. "*Nicht schiessen, nicht schiessen!*"

The MG 42 ripped the dark again. They ducked and the prisoner spun around to run, his overcoat rustling against the beets.

Arlen's rifle came up to his shoulder without a thought. He couldn't see the sights, but then there were two shots and the muzzle flash blinded him.

Paine pulled at his sleeve. "Let's go!"

Blinking away the silver-blue suns of the muzzle flash, Arlen tripped over a row of beets. "Get the prisoner!" he said, but Paine had done just as Arlen said, high-tailing back home. Still half-blind, Arlen stumbled toward the Kraut. He grabbed the overcoat and yanked hard. The prisoner did not resist. Arlen rolled him over and the prisoner flopped to face him. One round had punched his thigh and the other passed through the base of the throat. Arlen pulled the overcoat back. The grenade was still there, stuck under the belt. Other than his papers, it was all the Kraut had.

Lord, ain't this war a damn waste.

The MG 42 started its hateful drumming again. It was time to crawl.

When Arlen at last wormed his way up to their own observation post, the sentries were expecting him. "Halt! Who is it?"

"Sergeant Breckenridge."

The sentry threw out the challenge: "Clam."

"Chowder."

"Come on through, Sergeant. You're the last one."

"Every get back all right?"

"I count six including you."

"That's good."

"Better get to cover, Kraut's are gonna throw some shells our way after what you just stirred up. Oh, and Lieutenant Venters is looking for you."

"I'm sure he is."

It took a long time for Arlen to stumble back through the dark after leaving the company command post. The captain and Lieutenant Venters had grilled him over and over as to what happened, and Arlen had given them the crucial details. The officers plied him with coffee, trying to get him to say more, but Arlen simply handed over the dead German's papers as the last word about the patrol.

He wandered into Second Platoon by accident and they turned him around and sent him back in the right direction. The scattered arc of foxholes told Arlen that he had reached his platoon. There was his hole — he knew it by the shape. If only there were trees to cut down for logs for better protection.

Paine's voice rang hollowly. "Is that you?"

"I'm back." Arlen stepped down into the foxhole and collapsed against the back of it. His helmet came down over his eyes and he set it back in the right place.

"We made it," said Paine.

"Yep." Arlen rubbed his eyes. He should get some sleep, but his nerves still burned hot. He would stay awake and let Paine sleep. But the words that came out of his mouth had nothing to do with any of that. "Buddy, I messed up."

"What do you mean?"

"Back there at that Kraut outpost, I messed up bad."

Paine did not even hesitate to answer. "Tell me about it."

"Schaeffer and I went up there and I found that Kraut. I just went right up there and I got him with the blackjack in the head. Didn't stop to think, even. I just saw him and went for him, and he went down. And I jumped in and I don't know why, there could have been others, but I felt like there weren't. Stupid of me, but I reckon I came out all right. Maybe I just wanted that prisoner."

"For what?"

"I don't know." Arlen shook his head. "The looie wanted one, but did I want to get him one that badly? Don't know why I did it. Weren't my idea for the patrol in the first place, neither." He was quiet for a while. He wasn't even sure if Paine was still awake, but he spoke again anyway. "I went right up into that outpost and I hit him and he went down, hard. And I got Schaeffer to question him, 'cause I thought that we might find out if there was a patrol out there or what units were in the area. But then Schaeffer said he'd been callin' out for his buddy."

"Do you think they knew we were there?" said Paine.

"Maybe. There was a field telephone in that OP, maybe the other one went out to take a leak and when he came back he called it in."

"Shit." Paine was quiet. "That was close, then."

"Real close."

"I knew they were out there," said Paine. "I had this feeling."

"You did?"

"Yeah."

"When?"

"I guess, well, right before I fell in the shell hole. I kept thinking, those Krauts are out here somewhere. I felt like they were dug in deep, and like we were almost on them, or maybe we walked in between them and they didn't know."

"They would've known. We weren't that quiet."

"I think we were. You remember the wind blowing out there — remembered how it rustled the beet leaves and made it hard to hear?" Paine scratched his temple, pensive, but he kept on. "I remember thinking that I heard something or felt something move out there in the dark. It wasn't wind, I know that. I can't remember now — maybe I didn't hear it, but now I feel like I did. Maybe I only felt it, but at any rate, there was something like a click or a thud, like some Kraut heard us and was waiting to see us before he sounded the alarm. Or took a shot."

"You reckon we walked through a Kraut position or something?"

"Maybe, or close to it." Paine's voice was nervous, even here in the safety of his hole. "You know, maybe we crossed in front of it, before we circled back to the railroad line."

The details were becoming murky already. At their demand, Arlen had given the officers as many as he could recall, but they didn't matter to him. What he thought and feared and heard and could have done, that stayed, that was what was stuck in his head. The finer points faded to the background, still there but waiting for him to forget the vivid impressions of that night. If he ever would.

"We were damn lucky," Arlen said.

The wind whistled up over the plain of mud.

"I killed that Kraut."

"Which one?" said Paine.

"The prisoner."

Paine did not reply.

"He had a grenade on him."

"Shit. How did he hide that?"

"I forgot to search him." Arlen shook his head. "He had it on him and he got away. And I shot him."

"Them's the breaks."

"He didn't even go for the grenade."

"But he had it on him."

"He wouldn't have if I'd searched him before I gave him to Schaeffer. I reckon Schaeffer should have, too, but it was my responsibility. Well, maybe that Kraut was too afraid to pull it out and throw it away when we were marching him back. And I had to shoot him for it."

What would Wade have said? Or Great-Grandfather Alexander? Anything but dishonor was endurable, they would have said. But of course, they were not here. And so what they might have said was still unknown.

But someone had to say what Arlen had to hear. So it fell to Paine.

"Fuck him, Arlen. You think he was so innocent? What would you bet he was the one who called in arty on us? Huh? You think he doesn't have blood on his hands? Why does he get a free pass for putting an 88 up Mueller's ass while he's taking a shit, but you don't?"

"That ain't the same."

"That's right, he didn't get to see the person he killed. Just like a bombardier looking through the bomb sight. Or the gunner on a 105. Yeah, they get a clean conscience because when they kill, the Krauts can't surrender. But you gotta carry all that guilt around with you. Yeah, that's real swell, Arlen."

"You didn't—"

"I didn't see it, but I know," spat Paine. "Listen, if he had gotten that grenade off and killed one of us or all of us, how would you feel then? Huh?" Paine sighed. "You think it's about you and the Krauts. But it's not. It's about you and us. You kill whoever you have to get the rest of us home. I wish you would see that. That's what I've been doing this whole time."

Lord, forgive me. If only I knew.

The two soldiers were alive. As always, it was a miracle and a mystery. Neither could explain why, why them and not others. But they tried. Paine and Arlen kept talking for a long time, recounting the whole patrol over and over, talking about the same things once, twice, three or four times, using different words, recalling and wondering different things, putting it all into place. They had to speak to each other like this. It was the only way. If they did not, they would start to question the tight cocoon of cold practicality they had spun around themselves to protect them as they advanced toward danger. And they could not afford to have that unravel. They knew a man's fate was not his own. And yet it was his own and that of those next to him, in some immediate sense. For if he or any one of them was careless in his habits, if they all did not take survival into account in every single thing they did, blindly hoping to survive, then they would not make it. They all knew it, they had seen it. They had to speak of all they had done, and speak now, or else they would not remember perfectly and would never understand it. They had to speak, and to listen, and that was how they knew they lived.

After a long time, perhaps an hour or more, they fell silent. Arlen felt empty. There was nothing else to discuss about the past night. Here he was, and here Paine was, and that was it. Tomorrow would bring its own problems.

"Arlen?"

"Yeah?"

"Are you using your blanket?"

"Aw, shit, buddy, I forgot. You're still soakin' wet."

"Yeah."

"Here, take my blanket." Arlen wrapped it around his shivering friend. He was amazed Paine had said nothing the whole time they had talked. "You want my socks?"

"No, I've got on my dry pair."

"All right. Get some sleep."

"You too, Arlen. You need it."

He did need to, but he didn't want to. He would only dream of all he had talked of, the memories more set now than before they had spoken of them. That wasn't sleep. That was the same as waking.

XIV

There was one thing to be said for these brick and stone houses: when the artillery brought the walls and roof down, it buried the dead quite nicely.

Yes, Lord, it does, it seals up the bodies just like a tomb. Mighty convenient, ain't no one to bury. No bloated bodies fillin' up the ditches like back in France.

The shattered houses weren't American tombs anymore. They were for the Krauts.

Mighty tidy. Mighty German, ain't it?

"We're on the move!"

Arlen shifted his equipment and M1 on his shoulders, but it did not help much. His muscles strained under the weight of extra rations, a full canteen, extra grenades, and nearly two hundred rounds of ammo.

The G.I.s began to move. Ahead of Arlen, Lieutenant Venters and his runner set off at a brisk pace, following the rear platoon of Company L as it led the battalion up this muddy, churned-up road. Arlen stepped off and, once settled into his stride, looked back to make a count: Paine, Schaeffer, Wood with the BAR, Sayers the replacement, Hirsch, Smith and Hernandez who were also replacements, Jones, and Corporal Sedgwick bringing up the rear of the column. The men, strung out five paces apart, trudged on wordlessly. Soon the hamlet of farmers' houses and their entombed German dead were behind them and another emerged faintly ahead on the grey plain.

Arlen's skin began to crawl as the November morning march warmed him. He wished he could scratch, but he had too much gear, and there was no stopping. They had to keep a brisk pace. Their speed today was astounding. By Arlen's figuring, they had come three or four miles already.

Lord, let them brass hats finally get some sense about them. Ain't no good going back to taking a yard here and there, losing men right and left for each one.

For five days, the regiment had hit the Germans hard and fast, pounding them with artillery and aircraft and rushing in hot on the heels of the fire. Each battalion in the division took its turn giving support and attacking, leapfrogging forward over the others in quick succession. The speed with which they moved was dizzying. They thrust forward right into the Germans, and although Arlen was still expecting the inevitable return blow, the counterattacks never really came and the dogfaces just kept marching and fighting. The First Battalion boys had gone up in the morning to the sound of heavy fire against a little village called Langweiler. They took it. This next little village which they had passed through had fallen but twenty minutes before.

But objectives gained or lost were for the lieutenants and everyone else on up. Arlen's thoughts were on his men. Many had gone back in the last six weeks: a half dozen replacements, three killed, three wounded; some veterans, like Curtis, sent back maimed; and the broken men, Tuttle and Goodson, fatigued until they got careless. It was the latter who weighed on Arlen, for he could do nothing for them. They could get a rest for a few days behind the lines, but they could never get away for good — they were needed too badly.

But what could he do except accept them back as best he could? He had to take them on patrol, on advances through muddy fields, leave them on sentry alone in the dark, for there was no one else sometimes. All he could do was listen and watch and be there when they broke again.

Ain't the time to be thinkin' 'bout that.

The battalion halted beside the road. The attack was coming, they all knew it. The G.I.s settled down on the roadside, although each knew that if he made himself comfortable, they would be ordered to move out almost immediately. Few talked, as the older G.I.s had long since told each of the replacements, *Don't ask Sarge how much longer.* The soldiers smoked, burning through their packs of cigarettes, not knowing if they could get more and not caring if they would.

Arlen resisted the urge to look at his watch. Why the pause in the advance, he wasn't sure. But Arlen knew how it would pan out. They would go up the road and at the first sign of resistance, the whole battalion would be sent against that village ahead, and Indian Joe would put Second Platoon on the right, First Platoon on the left, and Third Platoon in reserve, just like always. Maybe it was sour grapes, but it seemed to Arlen that Third Platoon was always in reserve. Maybe it was because they came last on the list, their number the last in mind. Of course, King Company itself had seen its fair share of breaks, Arlen couldn't deny that. But it didn't feel like that when the time inevitably came. Arlen knew that it would probably be First Squad on the left of the platoon's advance, Second Squad the right, Third Squad in support. He knew but held his tongue. Nothing would change it.

He lit a cigarette and looked back at the squad. Wood was showing Sayers the replacement how to change a BAR magazine. He only did because Arlen had told him to. Most of the veterans — *Veterans and they ain't even been in two, three months, most of 'em* — did not want to talk to the replacements. Arlen had not either, once upon a time. He didn't want to get close to one of them, only to see his dumb head get blown off. But he was the leader now. He had to do what he didn't care for, not for himself, but for all of them.

"Let's go, up and at 'em!" came the call. Arlen flicked the butt away. "Let's go!" said Venters. Arlen repeated the same words to his squad in a sharper tone. They formed up, ready for the attack. But they just waited. Minutes turned into a quarter hour, twenty minutes, a half hour. Too much delay dulled the fine edge that anticipation put on the senses. Arlen checked the squad once again; there was nothing else to do: "Rifle: you got it loaded? Grenades: no, don't hang it by the pin. Don't care if you didn't know, it'll be all our asses that get killed. Don't do it again. Where's your aid kit? Good. Now check that rifle again: I'll be back."

After the one check, and a double check, the third double-check of the day so far, Arlen had nothing left to do. The small village was still there, waiting for them. Arlen pulled out two cigarettes, lit both, and walked over to Paine, who squatted with his back resting against a low wall. Arlen held the cigarette out, but Paine didn't seem to notice.

"Buddy, it's for you."

Paine didn't look up.

"Come on, I know they're Raleighs, but I ain't got nothin' better."

Paine was fingering his rosary. Paine yanked on the beads, jerking them apart with so much force it seemed that he would break the strand. He stared across the plain, at first a thousand yards, then a hundred miles away, looking deep into Germany.

Arlen shook the staring soldier by the shoulder. "Hey, buddy, snap out of it."

Paine looked up at Arlen. "Sorry, Arlen." His eyes still weren't there.

"You seein' something?"

Paine did not answer, but just took the smoke. Arlen watched him, his brow furrowed in concern. He waited, looking up and down along the squad. Finally, he said, "You want to tell me?"

Paine blew a long stream of smoke. His face was not normal. It said what words could not. Paine pulled the cigarette away from his mouth. "Are we attacking?"

"Reckon any minute now," said Arlen.

Paine took a last, long draw, then cast the unfinished butt down and ground it out with his heel. He let the smoke curl from his mouth and finished with a smoke ring. "Okay." But he kept staring.

The order came. The G.I.s fell into a double colum and the whole battalion started forward down the road. The strike and squish of their boots on the

142

road was muffled by the rip of outgoing shells. Company L peeled off and moved out into the muddy beet fields on the right side of road. Captain Reaser led Company K off the road to the left. Maintaining a quick step, platoons shook out into columns, arrayed just as Arlen expected. Arlen was at the front of the platoon's column, only the scouts and the captain with his command section ahead of him. Reaser stopped and peered through his field glasses as the men moved forward. There was nothing to see except the village ahead, no cover for the enemy to hide behind on the almost perfectly flat fields between here and the brick island of the farming town. Nowhere for the enemy, but nowhere for the G.I.s either.

But the artillery kept on beating against Langendorf and not a shot nor shell was thrown in return. It was all going well. Arlen looked back along his squad, seeing that everyone was keeping pace. No one fell behind today, not even the replacements.

The distance disappeared under their feet and almost as suddenly as it had started, the artillery stopped. Arlen checked his watch. *Ain't even been fifteen minutes.* They had gone quickly and had drawn too close for the 105s to support. There were no tanks to come with them. The dogfaces were on their own.

Arlen said nothing, for his squad knew what to do, and so they all listened impassively to shouted orders and the clank of equipment. It was not far now — if they could keep going quickly like this, nothing could stop them. A little bit farther and they would be over the threshold. No matter what the Krauts threw at them, they could assault through. They could push through the outer defenses and into the heart of the town and flush out the Krauts. But not yet. Still a little farther.

A quick searching burst.

Arlen's head spun. Over there, to the front right.

The second ripping burst snapped bullets over Second Platoon.

The long-gathered tenseness exploded from every man almost at once and they broke from their columns into the squads. Venters' voice sounded above the commotion: "Platoon! Double time!" Arlen passed the order along, but the men had heard it and had already broke into half-run, tripping through the unharvested beets. They had to close the distance quickly — there was nowhere to hide.

A wave of fire swept over the advance. Second Platoon and Company L took the brunt, for they were closer to the narrow-faced village. Every pulsating urge said to Arlen, *Stop your steps! Burrow flat! It's a dishpan out here! They can see you!* But, no, he would not. Everyone else pressed ahead. Others were getting it worse. Keep going, it's not bad yet.

He let his eye be pulled to Schaeffer, out far ahead as a scout. The boy's neck seemed to have disappeared between his helmet and shoulders. The helmet pivoted around and looked back at Arlen, as if he had missed an order to stop and take cover. Arlen gave him his hardest eye. The silent urge was best. Example must keep the squad moving forward.

Second Platoon on the right slowed to crawl and in rapid succession its men dropped to the ground as the machine gun and rifle fire became too intense. They began to return fire against the invisible defenders of the village, Langendorf. The aid man popped up and ran to a figure that squirmed about, his pain silenced by the distance and the chatter of gunfire.

Footsteps came from behind. Kiley, the platoon runner, grabbed Arlen by the arm. "Got a message from the lieutenant," he said between breaths.

"Where does he want us?"

"We're pushing ahead," he said pointing toward the open land north of the town. "To that farm."

There was what looked like a large house with several outbuildings and a grove of trees near it. "Gonna be a long run. The looie know that?"

Kiley never replied. He knew the answer. Of course Venters could see it was a long run.

But so it had to be. All this time they were moving, moving, moving, their legs never stopping, for that was the infantryman's lot in life. Engines could carry them across the world, tires could speed them in comfort, but when the objective was seen, it was all down to the dogface, walking a field in full risk to himself. This Arlen could understand in his bones.

A mortar round landed on their right. A second quickly followed. Rifle rounds snapped regularly between them and over their heads. The G.I.s were breathing hard. But not one scream was heard despite the intermittent shots and shells. Another mortar round went off, closer to First Platoon.

Good Lord, don't 'em get the range on us.

Fear roiled within, but Arlen's legs kept moving and that was enough. As long as they could carry him forward, all that fear would stay beneath for now, for he would not be stuck out there on the plain like a sitting duck. On and on and on, keep going, legs, and breathe, lungs, and listen, ears, for the orders and the shouts of the men.

The wall of bullets hit them at last. With surprise and inescapable fire, their usual method, the Germans poured rounds into First Platoon. Arlen fell through open air, straight for the German soil. He bashed his elbows and his jaw rattled. He burrowed down among the unharvested beets.

"Medic!"

Rounds from indistinguishable weapons snapped just above the beet tops. Carefully, Arlen raised his head. Crouched, hunched over, or almost flat on the ground, his men were spread in a ragged wedge formation. A mortar round burst close by and Arlen ducked. "Return fire!" shouted Arlen hoarsely.

Against what, Arlen?

He tried to swallow, but his mouth was bone dry. Working up some spit, he wet his lips and raised himself up again. Third Squad, on the right, was delivering a hasty return fire against the farm. Every now and then, there winked a flash, which was all you would see — you would not see smoke, German guns didn't make them.

Rising up as much as he dared, Arlen looked back to the squad, pointing forward. "Suppressing fire on the objective!"

Wood heard Arlen's command and turned his automatic rifle from silent. The rest of the squad followed one by one. The veterans were quicker, but the newer men were hesitant.

Dammit, why won't they shoot? Kraut points a gun at you, any greenhorn would shoot him down. But suppressing fire, you got to wring it out of them.

Onto his feet, Arlen dashed to the other section. He told Corporal Sedgwick to stay on the men and make sure they didn't let up. Up again and through a swarm of angry rounds Arlen ran back to his section, thinking nothing, all consciousness of his work gone, only the instinct of weary mastery there.

He threw himself back down and shouldered his rifle, a better one than the first one he'd drawn upon returning to the unit. He'd broken the old one on purpose in a fit of anger at its inaccuracy and had drawn this beaut — he knew that if he could put a target in between the width of that sliver of a front sight, he could hit it. He settled the front post down on where he had seen a flash. He squeezed the trigger slowly and steadily several times until the rifle *pinged* and he reached for a fresh clip.

Kiley threw himself down next to Arlen. "Orders from the looie."

Arlen finished firing and said, "Go on," reloading again.

"Your squad will take the trees and cover Third Squad while they take the farmhouse and the barn. Second Squad will be in reserve."

A couple rounds snapped close to them. "Sonuvabitch," said Arlen.

"Third Squad is taking too much fire to move, but they'll provide you a base of fire. Lieutenant wants you to move quickly, by bounds if necessary."

Shit. "You mean just us?"

"Second Squad will be in reserve in case you meet any resistance. They are there to watch your flank from any surprise attacks."

"Hell, ain't gonna be no surprises. Look out there. No cover, nothin'." Arlen let the rifle bolt slam home. "We gettin' any support?"

"Third Squad and the mortar will suppress the enemy position while you move."

Arlen gnawed on his lip. It was probably three hundred, maybe three hundred twenty-five yards to the objective. "Helluva long run. The looie want to come along?"

Kiley left without another word and Arlen looked to his squad, firing slowly and steadily. Their fire held the Germans and they traded weight for weight. Carefully, Arlen moved to Sedgwick, told him laconically, and then let him pass the word.

It would be very dangerous, for there was not a scrap of concealment or surprise to be had. The Germans would know what they were doing at every moment. There was one more thing that could be counted on: the platoon's mortar would make all the difference for them. *Lord-make-us-worthy-of-these-gifts-we're-about-to-receive-in-Christ-Jesus-name-Amen.*

Thighs shaking, Arlen launched himself forward, the first strides carrying him past the rest of his section. He swept them up with him and they rose and followed in his wake. Arlen's pace was beyond the double, it was a dead run, feet pumping up and down, scrambling for traction in between the beets. Not a shot came near, not a single round — the air felt clear and free. He pushed his tight, sinewy legs harder, trying to pull the whole squad after him, as if speed and speed alone would keep them coming. He looked back — there they were, olive drab bobbing through the beets, running erect, then ducking right as—

Arlen felt the sting and then the burst. It was the mortar. He lifted his right hand: a piece of shrapnel had grazed across the back of his hand and it leaked blood down his wrist. He kept running.

Another mortar round went off, much closer this time. It was not theirs. Arlen dropped to the ground, motioning for the squad to come forward to him.

Did they all make it?

He tried to count, but couldn't see well. Bullets passed between them, the crack of its path telling the G.I.s that the Germans could see them. Arlen could see flashes in the trees.

Got to keep movin'.

Arlen caught Sedgwick's attention and signaled: circling the hand, hand falling forward from on high, pointing ahead, then a clenched fist pulled down. Then Arlen turned to Wood. "Cover the other section, Private. Keep those Krauts' heads down."

"Yes, Sarge."

"Go on, now."

The BAR stuttered and Sedgwick charged ahead like the bull he was, battering a hole through the invisible wall of enemy fire so big that Hirsch and Hernandez and Smith could pass through abreast. They bobbed along behind him, see-sawing from one side to another, no fine parade ground step, just the movement of men hoping that the bullet will not come right then. Jones straggled behind, slower, almost limping. Perhaps he was hit.

Arlen's head whipped around. "Keep firing! All y'all!"

A cloud of black-gray aether and lumps of earth dribbled over the rushing section. Someone was missing. Sedgwick stopped and went back, the others taking cover. Another mortar burst and Arlen ducked. Then Sedgwick was hauling a man forward toward the others.

"Get ready to move," said Arlen. Then, as an afterthought: "Paine, you still got that smoke?" There was no reply from his buddy, who lay prone between the rows of beets. He rapped his knuckles on Paine's helmet. "Hello in there, you got that smoke grenade?"

Paine scowled. "What do you think?" He did not even look up at Arlen.

Sedgwick's section began to fire into the trees. At the first reports of the rifles, Arlen started ahead. The section gathered up in his wake again — Paine quickly with him, Schaeffer not far behind, Sayers lagging, and lastly Wood, moving slowly.

Arlen could not see the rifle flashes. He could not hear the reports over his own rasping breaths. Snap, snap, snap, snap: the rounds announced themselves all the same.

Paine swore right behind him. Perhaps he had been hit. Perhaps he had merely tripped. Arlen would look back later. Ahead, ahead, his churning legs would take him ahead because that was the only way offered to him and he had the courage of that certain kind of man who knows it and goes without complaint all the same.

Snap-snap-snap-snap-snap-snap-snap.

A swarm popped the air around him and Arlen fell straight to the ground. One more burst passed over and then the fire shifted elsewhere. Cautiously, Arlen rose up, looking behind and motioning the section on — it was useless to yell. They gained another couple dozen yards, sweeping just past Arlen before fire forced them to ground.

"Give 'em covering fire!"

Arlen raised up to fire. Snap, snap, right past his head. He saw the flash and set his front sight atop it, the post sliding down until the spot of the now-gone flash was bisected by the top of the sight. His finger took up the first stage quickly, then the second stage slowly, and the trigger broke.

Thump.

Thump.

Thump.

Three shots and he came back down out of recoil and raised his head. Paine and Schaeffer were covering. Wood was reloading the BAR. Sayers crouched beside Wood, magazines in hand, ready to pass over a fresh one.

147

"Sayers! He don't need no damn help! Get your rifle and fire on those trees!" shouted Arlen. It was the other section's turn to bound now. One man dashed forward, stopped, then moved ahead again. Another sprinted past his comrades. Another plowed steadily ahead. Each in their own steps, at their own speed, as fast as each could, all alone save for the man to the left and the man to the right. They bounded past Arlen and pushed farther and farther out into the cover-less field until something made them stop and flop down and begin to fire back at the Germans. Poof: a mortar round from the Krauts. A burst of machine gun fire. The Americans' own mortars fired back. The trees seemed no closer, but now it was Arlen's turn to lead the men up there.

And so the G.I.s moved, again and again, far out on the far left flank of the whole attack, bounding in turn, dodging rounds, hunkering down as German mortars seemed to get the range, then dashing ahead again. Chaotic, it looked, but those in it knew the tight swings and spins of this wild dance that would get them there, up there to the objective. And with providence, the next one, and the next one.

And Arlen's section came up beside Sedgwick's and fell to the earth there, right down in a little fold that was invisible from the rear. They were all out of breath and the fire was too close now. The suppressing fire from Third Squad slackened off — perhaps the other G.I.s had lost sight of them. Only the light thirty caliber machine gun stuttered its occasional support.

"Who's hit?" said Arlen. He knew they were minus two.

"Hernandez and Jones," gasped Sedgwick. "Jones got hit in the calf, I sent him back. Hernandez took shrapnel in the thigh and I brought him forward to dress the wound, but—" The big corporal shook his head. "He bled out. Must have been a tiny little piece, I could hardly see the wound. But blood everywhere."

Arlen said nothing. Ten minus two meant eight of them to get the job done. That was the only thing to think. They were safe from the enemy fire in this little depression, but the Krauts would get the range soon and plop mortar rounds down on them. They were about sixty or seventy yards from the grove of trees. That MG 42 could cut them all down in an instant if they tried to rush the last distance. But close that distance they must. Arlen gnawed on his lip.

"Hey, buddy." Paine tapped Arlen on the shoulder. "I found that smoke."

"Hot damn." Arlen took the grenade from him. "And it's Willie Pete, too, God bless." Paine said nothing and wormed away from his sergeant.

The smoke would help. He could start with that. Arlen gnawed his lip and thought the whole thing out in a few moments, each component of the attack coming quick on the heels of the other, each segment a simple follow-on that had been proven time and time again before Arlen's eyes. Then he turned to the squad and laid out the plan.

Wood inched forward, pushing the BAR over the top of the rise and dragging bandoliers of ammo with him. He looked back. Arlen nodded. Wood opened up on the trees. Two rounds, two rounds, three rounds, two rounds, three rounds. For a replacement, he was good on that trigger.

Without waiting for any signal, Sedgwick, Hirsch, and Smith began their half-bent run. Out of the little fold they scooted, making a left hook. Arlen peered over the crest, watching them go. Any moment now, any moment. Wood changed magazines.

The sharp rip echoed and Sedgwick and his men went to ground. They returned a brave fire, Kraut bullets all around them.

Arlen pulled the pin and heaved the smoke grenade. It disappeared into the grey sky and he fell down, head raised in hope. A silent white cloud billowed from thin air, drawn in every direction by tiny suns of white phosphorous.

Sedgwick and his boys heaved their own grenades.

Lord, I hope they're close enough.

Thud. Thud.

Thud.

The BAR rattled out lonely bursts.

The smoke cloud grew and drifted toward the Krauts.

And in no time at all, they were on the cloud: Arlen, Paine, Sayers, and Schaeffer coming from the right and running for the Kraut position. This time the other G.I.s were faster and they pulled ahead of Arlen and passed into the smoke.

A machine gun burst through the smoke went wide, missing Arlen and he entered the cloud.

He tripped and went down. He fell hard and almost shouted, but then he saw the body in the white haze. Schaeffer was face-down and there were two bullet holes in his upper back.

The BAR stopped. He could hear the Krauts shouting and Sedgwick saying to hold fire.

Arlen ran from motionless Schaeffer and tripped again, this time over Sayers.

"Sarge, where were you?" said Sayers, cowering on the ground.

Guttural shouts ahead. Arlen saw Paine, who stopped and looked back.

"Keep going!" Arlen shouted into the silence.

It was so silent, he could go mad.

Shoot, just shoot, dammit, kill those fuckin' Krauts, just shoot, someone, please, Lord, hear me

He grabbed Sayers by the shoulder and dragged him ahead. The replacement would not, could not stand.

"Dammit, get on your feet!"

"Sarge, you go first!"

Arlen dropped Sayers, not caring if he came. He ran in a blind charge.

Fast shots traded back and forth, the reports echoing off the trees. The grove appeared through the dissipating smoke. Paine stood firing into the trees. He was like a tree himself, stock upright, blazing through rounds, thump, thump, thump, thump, ping.

A Kraut fired — a sharp crack — and the bullet should have gone right through Paine. But the little guy reloaded and thump, thump, thump, poured fire back at the Krauts. Thump, thump, thump, thump, thump, ping.

Arlen pulled the frag grenade from his belt. "Paine! Get down!"

Paine fell backward and there was a sickening crack of wood and metal.

Arlen shouted in fright and dropped the live grenade.

But with a quick hand he caught it and with a sidearm throw snapped it into the Kraut position.

He threw himself to the ground, his helmet blocking out the light.

The explosion slapped his ears. There were screams. He heaved another grenade into the trees. Crawling to Paine, he took another one off his buddy's body.

Paine moved, squirming around.

"Buddy! Hold on!"

He heaved the third grenade over and it burst. There were no sounds for the moment. "Buddy, I'm here," said Arlen, scooting up next to him.

"I'm all right, I'm all right!" said Paine, swatting at Arlen's concerned hands.

Arlen did not understand, but he accepted Paine's dismissal. He peered over the earthen berm in front of a hastily-dug foxhole. There was a dead Kraut thrown against the back of the position. A broken tree, shattered by a mortar burst, shed light into the grove and revealed three dead Germans in the trees. Arlen carefully crossed the berm, poking his way along. The position was empty. He signaled to the rest of the squad to come up.

Returning to Paine, Arlen knelt down next to his buddy. His face was bloody, bits of wood and flecks of splintered bullet jacket peppering his cheeks and nose, but he seemed lucid. His rifle was split nearly in half — the bullet had hit the stock just as Paine had raised it to fire. Arlen forced a smile. "Good thing you had your rabbit's foot nearby, right?"

Paine was shaking. "Where were you? What fucking took you so long?"

"Buddy, I'm sorry."

"What took you so long?" he spat.

Arlen reached out to grab Paine's shoulder to steady him, but Paine pushed him away, fumbling for his cigarettes and his lighter.

Arlen felt sick. He stormed into the trees. Between the trunks, he saw the German squad was falling back. A Kraut with the MG 42 over his shoulder was straggling through the mud. He was almost to the farm house, made of sturdy brick and impregnable to all but a determined assault.

Pushing through the trees, Arlen came to the edge of the wood and as he planted his left foot, he snapped the M1 up. It wasn't far and the grey of the uniform made the front sight disappear.

Thump.

The Kraut tumbled over in a cartwheel gone awry. The machine gun stuck muzzle first into the mud, held upright for a second, and then slowly fell over.

The other Germans looked back, confused, angry, hesitating. A Kraut raised his own rifle. Arlen swung the M1: the rifle was slightly muzzle-heavy and when it reached the target, it settled firmly on it. Post, aperture, first stage, squeeze. Thump. The Kraut collapsed. Arlen picked another and fired, but missed. Two more rounds went wide and then the Krauts in the farmhouse got his range and opened up. He ducked back into the trees, reloading as he backpedaled away from the incoming rounds.

"Sarge!"

Sedgwick and the rest of the squad swept up behind him.

"Where do you want the light thirty?"

Lord, thank you for your many blessings.

"Right there. Get some fire on those bastards!"

From there, it all slipped beyond Arlen's control and he felt a sudden lightness that the fighting soul often does not know is relief. The machine gun suppressed the retreating Krauts and the platoon's mortars at last came to bear on the farmhouse. The rest of the squad joined in the fray, firing their anger away at the enemy that had nearly killed them all. The sickness still sloshed around in Arlen's stomach. He should never have told Paine to charge the machine gun nest like that. What a damn fool thing to do.

You would've gone yourself, Arlen. You would've sent anyone else, too.

But he had sent Paine.

A mortar round burst nearby: it was big, it was German.

Gnawing on his lip, Arlen inched forward to the treeline. Far out there, in the field beyond Langendorf, he saw a crew of men moving around tubes that puffed occasionally into the cold air. Desperate, they were, to be exposed like that.

Arlen passed his left arm through the rifle sling, wrapped it under, and then brought his hand back around. The sling was tight against his chest and arm, his hand firm on the stock. He knelt. Undoing the lock bar, he clicked up the rear sight and reset the lockbar. Tucking the butt into the pocket of his shoulder, he had set his head to the comb when there was a hand on his elbow.

"Where are they?"

His voice was barely audible through the din, but Paine was there all the same. Arlen pointed out the targets. He could make out the poofing vapor of the German mortar in the cold air. He set the front blade on a Kraut beside the mortar and let it settle into the rear aperture. Slack out of the first stage. Breath in, breath out. Thump.

Thump. Thump, thump. Thump. Thump.

Paine called the shots as best he could see them. Up one click, two clicks left, he said. Then Arlen had the range. Clip after clip, it was good shooting, it felt right. Paine said Arlen made one solid hit, maybe two. The Kraut mortar fire stopped. A smoke screen was drifting across the plain. The platoon's own mortars stopped and then the light thirty, too. Third Squad appeared and was on the farmhouse in a matter of seconds. Grenades in the windows drove panicked Krauts out the back. The men shot a couple down. Third Squad brought out prisoners.

Shivers came over Arlen. With numb, trembling legs, he gingerly sat down, resting against a tree trunk. Paine sat, too, and the rest of the squad collapsed one by one. Wordlessly, Paine lit cigarettes and handed one to Arlen.

They should consolidate. They should post sentries in case of a counterattack. But imperatives rang dully in Arlen's head. He would do it in a minute. Not yet. Not just yet. He drew on the Old Gold.

Second Squad trickled up to the farm single file, looking fresh, ready to take over. Lieutenant Venters led them with his carbine at the ready, as if a Kraut might pop out at any moment. Captain Reaser marched beside him. Arlen rose, some instinct of respect still flickering through his foggy head. When the two officers saw him standing up there by the grove, he touched his hand to his brow in an exhausted salute.

Reaser and Venters came up to the trees. The captain returned the salute and reached out to shake Arlen's hand. It was coated in blood and dirt and burnt powder, but the company commander did not blanch. "Sergeant, that was exemplary. Your squad, your platoon — indeed, this whole company — made the perfect infantry attack today. It was textbook." Reaser smiled warmly.

Arlen stared vacantly into the captain's eyes and nodded. This man, their commander, knew the hardships they did. He lived them as much as any buck private. He saw men die, saw them shredded by artillery, holed by bullets. There were bars on his shoulder, but he was a dogface, too. Yet, at the end of the day, what, and not who, was the measure.

Venters grinned. "Sergeant, assemble your squad." He pointed with a swagger. "You'll be in reserve, but we need to push out to those orchards and neutralize the threat to the battalion's flank." The looie shook Arlen's hand.

"I'll see to your casualties, Sergeant."

Venters and Reaser walked off with their command sections in tow. Arlen quivered a little, still not steady on his feet. Paine appeared beside him, lit another cigarette, and drew on it. He said dully, "In the textbook, they don't have casualties."

Arlen sniffled and spat on the ground. "Naw, they do. Reckon, though, they ain't got names."

XV

"Fuckin' First Battalion. Goddamn pigs, all of them."

William Buford Paine's voice rang from the cellar of the house beside the truck. He was a fast one. The convoy had hardly stopped and no order dismount their trucks had come. But he was already rooting around for a place to stay, just in case. Peering around the corner of the tarpaulin, Arlen looked up the street. It looked like a stop for sure. Arlen jumped off the tail of the deuce-and-a-half. For once, it was cobblestones and not ankle-deep mud. Before they could ask, Arlen told the men, "Y'all go on ahead and find yourself a billet." He peered up the length of the convoy. "Before Lieutenant Venters sees you," he added.

"Won't he be mad?" said Private Wood.

"You just let me worry about that. Y'all go on and burrow in like a tick."

Poking his head into the cellar, Arlen called out, "Buddy? You in there?"

"Fuckin' First Battalion . . ." muttered Paine.

Arlen descended into the stone room. It was mighty large and looked like a decent place for a billet, if a little chilly. "And what'd those boys ever do to you?"

"Look at this place. It's a mess."

Arlen's eyes had not quite adjusted to the darkness. "Looks fine to me."

Paine grumbled over in a dark corner.

"Buddy, if you want, we can take one of the upper floors."

Paine turned around. His scowl was sinister in the shadows of the cellar. "Are you crazy? The Krauts will know we're here."

"Oh, I reckon they already do. You know, there's a family up there. But we can run 'em out."

"Walking around up there, the Krauts would see me and call in arty on the house."

"We ain't close enough to the front for that."

"Then they'll shoot me through the window when I go to the crapper."

Arlen repressed a sigh. Sometimes his words just did not get through. "Reckon you want me down here, too."

"I'm not letting you get shot either," muttered Paine.

Arlen let him be. He shucked his musette bag and rifle and went out onto the street. The regiment had liberated this town nearly two months ago. Now it was a safe spot for the men to rest and relax. For weeks since their perfect infantry attack, the G.I.s had been out there on that awful plain of mud. They had assaulted and patrolled; they were shelled and sniped at; they struggled through quagmires and across swollen streams; they hauled their dead and wounded back the same way. The Krauts hid in the towns and the land around them; the G.I.s killed them amongst the bricks and in the mud. Now that awful offensive was behind them and they could get a little peace. A little was all they needed, a G.I. could make it go quite far. It was a week until Christmas. They would not celebrate in Berlin. But that was all right with Arlen. If he could just go down to the little church where the Germans sang carols, that was just as good. Just let there be peace in Kolscheid, even if not on earth. Then they could send him out again.

The rest of the squad was tucking themselves nicely into the adjoining houses. Some of the other squads had not even dismounted their trucks, still waiting for the order. Poor suckers, they would be left with whatever billets the officers didn't snap up. Arlen noticed a stack of empty C ration boxes outside the cellar door. He quickly snatched them and went back down into the cellar. Making a neat pile of cardboard cartons in the middle of the floor, Arlen lit them and began an important ritual. Canteen, cup, and instant coffee appeared from his musette bag. Quickly, he made a strong mix.

A tin can scattered across the floor, tinging on the stones.

"Daddy, you want some coffee?"

Paine did not reply. He scuffled across the cellar, nudging empty C ration cans with his toe.

"Get your cup, I'll make you some."

Paine shuffled over to his kit. He pulled out his blanket and wrapped it around him. With a grunt, he continued scuffling back and forth. The fire was smoldering. Arlen blew gently on the embers and the cartons finally caught and put up a strong flame. Arlen held his canteen cup of water over the fire and waited for it to heat. His dry, cracked hands prickled at the warmth of the fire. Paine kept making his circles, around and around the cellar, grumbling under his breath. He kicked a can again, sending it scattering into Arlen's little fire.

"Dammit, you quit that right now."

"Quit what?"

"All of it. The damn pacin' most of all. You keep that up, you'll wear a hole all the way to China."

Paine scowled. "Why are you in such a good mood today?"

155

"You ain't exactly a ray of sunshine yourself." Arlen looked back to his coffee. It was beginning to steam lightly.

Paine swore indistinctly, and he lashed out, trying to throw something from his hand against the wall. But his arm got caught in the blanket and the object disappeared into the folds, leaving Paine searching for it, swearing under his breath.

"What are you so damned angry about?"

"What do you think, Arlen? Those fuckin' First Battalion pigs left all these cans and cigarette butts everywhere."

He was still on about that. "Didn't know you cared so much," said Arlen.

"Well, I do."

"Ain't so sure we left our positions much cleaner when we left for Kerkrade."

What a place, Kerkrade. A few weeks back, the whole battalion had retired to the old monastery there for a couple days. It was their first real rest in months. The ancient halls were so ornate that Arlen could not believe men had the patience to carve stone like that. He would have admired the place for hours, but the sound of falling water snatched him away from his gaping. There were showers. Arlen had hung limply under the hot and endless stream like a flag in a summer rain. He had emerged flush, alert, and weak, and the clean towel had made his skin crawl. They ate bowl after bowl of stew and whole loaves of thick bread on captured German china. Others had played cards and written letters, their voices echoing up and down the halls of the college, but Arlen had just slept and slept and slept until he awakened the next day groggy and heavy-limbed. He could laugh and smile and snarl in anger again. Others had recovered, too: Paine had gotten his humor back, for a little while. That was what clean was. Was, was, was — things were always past tense for Arlen. He could remember after he forgot, and he remembered what others forgot. But these days it was harder and harder to think back, as if there was some limit, some bend in the earth where memory stopped. It seemed closer and closer behind him every day.

Arlen coughed, waving his hand in front of his face. The waxy smoke of burning cardboard was beginning to hang against the ceiling like a fog. He dipped his pinkie in the coffee. Just another few minutes. He stirred the dark liquid with his bayonet blade.

"Did you have to build that in here, Arlen?"

"You want me to go build it in the street?"

"The damn smoke is getting my eyes."

"I ain't got no heatin' tabs." Hopefully the looie would get them more. They needed more of everything. The Army could never seem to get them enough or on time. Arlen's toes prickled on pinpoints most of the time, for his

156

socks were wearing thin and they had received no winter boots. He had half a mind to write his mother asking for socks, for he had not received any from her. It wouldn't be much use to write her now, though. Once she received the letter, knitted a pair, and posted it, it would be too late. And she surely couldn't go out and buy a pair. Things were very tight for the family. He knew that from the last letter she wrote — the letters were always from Legenia, never from Wade, who proclaimed many a time he was no good with a pen. Arlen had already sent home most of his pay. He would not ask for anything more from his parents.

What about Rebecca and Elizabeth? Or Ruth? Maybe they could send a pair.

If only he knew their addresses. He could not remember.

Was there anyone else? Arlen felt there was, but he could not picture who it might be. It was so hard to imagine these days. Whatever it was, he had to see it in front of him or else it remained beyond that creeping horizon that shadowed his memories.

The carton fire was dying out. Arlen fetched more cardboard and returned to the cellar. He piled up the cardboard again and set fire to it again with his cigarette lighter. The flames let off black, waxy smoke again and he set his canteen cup over the fire to let it warm back up. Paine came scuttling over. His arms poked out from the swaddled-up blanket and he put his bare hands over the fire, pushing Arlen's cup out of the way.

"Buddy, you'd better cut that out."

"I'm cold."

Arlen's face flushed in anger. He was sick and tired of Paine's griping. He pushed Paine's hands out of the way with the hot cup. "Go on, now, get out of the way. Let me finish. You can have it after I'm done."

"Goddamn you, Arlen, you are so greedy." Paine stomped off to the corner and in between a hiss and a growl, said, "Can't you see how cold I am? Some fucking friend you are."

"You're one to talk!" snapped Arlen. "How about you just leave me be for once? How 'bout you quit doin' whatever you want and then come whinin' to me when things ain't like you like 'em?"

Over in the corner, Paine sat in a lump, his eyes boring a dull hole through some distant thickness. His lips twitched every now and then, but there was no audible mutter.

Lord, what do I do with him?

Arlen dipped his pinkie in the coffee again. It was almost warm enough. Arlen tasted the coffee. Another minute and Paine could come warm his hands.

"Sergeant?"

The voice boomed like an 88 in the cellar. Arlen jumped to his feet. "Yessir?"

Lieutenant Venters was hunched over in the low cellar door. "Get your ass out here," he said.

"Yessir." Arlen grabbed his gear and was out of the cellar in two leaps.

Lieutenant Venters' armor-piercing stare did not waver from Arlen as he spoke. "I had to get your squad out of these houses myself, Sergeant, because you were nowhere to be found."

"Yessir, I'm sorry, sir."

"No one told you to secure billets."

"No, sir, but I figured—"

The convoy cranked up one by one. Arlen's mouth hung open.

"Mount up, Sergeant."

Arlen hesitated for a moment, then disappeared into the cellar. The shelter was unnecessary, and Venter's wrath had been expended, short and sharp like the MG 42. Arlen emerged with Paine beside him. The blanket trailed behind his buddy and Arlen carried his gear.

"Lieutenant, I—" said Arlen.

"Sergeant, the Krauts have broken through. Launched an attack last night."

Like a knife stropped on old denim, Arlen's fear came sharp quickly, ready to cut the unknown small enough to handle. "Where'd they break through? Don't tell me Inden." Lord, anywhere but Inden, don't send us back there.

"To the south, Sergeant. Down in Belgium."

"Ain't there someone else they can send? I mean, why pull us off the line just to send us back out again? We're mighty worn out."

Venters was looking at his watch and not listening.

"Sir, we do all the damn fightin' in the Army, seems like. Do they have to send us? They sendin' the battalion? The regiment?"

The lieutenant raised his eyes to Arlen's. "They're sending the whole division, Sergeant. And many others."

"It's that big, sir?"

"The biggest yet."

Arlen gnawed on his lip.

"Sergeant, you're right. We've fought more and fought harder than any other division in the Army. We all need a rest. And these Krauts know that. They think they've caught us with our pants down. Well, we will show them."

"Sir—"

"They've left their defenses, Sergeant. All they have done is give us a better chance to kill them in the open." Venters grinned pearl-white. "And this platoon will kill more Krauts than any other in the division."

Arlen looked away from the maw of the gleeful shark. Paine was trying to pull the dirty blanket over his skinny shoulders with a single shivering hand.

"Sir—"

"Mount up."

Wordlessly, Arlen boosted Paine into the back of the truck and his buddy disappeared under the dark of the tarpaulin with the rest of the squad. Arlen threw in their gear and climbed in himself. The convoy rumbled into motion and as the truck pulled away, Venters leapt into the back. He hung from the truck, peering around the side at the passing town. His grin still shone brilliantly against the drab houses and grey sky. His thoughts were not with his soldiers. They were already in the fight ahead of them.

Don't matter to the looie what we can give. He'll get it from us.

Ask and you shall receive.

Arlen felt a finger on his thigh. Paine was feeling his pants leg. Arlen saw that it was stained. He must have dropped his cup without knowing it when he ran from the cellar. Paine wiped his finger across the brown mark and sniffed his finger. "At least it's coffee this time."

This time, at least this time.

A frigid gust of wind lifted the rear tarpaulin and the taped-up headlights of the following truck peeked in. The tiny beam cut across the hunched-over men like a miner's lamp through a crowded pit. The occasional ember of a cigarette traced the orbit of their heads bobbing on a turbulent tide of no known ebb or flow. Another gust came rushing in under the tarpaulin and chilled them all to the bone. The men shuffled around on the wooden benches, trying to find relief. Their rear ends were asleep and their toes were numb in their leather boots. After dusk had fallen for the second time on this journey, they all stopped asking when they would get there. The roads were choked with tanks and jeeps and trucks and refugees fleeing west, but these elicited no response from them except for the occasional "You got any smokes?" Yet another gust bellowed the tarpaulin and Arlen shivered. He tucked his head further into his thin jacket until his chin grafted itself to his Adam's apple.

The engine revved and the transmission yawned as the clutch searched for the gear. It engaged with a jerk, yanking everyone onto each other. The truck rolled steadily along at a faster pace. But as soon as the G.I.s settled back onto the benches, the truck slammed to a stop. The G.I.s grabbed onto each other and cursed. The engine coughed to a stop, then instantly ground to life again. The clutch caught and they crawled forward again in an agonizingly low gear. The truck swayed and shifted gears again. Arlen closed his eyes, feeling the truck beginning to gain speed. His heart jumped and his eyes opened to the dark as the truck banged to a stop again. The driver caught the lowest gear this time, and they sat idling for almost a minute before once again the wheels began to turn and they bobbed over the obstruction.

"Don't they know how to build a damn road in this country?"

Which country was that? Arlen peered through the gap in the tarpaulin. A glimpse revealed dark firs and fields dusted in white. Then the cold wind slapped his face and even his eyeballs went numb. He jerked his head back.

The convoy pounded along at five miles per hour at best. The cigarettes were all gone and it was completely dark now. The truck downshifted again and the shaking and jolting stopped. Smooth paved road flowed under the tires and every man felt the vibrations filter out through their fingers and toes. Relieved, a few fell asleep. The convoy climbed in elevation. Wind whipped stronger and stronger up the ridge as they ascended. Arlen tied the tarpaulin shut tighter against the wind. The miles, taken at no great speed, wore on and on. Arlen laid his head down on his knees and closed his eyes. He dozed off, his mind dropping off into a pool of blankness. He lay like that for some time before hearing the rush of water; he even smelled it. The convoy slowed, stopped, and waited. Someone outside was walking up and down, shouting to the drivers, who shouted back argumentatively. The trucks started again at a creeping pace.

And suddenly the engines reverberated on stone. Arlen opened the tarpaulin and saw houses of brick and carefully fitted stone. There was a sign: *Malmedy.* There were no lights in the town, but the streets seemed alive: fair-haired young girls and older women, a grandfather, a policeman waving the convoy on in a habitual yet unnecessary gesture, even a couple of young kids, all watching from street corners and doorways, revealed by the slight gleam of the truck lights. The convoy passed through the center of the town. The cobbled streets changed to paved road and the wind whipped up again. Nothing but darkness and, barely audible over the rumble of the trucks, the rattle of tree branches tossing against each other in a violent gust.

Arlen didn't look up when the trucks stopped again. He just sat, nose tucked beneath his buttoned-up collar, trying to wiggle each toe as much as possible. There was a bang of a falling tailgate, then another, and another. Only then did he look up, the cold nipping down onto his neck before he had a chance to adjust the collar again. The soldiers in the squad began raising their heads. Shouted orders and clamoring voices began to fill the sharp air.

"Well, reckon we're here."

The G.I.s jumped off the truck, wincing as they landed on cramped calves and stiff knees. "Y'all hold down the fort," said Arlen, and he immediately went in search of the lieutenant. Venters found him first. "Give me a minute to find out where we are headed, Sergeant. Smoke 'em if you got 'em."

"You got 'em, sir?"

The platoon leader tossed him a pack of Kools. Arlen went back to the truck, and passed out the cigarettes. The men took them reluctantly.

"Where are we, Sarge?" said another.

"I heard Belgium."

"Belgium? Why Belgium?"

Arlen did not answer. He tried to smoke his Kool, but it really was too much for a cold night.

"Sarge, are we retreating?"

"Yeah, I heard everyone's on the run."

"Ain't nobody on the run," said Arlen. "They're sendin' us to finish these Krauts off."

"Yeah, but what if our old positions got hit after we left? What if the Krauts are attacking all over?"

Arlen shook his head in the dark. He didn't want to listen to all this.

"The Krauts are out there in American uniforms. They dress up like G.I.s, I heard."

"Shit, so they can sneak past our outposts?"

"Yeah, and ambush us from behind."

"Those sneaky bastards."

The rumors went on and on. Nothing stood between the Krauts and the Channel, they were going all the way to Dunkirk, just like in 1940. Hitler himself was at the head of the lead panzer divisions and the SS had orders to take no prisoners. General Eisenhower was back in Washington and Field Marshal Montgomery would take over the defense of the Allied line. The last one angored Arlen. "All right, y'all can cut that out. I ain't gonna hear nothin' 'bout us fightin' for fuckin' Monty."

"But what if it's true, Sarge?"

"Shut up, all y'all," said Arlen.

Venters finally returned. "Captain Reaser says this is the end of the line for the whole battalion. Get your bedrolls out of the trucks, we've got to march to our positions."

"Tonight? In the dark?" said Arlen.

"The Krauts are out there, close by. We've got to get in a strong position and quickly. There might even be a fight tonight."

The men took the news laconically. They retied their boots, checked their equipment, and loaded their rifles. Hefting their bedrolls, they formed up in a squad column, waiting. One by one, the platoons moved out, each in a different direction, each to be on its own. Venters appeared again. He looked harried and Arlen felt a little knot twist up in his stomach. "Form up, Sergeant. First Squad's in the lead. Have your scouts fall in with Sergeant Proctor."

161

The scouts set out with Venters and Proctor, the platoon guide, and the rest of First Squad followed, each man of the remaining nine pausing until the soldier ahead was five paces ahead. Before them, an open field of snow sloped sharply upwards toward a crest covered with firs. The dim truck lights were gone and with snow-threatening clouds covering the sliver of moon, only the barest silhouette of the man ahead gave any indication of direction. The scouts, moving quickly and confidently, disappeared, and Arlen had to search for their boot prints to find his way. The wind blew stronger and stronger and their steps grew slower and slower. The snow soaked right through their leather boots. Arlen's feet went numb. Nearing the treeline, Arlen stopped and made a count of his followers as they trickled up to him. All eight. Without a word, he set off again, following the boot prints into the dark forest at the top of the ridge.

The firs were oppressively close, but they broke the wind, at least. Arlen still could not see Sergeant Proctor and the scouts, but he heard snatches of their voices in between the long gusts whistling through the trees. *We could fumble about here all night and never find our way out.* He stopped and looked for the rest of the squad. There was movement out there, darkness moving on darkness, visible only in the periphery. There was a loud clank and he heard someone swear.

"Y'all all right?" he said.

"Calloway ran into a tree," said a voice. It sounded like Hazlett, a retread like Calloway. His voice was tense; he had never done this before. Neither had Young, the replacement. Three new men: the latter green, the other two stripped away from their cushy jobs and sent up to the line. Was the Army that desperate? Was the whole enterprise stretched that thin, just like the line here in Belgium had been?

Good Lord, what if we've gone as far as we were ever going to?

He shivered. The firs rattled as a gust ran up the length of the ridge.

I want out of these trees.

Arlen left the private behind. His steps fell heavier and faster. He could not see the scouts. He lost sight of their trail through the trees and all he could do was fumble forward.

Twigs cracked like rifles underfoot.

The Krauts are out there, close by.

Venters repeated himself in his head. He could not shake the looie's words. The resident tactician had rented a room for good.

They were on the wrong side of the slope. They had to get up to the crest. It was safer up there.

Arlen thrashed ahead, kicking through any logs and limbs that stood in his way. Up and up he went, ducking and weaving between branches. He saw nothing except black forest. He had a vague sense of going uphill and so he kept on, tripping and crawling through the trees. Bashing his knee on a stump, Arlen stopped, holding in his swearing. He stayed stock still. The forest was dark and swaying, full of movement and not a sign of life. Where were the scouts? How did they move so quickly?

He dared not look back, but for what reason, he did not know.

Up the slope. Get up that damn slope.

Twigs cracked and snapped underfoot. The wind stroked the trees and the boughs overhead hissed.

Arlen stepped around a big fir and he felt that he was over the crest, headed down the reverse slope. He let out a long breath. If he met any Krauts in the woods, he was in the uphill position. At least that was to his favor.

Another hundred yards passed under his numb feet before he saw the tree line of the far side of the woods. There were figures squatting just inside the tree line. Arlen's steps slowed, instinctively, not willing to trust his first assumption. He unslung his rifle and lightened each step so he could listen. He heard nothing distinct — they all spoke in hushed tones.

Arlen stopped, catching his breath and composing himself. He waited in the dark until he heard movement behind him. At last able to look back, he held his hand straight up in a signal to halt, hoping that the squad would see it. Once the snapping behind him stopped, he cautiously approached the dark figures.

Venters was waiting with Proctor and the scouts. The lieutenant rubbed his hands together frantically to keep warm. "Sergeant, this is as far as we go tonight."

"We diggin' in here?"

"That's right, Sergeant. First Squad will be here on the right, Second Squad in the center, and Third Squad out there on the left."

"No reserve?"

"We're spread thin, but we have to cover as much ground as possible." Venters made a gesture in the dark. "There's a crossroads down there, Sergeant, and I want your squad to cover it and the road running out of it toward our position. Understood?"

"Yessir."

"Good."

"Lieutenant?"

"Sergeant?"

"We stayin' here long?"

"Things may change in the morning. But for tonight, prepare like we're going to stay."

"Yessir."

163

Arlen passed the word along to his men. Close to the edge of the forest, they spread out, staggering themselves in a rough arc along the treeline. Soon the sound of chopping on wood and the clank of entrenching tools drowned out even the wind. Arlen scraped away a thick layer of twigs and needles to get to the hard ground. He slammed the entrenching tool against the dirt, over and over, but he only knocked loose a few frozen clumps of earth.

Arlen stopped his rhythmic swinging as Paine sat down slowly next to him, settling as though a great weight bore on his shoulders, his arms dropping as though he was about to faint. "What is it, buddy?"

"Fuckin' lost my musette bag." Paine's voice was flat, drained of all feeling.

Arlen's face fell. "Where'd you put it?"

"I don't know."

"Don't know?"

"It's next to the tree."

Arlen looked back into the hopeless forest. He laughed. That short chuckle led to another, and one more, until he could say, "Oh, I know which one you mean. The tall one, right?"

Paine said nothing. Arlen saw his face disappear into the dark — perhaps he was looking down at the ground. Arlen rested on his knees for a minute, watching his closest friend. Then he went back to digging. *I'll finish it.*

He got as deep as he could go in the frozen ground, just deep enough. He set the entrenching tool aside, feeling the little bit of sweat he had worked up beginning to grow cold already. But the chill that would stay with him all night was not on Arlen's mind. He thought about Paine. Arlen scooted over to him. "Hey, buddy, you get down there in the hole. Just go on to bed. And don't you worry 'bout sentry. I'll stand guard all night."

"I'm cold. Really cold."

"Here, take my blanket. We'll find yours in the morning."

"Okay." Paine slid numbly down into the foxhole, taking the blanket. Again his eyes bored into the distant nothing, and yet they were the only part of Paine which seemed to hold onto life. The rest of his thin body and his grimy, gaunt face was beating a retreat. Arlen pulled the blanket up around Paine's neck and tucked it behind his shoulders. Paine hardly moved a muscle himself.

The boy needs to go home. Why won't they pull him off the line?

Lord, what do I do with him?

Arlen shivered and jabbed his hands under his armpits. He needed to check the perimeter. Slinging his M1, he made a slow clockwise trip around his patch of the forest. He found each of his men by their raspy breathing and coughs. Everyone was dug in good and deep. They would add logs to their foxholes tomorrow morning. The BAR, set at the apex of the position, was in good hands with Wood, and Sayers already had the spare magazines laid out. Everything looked safe as could be, way out here, the flanks in the air, the Germans out there in the snow and trees, headed who knew where.

After a few wrong turns, Arlen found the foxhole again. Paine was curled up in the bottom and Arlen slid in slowly so as not to wake him. He rested the M1 on the hump of earth he'd built up in front of the hole and settled down to wait.

His heart leapt when Paine spoke.

"Arlen, why me?"

Paine's eyes were fully open, though he lay curled up.

"What's that, buddy?"

"Why haven't I been hit?"

Arlen tried to answer as quickly as he could. "'Cause you've got me around, remember? Your lucky rabbit's foot?"

The platitude had no effect on target. "You weren't there at Mortain, and I didn't get hit there. Why?"

"Buddy, you ain't gonna be hit, all right? Ain't yours to worry 'bout. You know what to do. You just go with your gut and don't get careless and you'll be fine."

"No," said Paine, voice dull and hollow, "my number's up. Everyone else got theirs. You and I are the only stateside guys left. And you got wounded. You got your number. It wasn't the million dollar one, but you punched that ticket. You don't have to worry. But me . . ."

Paine stopped and was quiet for so long that Arlen's stomach began rising into his throat. The boy was so still.

Oh, Lord, don't take him from me now. Not like this, not out here.

His buddy spoke again, his voice just as empty as before. "I've gone so long — so many close calls — not even a scratch. Never even opened my aid kit." He went quiet again for a while. Then, thinly, he said, "When it comes, it'll be the real McCoy. The big one. It's coming soon. I can feel it."

And Paine went silent. His time had come, the well had run dry. There was no filling it back up again. Pain and fatigue had crystallized him into this man he was now — not malleable, adaptable, renewable, but hard, frozen, transparent to all the world's brutality. And the only remaining change in his nature was the right tap with the right force in the right place.

Arlen settled into the foxhole, his rifle in his lap and his back against the foxhole side, his bones becoming one with the frozen earth. Paine began to snore — at least he could sleep. At least he did not have to lay here knowing that there was no relief for him, that there was no returning to safety.

Lord, what can I do for him?

God spoke, but it was not the voice in the flash of light on high. The

165

inevitability of the thing to do was the answer.

But I'm already standin' beside him, Lord, don't you see?

And maybe he don't have to, but I got to fight. Even if he ain't there.

Lord, you didn't even give him a chance. You gave me a second chance, dammit, give him one, too.

Arlen wrapped his arms tighter around him and dug his chin into his collar. He looked at Paine. A thin curl of breath whistled between the young soldier's teeth.

What can I do?

Arlen stayed awake beside him all night.

XVI

"Sergeant, assemble your squad."

The old command, once again. How many times more must he hear it? Arlen just could not stand it anymore.

Nonetheless, duty, the prime mover of his breed, sat him up and cast off his blanket. He rolled it up quickly and shook his buddy awake. "Time to go." His hands and feet cold, Arlen slipped out into the dark, looking for foxholes. He woke each man in the squad personally. Returning to his foxhole, Arlen found Paine sitting there in the bottom. His eyes were fixed far off. His breath curled from his mouth shoved into his collar.

"Buddy, come on up out of there. Come on, get on your feet."

Paine did not answer. He was bundled up, layer upon layer, and draped in a white camouflage cape, improvised from a civilian's bedsheet. And Arlen had made sure Paine had been the first in the squad to get the new triple-layer booties that fit under his overshoes. He could not be cold. But his hands that rested on his rifle trembled over and over, playing a slow and silent crescendo. So this is how he was today. Arlen never knew what it would be. He had been all right the past day or two.

"Assemble your squad, Sergeant."

Arlen stepped over to Paine. "Buddy, come on, you've got to fall in."

Paine looked down at his rifle and tried to grab hold of it. His trembling fingers slipped a few times before he managed to get a hold, and he hefted it up with great effort. Slinging the rifle over his shoulder, he stood up. Arlen stretched out his hand. Paine reached out his own, grabbed on as tight as he could, and Arlen felt his own strong forearm wobbling in time with Paine's. The private went to step out of the foxhole and Arlen pulled to give him momentum. And he pulled more and more, until finally he had to use his whole strength to drag Paine out of the hole and into the snow. Arlen made sure Paine's bedroll was rolled up neatly and set next to his own, and then set to checking all of Paine's equipment. His buddy just stood there, face blank, silent, staring away.

Ain't no damn reason for him to be out here 'cept that the looie won't send him back. The hell we don't have anyone to take his place, he can't fight now anyway.

"Sergeant, fall in with your squad," snapped Venters as he trudged past. The platoon was falling into column.

"Buddy, come on." Arlen pushed Paine on the shoulder, as gently as he could, and guided him to his spot in the squad, right in the middle. Arlen then made a quick check of each soldier's weapon before taking his own spot at the front of the squad. The lieutenant stood waiting. "Are you finished, Sergeant?"

"Yessir."

Venters turned to his runner. "Let the captain know we're ready." The runner disappeared off into the twilight and the platoon stood, waiting. A stiff wind kicked up again, whipping snow off of the ground and driving it against them. Arlen tucked his face down under his collar the best he could.

The dark of morning was passing away and so too was its cover for the assembly. The runners and the officers moved about, faint dark shapes against the dim snow, getting the last elements in place. The battalion would go on the attack today. It seemed like forever since they had attacked. Arlen was nearly thankful for an attack, anything to break the monotony of cold rations, cold foxholes, cold winds, cold sentry. Nearly so: he still knew these were better than lying in the cold ground. This cold, awful foreign ground. What price would the Germans try to make them pay for taking it? Or even not taking it? He tried not to care for now. It was only tonight that they would know who did the paying and the taking. For now, he tried to think only of how their weapons might jam, of keeping the men camouflaged in white, of making sure no one fell out with frostbitten feet. He tried not to think all the way to the end.

The orders came back and the G.I.s moved in a rough column across the open, snowy fields. Off to their left, tanks roared and clanked, giving away the advance before it had hardly begun. The going was slow. Every G.I. had to break through the deep snow to set his foot and then extract it again to take another step. As they struggled forward toward their objective, the tall, unseen Hill 451, the sun gradually came up, lighting up the world from somewhere behind gray clouds, and the white-painted Sherman tanks took their place ahead of the columns. Still, the platoons were terribly exposed in the open fields. There was little choice. There were Krauts in the trees and Krauts in every town. There was nowhere for the G.I.s but out in the open. Arlen looked back. The squad, clad in makeshift white capes, struggling ahead with every step. Paine was going very slowly and Arlen wanted to go back and drag him along. But he forced himself to look ahead, looking for that big hill they were going up today.

The gentle slope of snow became gradually steeper until it was clear this was the base of the hill. The advance was slow, so slow it hardly seemed like an attack at all. A tank was nearly stuck, a huge mound of snow built up in the front of its hull. The tank commander leaned out of the top hatch, scowling at the slow progress. "Hey, you want us to give you a push?" shouted a wiseass.

On the flank, a machine gun fired a single burst. Arlen's head whipped around. Another burst of fire and rounds snapped over their heads. "Where's it comin' from?" he shouted out.

"House, up there," said Wood.

Arlen saw several clustered near each other. "Which one?"

"Second one, I think."

The squad went to ground as one of the tanks turned its attention on the offending house. A round burst against the house, but the high explosive barely broke the stout stone walls. Enemy fire began again, stronger this time, searching out the dogfaces around the tanks. The tank fired twice more into the house into the offending house and it was finally silent. Third Squad moved in to mop up as the rest of the company moved ahead up the slope.

Venters moved quickly between the squads, bellowing, "Don't worry about the flanks. We've got to take the top of this ridge."

"Tell that to the tanks," Arlen growled. But the lieutenant did not hear him. The steel fortresses were hardly crawling now, for the snow was too deep. The dogfaces pushed past the stalled Shermans, secretly hoping the brutes would miraculously find some stronger gear and batter their way through the drifts to the top of this steepening ridge.

Arlen looked back. Paine was there — he stumbled along, unscathed, face still blank. "Buddy, you all right?" he called out.

Paine muttered.

"What did you say?"

Paine made no recognition of him.

"Sergeant! Keep your men moving," shouted Venters, storming through the middle of the struggling platoon, picking up and pushing stragglers to their feet.

"Lieutenant, we really pushin' up there without the tanks?" said Arlen, gesturing up the hill.

"You worry about your squad. I'll worry about the tanks." The lieutenant stomped past Arlen, urging the men on and up toward the unseen objective.

Arlen just stood there in the snow. He just couldn't take another order. He knew what was coming, just as soon as they got beyond the protection of the tanks. He was no fool.

I have half a mind just to stand here.

Half a mind, but only half by a mile. For Sayers and Wood, almost inseparable by now, passed by him. Sedgwick, Calloway, Young, Hazlett,

169

Hirsch, and Jones slowly swept by on both sides. And there was Paine, struggling up the slope behind them. They broke trail through the snow without any of Arlen's urging. They were going up because they knew Arlen would, too. He would be there like he always had.

He put his right foot forward. His left went forward easy enough. Then the right again. And soon he was with the others, just a part of another advance.

The storm broke from the right this time. Automatic weapons from the woods cut into the company. Mortars fired from the high ground and the rounds blew spumes of dark earth across the snow. Far behind, a tank or two fired to suppress, but their rounds did not stop the barrage from the forest.

Arlen cursed Venters under his breath. If he could not get the tanks up here, couldn't the looie at least get them artillery support? Arlen turned to call out and saw Venters, down the slope, flailing his arms frantically. What was he trying to signal? Venters ducked as a burst of fire went over his head. When he popped back up, he cradled a body which was staining the snow red. The lieutenant called out fruitlessly into the din.

Arlen's legs started to give out from under him. Reaching out, he caught himself with the rifle butt.

Get up, you bastard, get up.

He pushed on the rifle with all his strength. Sweat poured down the back of his neck. He finally managed to stand and, finding his place on his wobbly feet, Arlen surveyed his squad and his platoon as bullets snapped close by. The G.I.s moved cautiously, pulled up the slope by the struggling example of their leaders but only barely. Clods of dirt and snow from a mortar burst fell around him.

What'll I do?

It was there, somewhere inside — he'd found it a thousand times before, in a thousand decisions of the battered but competent infantryman. But this time there was nothing, no answers, not even hints. Every old soldier finds that one day, that the impenetrable thickness of his worn-out head is the true fog of war.

His gaze wobbled around. A few G.I.s were returning ragged fire. Second Squad was inching its way forward. Wood was reloading the BAR.

Fire. Maneuver. Yes, those, the old standbys. *Fire and maneuver.*

Where? The German positions on the flanks were well concealed — there was nothing to fire on. The whole company was caught in a huge open draw, with high ground on the right, the left, and the heights before them, over another crest. There was nowhere to maneuver.

Arlen looked back again. Venters was going back down the slope, carrying the limp body with him. Even the lieutenant had one of his men he cared for more than anything else.

But that did not stop Arlen's blood from boiling. *That sonuvabitch, just leavin' us like that.*

Who was in charge? The platoon sergeant, but where was Sergeant Gates? Was he the one hit? But Arlen did not need answers to know.

I have to lead them up this damn hill.

Not just his squad, but the platoon.

I can fight, Lord, I can fight to get home, if that's what you want. But I can't lead this platoon up this hill.

But where else was home? Only forward, up the hill, up there with his men.

I'll die up there and the rest of 'em with me.

But there was only one thing he could do, and it was not a terrible thing. Arlen got to his feet. He heard a *plonk* behind him. He looked up overhead and caught the tiny speck of an outgoing mortar against the evenly gray sky. His gaze followed it down toward the ground ahead and there came a flash. Glowing trails of phosphorous arced out and burned bright against the snow and a cloud of smoke grew on the high ground on the left. *Plonk.* Another smoke round burst just beyond the first one. One more *plonk* and a third smoke round landed. The whole of the crest of the high ground was covered with smoke.

Arlen knew it was time to go: he roused his men, Paine, Wood, Sayers, Smith, Calloway, Young, Hazlett, Hirsch and Jones. Where was Corporal Sedgwick? Hit, came the word, a bullet through the side of his face. The aid man had to hold the corporal's jaw on with a fistful of gauze until the stretcher bearers arrived. So it was: Arlen did not ask if Sedgwick would make it, he knew all too well. He put the corporal behind him and sent the scouts out ahead and followed close behind. The wind came from behind them now, very gently, and pushed the smoke before them. With the wind at their backs, it felt a little easier to go up that hill, to be the example for the whole platoon. And so they were. One hundred, two hundred yards disappeared under their feet. Soon Second Squad was with them, just behind and on the right. The smoke dissipated gradually and the way ahead became clear: beyond a few undulating fields were the forested heights of Hill 541. Every man was exhausted — there was no rushing now. Each G.I. plodded ahead, one foot in front of the other. Small arms fire came from here and there — a farmhouse, a patch of woods. They threw assaulting fire back at it — quick rifle shots, bursts from the BAR, a rifle grenade — and kept on, stopping for nothing.

"Sarge!" Arlen looked back. Sayers was waving to him and pointing down to a G.I. squatting in the snow. *Shit.* Gnawing his lip, Arlen turned around and trudged back to the two soldiers. He was so tired. His legs twitched and burned and his sweat was freezing under his uniform. He stopped and knelt next to Paine. "What is it, buddy?" he said flatly. "You hit?"

"Arlen. Arlen."

"Buddy, I'm right here."

"Arlen."

"Paine. William Buford Paine, it's me. I'm here."

Paine blinked and looked into Arlen's eyes. "Arlen."

"What is it?"

"I told him we have to keep going," said Sayers. "But he wouldn't move."

"We can't stay here," said Arlen, taking Paine by the shoulder. A bullet snapped near them.

"Leave me."

Arlen's mouth went dry. "You can't stay here, buddy, you've got to come, too. Come on, now, let's go." Arlen grabbed a hold of Paine and tugged on him, but all the strength was gone from Arlen's arms and Paine was dead weight. Arlen felt his buddy's body convulsing, shaking uncontrollably from his torso out through his shoulders and arms. "Help me," said Arlen to Sayers. They hefted Paine up and Arlen threw Paine's arm over his shoulder, supporting the little guy's weight across his own shoulder. "Get up there with the rest of 'em," said Arlen to Sayers. "Don't let Wood fall behind, I want that BAR at the front." Sayers nodded and moved off. With steady steps, Arlen and Paine followed, the sergeant bent painfully over to keep his short friend's arm over his own shoulders. He knew he could not set Paine down for a moment lest they not get him up again.

The ground had flattened out and the platoon covered the next few hundred yards with less trouble. The scouts traded shots with snipers hidden in the woods, killing one and driving another out of the trees and up to the forested hill crest. The platoon gained the road below the treeline of the great hill. As they did, who should appear, but Venters, marching at the double, looking as if nothing had happened. The lieutenant signaled for a stop. The G.I.s collapsed against the snow drifts on the far side of the road. The air filled with their coughs and rattling breaths. The sound of fire rolled up to them from every direction — in the trees on the hill on the right flank; in the village back on the left flank; and ahead of them, around on the eastern side of the hill before them, an enormous din of small arms and mortar fire.

"Is that Love or Item over there?" said Venters between gasping breaths. "What a snafu." He looked at his map in silence for a few minutes. He nodded to himself, murmuring words of self-encouragement. Arlen had never seen him do that before. Venters put the map away and unslung his carbine. He let out a long, steadying breath, then said, "All right, listen up," to those that remained in the half-strength platoon. "First Squad on the left, Second on the right, and Third — Corporal Vinson's leading it now — in reserve. I will be leading from the front." He emphasized that point. "I want the squads spread out in skirmish lines, as wide as you can. Sweep any Krauts we find up that hill and don't pass any of them by. Understood?" They nodded in silence. Venters gave final instructions, made sure ammunition taken from the wounded was distributed, and that the mortar was in place. Arlen grabbed onto Paine's arm tightly, ready to drag the poor kid with him. At Venters' silent signal, the battered platoon stood and left the road behind, crossing a small field and pushing into the firs that crowned the hill.

Two steps into the trees and the world was dark. Snow on the high branches blocked light from above. The G.I.s thrashed their way ahead. Arlen plowed his way through a deep patch of snow, his rifle held at a high port. But he cried out in shock and pain and grasped for his leg. He dug down in the snow and touched his pants carefully — nothing felt amiss and there was no blood. Paine, right behind him, was terrified, shaking like a nervous dog. Arlen gnawed his lip and gave a big tug to free his leg from the drift. "Buddy, take care you don't hit yourself on a stob. There's plenty of 'em under the snow." Paine just stared back. There was hardly a breath from his lips. "Come on, buddy, we've got to get up this hill." Arlen stepped over a limb and reached out his hand to Paine, who gingerly took it and let Arlen pull him over. The kid was still shaking.

A machine pistol fired ahead of them. Arlen ducked behind a tree. Paine kept standing, staring up the hill, rifle almost dangling from his fingertips. "Get down!" Arlen hissed.

Another burst from the machine pistol — it sounded muffled here under the trees, as if fired from under a blanket. Rifle shots — an M1, it sounded like. Orders shouted: English, not German. Rifle shots — American and German. Another burp gun fired. Arlen craned his neck, trying to see where it was going on. The rest of the platoon had disappeared into the thick forest. Arlen counted his men — he couldn't see but three or four of them.

Bullets broke limbs around them. Arlen hunkered down further. Paine was hiding now. When the fire stopped, Arlen cautiously peered around the tree. He slid his rifle up beside him, then up to his shoulder. He saw nothing up the slope that looked like a uniform or a gun barrel. Someone off to his left fired a rifle once. A shout, then another rifle shot, then a shout. German words rolled down the slope. The BAR's long stutter cut them off. Arlen saw a flash of movement and he followed it as quickly as he could, firing twice, three times at it. He knew it didn't hit home. *Can't see nothin'.* He swung the rifle back again, looking, hoping. The artery in his neck tapped hard against the rifle stock.

"Sarge, they're up there," said Wood, "about seventy, eighty yards."

"Can you see 'em?"

"Every now and then I get a peek, but can't see much."

Arlen heard Second Squad thrashing ahead, shooting, taking fire. Someone screamed. Where was Third Squad? Did it matter? Arlen could only remember the lieutenant saying he wanted to sweep the Germans up the hill.

"I'm going up there, Private," Arlen said numbly. "Cover me when I do."

Wood fired a burst. "Me, Sarge?"

"Dammit, Private, I ain't askin' you to a dance. Just do it." Arlen did not wait, but stood up and dashed ahead to the next tree. He would go and the men would follow after him. He was sure they would. Empty, rattling logic told him they would. But before he took the next step, he turned back to Wood. "Bring Paine with you. Don't leave him behind."

"Okay, Sarge. Whistle when you're in place."

Arlen didn't hear him — he was already stumbling through brush, half-running, half-swimming through the snow to the next tree. Rifle rounds beat at the tree trunks around him — it sounded like one of those new German rifles, the automatic one with the big magazine. Arlen stumbled, fell into the snow, stood again, and thrashed his way to another tree. It was big enough to hide behind. He fell against the trunk. The tree cracked and leaned, rotten from the inside out. But his momentum hardly stopped — Arlen rolled away and kept one leaping stride following the other, hopping through snow and over downed limbs. He reached a big, thick fir and collapsed. He was pouring sweat. He panted so hard, he was sure the Krauts could hear him.

The whole hill was awash in small arms fire. The BAR was still stuttering, throwing rounds up the slope. Arlen peeked around the trunk. He was a bit closer to the Germans, but he could see nothing distinct. Where was the rest of the squad? *Don't leave me up here. Not now, boys, not now. Come on, now, get up here to me.*

A machine pistol fired ahead of him. Nothing was returned from Arlen's side.

He heard snapping twigs. Arlen closed his eyes and listened. The snow squeaked under foot, compacted under careful steps. Arlen rolled to the other side of the tree trunk. His heart leaped — he knew the helmet shape, the camouflage, the weapon each man held. Arlen shouldered his rifle, sliding it between a fir branches. There was no need to be precise — it was thirty yards at most. The aperture lined up with the post and he squeezed the trigger once.

One German pitched forward down the hill, rolling once and hitting a tree. The other sprayed his machine pistol toward Arlen and ran. The remaining enemy soldier shouted in German and was met by answering voices from up the slope. Another burst of rounds smacked the trees and sprayed up snow. He curled up tighter. If only he had a chance to roll away and run.

An M1 rifle fired nearby. Shouts in German overlapped each other, then came silence, then a machine pistol burst, and another pair of M1 shots. More silence. Arlen raised his head. He saw a figure in a white helmet and olive drab moving up the hill perhaps twenty yards to the right. It was Hirsch, stepping through the snow like a high-prancing horse. Arlen whistled to Hirsch, who saw and acknowledged him. Hirsch gestured with a grenade across the hill and to the left, and Arlen nodded. Hirsch drew a bead with his rifle as Arlen took a grenade, pulled the pin, and released the spoon. *One, two.* He lobbed it the best he could between the tree trunks, toward the German positions on the left. He hid behind the tree and felt the explosion. There were cries of pain and more shouted German, and Hirsch fired several times. Arlen turned his own rifle around the tree and fired at a white shape moving up the hill. Hirsch moved up the hill quickly and Arlen followed. Little by little, they gained ground, and one by one the rest of the squad caught up with them. The Germans fired furiously at the Americans, then faded into the trees. The G.I.s climbed cautiously, looking and listening. Somewhere on the right Second Squad was fighting, but Arlen could only hear the fight, not see it. The squad stopped to catch its breath. Wood came struggling up the hill, hauling the BAR and Paine with him. He pushed Paine forward and the little guy stumbled up, then collapsed on the slope below Arlen. There was no time to check on the poor kid — they had to keep pressing forward.

"Where are the Krauts, Sarge?" whispered Wood.

Arlen pointed up the hill, straight ahead. "I want you to anchor the right, while we move up on the left."

Wood nodded. "Let me get in place and reload and I'll be ready." He stepped quickly out from behind cover. A burst of fire rattled the tree trunks and Wood fell onto his side and slid down the slope, blood smearing the snow as he went. Rounds began cracking and snapping through the trees in a constant swarm. Arlen made himself small behind his tree. He could not reach Wood — he had fallen just out of reach and he could almost see the incoming bullets as they cracked the air between them. He heard the poor kid choking. "Medic!" Arlen shouted. "Medic!"

The German fire did not slacken. The chattering, knocking bullets blew around them, breaking branches, spraying splinters, and tumbling this way and that when they were spent. Wood writhed on the ground below Arlen, the snow turning red. No medic would reach them as long as this hellacious storm kept up.

The BAR had tumbled from Wood's hands and fallen down the slope next to Paine. "Buddy! Pass me that BAR!" shouted Arlen. Paine did not answer. He was curled up into a ball, both hands holding his helmet on, his whole body quivering. "Paine! The BAR, dammit!" Still not a move or a whimper. Arlen saw a muzzle flash and he snapped up his rifle and fired at it.

"Sarge! I got it!"

Through the hail came Sayers — of all his men, Sayers. He snatched up the BAR and leaped through the incoming fire and dropped behind the tree Wood had gone for. Arlen saw the soldier's face was shaken at the sight of his wounded buddy, but his hands moved resolutely, bringing the BAR into position and loading a fresh magazine.

"Tell me when, Sarge!"

Arlen thought for a second. Around to the left, take whomever would come with him, lob a couple grenades, and then clear out the Krauts. That was it. Nothing spectacular. Nothing to stop him, or any one of them, from being cut down. But he had to do it.

He signaled to Sayers and the soldier opened up.

To the left, he saw Hirsch and Sedgwick. They would go with him. He signaled to them and they started moving around to the left. Finding one of his grenades, Arlen readied himself to move.

But then he heard his name.

"Arlen. Arlen. Arlen. Arlen," Paine called out through chattering teeth and sobbing gasps of breath.

His voice was different this time. Arlen put the grenade away without another thought. He carefully inched his way down the slope to Paine.

"Sarge! You got to go!" shouted Sayers.

Arlen looked away from Sayers, from the rest of the squad, from the Krauts. Not now, he could not go right now. Paine needed him.

"Sarge, it's my last magazine! You got to move!"

Arlen screwed his eyes shut. It was just for a second — how could he take any longer? Then he picked up Paine and under the cover of Sayers' fire, moved him down the slope away from the squad. Sayers shouted after him and rifles fired out on the left, but Arlen paid them no heed. He set Paine behind a big tree.

"Arlen. Arlen."

"I'm here, buddy, I'm right here, all right? You hear me?" Arlen rolled Paine over and pried his hands from his helmet. "I'm right here."

Snot and tears covered Paine's face. "They got me, Arlen, they got me, they finally got me. They got me."

"You ain't hit. You're fine. Ain't hit at all." Arlen held Paine close. "Ain't hit at all."

The BAR had stopped firing. The German fire continued. The assault had petered out. The hell if it had. He had to be here with Paine and that, too, was not a terrible thing.

"My name. Got my name."

"Buddy?"

"Got my name on it, Arlen, it's coming, it's got my name. Got my name on it. Coming, coming, got my name."

And then Arlen heard it too. A mortar explosion, unannounced, and then another and another. Each burst and the trees rattled. One by one they drew closer — it was Kraut fire, incoming. The rounds exploded high against the tree branches and sent thousands of splinters in every direction. Arlen grabbed Paine and pulled him close, holding on with the last strand of strength left in his arms. Paine shook and sobbed and squirmed, and Arlen held on tighter.

Closer. The shrapnel and splinters knocked against the firs.

Arlen pulled his helmet down over his eyes. His long frame shrank smaller and smaller into a knot, and he felt that he could pull himself under the whole steel pot.

Closer again. A mortar burst severed a tree trunk and the top of a fir came spinning down and landed mere yards away.

Lord, Jesus, forgive me, forgive me, here I come, don't want to come, not one bit, you know what I want to do, what I've tried to do, just don't take me yet, Lord, not now, not now

But here it comes

There were many explosions, but they all felt as one. The world darkened around Arlen and he felt the trunks crash all around him, great tearing, rending breaks and the hissing of falling needles and snow and the great storm settled all around.

And Arlen opened his eyes, and Paine was gone.

There was no body, just the scraped spot where Paine had laid.

Can't be dead. Shell didn't get him, 'cause I'm still here.

Where'd he go?

Arlen raised his head cautiously.

A small figure was running down the hill, stumbling into trees, casting away his equipment piece by piece. He passed under an open patch in the canopy and in the light Arlen saw the olive drab coat and the familiar back of his dearest friend's bare head, clear as anything he'd ever seen. And the figure disappeared down the slope and Arlen lost sight of him.

Buddy, don't be gone for good.

Wind blew and Arlen felt a great chill on his face. He reached up and touched his cheeks — they were wet. He was crying. Arlen wiped his face with his sleeve, but it cleared away nothing. He searched for breath and his chest heaved as his lungs tried to fill themselves again. He smelled burnt powder and clean wet snow, and pine coated his tongue. His muscles were clenched up, unable to release themselves. He told himself to move, but he could not stand nor turn nor reach out.

The mortars came again, closer and closer, and he moved in the only way he could now, shrinking down into a little ball covered by his steel helmet.

Snow fell very gently, each flake taking the slowest, softest fall it could, drifting from side to side hardly at all, making only the occasional tumble or twitch to turn over a new side. Not a single one touched Arlen's face, nor his nose. His neck was pulled back inside his jacket. A pair of socks, wrapped around his neck to dry, served as a scarf. His helmet rode down low, creating a tiny slit from which he could look ahead, peering in safety from his own little pillbox.

There was snapping sound and the sound of a shout over on the left of First Squad's position. Arlen leaned forward from the trunk of the tree against which his back rested. His eyes searched frantically through the dark, looking for any movement or glint. His breathing held, letting his ears strain for the faintest snatch of guttural German or the cry of an American for help. He heard a heavy foot against brush, twigs snapping at first, then muffled by the thin creak of weight compacting light snow. Arlen pulled his right hand out of his pocket, reached down without thought to the M1 laying across his lap, and flicked off the safety. His mind ran far ahead of that moment, wondering how they could possibly take a German patrol infiltrating them, or, God forbid, a full-on night counterattack. *Where are they?* He realized he didn't know the location of his men. They were out there, to the left and the right, but he had not walked the perimeter as usual.

How many have I got?

Arlen had counted the men remaining after they had gained the heights, but he could not remember now. The number was trapped in that fog in his head, making no effort to get out on its own.

The snow had stopped, he realized.

How many?

He tried again, but couldn't find the number. From there, the well-tread path of thoughts of how to lead and repel an attack, so often followed with habitual ease, failed to materialize, hidden too in that fog, as if he did not know how to step toward what he knew was there but could not see.

Nasal English ricocheted off the trees from the same direction as the cracking brush. Someone gave the challenge, and another voice responded with the password. Everything went silent. Arlen leaned back against the tree. Fear ebbed away from its well-worn high water mark.

The snow started again.

He put the rifle's safety back, and his hand went back in his pocket. Then Arlen pulled it out again, and nervously patted his body all over, searching for, but not finding, the wound he thought he must have. *Maybe I just didn't feel it. Got to be there. Ain't no way I didn't get hit.* He felt his legs, even reaching his fingers under the tall leather cuff on the top of his boots to probe his ankles over and over, then back up his calves and to his thighs. He ran his numb hand under the piles of equipment around his waist and across his chest, feeling for the bullet hole or shrapnel wound. How could he have survived? He had lost Wood and Sedgwick and Paine that day — *Paine.* Arlen could not cry for his buddy anymore — he was dried up, in every way. He remembered that terrible feeling of seeing his best friend gone, broken, fleeing, the only clear memory left to him from that day. The rest of the attack was a hazy, absurd dream. There came to him, if he tried to recall, a great distance of snow, constricted on both sides like a tunnel, that they could not deviate from, that they could only go up against or recoil back from in defeat, the Krauts shooting down that long snowy corridor and men falling here and there like the last remaining trees methodically, calculatedly cut from the white expanse.

He didn't find any wounds.

The snow behind him creaked suddenly. Arlen almost jumped a foot in the air without using his legs. But it was only Staff Sergeant Gates. The weary soldier knelt next to Arlen and wasted no time. "I'm in charge of the platoon, Arlen."

"Is Lieutenant Venters all right?" said Arlen.

Gates shook his head. "I don't know. He'd lost a lot of blood by the time the medics got to him."

That damn courageous bastard. Venters had led Third Squad around the Kraut position, caught them off guard, and saved what remained of the platoon, though not himself. He had redeemed himself from every grumbling Arlen had made about him.

"Been a bad day." Gates said emptily. He leaned in closer to Arlen, trying to make him out better in the dark. "Jesus, Arlen, are you all right?"

"I ain't hit."

"No, I mean, you're shaking like crazy."

"Pardon?"

"You've got the shakes."

Arlen sat forward. The snow stopped again. He looked up. He'd been quivering so hard, he was shaking the fir against his back, knocking the flakes from the branches.

"Didn't have no idea. Can't feel much of nothin'."

"Where's your foxhole?"

Arlen said nothing.

"Arlen, you haven't dug one?"

Ain't got to explain myself to him.

179

"Dig one. That's an order."

"Fine." Arlen tried to stand up, but gasped in pain once halfway on his feet.

"What's the matter?"

It took a moment for the right words to find Arlen's mouth. He knew what was wrong, but just couldn't seem to say it. Finally, the words broke out from between his lips: "It's my feet."

"Pull those boots off."

With great pain, Arlen stripped the sodden leather boots from his feet. His socks were soaking wet and it took all his strength to get them off. Gates took Arlen's left foot in his hand. The clammy skin was white and shriveled, but sections around the toes were starting to take on a bluish tinge. "Arlen, why is this so bad?"

"Didn't do no dog show for the squad last night."

"You've got to keep up with the foot inspections. Trench foot will take a man out just as quickly as a bullet. Only takes a day or two."

"I know. I forgot."

Gates shook his head. "We can't afford to lose a single man from the line, not right now."

"I know, you ain't got to tell me."

"Why haven't you massaged your feet tonight?"

"Ain't — ain't got—" His throat caught and the fear and the guilt rested right there on the lump in it. Paine had always done that for him, as he had done for Paine. Arlen winced as Gates began massaging his toes. It was painful, a hundred pulsing pricks shooting up his nerves. Gates worked over the left foot, then Arlen's right. They said nothing to each other. When Gates finished, he tugged the dry socks from around Arlen's neck and slipped them on. Arlen watched his staff sergeant from far away, flying far above in the ice black night.

When he had finished, Gates slipped Arlen's boots on and laced them up. "Dig your position, Sergeant. Don't get careless. We need you." The sergeant disappeared into the dark.

Arlen slowly and stiffly rose from his position against the tree, pulled out his entrenching tool, and dug. He made the hole big enough for just one man. Then he wrapped himself in a blanket, Indian-style, and laid against the corner of the foxhole, his eyes half-open, trained to the platoon's front, seeing nothing, ears hearing nothing.

He was alone. He couldn't sleep. Someone had to stand sentry. He lay there, rifle cradled in his arms, motionless, his exhaling chest the only thing moving. He had to stay still, for he teetered on the edge. One false move and he would go over, over and down into that great chasm he had seen trap others, trap Paine, that irremediable exhaustion which he knew was there, always looming, but which he did not fear, for it was inevitable, but which he could resist all the same.

He stayed high above those great depths, at least for one night.

XVII

"Sergeant."

Faces flitted before him, distinct and indistinct, faces with names, the whole long list of them.

"Sergeant."

Moments, plucked from time and place and set right there in his head, playing through it like a newsreel — every moment of their truest qualities, every broken look and grimace of pain when they got it, got the one with their name on it, their number, the one meant for them all.

And it was not just the old ones, there were more now, more after the attack on Hill 541, even after Paine, who was now one of the many. Everything about Paine was distinct, yes, but he was all mixed in with recollections of Sedgwick and Schaeffer and Gunderson — *Gunderson, poor feller, where is he?* Arlen's thoughts wandered away for a moment, searching for his old sergeant, following after him, but the soldier disappeared and Arlen was lost, standing alone in a dark wood, no one around him, wondering how he got there. What had brought him here? He puzzled for a minute, a faint memory of faces lingering with him — but was that it? Faces, oh, yes, the faces — *Paine.* He remembered his friend, who was just a mask right now, moving here and there, hard to see, and Arlen set off after him through that dark wood. Arlen could see him more clearly with each step. He could see around all sides of that immovable mask, and then his buddy stopped — they were there, right where Arlen had hoped to be. And Paine's face disappeared as Arlen knelt down before all the memories of his buddy and touched them. The memories had been back there, somewhere, all pent up, but now under his touch they began to sluice out and run through Arlen's mind in no order, memories of the real life the two of them had shared: little habits, like Paine triple-knotting his shoelaces; silly conversations and Paine's practical jokes on the insufferable bores of the company; their confessions; and recounting shellings and attacks to each other, and poring over every close call, every man they killed, every comrade blown to bits instead of them, if only to give name to fear that sapped at them as they supped on hope—

"Sergeant, did you hear me?"

Someone was shaking his shoulder. Arlen blinked a few times and turned around. A bundled-up figure, face covered in darkness, loomed over him.

"Are you all right, Sergeant?"

"Yessir. Sorry, Lieutenant, I didn't realize it was you."

"Did you brief your squad?"

"Brief?"

"Brief them on the patrol."

Patrol. Patrol. Oh, that's right. "Ah, yessir. The patrol. They know. They'll be ready. Sir."

"Are they?"

"Yessir, I said they will be."

"No, now, Sergeant. We're moving out."

Arlen stood up and hitched his rifle up on his shoulder. "Yessir, I'll assemble them now." The memories were all gone now, packed quickly away, and the old pattern came once again to him, everything he had to do and look for, every little danger to anticipate, little different between patrol, attack, and retreat. Arlen roused all the men one by one and they assembled for the patrol, all six of them, the survivors. Five gone, three on Hill 541 and two more, Hirsch and Smith, the next day on Hill 551. The clouds were broken and the moonlight glowed blue off the snow. They would be able to see just fine. Arlen checked the squad, made sure that every man was armed and understood the mission. He had to dig around a little bit to remember what it was. Just a reconnaissance patrol, nothing more.

Just a patrol.

Arlen shivered and tucked his shaking hands under his armpits. It was just a patrol, just another one like he'd made a hundred times or more before. Nothing new, nothing to be afraid of. But everything bothered him. There was too much light from the moon, the Krauts would see them for sure. And if that moon disappeared behind a cloud, they wouldn't be able to see and they would stumble into the Kraut lines for sure. They didn't have enough men, and what was the lieutenant doing coming with them? The fool, he was new and he didn't know, he didn't know what it was like out there — all he saw was this mission, this patrol the brass had given to him, and he just opened up the manual and ran his finger down it and said, six men, six is how many I need and First Squad has six men and Sergeant Breckenridge is experienced, I'll take him. Arlen didn't want to go. But he had to go — the only thing worse than going was not going.

The new lieutenant, a Kansan by the name of Weston whose cheeks turned beet red every time he shaved, kept looking at the luminous dial on his watch. Finally, after a half dozen times, he said in a forced voice: "Okay, let's go."

Young was on point, keeping ahead of the body of the patrol, with Arlen leading the rest of them along. The lieutenant and his runner marched in the middle of the column. Arlen kept looking back, trying to throw a glare at the lieutenant, whose steps were loud and careless in the snow. The captain wanted a report and the lieutenant must have taken that to mean he had to see for himself, to go clomping off into the dark with field glasses in one hand and a compass in the other. These Officer Candidate School ninety-day wonders would be the death of this army.

They ain't been nothin' but bad luck for us.

Arlen wanted to smack his own head. *It ain't luck, Arlen. Ain't ever been, ain't gonna be. Don't think like that. Don't think like Paine.*

But he was still scared. He wanted to walk slower, crouch lower, dig a foxhole every time the patrol paused to cross a fence. But not with the men watching. He had to keep on ahead, keeping up this stupid bravery as tension ground all the strength from the fibers of his body.

The patrol went quietly and steadily through the snow, moving here and there as best the cover suited them. They stopped and listened and watched, then went ahead again, following fencelines across fields, stepping gingerly across an iced-over creek. With care, they reconnoitered along a road, then crossed it singly, and headed up a slope through deep snow. The ground opened up, all the trees outlining the fields disappearing, and the G.I.s had to make quick dashes over the white ground. They were going up there to the top of the hill, into the trees. They could get killed out here, just one little opportune moment of a German patrol seeing them and pop-pop-pop, that was it, dead or wounded or pinned down, no one to come help them.

"Sergeant, move," hissed Corporal Sayers.

Arlen saw a tiny black spot up the hill, unmoving. Was that Young on point? Or was it a Kraut?

"Sarge, go," said Sayers again.

Arlen dashed as quickly as he could up the slope, feet dragging and planting through the snow. A hard wind blew on his face and drained him. He couldn't go up there. The hill was too high, the wind too cold, this patrol too futile. But his legs carried him on. They would not let him stop — they had done this against all fear, all threats, all looming death for too long. Maybe they would stop one day, and soon, but not yet, at least not until he reached the trees.

Arlen knelt next to Young in a little undulation in the slope. The rest of the patrol come up behind them, wordless. The whole valley, from end to end, glowed blue-white and cold. The firs at the top of hill rustled in a wave as the wind hit them, then the sound faded and there was only the breathing of the G.I.s.

"One more dash, Sergeant," breathed Lieutenant Weston.

Arlen nodded reluctantly and signaled to Young. The point man moved up to the tree line and, one by one, the other men followed. They stopped at the edge of the firs, which covered the crest of the ridge. They threw a white cape over Weston's head and the lieutenant checked the map with his flashlight. He flipped off the camouflage. "We should move up to just below the crest there, about a hundred yards, and then we will turn east and move along the ridge for about seven hundred yards, Sergeant."

"Yessir." Arlen hardly even heard himself talk.

The lieutenant stashed his map in his pocket. "I'll take point with Private Young," he said. "Sergeant, you bring up the rear."

"Sir, don't think that's a good idea, you being out in front. German outposts might be out there."

"And we're here to find them."

"Yessir, but—"

"Sergeant, no buts. The captain asked me for a report and I want to make it."

Arlen gnawed his lip. *This ain't the damned Infantry School.*

"I'm more worried about a German patrol coming up behind us, Sergeant. You have sharp eyes and ears, so I want you back there."

This was not how things were supposed to be done, not one bit. He should be scared, not trying to improvise right from the start. But the lieutenant's face was set and confident, unreflective, as if this was the most natural thing in the world to be doing.

Arlen did not protest further and followed as the last man, relieved that the success of this patrol was in the lieutenant's hands now. All he had to do was watch out for himself and the men. He was well to the rear, walking forward, then walking backward for a ways, stopping and listening, then moving cautiously again. The trees rustled in the wind again and twigs and limbs snapped crisply and tumbled down in a constant patter. The Krauts could be right on them and neither side would know.

Yes, they had to be here, the Krauts. This was too good a spot for them not to be: dark forest, a ridge that stuck like a finger across the battalion's front, a hill on the far end that overlooked the battalion's flank. *Krauts have to be here.* Why had the captain not sent a bigger patrol?

The wind stopped and Arlen did too, listening carefully in its wake for the sound of twigs breaking underfoot, the last few steps made by a pursuing German patrol before they stopped in the cold silence. He heard nothing.

A shout echoed through the night. Arlen spun around toward the sound. Up the gradually climbing ridge line, deep in the darkness, he saw a flash and heard the fast drumming of a machine gun burst. He hit the ground and crawled to behind a tree. His men were shouting and the Germans were shouting and there was another machine gun burst, then another, casting flashes of light on the underside of the canopy. Arlen burrowed deeper, holding his rifle, waiting, listening.

Don't go up there. Don't go toward the fire.

Shouts of panic and tension, and rifle shots, and a wind blowing through the trees, howling in his ears, and those flashes up there again, and his throat was dry.

He could not stay away. They needed him.

You'll get yourself killed.

Arlen ran forward through the trees, his rifle catching and snagging on branches as he plowed his way ahead.

He saw a dark shape on the snow and then another ahead it, and that one fired a rifle and the muzzle flash blinded Arlen and left a little ember in his vision that glowed green-purple and then blue-yellow. He dropped to the ground, bringing his rifle to his shoulder.

"Sarge! Is that you?"

"I'm here. Who is it?"

"Hazlett, Sarge."

"What's up there?"

"Kraut O.P."

"What?"

"Kraut O.P.," hissed the soldier. "What do you want us to do?"

The machine gun fired again and the Germans yelled something indistinct and angry out into the darkness.

"Fall back, we're fallin' back."

"You sure, Sarge?"

"Yes, dammit, I'm sure. Go on, fall back, now."

Arlen began crawling forward through the snow, twigs scraping his face. A hand grabbed at his boot. "What?" he yelled back.

"The lieutenant's up there. That's him yelling."

"Dammit, go, fall back."

"Get the lieutenant, Sarge," pleaded Hazlett.

One by one, he found the men firing back in the dark and had them fall back. The last one he found was Young. Arlen almost had to drag him away from his position, he was so bent on staying. At last, Young relented and followed Arlen back down the slope. "What are your orders, Sarge?" said Young.

"We're fallin' back. Don't take the path we took comin' in. Go straight down the slope this way. Just keeping going downhill, keep close to each other, and follow the edge of the trees. Don't cross the fields. I'll bring up the rear."

They all stopped talking when they heard a desperate shout echoing off the trees. It was a call for help.

"Who's that?" asked one of the soldiers.

"That's the lieutenant," said Young. "I stopped because I heard something but he kept straight on ahead. I guess he wanted a better look."

"Are you going to go get him, Sarge?" asked Hazlett.

Arlen shook his head. "No, I've got to get y'all back. Go on, get movin', I'll bring up the rear. Young, you take point again. Think you can get us back?"

The lieutenant's shouts reached them again, a panicked, searching cry.

"Sarge."

"Get movin'."

Young silently started off down the hill. The rest of the men stared at Arlen sullenly before turning away to follow.

They shouldn't go back, not up that hill again. It was a fool's errand. Right into the jaws of the enemy, with a machine gun and who knew how many Kraut patrols out there on the flanks, closing in. The mission was done, over. Their goose was cooked. All Arlen could do was try to get as many out alive as he could.

The poor lieutenant.

He thought of Venters, of Iannucci.

We can't go back up there.

It was too much to ask.

I can't lead those men back up there. Can't get 'em killed like that, just for the lieutenant. He wanted to be on point, he got it.

Can't go back up there.

Calloway was the last soldier to start down the hill. Even in the dark, Arlen could see his searching eyes. Even in the trees of Hill 541, none of the men had looked at him like that.

Can't go back up there.

Arlen gnawed his lip. Who would go with him? Who would be there for him if he came back? Who would give for him like he could give?

Buddy, I miss you. Where are you?

The machine gun drummed through the night.

He set off running.

The G.I.s shouted after Arlen as he thrashed uphill through the trees. Enemy fire reverberated off the firs and rounds knocked into tree trunks and snapped overhead. He covered ground, his heart chugging in his chest — a grenade exploded and he was blinded again. Closing his eyes in surprise, Arlen ran right into a fir and fell over. He blinked away the spots in his sight and rose, moving ahead.

Rounds snapped around him, hitting tree trunks — he kept moving.

Muzzle flashes in the dark. Not toward him, but pointing uphill. He ran toward them. "Lieutenant!"

He could hear the Germans shouting from their observation post.

"Lieutenant!" Arlen stopped next to the body he saw on the ground and leaned over it. "Lieutenant!"

"Sergeant, get down!" The lieutenant grabbed onto Arlen, pulled the sergeant to the ground, then returned to firing his carbine at the Germans. He stopped, pulling out the empty magazine. "Jesus, Sergeant, I thought you had gone."

"Let's get you out of here, Lieutenant."

"Where's the squad?"

"Ain't here. Come on, let's go." Arlen tugged at the lieutenant's sleeve.

"Are they all casualties?"

"No, they ain't, they're hightailin' back down the hill."

"Sergeant—"

"Quit lollygaggin' and let's go." Arlen pulled harder on the lieutenant's sleeve, trying to drag him from his position. Rounds whipped in from the left and Arlen buried himself flat. The lieutenant fired back wildly in that direction, carbine casings flying from the breech and bouncing *ting ting ting* off the front of his helmet. Arlen grabbed a hold of the lieutenant's collar and belt firmly.

"Sergeant, let go!"

Arlen sat up on his knees, then, pushing with all the strength in his legs, rose to his feet, lifting the lieutenant up with him. He began to drag his commander back down the hill, his neck and cheeks flushing hot as he heard guttural shouts behind them and a machine gun burst and rounds in the trees and the lieutenant yelling and firing his carbine, and then there was a great whack to Arlen's head, and there was the flat ring of struck metal, and his head felt stunned and numb. He pitched forward down the hill and all went dark.

The light was bright in the house; it hurt his eyes after walking and observing in the dark for so many hours. But if it hurt, then he was still here. Wordless thanks ran through Arlen's head as he sat in a chair, poking his finger over and over through the hole in his helmet. The bullet had punched a hole in the crown, grazed the top of his head, shredded the liner, curved down the back of the helmet, and dropped neatly down inside Arlen's collar. The shards of metal from the disintegrated bullet jacket had embedded themselves shallowly in his scalp, and the aid man had plucked out as many as he could. The blood had congealed and matted Arlen's hair already — he couldn't put a hat on, though his head was cold.

The door to the headquarters billet opened and Captain Reaser was swept in by a bellow of cold air. His face was red from the chill. He shed his overcoat and came over to Arlen, who kept staring at the hole in his helmet and didn't acknowledge or salute the captain. Reaser stood over Arlen, quietly watching. "Sergeant, it's too late or too early, either way you look at it, but here's some hot joe for you."

Arlen shook his head. "No, thank you, sir."

"You need it."

"Sir, I feel mighty queasy."

"Sergeant, take it." The captain forced the coffee in front of him. Arlen took the cup and the coffee jiggled as his shaking hands tried to hold on. He avoided the captain's gaze. It was embarassing to be seen like that.

"Sergeant, do you mind if I ask you some questions?"

"No, sir."

"Why did you go back for Lieutenant Weston?"

Arlen said nothing.

The captain nodded toward Weston, who sat across the room at a table strewn with maps, clutching his own coffee. "The lieutenant here says you went for him back all on your own."

"Yessir."

"That's very brave of you."

"If you say so, sir."

"Did you send your squad back down the hill?"

Arlen did not want to say. But the captain was waiting and Arlen had learned long ago to answer his betters in this army. "Yessir."

"Why didn't you lead them back up the hill to take the observation post?"

His lips fell away from each other and a hole formed in his mouth above his tongue, but nothing came out of Arlen's mouth.

"Sergeant?"

"Sir, I didn't think we could. Not without gettin' men killed."

"That shouldn't have stopped you, Sergeant."

Arlen looked up at the captain for the first time, eyes set against his commander's. "It weren't a combat patrol. Didn't think it was right to go on the attack. Thought it best to get out of there and report."

"You did?"

In truth, he hadn't thought anything. There wasn't anything to think. But the captain wanted an answer. "Yessir, I did."

"Then why did you go back up the hill for Lieutenant Weston?"

Arlen kept staring at Reaser, but he said nothing. They were trying to trap him, to run him down.

"You were very lucky that the rest of the squad came back up the hill and laid down enough fire to get the two of you safely back," said the captain.

I did everything I could, didn't do nothin' wrong.

Reaser sat back on the edge of his desk. "Sergeant, how long have you been with this company?"

A puzzling question. It took Arlen a moment. "Nineteen-forty, sir."

"Nineteen-forty?"

"Yes, sir. I was a Guardsman."

The captain drained half of his own coffee before walking around to the other side of his desk. "You've been in every battle this division has seen."

"Not Mortain, sir. Missed out on that."

Captain Reaser flipped through Arlen's paperwork. "While you were in the hospital, I see."

"Yessir."

"That was your first Purple Heart. I see you got another when we were outside of Aachen."

"Yessir. Just a graze, that one. Reckon there've been a few more like that since, but it ain't worth the time to put in for one."

"We'll get you one for that graze on your head."

"No, sir, I don't need it."

Reaser drank the rest of his coffee, not looking at Arlen. "Sergeant, you'll take it, and wear it with your Silver Star."

"Sir?"

"From the attack on Langendorf. Don't you remember?"

"Never got no Silver Star, sir."

The captain rubbed his eyes. "I apologize. I put you in for it, but, well, things have been a little busy and I guess it slipped through the cracks." He looked at Arlen. "You'll get it, Sergeant, and maybe something more."

"Yessir," Arlen said evenly, his eyes cast down, boring through his cup of coffee.

Reaser looked to Weston and motioned to his foot locker. The lieutenant came over with a bottle of whiskey. Reaser poured a big slug into each cup, including Arlen's. "Sergeant, you've been a rock for First Platoon. A real leader. You always looked out for your men and you're a helluva fighter. An example to all of us."

Arlen tasted the coffee. The whiskey gave it a fiery pinch and it slid right down his throat.

"But Sergeant — and this is in no way to demean all you've done — you can't be out on the line anymore."

It was if a ramrod had shot straight through Arlen's back. "Sir, don't take me off the line."

"Sergeant, you're a liability out there," said the captain.

But Arlen wasn't listening. "Sir, the men ain't got no one if I ain't there."

"You can't make decisions and stick with them. You're tired, too tired to be on the line."

Arlen shook his head, not hearing the commander's words. "I'll be better, sir, I promise. I don't want to leave them, sir. Can't . . . can't stomach that, sir."

The captain was quiet, resting once more against the edge of his desk.

"What will they do without me, sir?"

Reaser finished his coffee and ran his tongue over his teeth behind his lips, eyes off in the corner of the room, weighing something. He went to Weston and whispered with the lieutenant.

Tighter and tighter Arlen felt, everything constricting around him. He tried to hold himself against it. He had to. His stomach boiled from the pressure and his throat felt as if it was closing around a rock.

The captain came back and spoke quietly to Arlen. "Sergeant, don't tell anyone this, but the division is being pulled off the line. We're going back to regroup, draw new equipment, and rest. Our fighting is done for a little while."

Arlen breathed deeply at last, long and searching breaths from the bottom of his lungs.

"We will draw new replacements, promote the leaders we have, and train everyone again. Your squad will be up to strength again. They will have someone to lead them. But it won't be you, Sergeant."

Arlen gulped the coffee. The whiskey was thick at the bottom of the cup and numbed his throat on the way down.

"You may be the last of the old Guard on the front lines. All the others are, well, elsewhere, we'll say."

Arlen screwed his eyes shut. He didn't know if he was trying to keep out all the old faces or trying to see them better, but there they were, playing before him. He had every regret that he was not with them, right now, dead or maimed as that might make him, even though going to them would take him from his men now, the living ones, whom he loved enough to regret abandoning for his old friends gone. And now he would not be with either of them. He would be on his own, and for what? For whom? There was only him now. *Oh, God.*

"Sergeant." Reaser set his hand on Arlen's shoulder.

Arlen opened his blurry eyes. "Sir?"

"You're getting a promotion and you're being reassigned to the rear."

The captain's words cleaved through the hundred thousand knots in him and Arlen came undone. There was no strength in him — all the tightly woven power had gone from his muscles, the tension in his bounds now slack. He felt he could hardly lift or push himself toward anything. The cup dropped from his hands and he buried his face in them, unable to stay upright. His cheeks and eyes sank deeper and deeper in the pits of his calloused palms, the hard flesh seeming to give way and swallow up this heavy head he had carried with him for too long.

I ain't any good anymore. All used up, broke down, can't even do what I know how anymore. They ain't got no use for me.

He grabbed after the old feelings in desperation, but they had fallen away as he unraveled. He clawed around, searching for any of them that remained, but all they left was him, just him, Arlen Breckenridge, there at the end.

When Arlen started breathing again, he slowly raised his head. "Where, sir?"

"Regimental headquarters. They can find a place for you there, maybe in communications or intelligence. You'll be doing good work, important work, but you won't be in the foxholes anymore." Reaser smiled a little. "I think you'll find the rest of your war will be pretty quiet, Sergeant."

The captain and the lieutenant quietly got up and took the whiskey bottle with them back into Reaser's quarters, saying nothing more, for none of their words would do any good after the thanks and the encouraging grips to the shoulder they each gave Arlen. He broke completely and cried silently, tears trickling down his cheeks and his nose dripping onto the floor between his feet. It was true, it really was. He had deceived himself for months, no, for years, telling himself that he would live, but only if he did this or that and if he was hard and sharp, honed down as far as he could be. And he had never fixed this day in his head — it had always been off, out there, real because he believed in it, but ever-receding. And now a blessing came as it always did, without warning or expectation, leaving shock and confusion like a wound that opened up part of him he hardly remembered.

VICTORY

XVIII

If you laid your head back against the bulkhead, you could feel the thrum of the engines. It made one's head tickle.

No one was leaning back, though. No, it was all forward, right forward into whatever was next, and next, and next. No one stayed in their rooms, they were all out in the corridor, crammed together like sardines. Laughs and shouts were a single seamless cacophony. Men piled in until it seemed that no one would ever be able to worm their way out, but then men went in search of cigarettes or a bottle of booze smuggled aboard and there was space to breathe and laugh and drink. Men pulled out trophies to show off: daggers, Lugers and Walthers, some with the cartridges foolishly still in them, and Nazi flags. The family men seemed to prefer silverware as their booty. Hand over hand, down one side and back up the other, went a Schmeisser machine pistol — an officer was bringing it back in his foot locker. Nobody was writing letters — that was pointless now. The *Queen Mary*, packed to the gills with every soldier of the division, was headed west across the Atlantic.

Arlen sat on the corridor floor, watching a game of poker. The cards changed and the pile of dollars grew and then melted away into one soldier's hands or another. They had stopped begging Arlen to join the game. The old man was too serious and morose for that. He had ridden the enlisted men in the intelligence section hard. He was respected, but not loved. All the better: he could not join them even if he wanted to. He had no money, he had sent it all home.

"Hey, Sarge, let me have a swig of that."

Arlen looked at the bottle of brandy he held in his hand. He had been drinking straight from the neck.

"You didn't leave any crumbs in it, did you, Sarge?" said the young guy. Arlen shook his head slightly, then silently handed the half-empty bottle over.

The kid shrugged and took a sip, laughed at a joke, took another, and passed the bottle around. "Straight!" someone shouted in excitement.

"Full house."

"Shit!"

Laughter again. The bottle paused in the hands of the last soldier in the circle as he flicked his cards back toward the dealer. A story started up and the soldier chimed in with his part of it. Arlen did not listen — he could only look at the bottle. *Go on, drink, you bastard, and be done with it.* But the brandy just hung from the G.I.'s fingers by the bottle neck and the brown liquid swayed back and forth with the motion of the man and the ship.

Suddenly the lights fluttered on and off, dimming just to the point of darkness before coming back to life. Arlen's heart seized up and everything went quiet to him. He watched the lights.

Hit.

Torpedo.

U-boat.

Abandon ship.

It could not be. The war was over. The bomb had been dropped not once, but twice. They had all cheered madly and drank themselves into a ecstatic stupor when Truman announced Japan's surrender two days before they left England. The war was done, never to return.

But the lights flickered.

Come back, good Lord, let the lights come back.

Perhaps there was one more U-boat out there, fighting on to the end? One last stand under the sea, taking down a troopship as it went home — were the U-boats no different from the SS troops or the Hitler Youth who had known nothing but war their whole young lives?

The lights went down, then up, then down again and stayed down.

Get your life jacket. Get to the deck. Get to the lifeboat.

He began to stand up.

The lights came on and stayed on. Nobody seemed to notice much. The engines were running still. No great rending bang from a torpedo. The ship dipped and swayed much as it always had. Arlen sat back down and breathed again. "Give me that bottle." Snatching the brandy away from the private, he knocked a big slug down his yawning gullet.

"Jiminy Christmas, Sarge."

Arlen downed another huge gulp and put his head back. He felt the hum of the ship through his skull. His stomach was queasy. It seemed to flutter with the ship. He stood up slowly and set the bottle down next to his men — yes, they were still his, whatever that meant, for a little while longer.

"You sure you don't want to join us, Sarge? I can lend you the money," said one of them.

Arlen didn't even acknowledge. He stumbled through the open door of his cabin and to his bunk. He collapsed on it, curled up like a baby on his side. It helped, but only a little. Closing his eyes only made the feeling worse. He opened them and stared at the gray bulkhead in front of his face. Everyone else felt good, and he did not. Everyone else was happy to go home, and he was not.

Maybe he was happy and he just could not feel it. Arlen could not feel much of anything these days. Like toes numb from trench foot, it took a mighty powerful jab to bring a feeling out of a man's soul. He did not get worried or excited or angry these days — all that was well past. His time away from combat had been good for him, and the memory of what he had been through made all difficulties pale in comparison. After they had pulled him off the line, the brass sent him to Paris for a week. Arlen had seen almost none of the famed city, other than the Eiffel Tower and the mighty Arc. Each day he slept for eleven or twelve hours straight, then took a hot bath, and ventured out at night for steak-frites and a single drink. By the end, he did not go out at all. He began to write letters again, but only to Caty. He confided nothing of significance to her; he merely told her he was okay and of his new assignment. It was remarkable: he had begun to think of her again and yet he could remember so little that he was spurred to write, as if it was a penance. And then the more he wrote, the more he remembered, and the more he wanted to tell her. He wrote more letters in a week than he had since the field hospital.

He had returned to the regiment feeling like a man again. Life in the intelligence section was easy. Most days he simply helped the lieutenant plan their missions. On rare occasions he did a little scouting here and there or he took charge of prisoners of war and made sure the interpreters interrogated them properly. It was boring work, with many reports to file and plans to organize, and Arlen had no mind for it. He could hardly use a typewriter except with two index fingers at a time. He made many mistakes, but only felt a little bad for it. No one chided him and they appreciated his hard if fair hand with unsure replacements and recalcitrant Krauts.

And he was with the division as it attacked into Germany and drove all the way to the banks of the Elbe. He rode along in a jeep, bored to tears, waiting, waiting, waiting. His war was over, but he was in for the duration — they would not let him go home. When the Germans had thrown in the towel, still he had to wait around even as thousands of other veterans got shipped home early and replacements filled in after them. Arlen did not have enough points to go home early, they said — somehow he had not done enough. Perhaps if he had taken all those Purple Hearts he had been entitled to, his score would have been enough to go home. Perhaps someone higher up just made a mistake. Whatever the case, he had said nothing and waited, tamed at long last by the Army. He knew where he was going and it would come soon enough.

And he would have to reckon with it. They were not sending him to Japan.

The war was done — they were sending him home.

I get to go home, and none of them do. Not a one.

Poor Paine. That poor kid.

He was out there somewhere, Paine was. He had survived running away through that mortar barrage, Arlen had found out, cracked up as he was. They had sent him off to convalesce. Where exactly, Arlen did not know. He had tried to find out so he could send letters, as he only had Paine's family's address. But nobody knew, or they would not tell him. Arlen was alone, with no one to talk to. That tormented him, even in safe billets back at headquarters. There was so much he had not settled. He and Paine used to talk over their close calls night after night. The others in the old squad had talked, too, and Arlen had heard and spoken the truth with all of them. They had to, for what they had seen was so horrible they could hardly believe. Those awful moments lived on only in the accumulated memories of the men who had fought together, each man adding what he knew, but only if he spoke, only if he shared, and every one of his comrades doing the same, their recollections and intuitions filling in the gaps of understanding left by words and restoring in the closest measure possible that which they had survived. Strip the men away, and there was nothing but a recurring flash of images, one's body feeling the fear again, muscles reaching involuntarily for a rifle.

Arlen had that with him and he always would, but he did not mourn for himself. There was only guilt that the others must suffer the same without him. He was not there for them, listening at first, then, his defenses broken, telling them all he knew and saw, each of them reassuring each other that it was right, that it was okay. They were gone and he was here, on his way home, without them.

Maybe they went home. Maybe some of 'em healed up and got home.

But that was no consolation. They all knew what the others meant when one of them said "to get home." It meant to get back just as they were, as they always had been, able to live like they remembered, like they knew no other way. To live as if forgetting was possible, forgetting the war and erasing its changes from themselves save for the lone satisfaction they could allow themselves: that they had done what was asked of them. Maimed, crippled, shattered — *like poor Paine* — that was not going home.

But Arlen got to go. He had been on the line longer than anyone else. He had seen more, killed more, had more close calls than anyone else. And he came back with a few scratches and a heart full of hurt, but nothing else. They would take him back, all those folks at home. He would fit right back in again, doing what he had always done. And that terrified the hell out of Arlen.

Lord, I'm sorry, I'm so sorry.

He should not have left his comrades. He should have bled more with them, cared more for them, died with them, even. He did not deserve this if they could not have it, too.

Is that what Paine would've wanted, Arlen? You dead? Or broken like him?

No, of course not. Neither had wanted the other to die or even to be hurt. They had tried all they could to keep the strange course of bullets and shrapnel from each other. They had not sought death, but neither had they shunned it so it might come between the two of them.

Such was the same for them all. Arlen had to find that truth again and again, to tell himself over and over — he could not remember it without his comrades here.

Boys, where are you?

Arlen looked back into that long dark tunnel of combat and they had not come out.

They ain't comin' and it's just me now. Can't forget them, though. Not for a minute, not for nothin' I do.

What an awful betrayal to just live for himself, for the thing he had gone for in the first place — his farm and his family, which were safe now, but not thanks to Arlen alone. They had all fought for each other's right to go back, and Arlen was the one that got to. His life, all the blessed things in it, was as much their doing as it was his own.

But what if those at home did not see that? What if they did not see what he had to do, but rather only what he had done: killing, killing, killing? And what if they resented him coming back, as if he had put himself first and let the others die in his place? A coward, a shirker, coming back to claim the good life and all the glory — no, the civilians would not let him have it. He could not let them let him have it.

Lord, ain't nothin' for me. Nothin' at all. I ain't a good man.

It was true: he was not good. He had simply done what was asked of him. He had no right to ask for anything, not even forgiveness.

Sick as a dog, Arlen lay on his side, hands clasped against his stomach, willing himself to sleep. The sway of the ship and the stuffy air of the cabin lulled him into a fitful doze. The same thoughts turned over and over, never abating, just appearing more hopeless with each reappearance. The brandy had done its work. He came awake quickly as a strong hand shook his shoulder.

"Sarge, are you all right?" said a voice behind him.

Arlen grunted numbly. His mouth was dry and tasted faintly of bile.

"Come on, get up." Many hands reached down and grabbed him under his arms. "Come on, Sarge."

"No," Arlen managed to croak. "I don't want to."

"Let's go up on deck."

Arlen screwed his eyes shut. *Why won't these sonsabitches leave me alone?* "Why?"

"Everyone is going topside. Come on."

"Leave me the hell alone." The other soldiers pulled Arlen to his feet. He swiped at them with leaden arms. "Leave me!"

"Sarge, cut it out, we're just gonna—"

"I don't want to—" Arlen said. He tried to make out the faces in the dim cabin, but could not. The light from the doorway pinched his eyes and he reeled backward, his head seized up. He hit the bunk and plopped down.

"All right, just take it easy." They lifted him up more gingerly this time and Arlen did not fight them. They held him as he slowly found his balance and then they led him, one on either side, down the corridor. He was groggy and his empty stomach reeled from the booze. The corridor was so stuffy, he had to get to some fresh air. Deck after deck they climbed. Suddenly they stopped. "All right, Sarge, get some fresh air." They let him go. Arlen stumbled out onto the main deck. It was crowded, men pushing up against the railing, leaning out into the night, pointing, laughing, shouting. The cool salt air wrapped around his head, poured down his open collar, and filled his stopped-up nose. Breath after breath, he felt better. It was night; he must have dozed in his bunk for hours. The G.I.s of his platoon made their way forward to the bow. He followed. Out on the open fore deck, there were even more G.I.s, some crowded up against the railing, other lounging on the deck, smoking, some drinking openly. The wind rippled over their heads. It smelled so familiar, but that time it had blown them across the Atlantic and this time they were going against it. It could blow and blow, but nothing could stop them now.

Good Lord, is it true?

It gusted and sent his hair a-flying. His hair stood on end and then after the instant rise, the electric shock dropped down through his limbs. His sinewy muscles suddenly acted of their own accord, separating the other strong, well-fed men from each other, and he broke his way through the crowd. He pushed and pushed and at last reached the prow.

And there ahead of them, across an ink water rippling with shards of light, blazed forth the city. Every light seemed switched on, not a single one was shrouded — the blackout was over. Columns of lights on the horizon stretched up and up right ahead of them, right where they were headed, and low clusters of lights stretched along the shore on either side of them. The ship no longer pulsed from the engines, but still they drew closer and closer, as little craft moved around them and the lights grew bigger.

"That's New York City, Sarge!"

He had never been to New York and never wanted to, but never had he ever been so glad. It was there, right there, it really was, and it was not something he had just imagined and told himself was real, a fine and flat image that his mind's eye recalled and recrafted to give him life. This was his place, his country — he had fought for it, for all that city out there, even if he had not meant to, and it looked so good to him. He laughed into the wind.

Boats cut all around the *Queen Mary,* from trawlers to yachts, carrying cheering people on their tiny decks. Men waved their caps and women blew kisses. Arlen squinted to see them in the dark. They were Americans, real Americans. They looked so happy and confident and healthy, uncowed, not beaten down by war and terror and hunger. They glowed in the light of the city, Manhattan right there, bigger and brighter and stronger than ever, growing closer and closer with each passing minute.

"Look there, Sarge."

Arlen gawked in amazement. "Well I'll be damned." It was the Statue of Liberty off the port bow, surrounded by tugboats that sprayed water in celebratory arcs into the air.

"And there — Ellis Island!"

"What's that?" said Arlen.

"You don't know Ellis Island?"

Arlen brushed him off, for he didn't know and didn't care. He could not take his eyes away from the city. The blast of ship's horns and cars honking rolled out across the water to them like a barrage, but Arlen did not fear a thing. He laughed and laughed. Here it was, almost within reach. And nothing would keep him from it.

The ship moved slowly now, guided by tugs, Manhattan slipping by on its right. The skyline burned in electric. His eyes were glued to the Empire State Building. He had never seen anything like that that glorious tall building, lit up from bottom to tip, built by men for man, and man alone. It stood taller and prouder than anything else out there, even taller than the woman with the torch in the harbor. Arlen did not know what to make of that, but right now he did not care. They had made it.

The tugs turned the *Queen Mary* and guided her gently to the pier. The elevated road on the shore was clogged with stopped cars, and drivers and passengers lined up along the side, waving and cheering. The ship gave a long blast of its own horn that smacked against the sides of the tall buildings and rolled back, with even louder cheering following in its wake. Windows in apartments opened and people waved flags, handkerchiefs, tablecloths, anything they could lay their hands on. Not a man on the ship could hear a thing for the deafening cheers and roars they bellowed out to all those welcoming them home.

Arlen stood tall against the prow, but not of his own strength. The crush of bodies had pinned him there and held him up. He still could not speak and he felt cold tears running down his face. He had nothing to worry about from this America of red, white, and blue and not a shade of gray. For all he had done and in whatever name, he was absolved. He could go home.

"Arlen?"

He must have been right behind Arlen to have made himself heard. The voice was familiar.

Paine.

He turned, but before he got his head around, he knew it would not be. It was not meant to be.

A face long forgotten matched that voice and it brought a grin to Arlen's face.

"Damn it all, Roy!"

There were children, children everywhere, playing in the streets, but the streets were filled full of water. Gushing water, the Roer River, after the dam had burst, flowing down the streets like a river should, flowing naturally through this tiny French town, where everyone stood outside laughing and pointing. "The Germans are over there!" The locals all spoke English. "The Germans are over there!" They were unconcerned. Here, have some wine. The G.I.s took it and laughed, simple, generous, heartfelt men of their own kind, bravely walking with glasses of wine through the flooded streets, German artillery falling from the skies, and Arlen saw the shells coming and he dove beneath the riffles on the cobblestoned streets, safe beneath the surface, where the shells came down and stuck, immobile, looking fearsome. And there was Second Squad down there, and Venters was with them — they were cooking K rations on the bottom of the river. And Indian Joe was driving a tank down there, too, and Arlen walked down there, down through the water as if it were a staircase, and Venters gave him a pack of Luckies. Arlen took them with a sharp salute and turned to go. Downstream, bobbing up and down in the current, was a Red Cross girl, fighting tenaciously against someone. She was tall, he was short, and his hands ranged all over her back, trying to get a good hold of her, and she was just trying to get some space so she could slap him. Who was that little guy? Did he know him? Go and see who that is. The little guy got the Red Cross girl to the ground and was about to rare his head back like a howling wolf. And then Venters behind him said, "Arlen."

"Yessir?"

"Arlen."

"I'm here, sir. Is it a patrol? We have a patrol? What's the objective? How many men?"

202

"Arlen?"

"Yessir? What do you want?"

Then he felt the hard grip on his shoulder, a real grip which sent hard light dashing through his head, clearing out everything just there. The air was humid against his neck and collar and he knew that feeling was real, because it was familiar like a scar, not like the echoes that build dreams.

"Arlen," said the familiar voice, "train'll be here soon. A few minutes, I reckon."

Arlen pushed back the service cap from his eyes. It was twilight. But he knew which way the sun was headed, for he smelled dry grass covered in dew, trees heavy with their fruit, red clay dust, and summer-soaked gravel — the humid heat of the day was not far behind. With one whiff, he simply knew, he did not have to believe: he was here, in North Carolina. It was not his farm, but it was home enough. Even more improbably, Roy was still sitting next to him, like it was the most natural thing in the world, like big Roy had just fallen back into the fold of earth where he belonged, the proper distance from his own lanky friend. Arlen wiped the sleep from his eyes. He felt very easy here. He had nothing to fear, nothing to adapt to, nothing to anticipate. He was built for this place; he was from it. And he was not even all the way there yet.

Roy yawned. "My head's mighty foggy. How 'bout yours?"

"Reckon I feel fine."

"Have you ever had so much to drink?"

Arlen shook his head. "I've never seen anything like it in my life. If you're wearin' a uniform, folks people would fight to buy you a drink. They told me I'm a hero and everything. I couldn't get away from 'em all."

Roy stood up and stretched. "That's the atom bomb talkin', Arlen. Folks are just so damn excited about it, they don't know what to think one way or another. So they take it out on us." Roy grunted. "And our livers."

Drink obscured much of the time since they met on the bow of the *Queen Mary*. They had joked and laughed and rough-housed and downed a couple toasts. In the dark hours, the regiment disembarked and was carried by train across the river to Camp Kilmer. The camp was chaotic swarm of checking records, turning in equipment, and making arrangements. The staff offered Arlen the chance to telephone his family, but as they had none, he sent a telegram instead. He sent one to Caty, too; he was gone before he remembered he could have called her. Everything signed, they let him go: thirty days of leave. Roy was waiting for him at the camp gate. Hopping a train to Philadelphia, they arrived just in time to pick up the *Crescent* in the late afternoon. There were no sleepers available, not even a Pullman berth, but it did not bother them one whit. They set up a zone of occupation in the bar and soon the miles melted away. They were past Washington before they realized they hadn't noticed the stop, so mirthful was the mood. They laughed and joked and entertained well-wishes from the passengers who ebbed and flowed through the car. Many joined in the reverie and instant friends were made, soon augmented by G.I.s coming forward to their car to see what the commotion was. More boys from the Old Hickory Division! The dining car closed and they wandered back to their seats. A dogface from Birmingham, built like a fireplug, fetched a bottle of Old Grand-Dad from his duffel bag. By the time they were belting *Rose of Alabama*, the conductor had enough. He quieted them down and suddenly they were all out like lights. It seemed like mere minutes later when he laid Roy and Arlen off in the dark at Salisbury. Arlen had bedded down on the platform, head resting on his duffel. He had slept soundly, unperturbed by his choice of bed. He was able to sleep out wherever and whenever, like his great-grandfather and father had learned to do in their wars.

The low washing rumble of the train reached their ears. They rose and stepped to the edge of the platform as a handful of other passengers joined them in the twilight that was cut for a brief moment by the front lamp of the green and yellow-liveried engine rolling slowly up to the platform. The train settled and some people got off and when they stepped aboard, everything seemed to brighten a full shade, dawn finally here. The soldiers settled into their seats. Only civilians made up the other passengers. With a slight jolt, the train started forward, creeping away from the platform and soon they were off, curving around a bend right away from the station and then settling into a long straight run to the west.

And here they went. The last movement, the last hurry-up-and-wait. In more than an hour, but less than two, Arlen would see his family and Caty. He really would. Real flesh and blood people living and doing things. Arlen looked out the window. A green wall of hickories and oaks flashed by for several long minutes, burly on high where the branches could not separate from each other, and spindly down below where the trunks were. The verdant wall broke and there were fields and roads and then more trees once again. The fields and roads came back in due course and there were white-painted farmhouses and smaller dwellings scattered around like the most humble fiefdoms the world had ever seen. People were set here and there, not jammed up against each other like over there, across the ocean; people lived with space and time to themselves, but never so far that they would not walk or ride to see a neighbor or kin when the desire arose on either end. Yes, that was how it was and how it always should have been — it had never ceased to be. Arlen pressed his forehead against the window. He knew it all by just a look. He knew how it all worked and played and the meaning of the place. Pressure mounted within him. It was all about to burst forth, the life of his in abeyance for so long, its long-delayed potential built up, waiting for Arlen to find a new strength to live it more thoroughly. He lost the beauty of everything passing by as his thoughts raced ahead toward the coming moment when he would find it all as it ever had been.

Arlen gnawed on his lip and bounced his leg up and down. He could not stand it any longer. He forced himself away from the window and looked over at Roy, who sat with his arms folded, looking contentedly out the window. "What are you gonna do when you get home, Roy?"

"Eat a whole damn pie by myself, that's what."

Arlen laughed. "I meant for work."

Roy rubbed a finger under his chin for a minute, still looking out the window. "We've still got to report back to Fort Jackson in month, you know."

"Oh, hell, they ain't gonna call anyone back up. Us especially."

"Well, either way, I ain't in the mood to work for a while. Reckon I need a rest."

"A rest? What for?"

"This war's been hard, Arlen. Don't you think it's time we took it easy?"

Arlen did not understand. "Ain't your pa gonna put you back on the tractor?"

"Don't see why he would. He's gotten by fine without me." Roy coughed once and refolded the arms across his broad chest.

"It ain't about just gettin' by," said Arlen. He almost said more, ready at last to offer good reasons for that kind of life, his kind of life, reasons that had distilled themselves to potency in these past years. But Roy grabbed control of the conversation:

"Danny's already gonna take over the farm. Ain't no room for me or Calvin or Paul. What'll I do, work for my brother rest of my life? No siree. Better to find my own way." He thumbed his chin again. "Maybe I'll join the Highway Patrol. Always had a mind for that."

"That's just what you need: a car, a badge, and a gun," said Arlen, shaking his head. "But you weren't no M.P., Roy. You were at division H.Q." It was astonishing that Roy had been that close for the whole war and he had not known it.

"It takes more than just a policeman to keep those brass hats from cat fightin' with each other. It's like tryin' to run a Junior League in a minefield." Roy laughed and with that changed the gears of conversation again. "Did I tell you last night about the time we hosted the Russians for a dinner? This was right after we'd reached the Elbe, but before the surrender. We weren't sure what was gonna happen, especially with the Russkies across the river, and I reckon General Hobbs wanted to put us on good terms with 'em, so the brass decided to put on a big celebration with the Red Army." Roy's arms were stretched wide, almost into the aisle, as he told his story, his huge shoulders and bulky chest straining the single button that held his uniform jacket shut. "We had quite a spread, on this big long table, hundreds of years old. Never seen anything quite like it. A bunch of them Russian officers came across the river in boats and we packed them and all the division staff around that table like sardines for a big ol' victory feast. And they put me in charge of organizin' this whole shebang, could you believe it?"

"I'll bet they said, 'Hey, roly-poly over there looks like he knows his way around a kitchen.'"

Roy chuckled. "I did my best on such short notice, that's all I can say. Well, table's set, food's ready, the Russians are here and everyone's seated. I was keepin' an eye on things from down at the far end of the table, where we put the division and regimental staff. And there's the Star Spangled Banner and the Russian anthem and a few toasts and everyone's being real nice, and I'm gettin' a little antsy, 'cause I don't want the food to get cold. But then the general gives me the signal and I tell the men to bring it out. And, Arlen, you ain't never seen such spread in your whole life. Our chef was good, and I mean he was a real chef, a Belgian feller who we picked up during the Bulge. Used to run a little restaurant before the war, but lost everything. A couple of the other men and I gave him a pair of G.I. duds and made sure he never spoke a word to any of the officers, so they never found out he wasn't an American. But here comes the Belgian feller, out to the big table, and I start sweatin' bullets. He ain't supposed to come out to the table. The first course was a bean soup, really delicious, and the chef has a plate with butter for the soup. And he knows how all the officers on the staff take their soup. But there's a new face — a woman."

Arlen leaned forward. "The big brass were fraternizin' with the enemy?"

"She wasn't a Kraut — reckon she was a nurse or a WAC. She was seeing one of the staff in the 117th on the side. Don't know why they let him bring her along. Anyway, this chef comes to this woman and he doesn't quite know what to do. Does she want butter or not? He figured he had to ask, so leans down right next to her. And, mind you, the only English he knows, he's learned by listening to us G.I.s at chow time. That's the extent of his vocabulary, that's all he's ever heard. And he looks like a perfect gentleman, and he's got the plate in one hand and the knife in the other, and you can tell he's imagined this day and what'd he'd say to first American lady he's ever seen. And then, in just the neatest, most perfect English you could imagine—"

"What?"

"He says, 'Madam, would you like some fucking butter?'"

Every fedora and each neatly bobbined head turned to their roaring laughter. They slapped their thighs and gasped for air, their sides stitched up.

After several minutes, they had caught their breath. "I nearly got court-martialed for that one," said Roy.

"Ain't surprised," said Arlen through residual chuckles.

Roy shook his head. "Arlen, ain't no one gonna ever believe what we did."

Arlen nodded knowingly.

They passed through Statesville and once into the country on the far side, Roy said, "You're going back to the farm?"

"That's right."

"You workin' with your pa?"

"That's right."

"You reckon he's ready to turn it over to you soon?"

"I'm takin' charge whether he likes it or not."

Roy crossed and recrossed his arms again. He was a little agitated. "You know, I just ain't in the mood to work." Roy raised his eyebrows. "Arlen, I ain't the same."

"Same here," said Arlen quietly.

Roy was looking right at him and so open was his gaze that Arlen had to look him back in the eye.

"I'd never treat you like Uncle David," said Roy. "I know you've seen ten times the fightin' I have, but I'll never ask you to say anything about it. It's done and gone. But if you ever need—"

Roy's words were stilled as the train rumbled out over water. Below them on either side of the trestle was the Catawba River. They were very close.

All other thoughts fell away. The two soldiers each sat forward, checking their duffel bags, lacing their shoes up properly, checking and double-checking everything as was their habit. The train stopped briefly at Catawba Station. The next stop, only fifteen or twenty minutes away, would be Newton.

"How do I look?" said Roy.

"Hold on, now." Arlen straightened Roy's tie, pulling the knot a little tighter against his thick neck. Roy's service ribbons were crooked and Arlen re-pinned them. There was a piece of lint on Roy's Combat Infantryman Badge and Arlen picked it off. "Now, how 'bout me?" said Arlen. Roy did the same, wiping brick dust from Arlen's shoulders and straightening Arlen's service ribbons with a tap of the finger.

The train made a slow, wide turn to the right, almost seeming to come back on itself. They were here, there was no more time. Both of the men stood up, donning their service caps. Roy looked at Arlen. "It's a good thing to come home." Arlen reached out and pulled Roy close. They hugged and gave each other a slap on the back, one that spoke more understanding than either of them ever would put in words.

The metallic *boo-woo-wooo-woooo-weeht* of the brakes was loud and clear, even above the murmur of the small crowd outside. The two of them stepped into the aisle and moved to the door. Those from the car behind merged with those ahead of Arlen at a shuffling pace and each singly descended to the ground near the platform. Before Arlen knew it, he was there himself, feet on the ground in the early morning light. He looked about for the family. They were all here, Arlen had no doubt.

Through the crowd around the door of the coach Arlen spotted, between the tall and wide, a familiar shape of hair. It was the right color, too. It disappeared behind a man in shirt-sleeves, but Arlen moved toward it through the crowd.

Maybe some people patted him on the back or welcomed him home — Arlen was unaware. He just pushed ahead through the bodies, fingers straining painfully against the bulk of the duffel bag. And there she was, and Legenia, too, and two of his sisters, fair-haired Rebecca with two children in tow and tall Elizabeth, who cheered lightly, somehow uncharacteristically restrained. But Caty seemed wholly real. She looked prettier than he remembered, her face was thinner than before, and her girlish behavior had been tamed, maturity come at last. She was smiling, not broadly, but genuinely. Arlen looked into her eyes and saw a touch of apprehension.

Smiling too, Arlen stepped forward as the women swarmed toward him. He dropped the duffel and hugged all of them at the same time, his arms never wider. "Oh, Arlen, welcome home, welcome home." He could feel his mother's tears dripping off her cheek and tickling their way down his neck. Arlen pulled away, grinning a little wider now. Legenia still cried, but her face was not joyful. Caty still looked concerned. He could not see why. He smiled, tried to dispel their emotion.

Then, after a quick thought: "Say, where's Pa?"

Legenia's tears stopped for a moment as she gathered enough composure to speak. "Arlen, your father passed."

What? Those words meant nothing. They were just words; they said nothing about the way things were. "What do you mean?" he said.

"He died, Arlen. He had a heart attack, the doctor said, out in the fields."

Arlen felt light-headed and his knees were weak.

"I found him out next to a tree . . . reckon he'd crawled there . . . didn't have enough strength to call to the house. He looked peaceful, though, Arlen."

The world went pale and wobbled. His hands shaking, his stomach and chest convulsing, he descended. The faces disappeared and shade covered him and he went down and down until earth caught him. No one could lift him up.

The car pulled up the driveway and stopped before the house. It looked the same as it ever had, although it badly needed a coat of paint. Weeds were sprouting around the corners of the porch. There was dust collecting on the windows. None of that mattered so much; the house could stand for years more. But what of the animals? The mules were out to pasture — who had put them out? What of the cows? Who had milked and fed them? The hogs? The chickens? The truck patch was full to bursting — who picked the okra and the beans? So much to do. He should set to it.

"Arlen?"

He felt Caty's breath on his ear. He shivered a little. "Yes?"

"Aren't you going to get out?"

He did not say anything.

"Arlen, I said you can come stay with us," said Rebecca, who sat behind the wheel. "We can make space for you — I've got a cot and everything. It'll be nice — you and me and Ma there too. Daniel won't mind it one bit. I'm sure he'd like to take you out for a beer when he gets a day off." She turned around in the seat and gave a hard look to her son and daughter who were squirming around on the floor under the adults' feet. They were quiet under their mother's demanding gaze, identical to Legenia's.

"You don't have to stay here," said Elizabeth, even though she was not the one offering space for Arlen to stay in and never would be. "In fact, I don't think you should be alone."

"Why's that?" Arlen snapped.

"You just got home. You should celebrate with your family. Rebecca's got a big dinner planned in your honor. Ruth couldn't make it today, but she will be there tonight. Don't you want to come eat with us?"

"I don't want a damn thing except to be here. That's all I've ever wanted."

Elizabeth folded her lanky arms and shook her head. "Well, you got your wish, I reckon."

Arlen looked into the back seat, glaring at his impudent sister. He wanted to yell at her, tell her what he really thought of her, or that he thought of her so little, that she meant almost nothing to him in the grand scheme of things, for she had left this little world here and gone as far as she dared, which was not that far, nor that daring, really, only Charlotte, but which she thought was Times Square compared to where she had come from. Legenia was next to her, and mother and daughter stared back at Arlen, their hard dark eyes seeing him but failing to grasp him. Only Caty's eyes were open. She put them out there for him, trying to meet him where he was. He would not disappoint Caty. He held his tongue.

"Arlen, you gonna get out?" said Rebecca in her hurried, frazzled voice. Good Rebecca, poor girl — the oldest but the sacrificing one, always run around and put upon by everyone else, especially Elizabeth. She suffered like Ruth, who had practically run off to Winston-Salem, unable to bear her older

209

sister either, and no boy from this part of the world looking at a Breckenridge girl after the way Elizabeth had poisoned the waters for any who came after her. Poor Rebecca, poor Ruth. The family he had known, loved, and fought for and would again, were all pulling their own way before he could step in to do what he should do for them, to hold them together in the last ditch. He pulled and they pulled the other way, and when he stopped, they turned around and pushed.

"Fine." Arlen threw open the car door and, his service cap in his hand, stepped out of the car. There it was, the smell of all his years which unspiraled before him. He smelled his childhood, his whole youth, the oldest part of him, in that earthy air. That clayey loam was all he really knew. The oaks and hickories on the wind and the thick green of the corn in the heat redoubled the sense. The house, the corn crib, the unchinked barn — it was all as it was, the old order, unchanged. He was here, in it, but his place was not clear yet. The sun beat upon his head as it always had. When it is hot, too hot to work, you go under the shade. He walked up onto the porch, the steps creaking in the same old spots. The front door was unlocked and Arlen went right in. He stood in the front hall, which was the same as it was five years ago. He got a nose full of musty wood and a lingering scent of soap from the kitchen.

Pa, I'm back. I made it. Don't you know?

If only he could proclaim it to the one man who would understand. Not just one who went and came back, but went for the same thing.

There was someone behind him — Legenia. She stood there with arms at her side, leaning against the door frame much as she ever had, except this time she was looking in.

"Ma, where did you bury him?"

"We put him in God's Acre, out back of the church, with the rest of his family."

"Not here?"

"What, on the farm?"

"Yes'm."

"No, Arlen. Why? Is that what you wanted?"

"It's what Pa would've wanted." Arlen shook his head. "I wish you would have waited."

"Arlen, it's August, it's just too hot to keep a body lying around. We had to. Besides, we didn't know when you were coming home."

Arlen swore, but kept it under his breath. He walked a few more steps into the house.

"I wish it hadn't been like this, Arlen. I wish you'd gotten the V-mail with the news in time. But you being upset ain't no reason to ruin your homecoming, and it ain't no reason for you to stay here."

Arlen whirled around. "Ma'am? You think that's what me coming here is about?"

"What else would it be? I know you miss him something awful, Arlen, but it ain't gonna do you no good to stay here in the middle of it." Legenia's eyes were hard and dark as ever. "It ain't gonna bring him back."

When did she become like this?

Arlen jabbed a finger at her, almost into her face. "You know, Ma, you're right. But that ain't got nothin' to do with me wantin' to stay here. I just want to be home. Right here."

"But what will you do?"

He did not understand how she could not see. "I'll work the farm. Pa's not here, so I'll do it by myself. I'll do it if you're here or not."

Her son had never spoken to her like that before. Legenia's eyes became harder. "But why, Arlen? That's why I can't understand. Maybe the girls do. They want to keep the farm in the family, but you know they can't help, they've got their own families. You're home, safe and sound and all in one piece, praise the Lord. Don't you want to rest and recuperate? You should celebrate. You need to enjoy this blessing God gave you. Take time and find yourself a good job in a little while when you feel like it."

"I don't need no job."

Legenia squinted and her lips pressed together in that familiar look of disappointment. "You'll end up like him, you know."

Then he saw it.

She thinks the farm killed him.

It can't be, don't she see that? What gives you life can't kill you.

She begrudged him his own life.

Arlen quivered with anger and he had to ball up his fists. Take away one piece of the whole and it all would teeter and fall. If he had not come home right when he did, what would have happened to the corn and the animals? Lose all that and the farm was gone, and yet Legenia seemed to have forgotten all about them in an instant. How easily it could have gone the other way.

But he did not run over such possibilities in his head over and over, like a younger man. To make a bargain or question was ingratitude. He had survived, he was here, and even if all Arlen had was himself — that hard, honed-down place he now started to fall back upon once again, accepting all the pain of the endless present and dulling it down with his resolution to remember what was and push forward until he got there again — it was enough. Enough to pick up that thin thread running far behind him and walk ahead with it, taking it hand over hand.

"Arlen, are you stayin' or are you coming with us?" Legenia's eyes did not

211

say it, but he could tell from the tone in her voice that she wanted him to come back with them, to live as they believed he was meant to, the brave young man, the veteran, their Arlen.

He was not theirs any longer.

"I'm stayin'."

Legenia nodded curtly, sealing their separation forever. "Come get your things out of the trunk, then." Her disappointment in him was palpable as she turned and left the house. Arlen followed her out. Legenia got in the front passenger door. Arlen did not look at her nor his sisters. All he saw was Caty slamming the trunk and coming toward him, bent almost in half, trying to heft his duffel bag over her shoulder.

Lord, no, not her too.

But her eyes were open, searching, honest as the day they had met. She struggled with the bag and it fell from her shoulder, almost pulling her to the ground as she fought with its dead weight. Arlen caught both it and her before they tumbled to the dust.

"Caty, we'll drop you by home," said Legenia from the rolled down window.

Caty brushed hair from her eyes and mouth. "No, ma'am, thank you. I'll stay here with Arlen for a while." The Breckenridge women stared at her. Whether they were scandalized or affronted, it was hard to tell. Caty looked to Arlen and smiled, her eyebrows arching in the middle a little. "He needs some breakfast."

Arlen bid his mother and sisters farewell, the obligatory, mannerful happy-to-be-homes and good-to-see-you and i-love-yous and i-will-be-by-soon-don't-hesitate-to-calls suddenly cutting through the icy resentment that had built over his own refusal to share in the life they thought he wanted, which they just knew he wanted, deep within, and which he would not take, for all his stupid intransigence, that silly boy. The war must have done something to him. So sad, isn't it? they would say.

He did not watch them pull out of the driveway, but turned away immediately, hefted his duffel and walked back into the house, Caty following behind him.

"What do you want to eat?"

He did not answer. He just stood in the dark front room, arms akimbo.

"Arlen?"

He was still queasy from his anger at his mother, but his stomach gurgled. He should eat. "Anything at all, Caty."

"Well, all right, it might take me a while to get a fire going, but you just have a seat and I'll have some coffee in there as soon as I can." She saw his face. "Don't you worry, I know where everything is. Go on, have a seat."

He would not sit, not in any of the chairs. Or maybe he just could not sit, could not physically bring himself to do it.

If the windows had been open, Arlen might have heard the corn creaking in the heat. He could have smelled the vegetables wafting in from the truck patch on the humid air. The grass was long, too, and it gave up its own dampness from its draped-over blades as the sun hit the midday peak. He heard the back door open. She was going for the firewood. She surely did not know where to go. But Arlen did not go after her.

His eyes wandered around the house, lighting upon one thing or another: the framed photograph of him as infant on Great-Grandfather Alexander's knee, the rocking chair in the corner, and the little side table with the giant hard-backed, cracked leather-covered Bible sitting on its low shelf. Already the Good Book had gathered dust. Five years gone and yet Arlen still knew what to do when he saw it.

I'll have to fix the family tree now, put Pa's dates in there.

Tears welled fast and he turned away from the scene of the front room in a flash. That was about as final an act as a man could have on this earth, done through his offspring's hands, his death year inscribed inside the cover of the old Bible, testifying that he was really truly gone now. Wade was not coming back, and it did not matter how much Arlen had fought and bled and steeled himself through suffering to see his father again, there was no chance of that coming to pass, not in this world, the one Arlen had fought so hard to stay alive in. To take up a pen and write in his ill-practiced cursive "1945" next to the birth year was to seal with his own acknowledgment that he was the only one left. That was too much.

But if he did not, no one would. And then no one from here on out would ever know.

Sucking the tears back in, Arlen walked back into the front room to the side table, and knelt down. He reached for the huge Bible, but his hand stopped. The dust had made a pair of oily fingerprints, so obviously Wade's hand, stand out to the eye. They were the last traces of the man. Wade's clothes had been washed and put away by Legenia, his smell gone forever. No phonograph had ever captured his voice; there were only a couple pictures of him, all of which his mother had taken. And when Arlen picked up that scripture, as he must do, for the generations of Breckenridges to come, so that they would know all this, his own hand would erase his father's forever.

The tears came again, but Arlen held them in. They grew to sobs that he barely suppressed. He rose from his kneeling position and collapsed into the rocking chair. Arlen's hands gripped the arms where Wade's had once done the same. He sat there, holding on tight, eyes screwed shut, breaths deep. His stomach boiled up and he felt the knot in his throat.

Pa, where are you? Why'd you have to go now? Pa, why now?

There was only silence.

He broke at last, sobbing to himself in the musty, still house. He cried and cried to himself, cried like he never had before in this house, like he only ever had for other men. Tears wet his cheeks and he wiped them away with his sleeve, the cloth catching on already-growing stubble. His eyes cast about. Here he was, right amongst all these things, touching the old Bible from the old chair, and yet it was all gone like it had been wiped from the earth. The things remained the same, the farm was still here, but what of the people that sustained it? Wade was gone; Legenia was gone. This farm would fall apart without them. And yet they themselves were nothing without the farm giving them all that it could — its security, its peace, its independence. Neither of his parents had that any longer — they both had lost it forever, Wade by death, Legenia by surrender. Arlen had fought for this and for them, and he had lost both of the latter.

Good Lord, what if I lose the farm, too?

He heard the clatter of Caty coming into the kitchen again, probably with an armful of firewood.

Can't have her see me like this.

Arlen forced himself out of the chair and went outside onto the porch. The screen door thwacked behind him and he stood outside it, still under the shade of the porch, feet spread by nature at parade rest. It was better here, looking out over the land. That still remained, the land and his father's mark on it. Arlen reached into his shirt pocket and produced a pack of Lucky Strikes. He put the coffin nail between his lips and with shaking fingers flicked his lighter twice, touching the pale flame to the cigarette and inhaling. The smoke coursed through him. His nerves settled with each puff.

Arlen stood at the brink once again like he had many months before: shaken, upset, but alive. He was looking at what might have been, and he could do nothing but curse at himself. He had lost nothing — it was his parents who had lost. He had had his fight, but so had his mother and father. Keeping this place going without him there had been an immense struggle — Arlen knew that much from the letters Legenia had sent of what she saw, and what she saw had surely only been a sliver of what Wade knew about the crop and the comings and goings of money and their prospects for the future. Arlen did not regret that it was so, that he had gone off and left the fight here to them — that matter was settled forever to him. For it would have all vanished had the Germans won. But over there he had forgotten that all was not decided in this world, not even here at home, not anymore.

Arlen had not lost, and his parents, though beaten, had not lost either. For he had made it. He was here and that meant something. Every sacrifice of those around him had put him here, the great end of all his striving. He had come to it at last, though not in the way he had imagined. It was only him now, without his parents to round the circle, and that meant he was not done. Not if it was to be what they had once made it. And he must do it without those who had been with him along the way.

Ain't got to mourn for Pa. He's at peace now. And he's got me here for him. Ain't nothin' else to do but to pick up where he left off.

The screen door banged like a rifle shot and Arlen jumped. He dropped the cigarette.

"Oh my, I didn't mean to scare you, Arlen." Caty reached out with both hands, holding a cup of coffee full out to him. "Just black, or did you start taking cream and sugar in the Army?"

"No, ma'am, just like it is. Thank you." He ground out the cigarette with his heel, took the brimming cup, and blew on it. He was trying to think of what to say to her. It was so strange, seeing her like this now — flesh and blood, right next to him.

She reached out and cupped his cheek with her hand. It was as small and soft as he remembered it. He quivered a bit. "Oh, Arlen, look at you. You're ashen."

"Am I?"

She did not ask what was wrong. "Come on, sit down. Just sit with me." She dusted off a chair and he sat down. She sat on the arm next to him. He took a sip of the coffee. "Is it strong enough?"

"Did a spoon stand up in it?" he said.

She laughed. "No, but you want me to get you one?"

He smiled and did not answer. He sucked a mouthful of the black strap down his smoky throat. She saw the contented look on his face. "Can I try some?"

"I didn't know you drank coffee."

Caty took the cup from him. Her fingers crossed his and again he felt that shock of life. She was more alive than anyone he had ever seen. He had only known the dead for a long time now, breathing and walking men who knew their time was up sooner or later. There was no trace of any of that in her.

She smacked her lips in satisfaction. "Now I know how you like it."

He was smiling. He had not smiled like that in a long time. She really was right next to him. She was not some figment of his imagination, some distant thought which only stirred up longing and self-doubt. He had nothing to fight his way back to: she was here. And after all these years! She did not reject him; she felt no strangeness in her proximity to him; indeed, she approached him with a womanly directness, not the playfulness of an overgrown girl. Had she

215

been unfaithful? He thrust the thought away. No, it was not that kind of directness, that comes from bodily knowledge. It was that she had been in his life and that thus she knew him. He had been gone from it, but she had been here where it took place, and now that he returned, she was no stranger to him.

An impulse came: he could not wait any longer.

Setting down his coffee, Arlen rose and opened his duffel bag. After a minute of rummaging, he found it. He turned around, not rising. In his hand was a clear sparkle on a thin band of gold. It was a fine piece; he had traded a sack of flour for it with the starving wife of some disgraced bürgermeister. Arlen raised his eyebrows. "Caty, you know I love you, and you know it ain't like me to ask for things, but I reckon I got to, so—"

Her voice went up an octave. "Oh, Arlen, yes, of course, of course."

He slipped the ring on her finger. He rose up and they kissed. He pressed her close, his whole body flushed at her scent and softness and the life that coursed through her, fluid and gentle. She held him, caressed his face, his neck, and his shoulder, and his wound for once did not even prickle at the touch. At last Arlen broke away. "Let's go right now," he said.

Caty's eyes were wide with fear and delight. "Where? The church?"

He shook his head. "No, not that. Your house."

"Oh."

"I have to ask your father, you know."

"Oh."

"Reckon we did it the opposite way we were supposed to, but, aw, hell, I ain't in the mood for standin' on convention." He swept her up in his arms and took her down off the porch and carried her to the truck. His face was set, seemingly unmoved by the moment, but there was gallantry in his arms. Caty touched his cheek gracefully. "Arlen," she said insistently.

He opened the door to the truck and put her inside. "Hush, now, you ain't got to worry about a thing. I'm back, ain't I? It's you and me now. I know what I got to do for us and, Caty, it's all gonna be all right. I love you."

She smiled appreciatively, but her eyebrows were arched. "Oh, Arlen, I know, I love you, too, but I . . . I was going to say, the fire is still going."

"Aw, hell." He went back inside and put the fire out. She was still smiling when he came back out and cranked up the truck. He reached into his pocket again and pulled out the Lucky Strikes. He placed one between his lips and flicked the lighter a couple of times.

"Here, let me." Caty took the lighter from him and struck it. She touched the flame to the tip and he blew out a long stream of smoke that hit and curled against the windshield. He rolled down the window and released it to the humid midday air. Caty still held the lighter with one hand and had her hand

216

open with the other. He put the pack of Luckies in her hand. She fumbled with the pack, pulling out three by accident, then trying to put them back in as neatly as they had come out. She put the cigarette between her lips as she had seen him do. Caty touched the lighter's flame to the cigarette and breathed in, very deeply. It got all down in her lungs. She sputtered, hunching over in her seat and almost dropping the cigarette from her lips. But she caught her breath, slowly sat back upright, and, with careful poise, began to smoke again. She rolled down her window just as Arlen did and they puffed away together. Arlen pulled the truck down the drive. The engine strained through the pedals and the shifter. The bald tires slipped and spun a couple of times as he pulled from the dirt onto the paved surface of NC-10, but they grabbed eventually. Caty reached over and set her newly bejeweled hand atop his on the shifter and it felt good. He headed east.

Her family's house was still right off of Startown Road. The house looked like it had a fresh coat of white paint and the garden was full. The family car was still there, with a B card rationing sticker on the windshield: essential to the war effort.

At the loud rumble of the Chevy and the crackle of gravel under tires, Mr. Cline came out onto the porch. He was dressed as if for work, even though it was a Saturday, with a white shirt and tie and gray slacks. Arlen stared at him through the open truck window, not believing it was the same man, the same drunk who had lost his job at the mill and only been saved by his brother-in-law's farm. This man had a swagger, as much as someone so stocky could swagger, and Mr. cline came right down off of the porch toward the truck. He was smiling and spread his hands wide in welcome. Arlen got out and Mr. Cline grabbed Arlen's hand and began pumping it up and down. "Arlen, good to see you, welcome home, good to see you. I wish had been able to come down to the station to greet you this morning, but I had to see to something down at the mill." He did not wait for Arlen to ask which one, adding, "Union Mills, in Maiden. You know it?"

"Heard of it, yessir."

"Well, well, never mind me, this is your day, son. Welcome, again, welcome home."

"Thank you, sir."

"Come on up on the porch out of the sun."

"Hi, Pa," said Caty, giving her father a kiss on the cheek. They went up on the porch, and Mrs. Cline came out and greeted them all. "Would y'all like some tea? Just give me a minute and I'll bring some out." Arlen sat down awkwardly on the swing next to Caty and Mr. Cline sat back in his chair, crossing his legs and showing off his neat cap-toe black brogues. He evaluated

Arlen silently. He seemed different somehow, Mr. Cline did, and it was not just the nicer clothes, nor the searching stare he put across the short distance toward Arlen.

"You look happy, Arlen," said Mr. Cline.

"Yessir, reckon I am." Arlen felt he should go ahead and say what he came for. You take what you have to do and do it right then and there and don't think about it too much. Anything less only makes it worse. He wet his lips and looked right across at Mr. Cline. "Reckon that's 'cause I've gone and done something, and I figured I should ask you if it's all right."

"Oh?" Mr. Cline leaned forward, pulling a handkerchief from his shirt pocket and blotting his forehead. "Go on, then."

"Sir, Caty and I are going to be married, and I'd appreciate your blessing."

Mr. Cline's face fell for a moment. This was unconventional, indeed. He was a run-down and rough man, or at least he had been back in the day, and yet even then Arlen would have still given him the courtesy of asking permission before proposing. But the clean, well-washed appurtenances of his new station implied that he was supposed to be more highly regarded by some quaint and half-believed standard of respectability, and Mr. Cline expected at least that and almost certainly more should be accorded to him. And as much as he might respect Arlen for who he was and the family he came from, rules had to be followed. Mr. Cline ran his eyes up and down Arlen, sizing him up as if he'd never seen him before. Then he gave a half-forced smile. "Arlen, I've heard you made quite the soldier. You've stood by our country, and stood by Caty all these years, too."

"Yessir."

"Then I reckon there's no need to stand on convention with me, you've earned the right to take life as it comes to you. It's the American way, ain't it?"

"Yessir," said Arlen, not caring if it was.

Mrs. Cline came out onto the porch with the tea. "Dear, Arlen and Caty are going to be married," said Mr. Cline to his wife. She feigned surprise — what could be more natural for youngsters separated by years of war than to get married — but her excitement was genuine. "Oh, congratulations to you both. We are so happy." Hugs and kisses all around, and more outpouring of thrill and exultation. Caty's mother poured glasses of tea and they all drank it down thirstily, the sweet iciness settling in their stomachs. Mr. Cline folded his hands on his belly as he leaned back a little in the chair. "Would you like something stronger to put in there, Arlen?"

"No sir, I'm fine, thank you."

They drank their tea for a minute. "We're so sorry to hear about your father, Arlen," said Mrs. Cline.

Arlen simply nodded. He could not bring himself to words over it now.

Think of Caty. Think of what you have to do.

"I saw him, Arlen, not too long ago," said Mr. Cline. "At the rationing board."

Arlen's eyes narrowed. "I didn't know Pa was on the board. No one ever mentioned it in their letters."

"He weren't. I am on the board and he came by askin' for an exemption for something. Can't quite remember what he needed, but it weren't the first time. Of course, I looked out for him, made sure he got it. We have to look out for those we know, don't we?"

Arlen said nothing. He refused to believe Mr. Cline. Times had been hard, but his father had not begged for anything in his life and could not have even in his most desperate moments. The land gave them all they needed, even though not all they wanted, but the latter was a matter of discipline, and they knew how to do without. *Ain't no way. Pa would have found a way, I know it.*

"How is the farm, Arlen?" said Mr. Cline. He was controlling the conversation now. Neither his wife nor his daughter spoke, waiting on him, watching for his lead. He was indeed different, a more powerful man. "Caty looked after the animals when your father died and your mother moved out."

Arlen looked over at Caty. She smiled coyly but proudly. Well, now, that was something. "Sir, it looks as good as it ever has," he replied.

"Is that so?"

"Yessir."

Mr. Cline took a piece of ice from the glass and sucked on it between his teeth. "That's what Caty told me. I will say, that doesn't sound like the picture Wade painted for us."

"Pa was always colorful. He could make you see what he wanted you to," said Arlen.

"You reckon you inherited that same gift?"

"I inherited one thing from Pa and that's the farm."

"Well, I hope for Caty's sake you didn't inherit all the problems he had with it."

"I don't know what you think they are, they ain't nothin' I can't handle."

Mr. Cline crunched the ice between his molars. "I ain't sayin' that, Arlen. But you are marryin' my daughter. I thought a bit of caution about tryin' to stick to the old ways was fair." He almost reached into the glass for another piece of ice, but stopped and let the glass rest on his belly, a wet ring growing on his shirt. "You see, Arlen, on the rationing board I get to see what a lot of folks don't. And sometimes it's what they can't even see themselves. Just like at the mill, where I oversee the spinning floor. It ain't what's right in front of you, but how the whole thing is going. Everyone has their own problems and thinks they're the hardest thing in the world and everyone wants a solution to 'em

219

and they always come to us, askin' to fix it. Sometimes we can and sometimes we can't, but the important thing is we know that. We see the whole picture of this county and we know what it takes to make it run smoothly. Got to keep folks from fightin' with each other over what little there is, that's a big part of it. And while I ain't braggin' on myself, it's a good thing that it's folks like me are in charge of things like the board, folks that run things. Maybe some other folks have a good heart and a good head, but it ain't no use to us if they can't manage their own affairs. That's how this county used to be run, back in the day and for too long. Well, I say it's a good thing this war happened, because at least it's shown us that — ain't nothin' for the old ways."

Arlen was stock still on the swing. Caty tried to gently kick her feet against the porch, but she could not move the swing in time with him and stopped. Mr. Cline's mouth moved and Mrs. Cline replied, nodding in agreement, but Arlen did not hear either one of them. His vision closed in, tightening up into that familiar old tunnel where he only cared for as much ground as he could see and as far as he could shoot.

That sonuvabitch. It ain't his place to tell me what works and what don't. He ain't never had to try and figure that out. Always had someone givin' his bread to him for whatever little they could pull out of him. He ain't had to account for what he does.

How did he get there? Folks like Wade would never have put a Mr. Cline in charge. And even those less recalcitrant and more modern than Wade would have seen reason when he set to convincing them. There was still the old heartwood in them yet. But here was Mr. Cline all the same, and from his words it seemed clear that there were many more like him, running the county as they saw fit. Maybe folks put Mr. Cline in charge and never protested what he did. Or maybe they did not choose him but acquiesced all the same. But what did it matter? Mr. Cline spoke for all the folks in charge. He was one of them, and yet it was clear, too, that the rulers were like him, people of the county, from messy and imperfect and ordinary backgrounds. They were the same as Arlen in many ways, or at least they had once been, in younger and harder days, but what about now? Surely they could not have changed that much. Surely they must see what Arlen saw.

They don't. You know that. Pa knew that, he told you as much. They've always been there, at least as long as Pa could remember, and maybe a little bit longer than that. They ain't nothin' new.

But their confidence was. If they were anything like Mr. Cline, there was no more propriety about what was a man's and could not be touched. There was no more convincing them or turning their arguments against them — their words and acts were complete, sealed, without petition.

All they got is their slander, Lord, slander of my father and his ways. He ain't around to defend himself, or defend us. I ought to pay them back for Pa.

But look at him: ain't gonna do no good to give Mr. Cline a piece of my mind. Ain't what Pa would've done.

Pa would've let it alone and gone home and worked harder. Built the farm up better, so that the closer they thought they got, the farther they were.

That's what I'll do. Same as ever. I ain't gonna leave no gaps in the line. I'll be on guard and I'll see 'em comin', every time.

Arlen just sat, his face a mask, though his stomach and chest ran hot and his neck was prickling. He had to keep them from seeing this shaking and boiling on the inside. He nodded agreeably, forced smile, and swirled the tea in his glass.

"Oh, you're bleeding."

He felt Caty's hand on his jaw and the scrape of a handkerchief across his stubble. Reaching up, Arlen felt blood from his lip. He tasted it, too, like water from an iron pipe. He had gnawed his lip too hard.

"Are you all right?" said Caty, wiping the blood from his chin.

"I'm fine," said Arlen, taking the handkerchief from her and blotting the rest of the blood.

"What is it?" she said.

"Just an old wound." The blood stopped for the most part and he folded the handkerchief back up and handed it back to her. "Ain't nothin' to worry about."

"How did you get it?" she asked.

Arlen said nothing. He did not look at her, but stared across to Mr. and Mrs. Cline. Their faces were unsure. They did not know what to make of this. The war was sitting on their porch swing. It was not the war they had read of in the paper, squawked by Edward R. Murrow over the radio, and felt in the tiny deprivations of day to day life. This war was angry, silent, enduring. Long minutes passed. Arlen felt the swing began to sway beneath him. He let his legs move with it and his body joined in the motion with Caty. Mr. Cline mopped his brow and took another piece of ice between his teeth. The sucking sound almost matched the *tong-tong* rhythm of the swing's swaying chains.

Mrs. Cline forced a smile. "Well, now, when should we expect the wedding?"

XIX

The doors to the church were flung open for Mr. and the newly-made Mrs. Breckenridge, letting the afternoon sunlight flood into the sanctuary that reverberated with the cheers of family and friends and neighbors. Arlen and Caty stopped for a moment to allow one of Caty's distant second cousins, who owned his own camera, to snap a photo of them. Arlen gave a slight smile, standing perfectly erect. He wore his uniform, replete with medals and a fresh crease down the legs from the old flatiron. He would have preferred a suit, but the second-hand one of Wade's looked like a potato sack even after his sisters' endeavours with needles and thread. In the end, he did not care a whit for his looks. He only cared about Caty looking serene in her pure white dress. It was very simple, with just a little lace and no long train, but very elegant all the same. Her own smile was not as subdued as his.

The photograph finished, Caty and Arlen stepped to the side outside the church door. The guests began to stream out of the church, led by Roy, Arlen's best man, and Caty's cousin, maid of honor. Everyone came and shook Arlen's hand and the women embraced Caty or gave her a friendly peck on the cheek. The guests were eager to push on past to the tables of food set in the grass between the church and parked automobiles, but still they knew to pause and offer congratulations:

"Best of luck to y'all!"

"If y'all aren't the finest couple we've seen in a long time!"

"Took your time, but y'all made good on it!"

The comments flew thick and fast. Arlen could hardly remember what he or anyone else had said. His hand grew sore from shaking, and he was sweating heavily in the very last of the Indian summer.

His mother approached, looking as worn as she had been a few weeks ago. It was not the shock of death that had given her that countenance — this was her new frailty. But her dark eyes seemed wider and happier than usual. "Oh, Arlen, I'm so proud of you," Legenia said, hugging him. "This has turned out wonderfully."

"Thank you, Ma. Ain't sure how y'all put it all together so quickly."

Rebecca, who planted a kiss on his cheek right after Legenia, said, "No need to say thanks. You just get right down to life with this beautiful new bride of yours."

"It's really all thanks to Mrs. Cline," said Elizabeth, who leaned in and gave Arlen a distanced hug. "You should be thanking her." Ruth, last of them all, gave Arlen a big hug, one full of strength for the tiny girl she was, wrapping her arms around his neck and hanging on tight. Arlen hugged her back and shook the hand of Rebecca's husband, Daniel, who smiled knowingly and said nothing. He was not a veteran of war, but he was a veteran of this family; he knew his place at times like this. His children were running around already, glad to not have to sit in the church any longer, and he nodded to Arlen and walked away after them.

Ruth finally released Arlen from her hug. He could see tears behind her stylish glasses; she did not bother to wipe them away. "I'm so happy for you."

"Thanks, Ruth."

"You just deserve it so much, after all you went through, being apart from Caty like that and the war — it's a blessing, Arlen."

"Yes, it is."

"Arlen, I'm . . . I'm sorry."

His brow furrowed. "What do you mean?"

"I'm sorry about Pa. I'm sorry you missed him. I'm sorry you have to take over that farm by yourself."

"It ain't 'that farm,' Ruth. It's our farm."

She hid her face as tears began to flow faster. "I only wish you could work it, Arlen. That's all."

"Why, Ruth, I—"

At that moment Mr. and Mrs. Cline came sidling up, as thrilled as anyone else there. Ruth turned away and disappeared past Caty, past the rest of the family gathered together, disappearing into the crowd of guests. Mrs. Cline planted wet kisses on the bride's and groom's faces and Mr. Cline pumped Arlen's hand up and down. "Congratulations, Arlen. You two look fine today. A shame you two couldn't have done this five years ago, but, well, better late than never."

Arlen nodded and grunted in concurrence, craning his neck after Ruth. She was gone, but he kept looking for her. And he did not want to talk to his father-in-law. If only folks would leave him to look after his new bride. No one let him, though. More guests shook his hand and embraced Caty and asked endless question about their future and Arlen dodged that question, as it was settled, and then they asked about Wade, or rather expressed their regret at his passing, and Arlen thanked them, though they could not know the half of it. Before anyone else, Wade should have seen this day. He should have been the best man. Or Paine, who was equally deserving. But that was impossible, and so Arlen had settled on an old friend of the same stock, on whom Arlen had never depended but knew like the back of his own hand.

And here he came at last, as the guests floated away toward the food and began to eat. His tie already loosened, Roy held in one hand a tall stack of Dixie cups and in the other grasped a heavy oblong object in a paper bag. "Get yourself a cup, Arlen."

"Ooooh, boy, I bet I know what this is."

Roy tipped the paper bag over the Dixie cup and clear liquid sloshed out.

"Oh, Roy," said Caty, shaking her head in the smallest kind of disappointment.

Arlen peered into the cup. "Shit, ain't no more Volstead Act, you don't have to keep it in the bag."

"I know, but some of the Baptists here might have something to say," said Roy.

"You never know," said Arlen. "Some of 'em are wet and it ain't 'cause they've been dunked in the Jacob's Fork." He knocked back the liquor and coughed once from the back of his throat. "Good Lord, that's smooth at first, but it's straight fire when it gets down far enough."

Roy filled up the cup about halfway again. Arlen held the cup out to Caty. She shook her head and crinkled her nose. "Oh, no, Arlen."

"Go on, have yourself a sip."

She took it reluctantly. She did not like alcohol, having seen what it did to her father when she was a girl. Barely a drop hit her tongue and Caty spluttered, forcing it back into Arlen's hands. "Y'all drink vile things," she said. The two men laughed and Arlen kissed her cheek. "Are you hungry?" he said.

"Starving."

"Well, come on, then." He held out his arm and she took it. They went and talked with a few more people and then filled their plates and made their way to the big table with his family and her family. They took their places and talked a little more and then at last got food into their bellies. They ate heartily and Roy came and refilled Arlen's cup and they shared a drink together. Then Roy went on around, filling up cups here and there at different tables, laughing, jesting with everyone, checking to make sure every one was well, setting problems aright — that was what he did by nature. Maybe he would make a good highway patrolman after all. Arlen watched him from time to time and was happy he was here. At least one of the others had made it back. Not the closest one, but a good one, who, even if he did not go as Arlen did, deserved his own life because he had helped end that war over there.

Arlen felt eyes on him. Both of the families were looking at his hand, which held his fork like a steam shovel. He was not at the mess hall, he did not have to pour the plate down his gullet in mere seconds. Arlen turned the fork around and ate slowly. They still watched him from the corner of their eyes, and Caty, too. Arlen would not have any of that. He leaned over for a kiss and she let him take it. Everything was all right between them. He offered her the Dixie cup again and she tried to brush it away. But he kept pushing it toward her and his sisters egged her on, and finally Caty took a sip. She choked and sputtered, but handled it better this time, a flush of red coming to her cheeks. She was beautiful, today and everyday. In mirth, Arlen drained the last of the moonshine from the cup. The sweet fire ran right down his throat and he began to glow from deep within. He tucked into the food with his original vigor. Roy came around with the paper bag and with a wobbly hand refilled Arlen's cup. He then scooted around to the far side of the table and filled Mr. Cline's. Arlen's father-in-law gripped Roy's paw and pumped it up and down enthusiastically. Roy moved on and Mr. Cline knocked the whole Dixie cup back in one shot. He picked up a fried chicken leg and, gnawing on it, said, "Arlen."

"Yessir?"

"I want to say I'm proud of you."

"Thank you, sir."

"I really am. You'll be a fine husband for Caty."

"Yessir, I'll do my best." *Wish he'd shut up.* Arlen took a bite of corn pudding, washed it down with a gulp of liquor, and began to turn toward Caty, who conversed with Ruth.

But Mr. Cline leaned on his elbows on the table, his tie almost in his food. "Arlen, tell me, what are your plans? Are you discharged yet?"

"No, sir, not yet."

"When will they let you out?"

"Oh, reckon in about another week I'll have to go down to Fort Jackson and report back in. Just to get my discharge, they ain't gonna keep me around."

"That's good, good news," said Mr. Cline. "What are your plans after that?"

Arlen wet his lips with another sip from the Dixie cup. What was he getting at? "Reckon I've had 'em made for a while. Don't you worry, they're all set."

Mr. Cline drank some more after Roy refilled his cup. "Are you going to collect that fifty-two-twenty benefit?"

"Ain't heard of that."

Mr. Cline's eyes went as wide as they could in their sockets. "Well, hell, I thought everyone has. Part of the G.I. Bill. Best damn thing this country has ever done!" His voice dropped as some folks looked askance at him. "It pays you a year of twenty dollars a week in unemployment. It'll help you and Caty pay the bills while you look for work."

225

Arlen swished the last of the liquor around in his mouth. "I ain't been unemployed a day in my life."

The comment made no impact on Mr. Cline. His hands crept up from wherever they had rested under the table and he began to gesticulate with fingers and palms that squeezed and caressed the air like he owned it. "Arlen, I know it's been a long war and a long time since you've worked, but things are gonna get movin' pretty quick in this country. Gonna be a lot of opportunities and it pays for you to take advantage of every single one you can. You'll have a wife to take care of, and some children, too, in the next few years. You ought to give them a good life."

"I will. Got it all planned out."

"Good, good to hear that." Mr. Cline picked up his fork and tucked into his food again.

At last, a little peace. Arlen looked to Caty again, hoping she would finish her conversation. He would rather walk around and speak with the guests than stay here.

Mr. Cline continued as if there had never been a pause. "So you've been lookin' for work, then? Whereabouts?"

He was just a dog with a bone. Arlen summoned his last reserves of patience and said, "Ain't been lookin' nowhere. I've been busy bringin' in the corn crop."

Mr. Cline's face lost its jovial tightness. "Don't tell me that's your big plan. Ain't no money to be made off farmin' like that."

Rudeness is judgment, son. We have manners so we do not judge others. Arlen could hear Wade's voice now. He thought of his father's own expositions on Scripture. Judgment must be met by the truth.

Well, let him have it.

"Yessir, I know."

"You know what?" Mr. Cline bawled.

"I know there ain't no money in it. And that's best. Never needed a lot of money, and if I don't need it, it don't need me."

Mr. Cline snapped his fedora onto the table with an angry flick of his arm. "Dammit, Arlen, don't you joke around with me. This is a serious matter. This is my daughter you're talkin' about here."

Arlen just sat and let him keep talking. Heads around them turned toward them and stayed glued to the two men.

"If you don't get movin', you'll be left behind. Someone else will take your place in the world, son," said Mr. Cline.

Heat prickled its way up to the top of Arlen's scalp. "I ain't your son."

"Well, you'd best take my advice like you were. Maybe you don't like that, but if you don't, there'll be a helluva trouble for you and Caty. I'm just tryin' to help you Arlen. You could be like the others and get yourself one of those low-interest mortgages for a house or maybe even go to college. The government will pay for it."

"Arlen never finished high school," said Elizabeth. Arlen's eyes snapped over at her. She was not repentant. Arlen's eyes moved to his mother. Legenia said nothing, sitting at her place, eyes ahead, looking up and down between her food and the distance in the autumn sky. There was no help coming from any of them.

"If Arlen will listen to reason, he ain't got to let that stand in his way," said Mr. Cline toward the other Breckenridges, though not really to them. "He don't have to stay on the farm because no one will take him. He's proved himself and the least he can do is take a hand up to get what's rightfully his: a good life, good job, good house, and plenty of money."

Arlen tasted blood as his teeth cut into his lip. *They don't see. Not a one of 'em. There ain't nothin' holdin' me back. I just don't want any of that. I have what I want. I have it all. Why won't they leave me alone with it?*

Mr. Cline waggled his thick finger at Arlen. "I'm not gonna tell you 'you'll see one day,' Arlen. Because that'll be too late. Too late for my Caty, too late for my grandchildren. I ain't gonna have that."

"Ain't yours to decide," said Arlen as he licked the blood from his lip. "It's mine."

An exasperated groan issued forth from Mr. Cline's thick throat and his fat fist crumpled the Dixie cup. "I don't know why we fought this war if we're gonna throw this nation away on the likes of you. Don't you know what's good for you when you see it? It's what's good for the country too — it's what we all deserve."

The truth was no less bare than any other time it had come to Arlen, and having seen it so often rendered in blood and steel, he was not perturbed by its bareness. There was no escaping Mr. Cline. He would keep on coming. He would keep demanding. Never would he let up. It was not the man — Mr. Cline alone was as weak as straw. It was what drove him on. Something had grabbed hold of Mr. Cline and tightened him up, like cinching up one's laces. That something had done it, or they had done it, whatever or whomever it was — but something drove him on and on, right at Arlen, and it was because Mr. Cline believed it. He would keep coming because he believed he would win — everything told him that he would and it would never get out of his head because he had forgotten otherwise. Arlen could see it in Mr. Cline's face — his weakness and inability in older days never registered; he did not recall that he had once depended on his brother-in-law's farm simply to eat. He took all the slogans of the world into his half-thinking, empty head and made them his own and whether they whispered like gossip or squawked like the radio, they

227

all said, Victory is ours if you will only take it. Take it, take it now, Cline.

He's like the fuckin' Krauts. Ain't no stoppin' him if you let him come. He'll get to you eventually.

Unless you put him down.

That sealed it. Arlen stood up quickly, knocking the table back with the force of his legs, the plates sliding almost to the edge. Mr. Cline's mouth hung open in mid-sentence. The man was startled, but not afraid, Arlen could see that. "Get up out of that chair," said Arlen.

"What the hell do you mean?" snarled back Mr. Cline, gaining more and more courage by the moment.

"Get up, or are you a coward?"

Mr. Cline started from around his side of the table and Arlen quickly came out too, and they would have come to blows right there had Caty not risen from her own chair and shouted, "No! Not here! Take it over there, you two." She pointed to behind the church.

Arlen and Mr. Cline shucked their coats and walked sideways away from the tables, half looking where they were going, half watching each other. Many guests had stopped their eating since they heard the conversation growing more heated, and now their heads craned around to follow them. Some rose from their chairs, wondering if they should intervene, but no one was quite sure what to do. The two men kept walking as the crowd's murmur grew louder and people began to follow after them. Looking the ground over, Arlen stopped when he had come to a good place and Mr. Cline stopped too, a little bit downhill from Arlen. This was good. They watched each other for a minute. Perhaps Mr. Cline thought that the anger would dissipate and they could go back to the table, the matter resolved. But Arlen remained there, unmoved, hardly blinking, staring down his father-in-law, whole body almost motionless.

Come on. Come on, you sonuvabitch, I'm waitin' for you. We're waitin' for you.

He came on, just like Arlen knew he would. The liquor flushed Mr. Cline toward him like a round, heavy bobwhite and the big man put all his weight behind a right hook. Arlen saw it coming and stepped aside, not even raising his own arms in protection. Mr. Cline missed and stumbled, and Arlen's left fist came down like an 88 on the side of his head. The man went down, right onto his face. Arlen took a few steps back, watching Mr. Cline gather himself up onto his feet. They stood apart again, judging each other. Then Mr. Cline came at Arlen again, but more cautiously, feinting several times before throwing another blow. He did not connect and Arlen hit him again, this time across the nose. Arlen felt the crack in his hand long afterwards, and Mr. Cline shouted in pain. But he did not fall down — it only seemed to make him angrier. One, two steps and he got to Arlen, managing to get a fistful of Arlen's shirt, and throwing a punch for Arlen's gut. It landed and knocked a bit of wind out of Arlen. The farmer stumbled back and caught himself as Mr. Cline came toward him again. They each exchanged a blow with the other and stepped back, pausing, breathing hard. Mr. Cline's nose bled all over his busted lip and dribbled down onto his shirt, but he was still in the fight. Arlen felt a sore rib, maybe cracked, but the pain hardly registered. He was good at this. His battles had become mere practice.

One, two steps and Mr. Cline was at him again, with one, two swings, the second one connecting with Arlen's jaw. Arlen's head buzzed and rang but he did not fall, as Mr. Cline grabbed his shirt again. There was another blow coming, Arlen knew, and it would not treat him well.

All restraint disappeared. He had held himself back, out of some lingering sense of the rules of this place he was from. Fighting was occasionally right, although not at a wedding. But what of the rules? Nobody abided by them anymore, at least the ones born out of the way of life he knew. He could not see that way of life at work amongst his people anymore. Did that way of life flee because it was too weak or did it die with hardly a whimper? Arlen did not know. Wade would have known. This much was clear: it was the onslaught of men like Mr. Cline that did it. There was no sense in giving the enemy the benefit of quarter, the clemency of old ways that had lost their fight against the fifth column of the clean and good-thinking people of the county.

Arlen's hand reached out, but not as a fist. He got it up and around the other man's arm which held him by his shirt. His fingers plunged through folds of flesh. The windpipe popped in between them and his talons latched on. His enemy's hold on him slackened. The strangled head tried to turn to look at Arlen. The skin twisted and features yawed — was that fear? regret? pleading? The right fist cocked back and dropped like a hammer. Arlen felt the man's head recoil away and then bounce back into place. Arlen hit him again, harder. Snapping and crackling reached him through the rush of hot blood in his ears, a familiar confirmation. He let go and the man fell straight back with a resounding thud to the ground. Arlen went right to him. The bloodied man tried to get up and Arlen stepped into the punch, hitting hard right across that broken nose.

"Arlen, don't go no further, ain't right, ain't worth it."

Arlen whipped around, brushing the arm from his shoulder, and drove his fist into the big man's chin. The blow hardly fazed the big man, though, for he just stood there, rubbing the spot. He saw the look in Arlen's eye and he understood. He turned and faced the crowd of guests that had gathered. With outstretched arms, Roy began to back the crowd up. "Come on, folks, give 'em some distance. Ain't nothin' to see here."

229

Arlen returned just as the prey had propped himself up on one arm, trying to get to his feet. Arlen gave no quarter. One strike and then another and another until he felt no more resistance from the lump on the ground. His fist cocked back one last time and held there as he heard only the gurgle of words through a mouth full of blood.

Arlen's hand went down again, but this time it grabbed a hold of hair. He lifted the man's head up and saw both eyes were swollen shut and his nose flattened and cocked to one side. Blood covered his chin and neck and shirt. Arlen, still holding on by the hair, began walking out into God's Acre, dragging his father-in-law into the graveyard.

"Arlen, Arlen, please, stop, please, I give up, I'm sorry," murmured Mr. Cline.

"Shut up, old man."

"Arlen, I'm sorry."

"You can shut your mouth for right now. Ain't me you got to apologize to."

Mr. Cline howled in pain and he tried to crawl fast enough to keep up with Arlen. "What . . . what do you want . . . me to do?"

Arlen dragged the man between the headstones, some new, many cracked and weathered, a handful broken and lying on the ground. Arlen stopped before one of the new ones and released his grip on Mr. Cline's hair, letting the short fat man collapse on the ground. "Get up. Go on, get up, get on your knees." With great but very reluctant effort, Mr. Cline tried to sit up. It was not fast enough for Arlen, so he grabbed Mr. Cline by the hair again and pulled him up instead. He pointed to the gravestone. "Who's that? Tell me, who is it?"

"Your pa."

"Who? What's his name?"

"Wade Breckenridge."

"That's right. You're gonna apologize to him, you understand? And maybe while you're at it, all the rest of the family around here too. 'Cause what you've done and said is real dishonor. You tried to make me what I ain't. And that ain't so much an insult to me as it is to them. They worked for what I still am just as hard, and it ain't their choice to be down there in the ground. They'd just as soon be up here with me, doing the same thing as me. But they ain't and I'm all they have left. I'll have my way, but you better apologize to them for tryin' to keep me from it. Hear me?" Mr. Cline didn't answer, so Arlen slapped him upside the back of the head. "You hear me?"

The battered, pathetic man gurgled an assent.

"Now you stay here and don't come back down to the party until you've had a good long talk with Pa. You'd better mean what you say, too."

Arlen rose up and walked back through the gravestones. His ears were ringing and the tip of his nose was numb. His hands began to shake. He felt his strength flowing out to sea. It was the weakness after the attack. Just as surely, he felt himself knot up, straighten up, begin to look around, knowing that now in his brief weakness was when the counterattack always came.

But it did not. He had won.

He reached the edge of the graveyard and looked down upon the scene of the wedding. The guests were no longer clustered about, waiting for the outcome of the fight. They streamed away, past the church, between the tables laid with plates of half-eaten food, headed toward their cars. Some had already pulled out onto the road and were driving off. Arlen watched them go. They had heard the argument. They knew of the Breckenridges and what they were. They would have known what was at stake. But they still streamed away.

They ain't on my side. Not any longer.

They're with him.

How could that be? These sons and daughters of sons and daughters of strong folk, who had fought and scraped and prospered in their own small and centered way, should have stood with Arlen. They would have before the war. But now they took Mr. Cline's side.

Arlen didn't know why they did. Had something high up had sucked them in unawares? He wondered what could do that. They seem to be trading away their birthright of hard independence, for allegiance to another's was as good as defense of their own. And for what? Arlen sure as hell didn't know. This old land was new to him, for if the people couldn't remain the same, then the land, the soil and the trees and the hills and the creeks running red after a hard rain, couldn't either.

Arlen couldn't help that. It was not his job to fight it. He would have, for it was his responsibility to others, but that took others' help too, and they were going away from him, going away with Mr. Cline and his ilk. Now he had only what he could do himself and what had ever been his family's responsibility to itself — to persist in the face of it all, in their own way. He knew this was truth. The world that had come to Catawba County had gotten everyone else, but it would not get him. Not now, even as almost everyone he had ever known and depended on streamed away from him. Down there Arlen could see Roy next to his sisters and his mother. The women were shaking their heads. He saw the truth again, from a further angle, and he gritted his teeth at the hardness of it, though he understood. It was not that his family was weak and that the war had gotten them. The war had gotten them all: family, friends, and neighbors. But the question was, who knew it? And who would put right what victory had made?

They wandered away from Arlen's gaze, and his eyes fell on a closer figure. Caty sat in a chair, alone, hands folded in her lap. She looked across the distance toward him, angry and sad in her silence, but nonetheless waiting patiently in her bridal dress, casting her lot as she did.

XX

The October sky was clear and chilly, even here toward the end of the day when the sun was at its greatest strength and was, for a little while, unmarked by airplanes. One saw them a lot now, some glinting in the sun, others in a darker drab color looking like gnats on high. Back in the day, one might have seen the mail plane overhead, but even that was rare. Now they often streaked the sky with their white lines and their engines droned slowly from one pitch to another as they passed overhead. But the sky was silent today. There were no birds out, either, and in this spot Arlen could not hear any cars from the road. The only sound came from the ground. As the mules pulled the riding plow across the fields that were gradually being turned to face that clear sky, metal clanked and wood groaned in rhythm with the steps of the animals. But those sounds were here and there, and a man could almost anticipate them if he felt the motion of the whole rig across the earth. In truth, what was really heard was the hiss of the soil on the face of the plowshare. That was the constant in the air.

In the middle of a furrow, Arlen glanced to the side and saw the other furrows already completed, and before he could take pleasure in them, he wondered if they were enough. There were many more acres to plow and he had done but a few today. He could have done more, or at least he wished he had. But even Arlen had to admit his skill was not what it once was. It was true, his rows were growing straighter and he put in each one more quickly as the day passed. But he desperately wanted his work to be its best right now. The farm deserved it, and to make such a gift was to gain a blessing in return come the right season. He knew this, he had seen it with his own eyes. Dismayed with his inability, which is the only constant every man has, Arlen looked to the mules, which moved along at the speed they always had, generation upon generation. He knew he could not will them on faster even for the sake of completing the work in the time he had envisioned. For driving the mules on faster would ruin everything. The plow would be harder to control and the row would be more crooked, not parallel to the one right next to it, and all the subsequent ones too. That meant fewer rows per field and

233

perhaps a smaller yield. And the animals would tire faster and he would have to quit sooner if he did not want to wear them out completely.

Arlen looked back down to the plowshare again and the sight of it was not as great to him as the hiss of the soil on metal. He was doing the work he should be, at long last, and there was that to be thankful for. The work at hand took his attention and set him to making this row as neat and straight as possible. Arlen pulled and loosened the reins by a hair, guiding the mules to the end of the field, where they, by Arlen's direction, swung the whole rig around. "Whoa," said Arlen in a low voice. The mules stopped against the pull of the reins and took many steps in place, to the side, and a few backward as the weight of the plow held them back. With his left hand, Arlen kept the slack out of the reins, and as the wobbling of the whole rig subsided and the mules found their balance again, he grabbed the lever on his right and pulled it toward him. He looked down and saw the plowshare sitting where it should be, almost parallel to the soil and hovering an imperceptible degree above it. Arlen looked up the length of the rows. This furrow would be as straight and close as the others had been. Arlen took the reins in both hands and said with a minimum of force, "Hyah," and the mules stepped forward with the same tenseness they had shown early that morning. The plow gave a start and then settled into a smooth run across the field.

Arlen looked back and down at the share. Before they moved, the share seemed as if it would skim just above the ground without ever touching it. But after a yard or two, the chisel had sliced right through the top of the soil and the whole plowshare seemed to cut deeper with each passing yard. Gradually the right wheel of the riding plow ran deeper in the adjacent furrow and the share ran more shallow. Arlen pulled the lever further back and the share ran at the depth that suited him. His eyes flicked back to the mules. They were the same size, but Zeb on the right looked smaller because he stood in the same furrow where the plow wheel ran and Zeke on the left stood a little bit higher on the unplowed ground. Their ears were set back at first as they strained to get the plow moving, but at last they were running right along as Arlen wanted and their tense hesitation subsided into a steady push.

He had covered a couple acres already today and could plow at least the same tomorrow. It boded well: nothing would break this rhythm he was finding again. Arlen reached the end of the row and lifted the share up. By a long slow turn, he positioned them for a run back across the field. This time he set the share on the left side down. Arlen said again, "Hyah." The mules stepped off smoothly and the plow jerked ahead until the share caught the earth. The soil turned smoothly and Arlen heard through the clank and groan of the rig the hiss of earth on metal.

Their path began to stray to the left. "Zeke," said Arlen. The mule kept on stepping at the same rate he had. Arlen could see the growing slack in the traces. "Zeke!" he said more sharply. With a little snap on the reins on his rump, the mule moved a little faster and the path of the plow straightened out. Arlen's sight swung back and forth between the mules and the share. He felt and thought of nothing while he did. For this was as far as he was meant to go. Everything else he did was only to get him to right here. Each night he could close his eyes knowing that the most important work lay just on the other side of sleep. And in several days, when he had plowed all he needed, Arlen could think of sowing and take comfort in knowing that it was almost at hand. It was a chance to do what was right and what he had wanted. Arlen prayed that such chances would not be taken away, even as they had just been given to him. He prayed every morning before he went out and every evening when he came back in, but the rest of the day was a prayer too. His labor was pure faith, for nothing said it would not hail on the crop or the barn burn in the night. Arlen knew all this and yet persevered without the thought it would happen, for to do nothing was to have no faith.

Arlen lifted his wrist up and looked at his watch. It was about four thirty. He had told Caty to have supper ready by then. Turning the mules about, he put in another row, waiting for her to ring the bell. But the iron clang never came. Another row turned over under the plow, but still nothing at all. The sun was falling, it would be dark in an hour. Arlen raised up the shares and turned the mule team toward the barn. There he unhitched the mules, removed all their tack, and fed and watered them. Arlen walked from the barn into the bare earth between it and the house and he could see down the slight slope to the road, where a car was turning up and onto the property. Arlen felt the top of his stomach cinch up at the sight of it rolling up toward him. It was the sheriff, he was sure of it, coming back to hassle him about the fight at the wedding, even though no one was pressing charges. But as it drew closer, Arlen saw it was not the lawman, and the car seemed familiar. The black Ford came up and stopped in the farmyard between the barn and the old corn crib and the house. The door opened and a man stepped out, putting on a coat and a hat as he did. Arlen said nothing, though he knew who it was. "Hello, Arlen. Welcome back."

"What are you doing here, Earl?"

The extension agent sauntered over around the front of the car. "Thought I'd come say hello and check in on you."

Arlen said nothing about his state of affairs.

Earl cocked his head. "How have you been?"

"Just fine." Arlen left it at that, his arms at his side, his stance a little wide, in case, just in case.

"Wanted to say I'm sorry about your father. He was a good man." When

Earl got no reply, he continued on. "I wanted to come check on you because the last time I saw your father, he was having some trouble. I know a farm changing hands from one generation to another can be a hard adjustment and I wanted to make sure you were doing all right."

"I don't see what business of yours it is."

"Well, it is my business, Arlen."

"Ain't always been. I thought we made it pretty clear once that we weren't interested in anything you were pushin'. Well, if you think that feelin' died with Pa, you're wrong, 'cause I'm still here."

Earl shifted his stance, the dust rising and settling on his captoes. "Regardless, Arlen, you should know that you are responsible for what your father was supposed to do."

That seemed obvious enough. A man inherits. But Arlen paused and reconsidered the words. "And what could you tell him that he was supposed to?"

"I told him to grow more."

Arlen laughed out loud. "You think you got the right to do that?"

"When it's for the war effort, I do. And it's been up to me to make sure every farmer does what he can."

"Says who?"

"Says the county war board."

"What right have they got?"

"Arlen, they had to make sure the county was doing all it could for the war, and the most Catawba can do is grow food. We know each farm, we know how much each one produces, and we make a plan with the farmer for each year's production. Everything the farmers do, we guide them."

"You mean push 'em," said Arlen.

Earl folded his arms. "Your father needed pushing, Arlen. You weren't here to see it, you don't know what it was like. All the young men were gone and there weren't many deferments for them to come back to the farms. We couldn't even feed the county, but we still had to grow food for y'all out at the front. So we had to be efficient with the land and the labor we had. And a lot of folks saw what we'd been saying for a long time — with fertilizer and pesticide, they get a better yield off the same ground year after year. I would have had every farmer get a tractor too, but that couldn't be managed. Your father grew corn, wheat, oats, had that little truck patch of his — we needed every bit of it and far more. I tried to talk sense into him, tried to get him to modernize, but he wouldn't listen."

"You reckon it was because you hounded him so many times before about it?" Arlen snorted. "Well, at least he stood his ground."

"Oh, he did, Arlen. He always tried to work within his means, and I can't fault him for that, I reckon. But it wasn't enough."

Arlen jabbed his finger at the agent. "Who're you to say what was or wasn't? If he was growin' what he could for the war, then you ain't got no right to squeeze more out of him."

"Wade did produce what he could, given his inclinations. I came over here and checked on him frequently. But that was as much to make sure he didn't drive this place under in the process. We couldn't afford to lose a single farm. Lose farms, lose the war, I said."

Arlen furrowed his brow. "What do you mean drive it under?"

"Wade was stretched pretty thin, Arlen. He was working all the time, Sundays even, and he still seemed pretty harried."

"Probably 'cause y'all were squeezing so much out of him. Only so much work one man can do in the fields," Arlen snapped.

"I think it was the money that had him worried."

"What money? He ain't taken out a mortgage or nothin'."

Earl raised an eyebrow. "The farm takes money all the same, Arlen. There's no getting away from that."

"Don't see how."

"Well, you should look closer. I'd hate for you to end up like Wade. Better that you be like others than that."

Arlen felt a chill pass over him. He knew what Earl meant by "others." Earl meant the other successful farmers, the Casses of the county. He did not want Arlen to give up the farm, he was not Mr. Cline. No, Arlen had to change it to Earl's liking.

Lord, ain't that even worse? Leave this place and I'd be free, but change and become like them, and I'll just be chained to it by all that debt.

He's houndin' us worse than ever. Lord, how can I hold out against him until I set this place right? Lord, set us on a firm foundation, firmer than ever.

God put no words in his mouth, though. The answers were for later, as they always were. Arlen had no maneuver, no deception, no ambush possible — he was fixed in place. All he had was his old familial defiance, in harsher tones than his father, for it was a harsher world.

"Get the hell out of here, Earl."

"You want me to leave, Arlen? You don't want my help?" said Earl.

"Like hell I do."

Earl cocked his head and smiled a little. "All right, I will." And just like that, he walked around to the driver side door.

Arlen weakened suddenly and lobbed one more insult. "Can't see why you keep takin' such an interest in us, Earl, if you know you'll just walk on like that."

"Well, Arlen," said Earl, "it's just that I've never seen anyone so deep in

237

debt refuse to do what he had to in order to keep a farm."

Earl started the car and pulled away, waving to Caty, who had come out on the porch. Arlen didn't even see him go — the agent's words kept running over and over through his head.

Do we owe money?

Pa, what did you do? What did you leave me?

He ran a handful of paces to the house and vaulted up onto the porch in the middle of his powerful stride. Caty stepped aside in shock as Arlen threw open the door of the house, leaving it open to the chill air, and ran to the desk that sat in the corner of the front room opposite the hearth. The desk was still covered with Wade's papers, but Arlen did not look at those. If the truth was anywhere, it was somewhere in the rows of journals stacked neatly above the desk. Arlen pulled all of the journals into his arm and carried them out of the room and to the kitchen table. He swept aside the place settings, the plates and utensils clattering into a heap on the end of the table. Dropping the journals on the table, Arlen sat immediately in his chair and picked up the first one on top of the stack. It said "1932" on the cover — Arlen put it to the side. He ran through each year of the Depression, all the way through the war, until he found "1945."

"Arlen?" said Caty, who stood startled at the end of the table.

"Hush," he said. He undid the twine that bound the hard-backed journal together and kept all of the contents shoved in its pages from bulging out. Contrary to what Wade had once told Earl, he had kept a book on the farm. But it was not what the agent had once expected or proposed, with careful columns in black and red ink, all the inputs and outlays categorized and accounted for. Instead, Wade had kept odd notes of what he did, sometimes day-to-day, or by the week. He wrote of what crops went in and how much seed he had used; what tools or equipment were needed or required repair; how much certain things cost him, so that he might remember in the future and not pay an inflated price; to whom he owed work and who owed him. If there were numbers inside, none were balanced in any careful way, but simply scribbled down here and there. They did not calculate the worth of the farm but simply told a story to him who had written them, matching the story he knew in his head — all of Earl's meddling did not seem to have changed that. Arlen turned the pages and saw collections of odd notes, like "Ninety bushels — by the 17th," or "Jon. fix harness?" or "Five dollars too much." In spots there were notes on the comings and goings of money — wages paid to laborers and small profits when the surplus crop was sold — and Arlen's eye grabbed onto them, studying every integer until he felt he was staring right through the page. The laborer's wages stood out the most. He found them here and there, and he could tell the rates were quite high. He grabbed journals starting in 1941. That first year he was gone, the wages were not surprising, but come 1942, the rates jumped quickly. He turned to the next year and the next, and Arlen saw that as he had fought each battle over there, the wage had jumped up and up. At last he ended up in 1945 again, the last mention in June of this year, showing Wade paid almost double the rate before the war.

Those sonsabitches, weren't right at all for 'em to demand that much. Don't they know they'll drive the farmer broke? And they where will they work?

But most of the young men had been off at war and the laborers could charge what they wanted, even if it was for poor work. And there had been no choice for Wade but to pay them. After all, the crop was one size, whether he sold some of it or all of it.

Was that truly enough to sink Wade into debt? Surely not. The answer must still be in the journals. Arlen turned back through the pages. He soon stopped on the month of March. He had missed these pages before. There were calculations, sums added, amount deducted, and at the bottom of the page a figure circled and next to it the words, "Income tax paid March 15." Arlen gnawed his lip. The amount Wade paid to Uncle Sam seemed enormous. Arlen flipped through 1944 until he found the tax. It, too, was a big amount. Going back, year through year, Arlen found the notes Wade had made on his taxes, calculations that Arlen had never been privy to, and he found that though the farm always made about the same amount, each year Wade paid more. There was a war to fight, and it was not enough that Wade had sent his only son and was working himself to death to grow food for the nation   he had to pay what little money he had.

But where is the debt?

The income tax was paid, the laborers were paid, there was no mortgage. Maybe Wade had bought on credit from the store? That was nothing, everyone had done that at one point or another.

That damn Earl. He's just tryin' to scare me. Wants me to give in.

"You ready for your supper?"' asked Caty.

"Yes'm, I am."

"You clean all that up, now."

Arlen shut the journal, and as he did, he felt something wedged in the back of it. He opened the back cover. Jammed in between it and the last page was a stack of envelopes held together with a cracked rubber band. He pulled off the band and began sorting through them.

Oh, Good Lord. His heart plopped into his stomach with a faint but heavy splash.

The top envelope had been opened by Wade, handled heavily, and then stuffed back inside. It was the property tax bill, unpaid.

His fear came roaring back like the heat from an opened furnace. The fear radiating up his ears and neck, Arlen tore out the contents of the other envelopes. They were notices on the unpaid taxes, several of them, the last just before Wade passed away. Arlen gnawed his lip.

It can't be. Just can't be. Why wouldn't he pay it?

Maybe there's a receipt in there somewheres.

Arlen picked up the journal and shook all the scraps of paper loose from the pages. They fluttered down into a pile, but not one turned out to be a receipt for the property tax.

"Arlen, what did I say? Clear it off for supper," said Caty.

"Not now. Later."

"But it will be cold. Do you want me to—"

"Caty!" he shouted at her. He halfway turned to apologize, but she had already disappeared back to the kitchen and he had no time to wonder if she was hurt. She would forgive him, he knew — the county would not. They would put a lien on this place if they did not get their due and then that would be the end of them. Over and over Arlen shook his head to himself as he sorted through the papers. He did not understand. Never had his father been so remiss, not once that Arlen could remember. It was not in their character as Breckenridges. They took care of what was the most important first, however hard it made the rest of life. Maybe Wade had to give a few things up to pay the bill, but he would have done it.

But he had not. Arlen found no receipt, no quickly scribbled note as to when payment was made. Arlen wanted to believe that it had been simply misplaced, but the truth was dragging him toward it, hand over hand.

But why? Why didn't you pay, Pa?

He fell back against the chair.

The answer was right there. Wade had paid the income tax, but not the property tax. Perhaps he had been forced to choose one or the other. The county would not have wanted to drive Wade off of the farm if the war board still had to meet farm produce quotas — that would have stayed their hand. But Uncle Sam would have demanded his cut, so the income tax was paid first. And all the time the taxes were going up, the laborer's wages were going up. It was the same size crop, it took the same amount of work to bring it in, but Wade had been intent on feeding himself first, not selling the whole crop, as they had always done. He could have sold it all and paid the bills, but then he would have had nothing to eat. He would have bought his pork and meal from the store, like folks in poorer days, and Arlen knew Wade: he would not choose to beggar himself in such a way. They had snared Wade into spending all his money: there had been no one else to help, no Arlen, no other men to swap work with in that nearly-dead habit of older days; no way to escape feeding the warring nation; and the farmer's produce was not enough, he was taxed hard to boot. Of course Earl and his allies would have blamed Wade. He could have borrowed money to put in big crops, filling out his acreage and making up the difference in the depleted soil with chemical fertilizers — then he would have made the money back to pay the bills and the taxes. But he had not. Arlen knew his father: stick to the rotations, let the soil rest, and keep each crop to what he could manage. And he had reaped no money. He had tried to keep the farm as self-sufficient as he knew how, free of debt in hope that the old balance might return. Yet money still got him in the end.

Arlen pounded his fist on the table. *Those sonsabitches. All of 'em. I could kill all of 'em.* Earl, Mr. Cline, the lot of them — this was their doing. They had killed Wade before he gave in. Now they would kill the farm too.

No, no, no. I won't have that. That ain't gonna happen.

It was going to happen. There was no doubt about that, if he did not pay this tax bill. The county did not need to worry about the war effort anymore. It would put a lien on the farm and someone would snatch up the land for a good price. The land would still be plowed, only this time by a tractor driven by someone else, and the land would get worked over and over by the money farmer whose way was opened for him into the rushing, growing America Mr. Cline had spelled out so clearly.

Arlen's lip bled as he gnawed on it. *What the hell did I fight for if it's come to this? This ain't my country. It's the same place, but things've changed.*

I ain't done nothin' different. I've done what's always been mine to do and what everyone said was right. I went and fought, and I've looked after myself and my family and my neighbors. And now they say that I have to give more. I have to give 'em what I can't give.

He wasn't just going to lose his land. He would lose with it the set habits and rigid principles that made it a good and peaceable place to live, without which the land was simply dirt to be used and traded until no one saw worth in it anymore and all those habits and principles had long since faded into irretrievable echoes and there was no hope of their restoration on the soil itself.

It was so monstrous he couldn't even think on it.

All he could do was keep them from taking it. There must be a way in the old ways. He was not Wade. He was younger, tougher, meaner. He could go for days and nights without sleep, without food, in baking heat and piercing cold. He could fight his way through. There had to be a way.

"Arlen?" He heard Caty's voice first and then he realized her hands were rubbing his shoulders gently. "What's the matter?"

He almost told her. He wanted to, very badly. But this was not his to burden her with. This was his fight. "Nothin'."

"You seemed mighty upset."

"It's the . . ." Arlen gnawed on his lip.

"Yes?"

"Nothin'. Just Earl. The extension agent." He shook from the inside out and he tightened his stomach to try and keep the vibrations in.

"Did he make you angry?"

"Him? Reckon he did a little. Ain't just him, though." *Shouldn't have said that. Said too much already.*

Caty leaned down and rested her chin on his shoulder. "Then who else was it?"

"Caty, don't you worry about it." He sat enjoying her hands on his shoulders. It was a good thing to have her, right here with him. Then something inside him ticked over and he felt the press of time. Enough minutes had been spent on this. He had more work to do. He reached out for the journal and turned the page, keeping on with his work even as the house got dark and the oil lamps gave the only light.

"Aren't you hungry?" she asked.

"No, not particularly."

"Why don't you put this away?"

He could not. The fight was here, right here at home, and he could not fail. Everything depended upon him. Wrapped up tightly in what he knew and putting it to work as thoroughly as he could, Arlen could find a way. Each day would be one day closer to that place where the ambiguous work of change had receded and they would be free to persist again as they always had.

Lord, it's got to be that way. It's got to be that way one day for us.

I will stick to those old ways, Lord, lest they be gone forever. Even if they kill me. I will not break with our ways.

But, Lord, forgive me, I'm gonna take that 52-20 payment under the table.

And with his mind set, Arlen buried himself back in the journal. But he was not thinking of the pages, only the way he was straining against her arms wrapped around him. The pressure in her hands built as she tried to pull him away. He resisted, but her arms pressed harder against his chest. The weight of her was too much. He felt himself sliding back in the chair. Caty kissed him on the cheek. "Come on, Arlen. Leave it."

He would not, but he rose from the table all the same. Caty blew out the lamps and Arlen went with her as she led him by the hand up to his bed. His mind and body turned to his wife, leaving the journal and its numbers on the table. They waited there for tomorrow, to see if the hands of a man could prevail for a day in spite of them.

XXI

"I need you for a patrol, Sergeant."

The disembodied words of Venters, resonantly confident, played over and over like a broken Victrola first from behind, then the right, then the left, then far off, as if in a grove of trees. The lieutenant was not with them in this dark, snowy field. There was a line of darkened figures stretching out to the rear and it was impossible to count all of them. The feeling of the number was clear to Arlen, but when he tried to make a head count, one, two, three, he could not. They had faces and he knew they did, and he knew who each one was if they came close, but he did not see them, not even so much as a profile in the light.

"Patrol, Sergeant. Patrol. Patrol, Sergeant. Sergeant? Patrol. Patrol, Sergeant." Venters' words droned on and on. The moon passed in and out of clouds rushing overhead in an unfelt wind. Arlen was not cold, but his fingers moved stiffly. He felt no pain in his feet, but he stumbled and rocked around. Looking down, he saw they were swollen into lumps of iced flesh. He felt not a shred of surprise. His rifle was weightless in his hands and he kept reaching up and down, touching the bolt to make sure it was in battery, feeling the operating rod was in place, checking that the safety was snapped off, fingers back to the bolt again. Fir trees knocked and tossed in the invisible wind and sped past the patrol, a long stream of identical trunks and limbs. Arlen trudged endlessly in place, never drawing closer.

"That's it, Sergeant. That's the objective."

Arlen saw in the moonlight ahead of them a town, not unlike one they had captured. It had the church of Langendorf, with the column of smoke and pulverized brick already rising from it — Arlen never recalled it any other way — and the houses of Malmedy and a big square, except covered with hedgerows and orchards, and it was as if this was the town they had always meant to take, it was all the towns, and Arlen knew it and hovered above it as if looking down upon a neatly made sand table. He waited for someone to reach out and touch the building with a long pointer, but no one did and he kept marching toward the town which kept retreating before him, so far and so fast even the vast forest of firs could not keep up and fell away from the outskirts of the town. The 105s began to tear it down brick by brick with their shells, but not a single building ever seemed to collapse. Venters did not speak again, but Arlen knew that the orders were to capture the town. The bastards, it was not just a patrol, but an attack on a village whose only purpose on the face of the earth was to be battered and attacked and captured.

"But I don't have enough men," said Arlen to no one. "It's just my squad." And he hated himself for sounding like such a shirker, making excuses for what he knew he had to do and should do. But he had to care for his men, too, all of them back there.

From the dark appeared Venters, sitting on the rear engine cover of a Sherman tank driving in reverse. The tank belched hot fumes right into Arlen's face and his thick growth of beard waved like grain in the wind. "You have to, Sergeant. Battalion is counting on you."

"But Lieutenant—"

"Fire and maneuver, Sergeant. Textbook. Perfect. You can do it. Textbook and perfect."

The words rang tinnily in his ears as Venters rolled away on the tank, staring at Arlen through his field glasses. The squad was silent. Arlen signaled the advance and started walking. Feet squeaked and crunched through snow. The town was out there now, larger than ever and on fire. The flames burned in silhouette behind the town and shell bursts sent roof slates cartwheeling through the air in a thousand directions. Little lights winked here and there in the houses, and long fingers of brightness reached out toward the men. The beams of light snapped lightly around them and Arlen felt fear — not the churning stomach or the dry mouth or anything of the sort, but just round, hard, well-polished fear, like an immaculate and heavy stone that he carried cradled in the crook of his arm all of his days. More tracer bullets reached out from the far, dark village and Arlen heard the screams and cries of his men.

He should turn back and help. It was his instinct.

But he had his orders. He had to take the town, not care for his men. It would do no good for him to stop and look back, to bring the whole thing to a halt here in the impossibly dark expanse that was also a pristine snowy waste glowing in the moonlight.

Arlen heard the whistle and splintering of the air, and he knew it was incoming mail. Everything rocked and flashed and he felt wet bits pitter-pattering on his helmet like rain. He reached up and touched it. His hand came away with snow and mud and liquified tissue and somehow there was a massive shell fragment there, clutched in his palm. And then the screams landed on him like a wave plunging to shore. He knew the voice in every shout of pain. The crook of his arm almost collapsed on him and Arlen struggled to pull himself and his fear back up. He stopped to look around for the casualties, but they were not around. He was alone right here.

"Sergeant, why did you stop? Keep up the advance."

Artillery went off like flashbulbs around him, but Venters was nowhere to be seen.

"We're takin' casualties, Lieutenant!"

"Keep up the advance."

"Lieutenant, the men!"

"Sergeant, you must keep up the advance."

None of them were there. Not Gunderson nor Schaeffer, nor Iannucci or Mueller. And above all the others, Paine was not there. Arlen called out for him from a man's heart, which speaks no words most times, but measures all love by look and deed. He could not be alone, not in this last attack — something told Arlen it was the last one and of course the biggest and worst one, because how else could it be? But here he was, for they had fallen back across the white fields criss-crossed with hedgerows and let him go ahead.

Buddy, willed Arlen's heart, *be here with me. I know you can't take any more, but you could make it with me.*

Paine, buddy, I can't do it. I wish you were here. Maybe then I would.

If I send for you, would you come?

"Arlen?"

It was Paine's voice.

"Paine?"

Nothing came back. The shellfire kept raining down around him and the tracer fire snapped across the fields and Venters would swoop in any minute in his fighter and yell at him from the cockpit. But Arlen knew he had heard it. "Buddy?"

"Arlen!"

Yes, it was Paine. But Arlen could not tell where he was. Perhaps he was to the rear. If he could, Arlen would go find him, wherever he was. But the tracer rounds kept winking out in long beams from the village and he had to go, and go now — he had to take the town, which he would one day. There was nothing else but to do it. Arlen's feet carried him along at a snail's pace even as the unfelt wind blew the world past him, in reverse this time, the distance to the town growing greater and greater, and yet he was no closer to the dead and dying behind him.

"Arlen!" Paine's voice was louder and fainter at the same time.

"Buddy, come on, stick with me!" shouted Arlen. "You gotta keep movin'!"

"Arlen!"

"Come on, stick with me, buddy! It's not far now, I promise. Come on, buddy, I'll look after you, I need you with me, all right? Come on, I'm right here, stay with me!"

245

"Arlen?"

"Paine!"

Arlen came bolt upright in the bed. He was perfectly alert; he knew where he was after just a second or two: his parents bedroom — no, his bedroom now, his and Caty's, a dark and still space. He blinked a few times and yawned, his jaw stiff. His hands felt cramped. He touched his mother's quilt across his legs — it was soaked all the way through with sweat. The wet cloth was freezing in the cold room. He jumped in place at the movement in the corner. After a couple of stuttering breaths, he was able to see Caty there, shivering furiously in her nightdress, her arms wrapped tightly against herself, facing him across the room. She would not come to the bed. "You were screaming, Arlen."

He grunted in reply.

"Who was it?"

"Ma'am?"

"Who were you yelling for?"

Arlen rubbed the sleep from his eyes.

"Arlen?"

"Yes?"

"Was it the war?"

He still said nothing.

"Arlen, answer me."

"Yes, it was."

Now she came right across the floor in three quick steps and up onto the bed and before Arlen knew it, Caty had wrapped her arms tightly around him and buried her face in his clammy neck. "Oh, Arlen, I'm so sorry. I understand now, I understand. I was so worried, I didn't know what it was. But it was just the war." She clung tightly to him, waiting for him to return her need for contact, which seemed so strong these days.

Arlen pulled back the covers and swung his legs out of bed. She still hung onto him, arms around his neck. It was only the war and, yes, it was terrible, but it was not him, it was just something he went through, and he was home, with her, all should be well, she could make it that way — he felt this in the tug of her arms back to bed.

He stood up and let her fall away. She collapsed onto her elbows on the bed and only slowly sat up, looking at his back going out into the dark house. "Arlen? It's still early. Where are you going?"

Arlen dragged his overalls with him as he took the stairs three at a time and he dressed at the front door, where he put on his coat and his boots. He still felt woozy and when he went outside onto the porch, he almost fell down the steps. His feet landed on cold, hard ground — it was December — and he fumbled for his pack of Lucky Strikes in the pocket of the coat. There was only one left in the pack. Arlen lit it and began to walk under the light of the moon which basked the hours before dawn. Forced breaths came from forced steps and the cigarette tip lit up brightly, leaving an ember in the corner of his vision. Then the nausea washed over him so powerfully it bent him over in mid-stride and he stumbled across the ground. He caught himself on the trunk of the big oak tree and vomited beside it. His stomach cinched up tight over and over, until nothing came up but bile. The cigarette was drowned in the watery remains on the ground.

He held himself there, head pressed against the deeply rutted bark. He wished he was back in the war. It was simpler there. He had a purpose there. Even if it was to destroy, that was easy and he knew how to do it well. But here he had to make things live and that was hard. Here each season always led to the next and came back around again. Every act was accountable, every moment was full of innumerable choices of what he could do, but nothing said what it was he should do. The habits of his head and hands felt inadequate. For if he picked one thing to do now, then his choices for the day, the week, or the season were both limited and opened, and yet there was no clear sign anymore if that decision was right. Because there was a right and a wrong now: not in a moral sense — that was never in question, never once in the whole time of his family on this land — but in what would work, what would keep their heads above the waves without betraying what the Brockenridges were.

Lord, you saw me through, you brought me back, and now you give me this?

This ain't no reward. It's a curse.

I never bargained on it being this hard.

Arlen could stand the work, day in, day out. He had grown up with it and what would have numbed some men's minds did not bother him. But there was that smooth and heavy weight with him again, which told all the ways he could fail. The worst was that he could not tell if his failure was his own fault or that of the world reaching in over the farm gate. If it was the world, he would not hate himself but simply try to outwit. If it was himself, he would chastise himself and change what he did. But now he could not tell. It was all wrapped up together. Arlen thought of the winter wheat in the ground. He would harvest it in the early summer and only then would he know if it was enough. Perhaps it was enough to feed himself but not enough to sell as surplus — then there would be no money. Or if he sold it all as surplus, would he get a good price, good enough to buy what he needed for him and Caty from the store? Perhaps not, but then it would be too late. Who was he to blame, who was in the wrong?

He wiped his mouth with the back of his hand and straightened up. He had to do something besides stand here in the dark. With a burning chest, Arlen walked to the barn. It was early still and the animals might be surprised by his arrival. But he did not care. He fed the mules and milked the cow all alone, no one to talk to. When he finished in the barn, he stepped outside and saw a lone light from the house, the only illumination in the farmyard now that the moon had almost set. It beckoned him, but he could not go back in. He needed work to do, any work at all, until the sun was up. Casting around, he saw the woodpile at the far reaches of the light from the house. That would do. Arlen fetched the axe and fumbled around with the unsplit logs. He set one on the battered chopping block and let the axe swing through its natural motion. The sharpened steel fell from on high and hit the log square on the top. The pieces fell away and Arlen set another log atop the block and swung again. He split log after log and after a little while he did not have to think about it or anything else anymore.

It was light, suddenly, when Arlen stopped to stretch his back and look around. He must have been chopping for a good long while. The sun was coming up. The trees and fields were frosted grey, for the golden light had not hit them quite yet. Split logs were scattered on the cold, hard ground, lying in heaps here and there at different angles. He smelled smoke and knew that Caty had the stove going. Arlen swung the axe again as high as it would go and brought it down on another piece of wood. The bit penetrated all the way to the block and sent the two pieces cartwheeling in opposite directions. They tumbled and lay indistinguishable from all the other fallen pieces. Arlen pulled the axe loose from the block. He was breathing hard jets of vapor into the air. There was no more wood to split. He would have to saw more rounds first.

The sound of the back door closing was quite loud, even louder than the round sound of the axe hitting wood. He knew Caty was crossing the ground toward him, but he did not turn around. Perhaps she was coming to tell him his breakfast was ready. He saw a log he had missed and set it on the block. Footsteps crunched on frozen earth and stopped behind him. "Arlen?"

He swung once more and the log split. One half spun up and over his head like a mortar round and he reached up and caught it before it could hit his wife. A splinter jabbed into his bare hand and when he pulled it loose, a little blood came out. It was cold, so he hardly noticed. Arlen turned around to her. "You got breakfast ready?" he asked.

Caty wrapped the shawl around herself tighter. "Well, not yet," she said.

"Mmm," he replied, turning to toss the wood into the pile.

"Arlen?"

"Yes'm?"

Caty bounced up and down lightly, trying to stay warm.

She's gonna ask me, ain't she?

"What happened last night?"

"Last night," he repeated.

"Yes. Was it a bad dream?"

He did not look at her, just at the axe bit. It needed sharpening.

"Arlen?"

"Well, it weren't a good one."

"I know it was the war, but what happened in your dream?"

"Caty, I don't want to talk about it."

She took a step closer. "Tell me, Arlen."

He shook his head. "I ain't gonna."

"I'm not scared," said Caty. "Don't you want to explain it to me?"

"No."

"Arlen, I want to understand."

He took her eyes with his own, and this time she was not entranced by their look. "No, Caty, you don't."

"If it's so terrible, then don't tell me the worst parts. But tell me something."

Arlen swung the ax with his right hand in a big arc and it thwacked into the chopping block. "Dammit, Caty, it ain't a damn box you can just pull off the shelf and rummage around in and put back whenever you feel like!"

She said nothing.

He walked away a few yards, hands on his hips, shaking his head.

Caty came closer and he could hear the hem of her dress catching on the rough edges of the split logs. "Arlen, don't you think you need a rest?"

"I don't want a rest."

"You're killing yourself, Arlen. All this work, all the time, never a day off, and you keep agonizing over it all."

She thought she saw, but she could not, not one bit. "I want to work this farm, Caty. That's all."

"That's all you want?"

He wanted much more than that. He wanted happiness and contentment for them. He wanted to make things grow by his own hand and to live off that. And Arlen wanted to explain why it had to happen in this old and set way. He had gone to fight for it and all the killed and maimed — Gunderson, Paine, Venters, Wade, all of them — had fought so that he could be here, living free like they never would. They could not be let down. He had to live life without compromise for everyone in his past and for a faint hope in a distant but real future.

You're thinkin' too damn much, Arlen. Quit all that and get to work. As he wrapped the cocoon tighter, he found his old self that knew nothing but the fight and that the end to the fight would come some day, one day, and with that self-assurance, Arlen leaned down and began picking up pieces of wood, tucking them into the crook of his arm.

"Arlen?"

"Yes'm?"

"Maybe you should try something else."

Instinct snapped like a trigger sear and he spun around, log in hand, arm cocked back, about to come down on his enemy that was trying to stop him. But Arlen saw something of her through the fog of war, by the grace of God: her tears glistening in the rising sun. He didn't know which would have covered the farm more.

Good Lord, what have I done? All the wood fell from his hands and he fell to his knees before her, once again, as he seemed to do many times these days. Arlen's quivering hands reached out and grabbed Caty and pulled her toward him. He pressed his face into her stomach. He murmured over and over.

"W-w-what?" said Caty.

Arlen pulled his head back and looked up at her. "Caty, I can't do nothin' else. There's this farm and you and me. We'll do just fine once it all works right, you'll see. You've got to believe me. But if it don't, well, you married me. You knew the man I was and what I come from."

Her red and puffy eyes looked her man up and down and she did not know him. She knew the old Arlen, but not this new one.

Lord, I hope she'll understand one day.

He rose and turned toward the logs, already thinking he would work the whole day until sunset and if she could bring him his coffee and victuals to him, then the work might go all the faster. The lonesome work — it was not meant to be so, but so it was.

Caty, her voice reedy but clear despite her tears, blurted out, "Arlen, I'm pregnant."

He turned around slowly. "What?"

"I'm going to have a baby."

"Are you sure?"

She sniffled. "Yes, Arlen."

He was completely silent.

"Arlen? Are you happy?"

He was astounded. Ready to be happy, he was even more ready to be fearful, for he knew the implications immediately. He was held to the way a man was supposed to live in this country. All the hard work he did day in, day out was in light of that. But now his future in its unforeseen iteration had arrived. A loving and patient wife — *she is that, oh so patient and loving if nothing else, Lord* — could fit into his way, but what of this child-to-come?

Suddenly its presence cast a doubt on his abilities. Moments before, the old order of the farm would have worked, if just barely, but now he thought that at best he could only try. In fear he felt himself turning toward that vast and growing camp where the money farmers all gathered in their perpetual flush times. Eat he would if he threw himself in with them, borrowing money to make it all back again — *but for how long?*

He could not repose in his doubts, as much as they had assured him across the years. Here was choice, thrust upon him, and to refuse the choice was to choose anyway. And whatever his choice, it meant nothing if there was nothing to inherit. For now there would be someone who would inherit.

He's got to live, to grow up here, and to take this place over from me.

Arlen saw what that meant.

I'll do it, Lord. I'll do it. Help me make it work, I pray, make it work for now, for as long as it has to. Until I can find a way out. And find the way back.

"Arlen?" Caty's plaintive voice reached him. He said nothing, but took off his coat and wrapped it around her. With a hand on each shoulder, he carefully guided her between the logs, back to the house.

XXII

The old truck shook something awful when it was out of gear.

Arlen gripped the steering wheel and the shifter. The engine idled and the whole truck shook as if it would come apart and Arlen gripped all the harder. It shook and shook and his vise-like hold did not stop it. He did not waver, though. He held on, his pale knuckles bulging like rocks about to split from within.

Caty touched Arlen on the arm. He almost jerked his arm away from her, but his grip on the shifter was too tight. "Arlen, turn off the engine."

He hesitated and when she patted him on the arm again, he quickly reached up and switched off the truck, then jammed his hand into his pocket, his fist clenched tightly. His hand jolted and jerked and the spasms reached up to his shoulder. He clenched his muscles even more tightly. Caty must not see his shaking. One, two, three, four deep breaths and Arlen was able to release his grip on the steering wheel and open the door.

The cold February air smacked him and he hunched his shoulders up, trying to get his coat further onto his neck. He shut the truck door and stood there, looking around Hickory's Union Square.

Caty came around the back of the truck. She smiled and put her arm out to hook it through the crook of Arlen's own. But Arlen did not move to meet her. He stood, jaw clenched, neck immobile, eyes darting across the scene of a bustling Monday. In front of all the shops, trucks were making deliveries and Negroes were hauling crates of Coca-Cola. Men in suits and hats strolled briskly, and a proprietor was hanging a SALE sign in his shop window, the last season's fashions out and the latest ones ready to roll in. He eyed them for danger, for though there was none to be seen, he felt it keenly all the same. They all depended on men like him, he knew that in his head, but he didn't much feel like it. This bustle and change seemed the true permanence now, the center of all creation that somehow needed no patience, care, or discipline. It seemed it would grow and grow until it surpassed even its old self and people would look back with misty-eyed fondness for the quaint and simpler hustle and barter that once was. Arlen would remember otherwise and keep on in his way, which so different now that he could identify it, the reversal so complete that it stood out as the exception rather than the unnoticed rule. But what would that way come to? Would he have any discernible effect on events, any impact save upon those he met on equal terms in daily life?

Lord, how did I get here?

The proprietor was staring at him suspiciously. His stomach popped and turned and he looked away.

"Arlen?"

"Yes?"

"Aren't we going to the bank?"

He did not look at her. He could hardly raise his eyes up from the street.

"I thought that was why we came to town," said Caty.

Arlen wet his lips. He had first thought to have her along, so she would know and understand what he was doing. But he chickened out. His voice low, Arlen said, "I was thinkin' that just I would go."

"Oh." Caty sounded disappointed. "I thought you wanted me to come."

"To come to town, but I reckon I should've said that it'd just be me going to the bank."

Caty cocked her head to the side. "Isn't it important? The mortgage, I mean."

She did not know how bad things were and he would not tell her. "Just a few things I need to clear up with the folks there, a couple of things to sign. Ain't gonna take long."

"Oh."

"Be mighty boring for you," he said. "Reckoned it might be better for you to go around and do a little window shoppin'."

"That's a mighty long time to be on my feet, Arlen. With the baby and all?"

That was true, he kept forgetting that.

"Maybe I had better find a place to sit for a little while," she said.

Arlen reached into his pocket and gathered up the loose coins he had in there. It was all the spare money he had right now. He poured them into her outstretched hand, which was chapped red and bonier than before. All that housework. "Go get yourself some coffee somewheres."

"How will I find you?"

"I'll come find you," Arlen said, and with that, he kissed her on the cheek and turned away with hard steps plunging him straight toward the First National Bank built like a pillbox on the side of the square. Looking just far enough ahead to keep from tripping over the curb, he marched on, his hands jammed into his pockets, his head woozy, his tight stomach shooting fire up into his chest. With each step, he was more unsure how he got here. Any man who walked this concrete and asphalt with regularity had no need to remember anything that happened before yesterday. But Arlen remembered, and he remembered what others remembered, and he knew this was not what they or he did, this was not their way, and he so believed it, he was sure he had never compromised before. But here he was all the same, stumbling toward that bank. His steps were not imagined transgressions, they were real steps, right here, across a space that he had crossed before without ever knowing he would endure this. These steps to the bank were all too easy on their own. But it was he who had made them even easier: he had gone and talked to Earl. He had struck a deal.

All that your family ever did for you, Arlen, and all that Paine ever did, and all the others, you gave it all up. You couldn't see it through.

Arlen, you sonuvabitch.

He raised his head up, wanting to look back. But that was no use. He was already there. He was at the bank.

Arlen nearly pissed himself in fright. Cars pulled up to the curb behind him, and men got out and pushed past him, brushing his elbow. They kept on straight through the double doors of the great white building with hardly a hiccup in their step. Other men exited, donned smart hats, closed their overcoats against the cold, and looked at Arlen from beneath lowered eyebrows. After a brief consideration, they walked on down the sidewalk with the satisfied look of men who leave church having heard what they wanted to hear and finding no trouble in their souls for anything that might have spoken to them otherwise. Arlen could not stand here any longer. There was nowhere else to go. For all he remembered and believed, memory was not a direction. Arlen opened the double doors and stepped through.

He felt the difference on his skin before anything else. The dry, sharp air outside was now still and cool. The smooth, hard surfaces of the interior were innervating and his steps slowed. He looked around in confusion. He pulled his sore, tense hands from his pockets and flexed them. He shifted his feet and felt the profaning scrape of his muddy boots on the polished marble floor. He gnawed his lip.

A clerk glided across the lobby. "Yes, sir? How may I help you?"

Arlen removed his hat belatedly. "Uh, yessir, I'm here for a meetin', uh, 'bout a mortgage. I was supposed to meet with, uh, Mister . . ." Arlen had forgotten the man's name.

"Yes, are you Mister—"

"Breckenridge."

"Mr. Breckenridge. Welcome. I will let them know you are here. You're little early, but that's no problem, it'll be just a few minutes. Would you mind waiting here?" The clerk gestured to a bench against the wall of the lobby.

Arlen nodded wordlessly and sat on the bench quietly, like a good boy.

All the heat and churning of his fear had stopped. Stilled almost to lethargy, he numbly gathered in his surroundings. Men in suits made brisk exchanges with the tellers. Plump women leafed carefully through checkbooks. A few farmers, better dressed than he, waited solemnly in line. As the liturgy called them forward one by one, each maintained the proper composure. On the other side of the lobby, a handful white-haired men sat on a bench. One was perched right on the edge, resting his hands on a cane, and the others sat against the back of the bench, their heads rigidly erect. Their gaze was trained across the room to a long narrow board above the tellers. Numbers, abbreviations, and fractions scrolled across the board. "BS: 100.s.87 1/4" it would read, the symbols flitting across and disappearing through the other side of the board, never to be seen again. There was a short, sharp shout. One of the men in the line, smiling, clapped an adjacent man on the shoulder, grinning and gesturing to the board. The exciting number had disappeared, but the blush of ecstasy still filled his cheeks.

A suited man passed behind the battery of tellers and came out into the lobby, moving unctuously toward Arlen. It was the banker — the time was now, there was no delaying, no hurry-up-and-wait, this was the moment. "Mr. Breckenridge, how are you today?" he said, hand extended.

Arlen could not remember rising up or what he said or what the man's name was. They exchanged pleasantries and then Arlen was following him to the back, his dirty soles scratching grittily on the marble. Entering an office, the banker shut the door behind them. Frosted glass and wood sealed them off from even the low hum of the front end of the bank. The sunlight through the window was a beautiful color, but it warmed nothing. "Please, have a seat," said the banker. Arlen sat himself down squarely, his arms on the chair's arms, feet set apart, ready to talk about what this man could do for the Breckenridges. There was no avoiding this any longer, he had to do it, so he might as well go in like the man he was.

"Well, Mr. Breckenridge, I know you are here about the mortgage. What can I tell you about it?"

Arlen started to open his mouth, but then he realized he did not know what to ask. No one had taught him anything about the very thing he was supposed to avoid like sin itself.

The banker went ahead. "I talked with the extension agent—"

"You talked to Earl?" said Arlen.

"Yes. He told me everything about the situation. I understand you are looking to modernize the farm, get progressive with your production?"

"I just want to make it work. Mighty hard these days."

"Especially with your situation."

Arlen's brow furrowed. "My situation?"

The banker nodded. "Yes. Earl told us all about it. Owing back taxes is serious, although we have seen it before. Normally we don't undertake mortgages with farms that have serious tax issues, but he assured us that this was not a product of negligence on your part, but simple misfortune. He commended you on the highest level of work ethic and determination and said that you would do everything you could to make the farm profitable."

Arlen nodded, feeling odd that his old adversary would make such a flattering comment.

"Intangibles like work ethic are a nice icing to the cake, Mr. Breckenridge, but it takes good collateral to overcome financial straits such as yours." The banker lifted a piece of paper and put his glasses down to the tip of his nose. "This report by the extension agent on your land is quite comprehensive. A good location, some upland and some lowland tracts. It appears you have looked after your land."

"Yessir. It's everything."

"You practice good erosion control, I see."

"Yessir, I try."

"And crop rotation."

"Yessir."

"Not much in the way of modern improvements to the property, I see?"

"Sir?"

"Buildings and such."

"Oh, no, sir, not recently."

The banker nodded and set the paper down. "What are you looking to do with the loan?"

Arlen spoke the words with a heavy heart: "I need to buy a tractor, plow, cultivator, harvester, and fertilizer and pesticide, mostly. Want to bring up my yields, maybe diversify into other crops."

"I see."

"Might get a new truck and make some improvements to rest of the place if I can afford it in a year or two."

The banker leaned forward onto his big desk. "That squares with what Earl told us. Given your modest objectives, I think that the quality of the land itself warrants the mortgage you have requested."

I knew it, knew I could get it from them. Now I just got to get myself a fair rate.

But the banker pushed the stack of mortgage papers across the table and handed Arlen a pen. "If you'd like to start signing, we can get the whole process underway."

"What's this?" said Arlen.

"Oh, we went ahead and drew up the contract for you, Mr. Breckenridge."

"Pardon?" Arlen wet his lips. "What about the terms?"

"What about them?"

"You ain't asked me what I want."

The banker frowned. "Mr. Breckenridge, for a man in your situation, there is really not much room for negotiation. It is a risk on our end and we are making an offer that the extension agent thought was fair and which is perfectly within your ability to repay, provided that you have good returns on your crop for the term of the mortgage." He waggled the pen at Arlen again. "This is the best we can do, and it will be the best for you too, Mr. Breckenridge, so long as you can repay. Come on, now, we've already drawn up the papers for you — might as well go ahead and sign."

Arlen saw it, the very thing, the works, all of it all at once in an enormous flash like an artillery burst in the dark. Here it was, right before him, reaching out to him through a pen from an empty three-piece suit, just as Earl and Mr. Cline reached out and into his world. It had been there all the time, right under the family's nose all those years, waiting, watching, biding its time, building strength, apprehending the crisis that would give it the chance to do this, just this, the taking of Arlen's farm by his own hand marking ink across a blank line. He had thought the war had done it, and the war had, but it was only the opportunity that the war had given. The war accelerated everything that was going to happen anyway, everything coming quickly to the logical conclusion that had begun so long ago, years, decades in the past. They, those men like the banker and all the extension agents and the industrial men and the politicians and the rationing board members, had planned it. They had seen what the future held because they knew what they would demand from it, and the future would give it because it was willing. And Arlen and his family had taken nothing beyond what was theirs, because they were not prepared to sacrifice what they knew and what was theirs fair and square and what gave them an honorable living. They never had taken, they had hardly even asked, generation after generation, and here they were, squeezed out of the last thing that kept them who they were: their land. Free and clear, it kept them from envy and kept them from destitution; it kept them from slavery and kept them from decay. But the old ways could not save the land. These men and their demands could take the land with just the stroke of a pen — not take it in name or by force, but in making a man work unceasingly to maybe, possibly get back what was rightfully his. It was Progress, and they called it that no matter who called for it: the bankers, the politicians, the factory owners, the salesmen, the scientists, the whole lot. Even when they fought each other, they did not fight over whether it would happen, only over control. Each sought to run the whole thing in the direction they wanted, but there was only one way it would go. Who ran it did not matter to a man like Arlen.

For here he was at the receiving end, with incoming mail crackling in overhead, ready to detonate atop him. He could sign over his land right now and the banker would take it and give him money for it, and what Arlen did with it was of no consequence. The banker and his kind of men had no stake in Arlen's success. Certainly if there were enough years of good crops, the banker would be happy. But if not, then no matter, he would have the land instead of the repaid money. The bank would resell it to someone else and with the nation and the economy — which were the same thing these days — going the way they were, the money would be recouped in no time and Arlen and his land would be quickly forgotten. But it was not the banker's fault, even though it was. It was his habit, just as Arlen had his own habits, and each came from a certain logic. And no logic ever sprang up fully-formed on its own, but always came from a change of heart. They might have been from similar families long ago, but this man's ancestors' hearts had changed and so did the habits with each passing generation. The desire to live in the contented image of what had been, which was its own kind of logic, had disappeared. This man, holding the pen and pushing the glasses back up his nose, was the kind of man who reasoned that things must change and there must be Progress, even though he did not know where it would stop, because there was no end to it. But such men told themselves that some day, one day, things would have changed enough that they would be satisfied, even as there was still more to change, and that they would never again have to worry about going back to the bad old days — the change would be permanent. They repeated this over and over until there was not a shred of doubt in their minds — men could become less destitute and less awful to each other by endless work, greater riches, and making demands of each other and taking from others without ever having to give anything up, and this they thought was the true calling of man. So they did what they did and justified it by the yearning inside.

And it started from on high, in the hearts of the highest, but that had begun long ago. Arlen could see this was no new and wild passion in these men's hearts — this was carefully tried and tested, a formula endlessly repeatable. This was what his family had feared for all those generations. This was what they had seen coming, but could not articulate in fancy words. He could not either, but he felt it keenly at this last moment. From on high it had come down and down and down until it had reached even the small places like here in Catawba County. It had been here for a long time, building itself up, refining its words and phrases, taking captives here and there, turning men inside out and sending them off with new convictions so that they might do the hard work. Men all around Arlen were its front rank and they did the work. They did the convincing, the maneuvering, and the securing. They got people to lend, to borrow, to buy — when it was needed, they took ground. And they did it not for themselves, though they had newfound rank and wealth from it, but for those elsewhere, faraway, high up, and unseen, whose hearts were the same and who never had to see what really happened here in bank offices and in corn fields and on factory floors.

Arlen saw the enemy only now and it was not what he thought it was. But it was too late to wheel about and defend himself. They had him overrun. There was no more resisting. The clear image of the whole inhuman project dimmed like the night rushing back in after the artillery flash, and the sight of the fighting ground was gone for good save a bare silhouette in his memory.

"Mr. Breckenridge, are you going to sign or not?" intoned the banker.

His teeth did not gnaw on his lip. Arlen took the pen and signed his name on all the lines. The bottom dropped out from under him and he went down, even as the chair held him firmly. He slumped lower and lower as the banker talked at him and he heard not a word. He hid half of his face in the palm of his hand and just nodded over and over until he heard the banker stop talking and rise from his seat. His stomach clenched against the sickness pushing up into his chest. The banker put out his hand and Arlen shook it. He almost felt more guilty at that than anything.

Good Lord, I did it. Forgive me.

All the trappings of the mortgage were handed to him in a neat manila envelope. The money would be his soon and he could buy what he needed with it, but the farm was already theirs. They let him loose, and once into the lobby, Arlen stumbled his way to the exit. He felt very light-headed. He pushed through the front doors and felt the unobscured sun in his eyes. It worsened his headache and he felt even sicker. There were people coming and going from the front of the bank and Arlen pushed away from them, going around the corner, his hand running along the stone facade, ready to catch himself. He rounded the corner and after several shaky steps, he stopped, dropped the envelope, and leaned against the side of the bank, his head hanging down and stomach swirling.

A shame, Lord, it's a shame and I'm a shame. Better to have lost the whole farm than to give in to 'em like that.

His screwed his eyes shut, waiting for the tears. But he was dry.

The passing minutes were the distance between what he had done and where he was now, between what he had been and what he would be. Already he was far from doing anything, from making any bold and determined move toward a hard and fast truth. In his all his newfound wealth birthed from the mere exchange of paper, he had less. He could not stomach that thought. No, he would not consider it — it was not real. He had things to do — like find Caty. She was probably spending his last bit of change.

He crossed right through traffic, ignoring the honking horns, and began walking the storefronts, peering into each window looking for her. He saw her at last sitting and sipping on something warm, looking idly at a magazine on the table. Arlen stared through the window at her, wondering if he should go in and say something. Her gaze shifted up to the figure casting a shadow through the glass and she jumped a little at the sight of him. She smiled broadly and waved her hand a little, then rose out of the chair, taking the magazine with her as she exited out into the sunny chill. "Are you finished?"

Arlen nodded jerkily.

"Well?" she said.

"Ma'am?"

Caty looked back at him, waiting. "Don't you . . ."

He took her by the hand. "Let's go."

Her shoes clopped as fast as they could to keep up. "They gave you the mortgage?"

"Yes'm."

"Oh, that's good, Arlen. Was it what you wanted? I know I don't know much about these things, but I could get Pa to look over it for us, maybe he would have something to say. Oh, I know it's too late to do anything about it, though, but still, it wouldn't hurt. Don't you think?"

Arlen held her hand tightly in his and just walked to the truck.

"Arlen? Don't you think?"

"What?"

"Aren't you listening? I want you to tell me all about it."

"I'll tell you later, when we get home."

Caty screwed up her nose at the thought. "Home?"

"Yes, we're going now."

She sighed. "But you said we were going to do some shopping. I have a whole list of things we need."

"Not today."

"But when, Arlen?"

"Not today, Caty."

She stopped dead in her tracks. "No, I don't want to go home. We came all this way. I don't want to go."

"Dammit, Caty, not here, not right now. I ain't gonna put up with this today."

Caty jabbed a finger at him for the first time ever. "Don't! Don't you — don't you swear at me, Arlen!"

He could not look at her. "I'm sorry, Caty."

"You aren't, you are not." Caty shook her head. "What has come over you, Arlen? You don't tell me anything, you don't include me in anything, you just do it all yourself. And I know there are things I need to know, Arlen, but how can I? You keep it all to yourself. You just expect me to know what to do, when I need you to teach me. Won't you?"

Arlen grabbed her by the arm. "Come on, we're going right now. We have to get back."

"You aren't gonna tell me, are you?" Caty let him push her along to the truck, but she fought back in words. "This isn't the war, Arlen. Don't you tell me that it is. Don't you say that you can't tell me, that I wouldn't understand. I do understand, Arlen, I understand you, and I know this is different."

But she don't understand. If she did, she wouldn't have ever said a word. She'd have just known.

He kept on marching toward the car and she kept on talking. "You can't hide this from me, Arlen. You can't. You have to tell me. I have to know, so I can help you. We have to do this together. I'm not saying that I'll be as good as you at what you do, or you at what I do. But we both have to know what each other is facing." She tried to reach up with her other arm and touch him on the cheek. "Don't you want that?"

Arlen wanted that. He wanted it so badly. But he could not let that happen. For if she could not see already who he was and all that he had fought for, if she could not understand that he had to bury many things in the hope of living, if she could not intuit all of his deep, inherited ways and match her rhythm to his, then there was no hope. They could not live as complementary halves. Perhaps he had not instructed her enough, perhaps he had not taught her the way. But was it not simple? All she had to do was just be there for him. That was all he asked. For her to care for the things he could not and to be his refuge from difficulty. But she wanted a part in the struggle. She wanted to share. He could not endure that. He would not let his love for her die with her when she put herself into this fight of a humiliating mortgage and cash crops.

"Arlen!"

He opened the truck door and pushed her inside, shutting the door against her protests. He drew long breaths, oblivious to the passersby whose heads swiveled around, interested but not enough to stop.

Can't fail now. Got to keep on, got to see this through. Got to, for her sake, for the baby's.

He screwed up his courage, not just to face her, but to drive back to the land he had betrayed through no fault of his own and to settle down to work. He would keep things going as they had. He would pay off the debts and the time would come. It would not be soon, like he had expected at his homecoming. It would be years off, at least. But it would come. And he would protect and preserve everything he knew, and he would make the old live again. He vowed it again.

And in vowing, he forgot the town and the square and instead his mind turned to the minutes here before him. He was ready to meet each moment, confident in his ability, but ever fearful of and vigilant against error. It was the one thing he had left. He climbed into the truck, started it up, and pulled away from the square.

XXIII

When he came out the front door, Arlen could see from the light itself he was late. *Must be nearly six o'clock.* He should have started plowing an hour before. But there had been other things to do. Arlen shut the front door behind him, and went down the creaky steps to the bare dirt before the porch. The morning air was cool, but he did not feel the clean, blank refreshment of a new day's possibilities. He had been awake for almost the whole night and yesterday had run into today. There had been no sleep to cleanse him of the weight. Now, the start of planting had always occupied his thoughts and grabbed his attention away from other concerns, but he had long felt satisfaction with getting down to it, even in the preparations that took days or weeks before. But not this time.

He shivered a little bit as he walked down the drive to the road. Rising and working felt odd — the pattern was off. It must have been because he was getting a late start in the season. The last frost had been in the first few days of the month and he was free to plant not long after that. But he had not. He had waited. The following weeks had been unexpectedly dry, with little rain, and it would have been perfect to go ahead and plow and put seed into soil. But Arlen had not. He had waited, for he needed the machines which had not yet come. And the anxiety of anticipation, of habit deferred, had wormed around inside him and he could focus on nothing. Every fiber of him had wanted to set out with the riding plow and the mules and turn the ground, because he knew it would do well to go ahead and plant. It might not be the best, the yield they wanted, but he knew it was as good as he could ask for. It was not a guarantee, but it was close to it, having the seed in the ground when Creation gave you an opportunity. To wait was to tempt events too much.

But he waited, even as his instinct rang like a fire-bell in the night, and he made himself busy gathering all the supplies necessary for a big corn crop: fertilizer, pesticide, and a new variety of seed. Oil and fuel and spare parts, too, and tools for working on machines whose delivery had been delayed for so long. They had promised it to him, but everyone wanted one now and even though Arlen had paid his deposit promptly, he still had to wait. Time mattered to him, for it mattered even more to the constantly revolving seasons, but no one else seemed to care. All the consequences were on Arlen. He had almost given in and gone out with the riding plow, but then the tractor had arrived on the back of a truck the day before. They had rolled it down into the yard and left him alone with it. Now he had this thing which he had never used and could only struggle with, for he had never grown up with a machine like this. But he had paid for it, he should use it. So late the previous evening he had fueled it and tried to make sense of how it ran from the manual. He drove it around in the failing light for a while before parking it under the overhang he had built off of the old barn and going inside to toss and turn all night, thinking of how he could make up for lost time.

He could make it up. He told himself that and it hurried his feet down to the road. Arlen opened the front gate and stepped to the mailbox. The gritty creak of the hinge made Arlen wince. He almost feared to disturb the sleep about him, as if the birds who had not yet begun singing would begrudge him for it.

Hell, that tractor ain't gonna be quiet neither.

He pulled out the mail that he had forgotten to get the day before. The letters went without a look into his back pocket. Arlen turned the envelope he carried in his hand over and over, checking the stamp, the address — *Mr. William Buford Paine, c/o Mrs. Alice Paine, Post Office Box 1497, Gary, Indiana* — and the return address once, then again, in the growing light. He hefted the envelope in his hand. He had begun the letter a long time ago, but he had had not known how to finish it. What could he say to his old buddy? Events had carried them apart and Arlen wondered if he was well again. He was not sure if Paine was at home or not, and he did not want to disturb Paine's healing if he could. For to talk to his old friend was to bring up the one thing they really had in common, and that meant too many memories of too many bad places over there. But if Arlen waited, there might never be a time. For things had not gone as he had expected and he did not know when they would. So, a few hours before, Arlen had risen, lit the lamp at the kitchen table, and finished the letter. And though he had not read them again, the words kept playing through Arlen's head.

Come visit and stay a while. There's work for you if you want it.

But not yet. I have to get a few things right first, running like they should be, like I always said they would be, before you can come down.

I'll let you know when they are. It won't be long, buddy. I promise.

One last thing: from his shirt pocket he pulled out a photograph. They looked so young, with clean faces and muddy clothes, in that field in France. He put it in the envelope, licked the flap, and pressed it shut.

Arlen laid the letter in the box carefully, shut the squeaky door, and walked

264

back through the gate, locking it behind him, hoping that Paine's mother, if she saw him, would give him the letter without reading it. Arlen marched back up the drive and past the house. Caty insisted on making him breakfast, even at this hour, but he had not eaten much. Hunger would come only when he had found the new way of things and settled into it.

He ended his walk at the overhang off of the side of the barn. The brute sat under a tarpaulin. Arlen whisked the cover off. He still thought it should be olive drab, not gray. Arlen pulled the choke, set the machine in neutral, and went to the front of the machine. He bent over and turned the crank just like he had learned the night before. After a half dozen turnovers, the engine roared to life and spewed its rolling thunder across the still morning. Arlen stood with arms on his hips, listening to the cycling of the engine regularize as it warmed up. He imagined Wade spinning in his grave, the dead man's revolutions synchronized with the Ford's crankshaft.

The chugging of the engine steadied. Arlen still watched the machine, hesitant to climb up on it. He wondered if he had expected something different from this moment, something different about the machine or himself or what had to be done, both of them together. But he could not find any predictions he had made. That imagining part of him was long gone.

Lord, just let me do it right and be done with it.

He felt the instinct to pull his helmet down lower over his forehead as he stepped up and into the seat. But his old steel pot was not there.

Situated just right in the seat, Arlen shifted the tractor into gear and ducked to avoid the roof beam as the Ford pulled out from cover, the plow already in tow. Ten minutes later, he put the first furrows into the thin loam and the red clay just beneath.

A couple of hours passed and the plow kept cutting earth. He was fairly well along. The first couple of acres looked terrible. It was one thing to drive the tractor and to make practice turns with the plow in tow, but quite another to put the shares into the ground and actually till. The furrows on those first three or four acres were so damn crooked that Arlen wondered how he would follow them closely enough to get the seed in. After that, though, he'd gotten the hang of it and felt himself improving with each pass up and down the field.

With a recoiling jolt, the tractor stopped suddenly and strained to move forward, the engine running through its revolutions with a painful rumble. Arlen spun around in the seat. It looked like the plow had gotten caught on a rock.

Mighty peculiar. Ain't never got the old plow caught here before.

The engine whined and he shifted out of gear. He sat looking back at the plow. *Maybe I've got the shares set too deep.*

265

Arlen gnawed his lip. He set the brake and climbed down off of the tractor. He ambled around the plow. It was a rock, all right. He could not tell how big it was, but the top of it seemed to have caught the share and sucked the whole thing almost underneath. Arlen stood glaring at the tractor. *Hate this fuckin' thing already.* He would have to dig out the share. When he reached up to turn off the tractor engine, Arlen got a look at the sky. Rolling in from the west were pale gray clouds, gradually darkening to steel by the horizon. They were low enough to have just grazed the top of South Mountain as they came east. They were thicker than the ones which had zipped by over the past weeks without so much as an errant drop.

Arlen looked to the ground, the tractor, the ground again, then back to the sky. His instinct told him everything. It said to go in. It said to stay out and plow. If he had been with the mules, he would have packed up and headed back. But the mules were just out to pasture all the time now, and he had this tractor here. Time had been lost, and he could make up time with this tractor, couldn't he? That's what the people said — it did more work than a whole team of mules, and faster.

Hell, I ain't so sure. Nothing matched up any more.

Arlen looked to the clouds, expecting thunder, but they were silent and slow. Would they hold?

Ain't got no time to wait and see. Waited long enough. Put it off any longer and I risk everything.

He left it at 'everything' because he knew where that word went. Everything was a risk with a mortgage hanging over you.

He had to get the plowshare out from underneath the rock. That before anything else. Arlen switched off the tractor engine and took the long walk back. He crossed dense earth crosshatched with the cuttings of last year's stalks and stubble, and rose up out of this lower piece of land down by the thinly flowing branch, crested the slight rise, and continued on across the upper piece. He crossed the farmyard to the old corn crib, as old as Great-Grandfather Alexander. He had turned it into a tool shed now that they would build a new one. Undoing the padlock, Arlen swung open the creaky door. The air was cool and damp inside, amplifying the heavy smell of steel, cast iron, solvents, and kerosene. On the wall, beneath the old crosscut saw, its blade faded to an eggshell patina of purplish rust, was the tamping bar he needed. Taking it down, Arlen grabbed a shovel from the adjacent wall, then locked the shed again, and headed back out into the fields.

After he had backed up the tractor a bit, he could get at the rock. He could see it was close enough to the surface that he did not need the shovel. He scraped away with the chisel end of the bar, then began worming that end underneath the rock. Levering up and down, Arlen worked the bar under the full width of the rock and with a final heave, tossed it free of the hole. Brushing off as much soil as he could, Arlen hefted the rock into his arms, cradling it like the world's heaviest watermelon, and stumbled off a good fifty yards to the edge of the woods, where he dropped it and watched it roll almost over the bank of the branch. He turned to walk back — oh, now look at those clouds. They had played a trick on him — dark and thick, they were almost overhead. *Shit.* He didn't want to go in. He felt good about what he was getting done, about what he learned this morning. And the day itself, all that it stirred within him, new and old, gave him pleasure. He didn't want to go inside and sit in that house, waiting out the rain.

Hell, I can get this whole field done right quick. Raise up those shares a bit and I ain't gonna hit no more rocks. So he got back on the Ford and finished the row. Turning the tractor back to continue the furrows, he raised his head slightly, and the first drop of rain hit his face, cold but soft. There was a long moment where there were no more drops. Arlen looked higher, peering at the gray clouds spreading and settling over him. Then two drops hit his nose at the same time. A half dozen more sprinkled across him, from chin down across chest. Then the rain hit like a wet curtain. The metal tractor rang like his old helmet.

"Sonuvabitch!" he shouted.

There was no continuing on now. He should have taken warning earlier. He raised the plow up and out of the ground and turned the tractor around to go back to the barn.

You bastard, you fool.

The rain came down in rolling torrents. Arlen was soaked completely through already. Surely this sort of rain, as heavy as an upturned bucket, couldn't last very long. Yet the rain fell stronger and the drops grew thicker, as if the clouds were making up for lost time. Arlen looked to the tractor wheels, which were now bearing the weight of that heavy plow on the back. The tires were digging into the quickly softening ground and red clay was caking up on them. There was too much weight on the rear end.

Arlen stopped the tractor and looked about. The house was too far off and there was a incline to get to it. He dwelt on the problem for only a couple of seconds before jumping off the tractor. He undid the pin from the hitch and jammed into the back pocket of his jeans. *Hate to see this plow get wet, especially it being so new.* The plow might grow its first patches of rust, but the tractor's complicated and more expensive engine was far more important. Arlen could not fathom tearing the Ford apart to dry and oil every little part. Imagine how far behind it would put him in planting. And if the crop wasn't in at the right time, the yield might not be enough, not to cover his loan for the tractor, the fertilizer and seed, and every other expense staring at him from a ledger book which he could hardly read, the ink of the figures writing out a new meaning of time for him. Time was rarely with the farmer, but now it had reached it greatest, most fleeting compression.

Can't make no more mistakes. Not now.

Arlen put the tractor back into gear and started off toward the barn as fast as he could.

The churning wheels began to slip on the steeper and ever-more soggy ground. But Arlen didn't think to shift to a lower gear. He just sat in the tractor seat, gnawing his lip, anxiously watching the wheels slip and spin a little more with each passing yard. All he could do was will the tractor on: *Come on, baby, come on, make it, make it.*

The tractor dipped into a slight depression, canting forward and to the left, as it continued on through the rain. As it rose up out of the dip to climb the slope where the topsoil was thin and the clay shone through, the Ford reached its limit. The left wheel spun madly and the momentum came to a halt. Arlen pushed the throttle a little bit further, straining the lever, trying to eke whatever last bit of effort he could out of the engine. But his efforts only dug deeper the trench in which the left wheel spun. A spume of red clay from the churning wheel arced across the sodden earth. Arlen throttled back the Ford's engine and the left wheel settled into the rut, the uphill slope and the uneven dip putting all the tractor's weight on it.

Sonuvabitch.

Arlen nearly stopped the engine, but then thought he might not be able to start it again if the rain, now blowing diagonally, almost horizontally at times, soaked it through. Dismounting, he knelt next to the tire. It was certainly dug in, but the suction of the mud held it more than anything.

Just got to break it loose.

Reaching behind the seat, he pulled out the tamping bar from where he had wedged it. He worked the prybar down into the gummy red morass next to the tire, digging little channels for air to work its way to the buried tire. After a few hard minutes, the effort became a little easier. The sucking sounds became louder and more satisfying. *Close, real close now.* Full of enthusiasm, glad to know his efforts were not in vain, Arlen jabbed the chisel end of the tamping bar well under the tire and bore down on it with all his weight. He'd break the suction now.

But the bar slipped going in. The chisel end was only sharp on the corners, but that was still enough. The bar cut a small, jagged hole in the tire wall. Arlen heard not a hiss, but a gurgle, as the air bubbled up through the watery clay. The tire began to shrink visibly, then sag. Finally, after a couple of minutes, the whole tractor settled onto the back left wheel.

The rain had never felt colder. All Arlen could do was sit there and stare at the tractor, the expensive tire ruined and rain seeping down into the finely-milled parts of the puttering engine.

But it wasn't the destruction of his things that hurt the most. It was his own ruination.

Arlen would not have cared so much if it had been only him. But it was not only him.

He had sensed someone watching him as he had stood there, watching the tire deflate. Arlen didn't turn around for a good minute or two afterward. When he did, he saw Caty.

Caty. She stood under an old, worn-out umbrella that Wade had bought secondhand as a joke years ago. The black fabric was nearly soaked through and it hung limply on the side where two of the wooden ribs were broken. She held it in her right hand, her left hand tucked beneath her right arm, helping to keep her shawl wrapped tightly around her.

Why is she here? To check on me? Is she worried?

She shouldn't be out here. Not like that. The air was already cool and felt colder thanks to the rain. His worry was not so much for her, but for what she carried. Caty's dress, wet and nearly transparent, clung to her bulging stomach so that he could see every contour.

"Arlen?" Her voice matched her face. There was no worry, nor fear, not even pity. She showed only grief. But not at him — with him.

He had nothing to hide behind now. All he could do was stand there and see her looking down the slope at him, flecks of dirt dotting her shins up to the knee.

"Arlen, just come on in."

Arlen looked over at the tractor.

"Arlen, it's fine. You can leave it."

That edge on her voice when she talked like that — it wasn't demeaning, like to a child. It was consoling. She had only ever wanted him to be happy. She just wanted him to be the man that she had known before.

Can't be that. Not for her. Not me.

Can't give her what she wants. Ain't in me. All I can do is give her what she needs.

"Come inside, Arlen."

He wanted to go with her so badly. He wanted to stay here, too, to dig out the tractor, as futile as it might be.

He had hoped for more than this, envisioned life as so much more. But in the end, this was it. This was all there was. As much as he might strive and try his best by the principles he could not escape, he could not create any more than what was here. It was just Caty and him, just this mortgaged-out farm and a ruined tractor.

Can't make nothin' happen. Can't bring it back.

Arlen felt as though a stone within his chest had come loose and rolled away. He took several sudden, gasping breaths.

Ain't my fault. Ain't for lack of tryin'. Just the way things are right here and right now.

The vestiges of his family's world were finally dead and gone, save for him. All that had made him had finally vanished. Arlen was the last, carrying on in a way that had no bearing on this strange reality. He carefully did what was right, all those long-refined acts that had been passed on to him, and the world hardly noticed it anymore than an errant puff of wind. Arlen had changed a little, but not enough to make it. He was doomed to popping tractor tires, in one way or another, for the rest of his days. He had not come home.

"Arlen?" Caty's voice was worried.

If I'd been born back then, I could've lived a good life, doing what I know.

He would not, though. His life would be hard. The balance of pain and struggle with the joy and grace of a man in his proper place would never be.

I ain't chose it. Ain't never chose being like this. Something else did.

Gonna keep on, Lord. Maybe I'm a sonuvabitch for it. But it ain't nothin' I can change.

A strange sense of peace came. All the knots of care and concern, of the imperative burden of making those old ways live in this world by force of his own will, dissolved as the great fact of his powerlessness covered Arlen.

A curtain of cold rain slapped his face. Arlen looked at the tractor and the messy furrows stretching across the field on the other side of it. A still soul would not get this tractor unstuck. Peace would not put seed in the ground and food on the table. Bills were coming due, and he had his sinewy body to offer up as payment.

No keeping, nor bringing back. No fulfillment. Just toil.

For the first time in their brief life together, Arlen looked at Caty and gave her a genuine smile. It was not wide nor open; his mouth was tensed at the corners with anguish. She looked at him expectantly. He almost said something.

Then he grabbed the shovel from behind the tractor seat, stepped to the sunken wheel, and began to dig.

Author's Note

This book has been years in the making. While much of the writing life is solitary, it is nonetheless sustained by the unflagging presence of others who give whatever they can to the writer and, unwittingly, to the work itself. The people in my life, some close by, others separated by distance or years, have shaped this book into what it is. Without them, it would be a vanity project. My heartfelt thanks go out to the following:

My wife Jina. Your perpetual encouragement and confidence made the book more than it was supposed to be. I love you.

Mom and Dad. Y'all let me read and write to my heart's content in youth, providing every resource along the way, and have always had patient love for the work of one's child that only a parent knows.

My brother Stewart, my sister Shelby, and their spouses Davie and Ryan. Thank you for your continued interest, excitement, and encouragement even when I was lost in the weeds.

My grandparents, for their stories, their personal examples, and their love.

My friends and extended family, for remembering that I was writing when even I forgot at times.

My Patreon backers: Richard Harrington, Matt Sohner, Stewart Brenegar, Anderson Ellis, Jay Forsythe, Barbara Potter Pinto, Don Scott, Robbie Broyles, Michael Roope, and Drew Henderson. Thanks to your financial support, I am able to publish a book for the rest of the world.

I am indebted in particular to Warren Watson of oldhickory30th.com. His labor of love has preserved an enormous amount of material on the 30th Infantry Division, the Workhorse of the Western Front, and he pointed me in the direction of resources that I never would have found otherwise. May the memory of those who fought never be forgotten.

Thank you as well to Alex Floyd and the other staff at the Catawba County Library Rhodes Room. I slipped in and out a number of times without ever letting on what I was up to. Y'all never pried. Thank you for preserving a good county's history. I hope I have honored the place.

Finally, to all generations of the faithful heart. All those who set down, store up, pass along, give over, and persevere through are the blessed of this earth and the makers of everyone walking around. Your efforts are never in vain.

- Troop Brenegar, October 2022

www.ingramcontent.com/pod-product-compliance
Lightning Source LLC
Chambersburg PA
CBHW021003260626
47169CB00006B/1924